"Look at Me."

Elliot needed Deb to look at him, really look at him. And not just for a second before sinking back into that silent realm where despite her eager response to his touch, he still suspected she couldn't be reached. Before they went any further, Elliot needed to believe, thoroughly and wholeheartedly, that Deborah was making love to him, not to some memory of the husband she had lost.

"Who am I?" Elliot whispered, his breath warm along her ear. "Who am I, Deb?"

Deborah peered up at Elliot, her best friend, as if she were seeing him for the first time. She looked at him harder and longer than she ever had before. And then she understood.

"Elliot." There was no hesitation in her voice, no confusion. "Elliot."

The hand that had been resting on his chest now pulled him closer, and, in the lifetime before Deborah's mouth found his, she repeated, "You're Elliot. . . ."

When a Man Loves a

Woman

Alina Adams

A Dell Book

Published by Dell Publishing, a division of Random House, Inc.
1540 Broadway
New York, New York 10036

Dell® is a registered trademark of Random House, Inc., and the
colophon is a trademark of Random House, Inc.

ISBN: 0-440-23510-3

Printed in the United States of America
Published simultaneously in Canada
April 2000
10 9 8 7 6 5 4 3 2 1
OPM

For the two men loved by this woman —
my husband, Scott, and my son, Adam

Prologue

June 1984

James Elliot was the best friend Deborah Brody ever had.

After tomorrow, she fervently hoped she'd never see him again.

Lying in bed that night, she told herself that was because in five hours it would be Matching Day. The day when Deb and Elliot, bloated with the self-importance of graduating from the University of California at San Francisco Medical School all of twelve hours earlier, learned which hospitals had accepted them for residencies.

They'd each applied all over the country—"Just to be safe," they said—but both had their hearts set on getting their first choices: Deb in San Francisco and a specialty in neurosurgery, and Elliot in Los Angeles, for trauma care. If both got the selection they wanted, odds were high they'd never see each other again.

It was almost four AM, and Deb had been tossing and turning since midnight. She assumed she was worried about not getting the placement she'd requested.

After all, what else could be filling her with this nameless sense of deficiency, this feeling that she'd forgotten something? The only time she usually felt like this was when Deb left for vacation, and passed the first hour of her trip wondering if she'd turned off the water, and shut off the gas. But, right now, as far as she knew, Deb was not on vacation. When it came to the results of Matching Day, everything that could be done had to already have been done. Her staying up and worrying was not going to magically rearrange the letters inside of her envelope. Deb knew that. She understood it intellectually, and had thought she'd already let it go. Yet, here Deb was, lying awake and feeling like there was some question still terribly unsettled in her life.

It was getting ridiculous. With all her tossing and turning, she was getting a better aerobic workout in bed than she usually managed at the gym. And she refused to exercise involuntarily.

Gingerly, Deb slid out from beneath her blanket, reluctant to fully lift it off her body, for fear of waking up Max. She padded, barefoot, out of the bedroom and into their apartment kitchen. She picked up the phone on the wall beside the counter their landlord had oversold them as a "dining area," and, wincing at each click of her nails against the buttons, dialed Elliot's home number.

He answered on the first ring, as if he had been sleeping with his hand on the receiver. He sounded groggy, yet functional. A doctor for less than a day, and he already had the tone down.

"Elliot?" Deb couldn't fight her impulse to whisper. As if whispering could make up for waking the man up at four AM. "I—I . . ." Good Deb, now that you've got him up, maybe you should think of something to say. "Elliot, I need to talk. Do you, maybe, you know, have a few minutes?"

From the other end of the phone, she could hear Elliot stretch and smile lazily. Somehow, no matter what inanity slipped out past her lips, he seemed to have a knack for decoding the meaning underneath. Elliot took a moment, then drawled, "You bring the cards."

Deb's whole body exhaled. "I'll be right over."

Luckily, medical school had taught her to dress in a matter of minutes, in the dark, and in absolute quiet. Still, as Deb riffled around in her desk for a scrap of notepaper and a pencil, Max heard her and, stifling a yawn, rolled over on his stomach, propping his still sluggish head up with one hand. Eyes at half-mast, he took in Deb's jeans, her UCSF sweatshirt, her sneakers, and the Toyota keys pressed in her left hand. Rubbing the bridge of his nose with a knuckle, he asked, not unpleasantly, "Going somewhere, hon?"

She straightened, giving up the hunt for writing material, and confessed, "Elliot's."

"Something wrong?"

"Uhm, no. Of course not."

"A four AM social call, then?"

Deborah responded automatically, reassuring him, "Everything's fine. Don't worry." The last thing Deb wanted was to put Max out. And she knew that, if he found out just how frazzled Deb really was feeling right then, he would be very put out.

Not in a bad way, of course. She meant he would be terribly concerned, and he would ask her, over and over, what he could do to help. Problem was, there was nothing Max could do to help. But she was reluctant to let him know that, and leave him feeling helpless. So, in addition to her reassurance, Deb showed him a dazzling "no problem" smile. The one she always showed him, no matter what.

This time around, though, it didn't work. Max sat up in bed, blanket puddling his waist. "Try me," he offered softly. "Just once, try telling me what the matter is, Deb. You never know, if you explain it to me, slowly, I just might understand."

She really did wish she could unburden herself to him. She knew how much Max wanted to be the one to help her. She knew how much he wanted to be the one who slayed her dragons. And, most of the time, he was. Except when it came to work. Not because Max didn't understand her work. Granted, he wasn't a doctor, but he was intelligent and could promptly understand anything technical. What he didn't understand were the emotions that whipped around and tore at you when you least expected it. But it wasn't his fault. It was Deb's. She didn't have the adequate words to explain it all properly. That's why, when the difficulty was work-related, she needed help from somebody who knew precisely how she felt, without her having to struggle to articulate it. She needed Elliot.

Lamely, Deb attempted to answer Max's plea, more for his sake than for hers. She stammered out, "I—it—it's Matching Day."

"I know," Max said. "I also know that my brilliant, talented, *A+* pupil of a wife couldn't possibly be worrying about not getting her first choice of residency. Because, that would be absurd."

He looked so eager to please, it was all Deb could do to keep from reaching out and ruffling his hair. He thought he was telling her what she needed to hear.

Unfortunately, such unabashed confidence in her was the last thing Deb needed to hear.

But it was also the last thing she would allow Max to know.

"You're probably right," she said brightly.

"If I'm so right, how come you still look so jittery?"

"Too much coffee?"

Max guessed, "This is about more than Matching Day, isn't it?"

She didn't want to lie to him. But, then again, she also did not care to tell him the truth. So she settled for hedging. "It's . . . you know, school stuff."

"Nothing I could help you with?"

"Max . . ."

"I understand," he kidded. "I know when I get all worked up over stocks and bonds, only another commodities trader will do."

"Don't be upset, Max. It's nothing. I just need to run a couple things past Elliot. Doctor things. I'll be back soon."

He looked at her, then, like he wanted to say something or to ask something. But in the end, all Max did was blow Deb a kiss. "Good luck," he said. "I hope Elliot has the answers for you."

It wasn't until after a still-drowsy Elliot had already opened his door to her that it occurred to Deborah that he might not have been alone when she called.

Her first clue was the uncommon cleanliness of his apartment. Granted, the man was a doctor. But he was also a bachelor. His idea of cleanliness was that there should be nothing growing in the shower that wouldn't be more at home in the lab. Yet, crossing the threshold, Deb noted a discernible lack of dust on the table, under the couch, and even along the two paintings he'd bought because they were the perfect size to cover the water stains on his walls. In addition, his books, commonly strewn about the floor, now sat on the shelves. Horizontally, but it was a start.

She observed, "Fee-fi-fo-fum, I smell a woman, Doc."

Her observation visibly startled him.

That is, if one could use the word "visibly" to describe a man whose greatest expression of shock was the upraised eyebrow.

In this case, however, Elliot not only raised his eyebrow, he cocked his head to the side, and guessed, "Perfume?"

Deb shook her head. "Furniture polish."

And then it was her turn to guess. "Emily Delmore?"

Elliot nodded. But he didn't repeat the name, or advance any additional information. Instead, almost as an aside, he scratched the back of his neck and asked, "Do you like her, Brody?"

"Sure. She's terrific. You two make a terrific couple. She—Is she, uhm, is she still here?"

In a square, studio apartment, there really weren't a lot of places Elliot could have hidden her. Nevertheless, he joined Deb in looking curiously around the place, before asserting, "No. She left about a half hour ago."

Deb gulped guiltily. "Not because of me, I hope."

"No." His tone, or lack thereof, hardly invited a follow-up. Instead, he offered a question of his own. "What's wrong, Brody?"

"What makes you think anything is wrong?"

Another man could have thrown any number of facetious, flip, and/or downright rude responses at her. Especially another sleep-deprived—and God only knew what else—man. But Elliot merely smiled, sticking his hands in the pockets of his jeans and leaning back on his heels, rocking slowly back and forth, as if he had all the time in the world and would be content to wait forever until Deb felt comfortable enough to start talking. He was twenty-seven years old, and yet Deb wondered how, in that instant, Elliot could manage to seem both so patriarchal, so wise—and so young.

The young part was easier to understand. Dressed in jeans and a T-shirt, no shoes, and sporting raven-black, curly hair that could have used a trim at least several weeks ago, Elliot looked less like a board-certified MD, and more like the kid who still spent several nights a week playing hockey and broom-ball at the local ice rink. He stood a touch over six feet. Not skinny, just lean. His arms, thighs, and chest were covered in muscle. In body type, he might have been more aptly built for track and field. But Elliot wanted to play hockey. And Elliot tended to get what he wanted.

That's where the seasoned and wise portion of his looks kicked in. No one ever said no to Elliot. And not because he threatened or bullied or even intimidated. But because he never gave up.

"The trick," Elliot once explained to Deb in the same laconic, tranquil manner in which he did all things, "is to keep smacking your head over and over again against the wall, until the wall breaks."

And all walls broke for Elliot. They broke when he wanted to go to Yale but wasn't given enough financial aid to afford it. They broke when UCSF balked at admitting a candidate who'd taken a year off to earn his tuition by, among other unusual jobs, driving a truck loaded with nitroglycerine across the country.

"Tell me what's wrong, Brody," he repeated. But then, rather than making Deb ill at ease by continuing to stare at her expectantly, he took a step backward, settling comfortably into the depths of his couch. His palms rested atop his knees. Elliot asked, "Did you bring the cards?"

Finally, a question she could answer. The relief of having something to say brought a grin to Deb's face. She eagerly pulled up a chair, settling to face Elliot across his somewhat scratched, secondhand coffee table, and, reaching into her purse, withdrew a brand-new deck of playing cards.

"Ranch-style, or high-rise?" Deb inquired politely, breaking the plastic seal.

"Oh, I don't know." Elliot's eyes danced. "I was kind of in the mood for a nice, prewar Tudor."

Because regular, uncreative people may have used playing cards for such mundane activities as Poker, Twenty-One, or Go Fish, Drs. Brody and Elliot built houses.

It started out as a simple bet. Each was trying to prove they had steadier surgeons' hands than the other. Over four years, however, it had developed into a passion. Deb and Elliot played every chance they got. After a day of cramming for finals and boards, it was frequently the only thing that could make them relax.

Deb put down her opening card without a word. Elliot followed her lead. It wasn't till they'd silently and painstakingly erected the first floor and were diligently working on the second that she got up ample courage to inch toward the true purpose of her visit.

Without raising her eyes from their edifice, Deb concentrated on sounding casual as she wondered, "Elliot?"

"Hm?" He, too, did not raise his eyes.

"Do you think a person can be precocious at forty?"

It was one of the stupidest questions ever uttered. Yet, for some reason, Elliot—God bless him—elected to respond like it was the most reasonable query in the world. "How do you mean?"

Deb tucked a loose strand of chestnut hair behind her ear and bit her lip, focusing on balancing the six of diamonds in her hands just so against the jack of clubs Elliot had erected earlier. She said, "When I was two, three, four years old, if you'd asked me my name, I probably would have told you I thought it was 'Precocious.' It's the only word anyone ever used around me. I skipped first and third grade. I started high school at thirteen, graduated in three and a half years, and still had the highest GPA in my class. My entire life, I defined myself as someone precocious. Know how some kids love to whine about the hardships they suffered being brighter than their peers? Well, I loved it. I loved being smart. I loved being smarter even more. And I *really* loved being the smartest."

"I've sat in class with you for four years," Elliot reminded her. "Somehow, I picked up on that."

"Precocious doesn't last." Deb sighed. "I used to get such a kick out of doing something really great or saying something really insightful, and having folks ask me how old I was. And they were always so shocked to find out I was *only* fifteen, or only twenty. Well, you know what, Elliot? I'm twenty-five now."

"I'll call the old folks' home."

"You don't get it, do you?" She wanted to growl in futility. Not at him, at the universe. "I'm growing into my brains, Elliot."

He didn't laugh. To his eternal credit, when Deb admitted her deepest, darkest, most embarrassing secret, Elliot did not laugh.

He only looked up from the cards, eyes meeting Deb's for what suddenly felt like the first time ever. He said, "I understand."

She thought she might burst into tears.

Tears of relief, and tears of joy. Because she believed him.

With anyone else, she would have felt sure they were humoring her, claiming commiseration while, inside, they were busy trying to recall the phone number for the nearest mental hospital.

But when Elliot said he understood, she believed him.

Her subsequent words spilled out of her like a hemorrhage from a severed artery. She barely remembered to breathe in between.

Deb confessed, "It scares the hell out of me, Elliot. I mean, precocious is who I am. It's how I define myself. It isn't about ego. It's about identity. If I'm not this precocious, little Girl Genius, then who the hell am I? How am I going to impress people? How am I going to get anyone's attention? A six-year-old who's got the whole periodic table memorized is someone special. But people kind of expect it of an MD, right?"

Elliot actually considered her question. Unlike most people, who barely waited for the asker to complete their thought before jumping in with some useless platitude or a lame personal anecdote that had nothing to do with the issue at hand, Elliot actually took a moment to think about what Deb asked.

Finally, putting down the card he'd been holding, he linked his fingers in front of him, staring contemplatively first down at them, then up at Deb's panic-seized eyes. He cleared his throat and calmly, rationally, soothingly offered, "Listen to me, Brody. You don't need a periodic table to get people's attention. You are an amazing human being, and your spectacular mind is only a small part of it. Precocious may be a temporary condition, like the flu. But kindness, compassion, decency—they're chronic. You're a good person, Brody. And that's going to be an attention-getter no matter how old or how young you are." He moved to pick up a new card. Then, so nonchalant that an outsider watching might have thought the answer was of no consequence to him whatsoever, Elliot asked, "Is that why you've been so uptight about Matching Day?"

Leave it to Elliot to ask the 25,000-dollar question. Deb hedged, "Sort of."

"You're afraid if you don't get your first-choice residency, there goes your precocious status?"

She said, "I've got a major reputation to protect, you know. People expect great things from me."

He tapped a king of hearts against his lips, cocking his head to one side. He dared, "You know, everybody who really loves you will, quite likely, continue to do so whether you get a top-notch residency or not."

"Can I have that in writing?" Deb joked.

He dropped his card in place, allowing himself a scanty smile that first wavered for a moment, then settled firmly. He raised his chin defiantly, looking Deb in the eye. He said, "Yes."

Deborah Brody had never, in actuality, been swallowed whole by another creature. She'd only read about the experience, with highlights coming from the Biblical Jonah, and Pinocchio. Yet, in that moment with Elliot, she felt . . . swallowed.

No. More than that. She felt . . . consumed.

In the past, Deb had, once or twice or a half-dozen times—no more than a dozen, certainly—looked up from her books in the library, or turned around in her seat in class, or shoved aside a cadaver they were dissecting, and, by accident caught a glimpse of Elliot looking at her. Looking at her with enough force to effectively suck all the air out of her lungs, and leave Deb feeling gutted and bloodless and drained.

But not in a bad way.

She only wished it had been in a bad way. Because then, two years ago, she wouldn't have made the faux pas of blurting, "No. Don't stop," when she realized Elliot had spied her looking at him looking at her and he responded by ducking his head.

Deb didn't know who came out of that exchange feeling more embarrassed, her or Elliot. And she certainly never got the chance to find out, because neither of them ever mentioned it again.

But from time to time, Elliot still looked at her.

These days, though, Deb was a lot more careful about letting him catch her looking back.

Except for right now. Right now, she was enjoying herself too much to even pretend she wasn't. With one word, Elliot had calmed her, and reassured her, and made Deb more joyful than she'd been in weeks, maybe months. She wasn't about to let that feeling go.

Then, Elliot asked, "What about Max?"

Deb blinked. "Max?"

"Don't tell me you believe your husband will stop loving you if you don't get the residency you applied for."

"Of course not." The notion was absurd. But. On the other hand . . . Deb said, "Max has sacrificed so much for me. He was a senior at the University of Chicago when we met. I was a sophomore. He always planned to return home to the Bay Area when he graduated. He ended up staying an extra three years in the Midwest because of me. I really wanted to make it up to him. That's why, even though I got into Yale Med School, and they're number one—"

"Stop showing off, Brody," Elliot teased.

"I decided to go to UCSF, anyway."

"We're number two, we try harder."

"I did it for Max. Same with this residency. If I get it, we can stay in town. I don't want to have to ask Max to move, again. I've already asked enough of him. I've asked him to put up with an awful lot these past four years."

"So, that *is* what's been worrying you? Max?"

"Yes," Deb said. Then, "No." Then, for no particular reason, she said, "I love my husband, Elliot."

Elliot said, "Hm."

"It's because I love him that I can't tell him how I feel. It would only upset him. He would reassure me, and tell me it didn't matter. He'd tell me he believed in me, and he would go along with anything I wanted—about the residency, I mean. But I'd keep on feeling guilty. Like I let him down. Like I betrayed him. You—you do understand that, don't you?"

He shrugged. He asked, "Why are you telling me this? Don't get me wrong, I don't mind the dawn's-early-light assembly; hey, I had nothing penciled in on my social calendar for six AM, anyway, but I am curious why you chose me to unburden yourself to. You do have other friends."

"Yes." Now that she understood his question, the answer could not have been easier. "But you're my best friend, Elliot."

"Oh. Right."

With those words, Deb sensed herself evaporating, dissipating, almost. It felt like being forgotten. It felt like dying. She didn't know what to say, and yet she was certain it was imperative she say something.

"Elliot," she all but called out.

When he glanced up in response, Deb got the sensation of being looked at from a distance. All scientific, spatial evidence to the contrary, she frankly thought that, if she reached out for him now, her hand wouldn't prove long enough.

"You do believe me, don't you, Elliot?" She was pleading, and Deb hadn't the faintest notion why, or for what. "You believe that you're my best friend. I wouldn't lie about something like that."

"I'm sure you wouldn't."

She stammered, "You—you matter to me. A lot."

"You matter to me, too."

She was losing him. He hadn't moved an inch, and yet Deb felt Elliot pulling further and further asunder.

The only way she could think of to make up the distance was to lean forward in her chair, to shorten the physical gap between them in the hope of somehow bridging this other thing—she didn't even know what to call it—as well. It was a difficult trick to pull off, with the precarious dwelling of cards growing squarely between them. Moving too fast, or even breathing incorrectly, would cause everything they'd worked so hard on for so long to crumble.

"Elliot," Deb said, inching her chin and neck hardly a smidgen forward. "Listen to me." Her voice grew softer. "You're the best friend I ever had. You are very important to me. I realize now that I never said it before, so maybe you didn't realize I felt this way. Maybe you thought I was just using you as a sounding board, or as the only kind soul willing to talk to me in the middle of the night when I got into one of my little panics."

She had his attention. Neither one of them was moving, but Deb felt the distance shrinking between them like a kite returning home. Elliot's eyes were, once again, unabashedly meeting hers.

Only this time, the steam they radiated seemed to be flowing both ways. She wasn't just being passively consumed, she was also the one doing the consuming.

A part of Deb wanted to stay this way forever. Another part of her knew that it was impossible, and yet a third reminded her that there was no way she could stay this way forever, unless she kept talking. It was her talking that was keeping Elliot tethered. One wrong word, one wrong move, and he would be gone. For good this time. She was certain of it.

Deb said, "I guess I never noticed. These entire four years. Jesus Christ, here I was supposed to be the precocious one, and I never noticed I was mistreating you. I behaved like you were this instrument created solely to make my medical school experience more bearable. I leaned on you, hell, I pretty much *exploited* you. And I never said so much as a casual thanks. I never told you how much I appreciated it. I never told you how much you've meant to me."

Elliot's breathing quickened. Or maybe it was just Deb's that did so. She couldn't tell where one of them started and the other one ended anymore.

"I never told you how much you've meant to me. As a friend."

Elliot smiled. His lips parted, a dimple on the right appearing and disappearing before burrowing in permanently. The cleft in his chin deepened. Even his teeth seemed to glow.

He shook his head ruefully from side to side. "You don't owe me anything, Brody. I'm the one who should be thanking you."

"For being a pain in the neck?"

"Yes." Elliot chuckled. "That's it. Precisely."

He sounded like he was kidding. Except that he also sounded dead-serious. Deb didn't know what to do. The only thing she knew for sure was that she couldn't let it—this—him . . . go.

Face-to-face, she could feel the warmth of his breath on her cheek. It ruffled her hair just hard enough to tickle. His eyes appeared bottomless, and possessing the secrets of the ages.

He opened his mouth, tongue gently pressed against its roof in preparation for speech. Deb couldn't even begin to guess what he might say. She only knew that, whatever it was, she was destined to agree with it. Elliot shifted his weight forward. He ran his tongue against his teeth. He took a deep breath. He said a single word. That word was, "Max."

He whistled too hard on the final *sss*. It created a breeze.

Their house of cards crumbled.

Chapter One

September 2000

Dr. James Elliot was waiting on the brilliantly sunny roof of Los Angeles Valley Hospital even before the chopper, carrying his eight-year-old Caucasian male victim of a fall from a seventh-floor window, landed on the helipad. When the doors opened, Elliot was the first to reach the gurney. He smiled reassuringly at the boy with the plastic collar clamped around his neck, before firing off a succession of questions at the paramedics who'd brought him in, all the while running alongside the gurney on its way to the Code Room.

Once inside the Code Room, Elliot allowed Jeff Greenwood, a Second-Year resident, to take over the initial examination. Valley was a teaching hospital, after all. They were big on the learn-by-doing method.

And all the residents rotating through the Pediatric Emergency Room were supposed to learn from Dr. Elliot. He may have been only forty-three years old, but in the eyes of the residents, he was the Grand Old Man of Pediatric Trauma Medicine.

Elliot hypothesized that was because, before he showed up, no one actually believed something so specific should be a specialty. The medical establishment figured that what worked in Adult Trauma should function just as well with kids. And then they wondered why the mortality rate was so much greater among children. Creating a trauma unit especially for the under-eighteen contingent opened a lot of eyes, triggered a mountain of journal articles, and earned Elliot a nationwide reputation as *the* specialist in his field.

Tongue firmly in cheek, Elliot told anyone who asked that his extensive experience was the reason for the "Old" in "Grand Old Man of Pediatric Trauma Medicine." It wasn't the gray he periodically noticed streaking his otherwise raven-black, curly hair. Because, save that, Elliot was in the same shape he'd been in college, when playing semipro hockey helped foot the medical-school bills. These days, however, he stuck to a set exercise schedule—mostly because of the physical demands of his profession. In Emergency Medicine, every second counted. When Elliot wasn't sprinting toward a patient, he was slicing a human chest open practically with his bare hands, or standing for hours, plugging bullet holes gushing from a drive-by shooting victim. If Elliot wasn't in perfect shape, his patients risked suffering for it.

Just like the patients risked suffering when their attending physician was only a Second-Year resident, still wet behind the ears. That's why, when Jeff Greenwood, in his haste to check out the ABC's of elemental trauma—airway, breathing, circulation—overlooked the harsh scratchiness in the little boy's voice as just the result of hoarse crying, rather than a potential lung problem, Elliot stepped in. He called for an X ray, followed by blood gas. The numbers he got moments later from the lab confirmed his fears: a collapsed lung. With a twitch of his finger, Elliot signaled for the thoracotomy tray. He stretched on his surgical gloves, reached for the syringe of anesthetizing lidocaine, and inserted the needle between his patient's fourth and fifth ribs. Their boy had stopped crying. The collapsed lung was making it painfully impossible. He squirmed and struggled inside his restraints, but had yet to utter a word. That disturbed Elliot. Most kids would have been cursing him out quite colorfully by now. He liked it that way. Screaming kids were kids with the will to live. It was the quiet ones that made a Pediatric Trauma Surgeon's heart beat faster.

Still, his immediate priority was the collapsed lung. Elliot asked for a scalpel, and made an incision beside the pinprick left by his needle. He stuck his finger into the hole to keep it open and prevent it from bleeding, then asked for the chest tube. Mouth slit in concentration, Elliot threaded the clear, plastic tube past his finger, into the surgical wound. He kept pushing until large, pink bubbles began burping into the tube. Pink bubbles. Not red. Not bloody. Thank God. The lung was working again.

Score one for the good guys.

Elliot turned to his patient. "Say something for me, kiddo."

The child just stared back, blankly.

Not a good thing. But at the moment, not a primary thing.

With the lung crisis out of the way, Elliot and Jeff completed the rest of their exam, patching up each critical injury as they went along, in order of severity, and double-checking that the boy was stabilized. Finally, at the end of a very long morning, they turned their attention to his baffling muteness. Unfortunately, as far as they could see, there was no physical cause for it.

Which, under no circumstances, meant that there was actually no physical cause for it. It just meant they couldn't see it.

Greenwood suggested to Elliot, "Maybe we should ask Dr. Brody in for a consult."

Deborah Brody was their Chief of Pediatric Neurosurgery, and an expert in juvenile neurological injuries. She'd been with the hospital for eight years, ever since Elliot, after half a decade of phone calls, had convinced her to leave her boring post in San Francisco for a place that really saw some action.

Elliot told Jeff, "Good idea. Brody's in today. Go ahead and page her."

"Actually, Dr. Elliot"—Jeff massaged an X ray between two of his fingers, leaving a smudge on the file— "I was hoping you could do it. See, I . . . Frankly, sir, she scares the hell out of me."

Elliot didn't try to disguise his smile. In all seriousness, he observed, "She'll be happy to hear that."

"I know," Greenwood said.

Elliot dialed Brody's pager number and recorded a message. While they waited for her to arrive, Jeff asked, "You and Dr. Brody, you two go back a really long way, right?"

"Twenty years," Elliot said. Then, because there was nothing else to do for the time being, and because the account came with a moral to young doctors about making snap judgments, he told Jeff about how, when they met on the first day of medical school,

Elliot thought Brody was the biggest idiot he'd ever encountered.

In retrospect, Elliot still asserted he couldn't be blamed for jumping to such a conclusion. After all, what was he supposed to think, when the woman sitting beside him at the second best medical school in the country couldn't remember her own name?

The professor had roll-called, "Brody?"

Deborah continued sitting there, hands primly clasped in front of her, blank as could be. It was only after the second "Brody?" that she jumped to self-conscious attention, awkwardly raising one hand in the air to announce, "Oh, that would be me, I guess."

A first-class idiot, Elliot decided on the spot. She just had to be sleeping with someone important on the admissions board. And all Elliot had to say about that was, she better be damn incredible in bed, because, on the surface, the chick wasn't much to look at. Oh, sure, she had that all-American thing going for her. Blushing cheeks, peaches-and-cream complexion, big hazel eyes, and gushing chestnut hair that she rolled up in a bun, probably hoping to look more professional. If you liked that sort of thing.

Elliot, personally, preferred the more sophisticated type.

It wasn't until he and Brody ended up, against his wishes, in the same study group, that Elliot learned the reason for her ditziness on that first day. Deb had gotten married to Max Brody two weeks before the fall quarter started, and medical school was the first time she heard herself called by her new last name. Elliot also learned, a touch to his chagrin, that the young woman sitting beside him was about as far from a first-class idiot as . . . as . . . well, as Elliot himself was.

And Elliot was not a man prone to low self-esteem.

As a result, he and Brody spent their four years of med school constantly trying to one-up each other in the classroom. One day he'd be top of the stack, the next day she'd be. When it came time for them to graduate, for the first time in UCSF academic history, two students were named number one in their class.

And the *precocious,* straight-*A* twentysomething she'd been then was still visible in the forty-one-year-old woman who bustled into the Trauma Room in response to Elliot's page. Having heard Jeff's opinion of her, Elliot watched with amusement as a pair of First-Years actually seemed to flinch when Deborah walked by. He didn't blame them. While Dr. Brody wasn't condescending or cruel, like some of the other senior staff, she did have a very, very low tolerance for incompetence, unpreparedness, or plain, old-fashioned stupidity. She expected things done right the first time, and if the resident in front of her couldn't hack it, she would find someone who could. There were no second chances in brain surgery.

Which was precisely why Deborah had chosen her specialty.

That, and one more, rather personal reason.

Years ago, Deb confessed to Elliot, "My mother was an amazing woman. She ran a household, raised four kids, chaired all the PTA meetings, sat on the board of five local charities, and put up with my father. But, still, no matter what she achieved, my dad would get this condescending smile on his face, and he would remind her, 'Well, it isn't exactly brain surgery, is it, Elaine?' That's all I ever heard growing up. And that's what made me decide, if brain surgery is considered the pinnacle of what a woman could achieve, then, by God, I was going to be a brain surgeon."

She'd just begun reviewing the compiled test results that Jeff slid before her, when Deborah's beeper sang its five-tone concerto. She excused herself, picked up the nearest telephone, and dialed her assistant while exchanging bemused smiles with Elliot behind Jeff's back about the resident's anxiety in going toe-to-toe with her.

"Yes, Francie," she said. "What's the crisis?" Deb listened closely. "I see." Then, "I'll be there as soon as I can." Brody hung up the phone and returned to the test results.

"Do you think maybe the—" Jeff began.

Deborah cut him off. "These look fine. Whatever the reason for your boy's silence, it isn't neurological." She turned toward the exit. "I've got to go."

"But." Jeff's mouth opened and closed like a fish. He looked from Elliot to Deb, confused. "Dr. Brody. Wait."

"What?" She pivoted, visibly in no mood to be second-guessed, especially by a Second-Year.

Concerned, Elliot took a step forward. Deborah Brody may not have suffered fools gladly, but it also wasn't like her to be this brusque with a resident. They were, after all, a teaching hospital. They were there to make better doctors, and Senior staff mentoring the Junior ones was a huge part of the process.

Jeff shifted his weight from foot to foot, and managed to look everywhere in the room but actually at Deb as he asked, "Are you sure—I mean, how long did you take to look at the test results?"

"Sixty seconds."

The brutal honesty took Jeff by surprise. But it also gave him the courage to pursue his initial objection. "Well, I've been looking at them for the last hour. How can you just come in and, after sixty seconds, decide there's nothing wrong?"

The younger doctor had a point, and Elliot expected Deborah to acknowledge it. She was tough, but she was also terribly fair, and Greenwood was voicing an opinion she herself often gave. In fact, of all the doctors Elliot knew, Brody spent the most time checking and rechecking and rechecking test results. He'd lost count of the many nights he'd swung by her office on his way home only to catch her, coat halfway on and dangling off her shoulders, eyes glued to a particularly bothersome CAT scan.

Deborah said, "Actually, it took me thirty-five seconds to see there was nothing wrong. The remaining twenty-five I spent musing why a Second-Year resident at one of the best teaching hospitals in the country couldn't figure that out for himself."

Stung, Jeff dug in his heels. "I was being careful."

"You were wasting time. Time that could have been better put to use figuring out what is actually wrong with this patient. You kids just don't get it, do you?" Deborah's eyes drifted to Elliot, as if seeking his support. But he was so stunned by her uncharacteristic behavior, that he could do nothing but look back at her, confused, and worried. He was hoping she might give him a clue as to what in the world was wrong with her. But when Brody realized he wasn't about to back her up, she simply shifted the bulk of her attention back to Jeff, telling him, "We've got the best equipment, we've got the best doctors, the best research space. We should be able to work miracles here for every single patient. But you know why we don't? Time. Time, Dr. Greenwood. It's the only thing none of us can control."

And, with a swish of the swinging doors, she was gone.

Jeff watched her leave, finally offering only a

dazed, "Wow." Followed by the more articulate, "What the hell was that?"

Elliot shrugged, equally dumbfounded. It wasn't like Brody to do anything half-assed. And it certainly wasn't like her to grant a CAT scan barely five minutes of attention before offering a snap diagnosis. Not that Elliot didn't trust Deb's snap decisions more than he trusted another neurosurgeon's two-hour meditation. But it still wasn't like her.

He was on his way to pick up the phone and call Francie to ask what was going on, when the emergency-room doors flew open and presented him with a nine-year-old girl covered in third-degree burns over seventy percent of her body, and a hysterical mother who apparently thought an incessant repetition of "I told her not to go near the stove" would somehow help the situation.

By the time Elliot got that crisis under control, there was a two-year-old who'd nearly strangled himself with a living-room drape cord to take care of, followed by a teenager who'd been struck by a car when she coasted her skateboard into traffic.

The whole afternoon and half of the evening disappeared into a vacuum of emergency tracheotomies and barked orders and soothing talks with frenzied parents before Elliot had the chance to catch his breath and take the elevator to Deborah's office.

He found Francie at her desk, headphones on, typing up one of Deborah's patient case histories from an audiotape, and dabbing at her eyes with a tissue, a crumpled pile of which already littered the wastepaper basket at her feet. Elliot thought nothing of it. Francie was famous around the Doctors' Lounge for crying at the opening of an envelope. To an outsider, the tendency might have suggested that, perhaps, medical secretary might not be the best choice of vocation for her. But Francie never broke down in front of a patient, and she claimed her tears were cathartic—"After I see what these poor little lambs suffer, it makes all my problems seem silly. It's really helped my home life, believe me. My Jack used to get so furious about my crying all the time. Now, I get it all out at work, and come home fresh as a daisy." Besides, Francie worshipped Deb. And she was the best assistant any of them had.

Elliot waved his hand on the periphery of Francie's vision, hoping to get her attention over Deborah's dictating in the headphones. Seeing him, Francie instantly turned off the recorder, and pivoted to face Elliot, her eyes filling with fresh tears.

"Oh, Dr. Elliot. Isn't it awful?"

"What is?"

"About Mr. Brody."

Max, naturally, had relocated to Los Angeles with his wife. He agreed that Chief of Pediatric Neurosurgery at Valley Hospital was too splendid a professional opportunity to pass up. Even if it did come from Elliot. Not that Max ever phrased it that way.

In the beginning, Elliot, trying to do the right thing, had attempted to reassure Max that nothing was going on between him and Brody. But Max merely waved his pledges away.

Elliot wasn't sure what to make of the dismissal. On the one hand, he was pleased that Max didn't have a problem with all the time Elliot and Brody spent together. Not only the four years at med school, but afterward as well. Even though both he and Deb got their first choice of residencies, and, for eight years, lived at opposite ends of California, they continued to keep in touch. They may not have phoned each other too often, but when they did connect, the conversations had a knack for stretching into hours.

Max didn't complain. The closest he ever got to acknowledging the situation was, once in a while, if Brody and Elliot's marathon chat swept over lunch and through dinner, he would fix his wife a sandwich and set it down quietly next to her.

Elliot supposed he should have been grateful his best friend's husband was understanding. It would have been awful if Max opposed their utterly innocent relationship. But, on the other hand, Max's indifference could also have read like an insult. Like Max didn't think Elliot was a rival even vaguely worth worrying about.

Shouldn't he have been at least a little . . . curious?

A decade earlier, Elliot had asked Max, "Are you that confident in yourself?"

"No," Max said calmly, his voice reasonable and fair and never the least bit patronizing. "I'm that confident in my wife."

And once Brody and Max relocated to Los Angeles, Max's confidence, whether he liked it or not, extended to finding his wife and Elliot together in the middle of the night. Building houses of cards.

Twenty years had passed since they erected the first one, and they were still keeping score.

Less than ten hours before Elliot and Brody found themselves leaning over the puzzling test results of a mute little boy, Max had walked down the stairs of their house, at seven AM, ready to head out to work, when he came upon Elliot and Brody, who had left the hospital two hours earlier, sitting in the living room, lips pursed in concentration, working on the fifth story of a shaky card house atop their coffee table.

"Elliot," Max remarked casually. "Are you still here?"

Deborah's husband stood a few inches taller than Elliot, with broad, muscular shoulders testifying to the linebacker he'd been in college, and cunning green eyes to remind of the master's degree he'd also picked up along the way.

"Elliot is still here." Deborah carefully balanced a queen of hearts against his six of spades. "Because he's losing."

"It's two to one," Elliot said. "And I'm not budging until we settle best three out of five."

Max shook his head, stopped to kiss his wife good-bye, waved to Elliot, and strolled out the door.

Had that really been only ten hours ago?

It felt like a week. But, then again, so much happened at the hospital in a single day, it was difficult to keep track of regular time. Now, in response to Francie's tears, Elliot inquired, "Max? What's wrong with Max?"

"He had a heart attack, Dr. Elliot. He's dead."

The beauty of being head of the Trauma Unit was that Elliot didn't have to get anyone to cover for him. He could just rip off his white coat, grab his jacket, checking to see that his car keys were in the right pocket, and screech out of the parking lot without a word of explanation to anyone. He drove to Deborah's house with unbelievable speed, figuring if a cop had the audacity to pull him over, he'd refer the bastard to his MD license plates, and keep going. An unfamiliar car was parked in Deborah's garage, leaving Elliot to skid his to a stop practically in the middle of the street, as he hopped out and flew up her front steps.

He rang the doorbell once, then twice. Finally, it opened. And he was facing a woman he'd never seen before.

Too concerned about Deborah to be flustered, Elliot demanded, "Is Bro—is Deborah home?"

The strange woman's eyes narrowed. "Who should I say is—"

"Elliot. Dr. Elliot. I'm a colleague of hers. Where is she? Is she alright?"

"Wait here, Doctor." Elliot couldn't determine if it was his title, or him in general, that seemed to be peeving her so. "I'll get her." She closed the door in Elliot's face, and padded off.

He waited on the damned stoop, nervously jiggling his keys, sneaking glances at his haphazardly parked car. After what felt like a lifetime, the door opened for the second time, and Deborah, the unfamiliar woman hovering behind her like a suspicious college den mother, stepped into Elliot's view.

He'd never realized how small she was. Despite knowing that she stood barely five feet three inches tall, Deborah had never seemed small to Elliot. At the hospital, she carried herself with enough authority for ten women. He couldn't remember ever having to look down in order to meet her gaze. Yet, under the porch light, she suddenly seemed painfully petite. And fragile.

She wore jeans and an oversized men's shirt. Elliot recognized it as one of Max's. She'd rolled up the sleeves so that they didn't flop all over her wrists. They wouldn't stay up, though. So, every few seconds, Deb had to nudge them back up with her fingers, rubbing her palms back and forth against her forearms, as if she were freezing.

Noting Elliot's recognition of Max's shirt, Deborah shrugged apologetically and explained, "It smells of him."

Elliot nodded, mutely, suddenly at a loss over what to say or do. With her hair down out of the bun she usually fixed, and only pinned back with a clasp at the back of her neck, Deborah looked as young as some of Elliot's patients. And just as lost. His first instinct was to hug her, like he did numerous times a day with his kids. But, the problem was, in spite of their closeness on so many other levels, his and Deborah's had never been a physical relationship. Never, not even once, had they crossed the line from friends into something inappropriate. Not even that one time, on Matching Day, had they done anything wrong. And besides, that didn't even literally count. They'd both been young, and anxious, and sleep-deprived. And young. They had both been confused. Still, even then, they'd done nothing wrong.

And both were determined to keep that record intact.

To that end, they may have kissed each other on the cheek at Christmastime. But that was all. Any other physical affection would have been professionally inappropriate. And now, with that strange woman breathing down their necks, it just would have been awkward. So, instead of following his instincts, Elliot merely asked Deb softly, "How you doing, Brody?"

She tried a smile, but it died in the development stage. "You tell me, Doc. What does it mean when it hurts to take a breath?"

"It means"—Elliot ached to at least reach out and take her hands in his—"your heart is breaking."

Deborah inhaled sharply, but her voice came out agonizingly resigned. "Yes. That was my diagnosis, too."

She looked over her shoulder at the woman. "Sarah, please. Do you think, maybe . . ." Deb indicated shooing with her chin.

The act drew Elliot's attention for the first time to another strange woman—bearing a remarkable resemblance to the first—and an older man, standing a few feet away from the door, all of them watching Deborah intently.

"Max's sisters," Deborah explained. "And his dad."

"Oh." Elliot nodded hello, which also served as a good-bye to Sarah, who, honoring Deborah's unstated wishes, moved a whole yard away from them, huddling with her sister and father.

He'd known the Brodys for twenty years. But Max's relatives were strangers to him. Geography was the culprit. Max's sisters and father lived up in northern California. They came to L.A. only for the rare family gathering like Thanksgiving. And the rule was, Elliot never attended any family-only gatherings. It was one thing when Deb had thrown a large bash for her fortieth birthday last year, or the twentieth anniversary party she and Max hosted for three hundred of their closest friends. But when it came to events like Thanksgiving or a family Christmas Day dinner, Elliot stayed away. He couldn't remember how this rule had come about either. He just knew that they both stuck as firmly to it as if it'd been part of the Hippocratic Oath.

"Is there anything I can do for you?" Elliot asked, hearing the banality of his platitude even as he spoke it. "Is there anything you need? Do you want me to stay—"

"No." Anticipating his question, Deborah shot out the reply before he even had the chance to finish asking. "No, no, Elliot. I'm okay. Besides," she lowered her voice. "Max's family is here. It wouldn't look right. For his sake. You understand."

Of course, he understood. Usually, it was Elliot who had to warn Deborah about things not looking right. Because, while Deb was content with her position as Chief of Pediatric Neurosurgery, Elliot had his eye on bigger prizes. It wasn't enough for him to be Head of the Trauma Unit, and chair three of the hospital's most notable committees: Surgery, Credentials, and Budget. Elliot's ambitions for the future included being named Chief of Staff, and, ultimately, heading a presidential commission on Children's Trauma Care. He also wouldn't refuse an offer to become Surgeon General. Hell, C. Everett Koop was a pediatric surgeon, and he didn't do so badly, political-wise. As a result, Elliot was always conscious of how things looked and what people thought of him. That was another reason for his and Deb's lack of physical contact. The last thing Elliot needed was to feed the hospital gossip mill, and risk losing respect, or worse—becoming a laughingstock.

Laughingstocks did not head presidential commissions.

"I totally understand," he told Deborah.

She nodded, hugging herself tighter, no longer even pretending that she was fixing her shirtsleeves. The urge to wrap her in his arms and keep her safe struck Elliot with enough force to bruise. But the trio of haunting Brodys effectively put a stop to that plan.

"Thank you, Elliot." For a moment, he thought she might be the one to reach out and lay her palm along his arm. But Deborah just smiled weakly and shook her head, as if banishing the thought from her head. "Thank you for coming by. I—I'll let you know about the . . . about Max's funeral." Her voice cracked on the last word, and, horrified, she covered her mouth with her hand.

He wasn't accustomed to feeling helpless. That was the other joy of Elliot's profession. When faced with a circumstance that made others feel powerless, Elliot could actually do something.

Except that now, he found himself floundering with the rest of humanity. Still, this wasn't about him. This was about Deb, and making the next few days more bearable for her.

He would play it her way. No matter what his instincts said.

And so, instead of grabbing her by the arm and yanking her out of this house and away from these people, and taking her somewhere where she could yell and scream and let her feelings out, Elliot just nodded thoughtfully. "Okay. Thanks." But he couldn't help adding, "If you need anything—anything, Brody—call me, okay? I'm here for you. Anytime, anyplace."

"I know." She raised one arm and ever so briefly stroked his right cheek, before remembering where she was, and guiltily jerking it away. "That's about the only thing keeping me sane."

Chapter Two

The day of Max Brody's funeral, Los Angeles unrolled a typical September morning, complete with blindingly azure skies and so much sunshine, Elliot stuck a pair of dark glasses in his jacket before heading for the cemetery. He found the weather most inappropriate. Funerals were supposed to happen under overcast skies, with frigid winds and drizzle turning the ground muddy.

Deborah was already standing beside the grave site when Elliot approached. On her left was Max's father, on her right, his sister Meg, and her husband. The other sister, Sarah, was mingling among their mourners, playing hostess. If Sarah was happy to see Elliot, she hid it beautifully.

He ignored the slight, pausing only long enough to

acknowledge greetings from the various hospital colleagues also at the service, but his destination remained, at all times, a more or less straight line toward Deb. She wore a black skirt with a matching tailored blazer, her hair pinned up, her only jewelry the engagement and wedding rings Max once gave her.

She turned and saw Elliot making his way to her through the throng. Her eyes momentarily lit up. Then, she remembered, and, regretfully, shook her head, expression apologetic, but firm. He stopped in his tracks, noting how pale she looked, and how alone. In spite—or maybe because—of the honor guard surrounding her.

Elliot raised his palm and waved it briefly from side to side to indicate that it was alright, he understood completely and would keep his distance. He was striving to reassure her, but, when Deb turned back toward the grave, she looked anything but reassured.

He couldn't take his eyes off of her all during the service. It wasn't often anyone got to see Deborah Brody absolutely still. She was typically in a state of perpetual motion, rushing from consult to consult, or to the OR, one hand on her beeper, the other juggling a stack of test results and files. She moved so quickly, she left a blurred outline hovering in the air in her wake, rather like a puff of dissipated smoke. It made for quite a sight.

Except that, at Max's funeral, the energy she normally exuded seemed to, for the first time, be directed inward, strains of tension coiling round and round each other, threatening to choke her like a cobra gradually slithering and squeezing Deborah's neck.

She managed to fight off the beast for the verbal duration of the service. But as Max's coffin commenced its creaking descent into the ground, Elliot saw she wasn't going to make it. He saw Deborah lock her knees, flatten her back, and square her shoulders as if being held up by two invisible hands from heaven. In twenty years, Elliot had witnessed Deborah reenact that stance precisely twice. The first was after a fifty-hour straight cramming session for the medical boards. And the second was following a three-day residency rotation in the emergency room that coincided with a pileup on three major L.A. freeways. Both times, Deb had made certain she'd fulfilled every one of her assigned duties before standing up, locking her knees, flattening her back, squaring her shoulders, and crumpling to the ground.

She didn't faint. She remained perfectly conscious the entire time. She had simply worked herself to exhaustion, and, as soon as the crisis passed, her body shut down.

When Elliot saw her standing upright as a sentry by the edge of the grave, he knew what was about to happen. He also knew that he was the only one who knew what was about to happen. Elliot had a split second to decide what to do and, as the costly milliseconds ticked by, he hurriedly evaluated his dilemma.

Deb had specifically asked him to keep his distance from her while at the funeral. She was uncomfortable with what people might think. Not about her. She most certainly didn't give a damn about her own reputation under the circumstances. But Deb was damned if she'd have others drawing negative, inaccurate insinuations about Max, because of her friendship with Elliot.

If he honored her wishes, he should just stay away. She had family there. They'd take care of her. He should let Deb fall.

But Elliot could not let Deb fall.

He knew it as soon as he saw her start to waver, and, without giving the notion a fair trial, Elliot felt his legs propelling him toward her, reaching Deborah in four strides.

He wrapped his arms around her waist a mere nanosecond before her strength gave out and her knees buckled. He caught her in his embrace and held her up until she regained her balance.

His face pressed against the back of her head, Elliot couldn't gauge Deborah's reaction to his intervention. But he had a front-row seat for the astonished expressions among the congregation of mourners gathered by the grave site, not to mention the acidic look Sarah was giving him. He felt Deborah stiffen in his arms, and Elliot mentally kicked himself for having made this excruciatingly tough day even more difficult for her. He should have just stayed away.

But he couldn't let Deborah fall.

He couldn't.

Sensing that she'd begun to recover her equilibrium, Elliot gave Deb a slight squeeze—a combination of reassurance and sincere apology—and tried to untangle his arms from around her waist.

But instead of pushing him away like he expected her to, the minute Elliot moved to withdraw his clasp, he felt Deborah's hands—ice-cold, despite the southern California heat—grab on to his wrists, and clutch them tightly for the remainder of the burial.

At the gathering following Max's funeral, Elliot counted seven casseroles, five salads, four Jell-O molds, and two sponge cakes in Deborah's refrigerator. The payers of respect had really outdone themselves with edible condolences. What a shame their efforts sat wasted on Deb. She didn't touch so much as a bite. Despite continuously wandering from her kitchen where the food was stored, to the buffet laid out along her mahogany dining room table, the plate Elliot had set aside for Deb remained pristine. Instead, she made a point of going around to each guest, thanking them for coming, listening to their stories about Max as if she hadn't woken up next to the man for twenty years. At least four times that Elliot saw, she took special care to seek out Max's father, making sure he was alright. She patted his hand, gave him little reassuring hugs, and basically kept a stiff upper lip for everyone. Though, based on how rigidly she held herself in check, as if any wrong action would shatter her into a million pieces, Elliot suspected it was the last thing she really wanted to do.

Deb's own father was in attendance, as well. Elliot hadn't noticed him at the cemetery, and suspected the older man may have flown in at the last minute. Relations between Dr. Deborah Brody, and Brain-Surgery-Fan and Retired-Salesman Peter Gordon were, even under the best of circumstances, strained. They didn't hate each other, and they didn't antagonize each other deliberately—they just rubbed each other the wrong way. At least, Elliot knew that was how Deb felt about the situation. He figured her father knew it, too. That was why he'd chosen to make just a token appearance, so no one could say he hadn't, and then get the hell out, again.

Elliot had met the man a few times, most recently at Deb and Max's twentieth anniversary party. He figured it would only be polite to say hello, and so made his way over. Mr. Gordon appeared to remember Elliot from the party, as well. He knew Elliot and Deb were friends, and so felt no qualms pointing to her, and sighing, "Same way she acted at her mother's funeral. Busy running around taking care of everyone else."

"If it helps her deal with it . . ." Elliot offered.

"Her mother was the same way."

"Hm," Elliot said, reluctant to admit that, over twenty years, he'd heard quite a bit about Elaine Gordon, and quite a bit of it not particularly complimentary toward her husband.

"Did you know Max very well?" Mr. Gordon asked.

It was a great question, and one that, honestly, Elliot wasn't sure how to answer. He settled for an honest though noncommittal, "I met Bro—Deborah, a couple of weeks after they got married."

"I never understood that man." Mr. Gordon shook his head, and shrugged, apologetic. "It's a hell of a thing to say, but I never understood what he saw in my daughter."

Yes, Elliot thought, this certainly was the Peter Gordon Deb had told him about. A most unusual father.

"Don't get me wrong, now. Deborah's a handsome girl. Smart. Too smart, if you ask me—brains like that only mean trouble for a girl—but, I guess some men like that sort of thing. Keeps 'em on their toes, or something. First time she brought Max around, I could tell he was crazy about her. Problem was, the longer they stayed married, less I could figure out why."

"Hmm," Elliot said again, this time because he presumed a wake was the improper place to challenge a man thirty years his senior to a duel.

"What the heck kind of wife was she to poor Max? Constantly working, never home. Two separate people sharing the same house, that's what that marriage looked like to me. I could have never stood for it. I used to look at Max, and wonder, how long till he cracks? Finally, last year, before that big party of theirs, I figured, gotta ask him before I die. My daughter may think I was less than the perfect father while she was growing up—what she doesn't understand is, I was always looking out for her. In my own way. Telling her not to be too smart, hell, that's just my way of protecting her. Same thing here. Who knows how long I've got left kicking around this earth, and if that husband of hers was planning on taking a powder any time in the future, well, it's my job to see that Deborah was left taken care of. So, I flat-out asked him. I asked Max, 'What the heck is keeping the pair of you together for these last twenty years?' And you know what he told me?"

Elliot did not know. However, he ardently wanted to know. For a conversation he'd started only to be polite, this little chat was currently seizing his attention like nobody's business.

"Max looked me straight in the eye—you know that way he had of looking right at you, so you wouldn't think there might be something funny going on—and he told me, 'Pete, your daughter, she's low maintenance.' And then he grinned. Grinned real big. He told me, 'Deb and I, we both love what we do. We love our work, we love our lives, we fit together perfectly. I don't ask her for anything she can't, or doesn't want to, deliver, and, here's the key part—she doesn't ask me for it, either. See, the thing about Deb is, she wants everyone to accept her just the way she is, no asking for changes, no complaints. But the beauty, the justice of it is, *Deb gives the exact same thing in return.* I've never known anyone else like her, man or woman. Think about it, Pete. Who, in the average life, is ever utterly nonjudgmental, utterly supportive, utterly noncritical? No one. No one except Deb. Just having her in *my* life has given me such confidence, such conviction. She makes me feel good about being me. Do you know how rare that is?' "

Elliot had an answer for Peter Gordon's question, now. To the question, "You know Max very well?" the only possible answer was, "No. Apparently, I didn't know him at all."

He'd never heard Deb's appeal to people stated so eloquently, and so aptly. And he'd never identified with Max Brody more.

Elliot's conversation with Deb's father went on for another ten minutes or so, but he, honestly, heard very little of it. He was too busy staring at Deb in a new— well, at least a different—light. Not that he dared approach her.

So, for the remainder of the gathering, Elliot spent more time mingling and making small talk with absolutely everybody else, than he did with the one person he'd come here to see. His display at the grave site had been enough. After viewing her desperate clutch at Elliot's hands, Max's sister, Sarah, now surveyed Max's wife as if Deb were personally responsible for stopping Max's heartbeat.

Elliot felt sorely tempted to knock said sister up against the wall, and politely advise her that Deborah Brody was the best thing that ever happened to her little brother. He thought he'd known it before today, but, thanks to Mr. Gordon, he knew it so much better, now. Elliot yearned to tell Sarah that Max had adored Deb, that he didn't simply light up when she entered the room, he beamed merely thinking about her. Elliot knew that as certainly as he knew the Latin name of every cranial nerve. Deb and Max had been the real thing, and he wished he could make as much clear to Max's sister. But Elliot also figured he'd done enough damage for one day. So, after an hour of chatting with everyone else in the room, he made a show of consulting his watch, and, pausing to offer condolences to Max's father, took his leave. The last thing Elliot saw before the front door was pointedly shut in his face was Deb looking up from a tense conversation with

Sarah and Meg, her eyes registering a heartbreaking combination of surprise—and gratitude—at his early leave-taking and all-around desperation.

It wasn't till Elliot was sitting behind the wheel of his car, key in the ignition, engine purring for every one of the plentiful thousands of dollars he'd lavished on it, that Elliot understood he couldn't just abandon her like this. No matter how uncomfortable being in that house made him, Elliot couldn't just throw Deborah on the mercy of total strangers—kind or otherwise.

And yet, he knew she wouldn't want him to come back.

Not now.

So, Elliot waited.

Despite the lack of engrossing reading material—there were just so many times one could leaf through one's Triple-A booklet before the story lost its suspense—despite the cold seeping in as a typically warm L.A. day turned into a typically chilly desert night, despite his common sense wondering what the hell he thought he was doing, Elliot waited, sitting in his car, for the last guest to depart. He expected those last guests to be Max's family, but the three had an evening plane to catch back to San Francisco, and so were, actually, among the first, after Elliot, to depart. It took another two hours for everyone—including Deb's father, who awkwardly hugged his daughter, pulled back, then, more sincerely, pulled her to him, again—to clear out. And only when he'd made sure that the final car had pulled out of Deborah's driveway did Elliot, grimacing at the cramps in his legs, climb out of the front seat, and hurry up the steps to ring her doorbell.

She answered, expecting one of the more recently departed to have forgotten something, and be returning to fetch it. When Deb saw Elliot, her features shifted from a picture of resignation, to one of wonder. She opened her mouth, then abruptly closed it, not saying a word.

What had sounded like a really great idea while he sat in the Lexus now struck Elliot with its reality. He was being intrusive. After the kind of day she'd already had, Deborah probably was in no mood to see anyone. Especially not a colleague she'd specifically petitioned to keep his distance.

When she opened her mouth the second time, Elliot felt certain Deborah was about to ask him to leave; maybe even reprimand him for making such a nuisance of himself.

But the two words that actually did come tumbling through her lips caught them both by surprise.

"Thank God," Deborah said.

Her refrigerator was stuffed with consoling leftovers, but Deb said simply looking at them made her nauseous, so the role of their makeshift dinner ended up being played by two scoops of chocolate ice cream, drenched in whipped cream, hot fudge, almonds, and candy sprinkles. They sat, facing each other, at the kitchen table, out of sight of the dining room, which still showed the aftereffects of a guest platoon. Deborah had discarded the dark skirt and suit she wore to the funeral for a simple, blue, terrycloth robe. When the edge of her sleeve dipped into the ice cream, smearing a chocolate stain, she didn't appear to notice. To be honest, she didn't seem to be noticing much of anything. She stared straight ahead, not at Elliot, but right through him, her hazel eyes vague and unfocused.

He felt there was something he should do or say that would, if not make Deborah feel better, at least distract her from her agony. But before he had the chance to conjure up a profundity—now he knew what he should have been doing in the car instead of rereading the Triple-A booklet—Deborah looked up from where she had been stirring her ice cream into discolored glop, and, with no preamble said, "Max loved this junk. The sweeter and richer the better. I used to warn him it would drive his cholesterol through the roof."

She jammed her spoon into the sugary mixture, and, in the same gesture, shoved it away from herself, nearly overturning the bowl.

Elliot caught it before the ice cream went splattering across her table. Gently, he slid the plate back toward Deb. His voice level and firm, he told her, "You didn't kill him."

"I know," she snapped; obviously she had been thinking precisely that. She squeezed her hands tightly, so that her nails left half-moon imprints on the backs of her palms. Deb took a deep breath, then let it out slowly. "But I didn't save him, either. Night after night, he sat right here, and he ate crap like this, because there wasn't a speck of food in the refrigerator, and he didn't know when the hell I might feel like coming home."

"Stop it." If he could have grabbed Deb's shoulders and shook her until she quit thinking this way, he would have done it. But considering how awkward he found it to reach out to her in sympathy that earlier evening on the front stoop, Elliot felt even more reluctant to touch her now. "Stop with the damned, wifely breast-beating, okay? Stop thinking his heart attack happened because you weren't around to cook three square meals a day and darn his socks, and whatever else it was Donna Reed did with all her free time."

He'd been hoping for a smile. But all Elliot got in

response to his outburst was Deborah shaking her head, and swearing to him, "I wasn't the wife Max deserved. I accepted that a long time ago. What kills me is that I sacrificed being the wife he deserved, so I could be a doctor. Now, I'm a doctor. And I couldn't save him."

Stunned by her harsh assessment, Elliot could only remind her, "He wasn't a kid with a tumor."

"No," she agreed. "Kids with tumors, I find time for."

"You're not a cardiologist. You couldn't have treated him."

"Well, I could have damn well given him a referral."

This time, Elliot wasn't quick enough to keep her from shoving her bowl not only away from her, but off the table entirely, so it splashed to the floor in a puddle of wet cream and broken ceramic.

"Shit," Deborah exclaimed, leaping from her seat, and reaching for a dish towel to sweep away the mess. She sunk to her knees, mopping up the floor with both hands, until, abruptly, she stopped. She let the towel slip through her fingers, and, like a patient contracting from a stomach spasm, slowly hunched over, shaking, her eyes clamped tightly shut, until her forehead smacked against her knees.

In a flash, Elliot was crouched beside her, resting one hand on her back, the other on her hair, patting it ineffectually, and, probably more for his benefit than hers, soothing, "It's alright, Brody. It's okay. Don't cry."

"I'm not." Her voice sounded muffled against her lap, and he had to strain to make out what she was saying. After a moment, Deb straightened up and faced him, her eyes raw but visibly dry. "That's the worst part of all this. I'm not. I haven't shed a tear since I heard. Everyone else has cried enough to charge a de-salinization plant. Francie . . . well, you know Francie. But also Max's father. Meg, too. And her husband. And Sarah, and Sarah's husband. Hell, half the people at the funeral were reaching for tissues. But not me, though. Not me. Is it any wonder, at the end there, Sarah was watching me like I was the whore of Babylon?"

"I suppose my behavior didn't exactly help," Elliot offered.

They were both still sitting on the floor, Deb having tilted a little so that her legs were now tucked by her side, while Elliot leaned back until his shoulder blades reclined against the cabinet directly behind him. The air smelled richly of chocolate and nuts, plus left-over cigarette smoke from the earlier gathering.

They were sitting barely half an inch apart. And yet, as soon as Deb straightened up, Elliot had recoiled guiltily, so that not even a fraction of their bodies was touching along any juncture.

Deb unthinkingly bridged that self-imposed gap, though, when, in response to his speculation, she reached over to rest her palm reassuringly along his knee, her fingers lightly brushing back and forth against the silk of his only black suit. "You didn't do anything wrong. If you hadn't come up when you did, I would have gone headfirst into the dirt. Hell"—she raised an eyebrow—"maybe that would have satisfied Sarah's quota for my self-flagellation."

Even not looking, Elliot could still feel Deborah's hand atop his knee. It squeezed the cap gently, fingers pressing against the indentations. Elliot said, "She really is some piece of work, your sister-in-law."

Deborah shrugged. "She loved Max. I've got to give her that. Both his sisters adored him, and they never felt I measured up. I can't condemn them for that. My priorities seemed warped to them. And, then there was ..." She looked away, sighing. "Max may have understood about you and me, but he never expected others to."

"The man was a saint," Elliot said, meaning every word.

"No." Deborah smiled, remembering. "He wasn't. And he hated it when people called him that. Max said that he merely acted like a decent human being. Which most folks, out of unfamiliarity, mistook for sainthood."

Elliot needed to laugh at that one. He no longer cared how it might look to anybody else, him and the recent widow sitting on the floor in her kitchen, laughing uproariously. He had to do it.

Deb took no offense. She said, "He was so understanding about our friendship. More understanding than I had any right asking him to be. He never voiced it, but I know it bothered him to hear the rumors about us, the speculations, the alleged 'friends' who looked at him and saw a blind cuckold of a husband. But he never asked me to see less of you. Because he knew it would hurt me. And Max would have rather put up with the whispers than hurt me."

Elliot nodded, wondering why it was that, in spite of hearing that Max never suspected them of doing anything wrong, and in spite of knowing that they never did anything wrong, he now sat devoured by a paroxysm of guilt unparalleled since the first time he exited the UCSF medical library and accidently bumped into Deborah Brody's husband, needing to fumble through an introduction.

Deb went on, "That's why it was so important to me today, that everything look perfectly proper. That nobody think, not even for a minute, that you and I ..." She waved the balance of her thought aside with the drenched towel. "It wasn't for me. Hospital gossip never bothered me, as long as I knew what was what. It was all for Max. I wanted this one day, at least, to be free of the nonsense he had to put up with because of me while he was alive. I wanted him to have his dignity. Damn, I wanted that. I will not have a noble man like that remembered as a buffoon who couldn't see what his wife was up to, right under his nose."

Which brought Elliot right back to the issue of the two of them, sitting on Deb's kitchen floor, her hand on his knee. He scrambled up with what he, watching from the side, could tell was not exactly a plethora of grace. Still, it got the job done. He was standing.

"I should leave," Elliot said.

"No." The swiftness of her reply once again suggested Deborah had been giving the concern a great amount of thought. Kicking the dirty towel toward the trash, she stood up as well, taking both of Elliot's hands in hers, and staring him directly in the eye. She said, "This afternoon was for Max. The rest of my life is for me. Except, I don't know what to do. Three days ago, I had a husband. I had a life. Today, I feel like there's nothing left. How am I supposed to get through this? I need help. You're my best friend, Elliot. I need *your* help. And I'm not about to let some shallow, dirty minds keep me from asking for it."

Well. That little speech certainly left Elliot with a myriad of choices, didn't it?

At least he no longer had to decide whether he really wanted to go or to stay. Deborah had made the choice for him. Her house could catch fire now, and Elliot would stay.

He smiled, and, at the same time, slipped his hands out of her grasp, linking them behind his back, one arm clasping the wrist of the other, like his grandmother used to make him walk around her house, to deter him from reaching out to touch any of the many pretty

knickknacks lying about. Because Elliot didn't know
how precious and fragile they were, and he could
naively break one of them. Even if he didn't mean to.

Elliot said, "I'll stay as long as you ask me to."

She bit her lower lip, catching her breath, and
when Deborah finally exhaled, it sounded like a sigh of
relief.

"Thank you," was all she said.

For about an hour there, Elliot actually thought
he'd managed to distract Deborah from the events of
the day. Out of habit, they went back to building their
houses of cards, both pretending not to notice when
their usual best-three-out-of-five stretched into seven-
out-of-ten, and beyond.

Working on the second story of a Spanish hacienda
made solely out of suits, Elliot kept up his rain of chatter, not caring if he sounded like an idiot, as long as he
kept Deborah's mind off of Max. He thought if he kept
rambling about the hospital—gossip, office politics,
hell, if he thought it would help, Elliot would start
reciting patient histories—they might both, temporarily, believe it was just another day. That Elliot and
Deborah were here on a few hours' respite between
shifts, and that Max was due to walk through the door
any minute.

Except that, even as he tried to unload that bill of
goods on Deborah, Elliot couldn't believe it himself.
Max was dead, and the incredible woman sitting on the
couch, across the coffee table from Elliot, was never
going to be the same, again.

Which meant, of course, that neither would he.

Pretending to work on the two cards that made up
the initial foundation of their paper sculpture, Elliot
studied Deborah from beneath his downcast lids. He

couldn't shake the impression that there was something different about her this evening. It wasn't merely the grief, though that did show itself in the dusky circles under her eyes, the way the pulse at the base of her neck quivered with each breath, and in the way, every few moments, she'd suddenly start, jerk up her head, and glance around the room, as if looking for the source of a noise only she could hear. And it wasn't her casual attire that was throwing Elliot off. Although he did note, in spite of himself, the way the closed ends of her bathrobe parted slightly whenever she bent over to add another card to the edifice. The funny part was, Elliot had seen Deborah, on other occasions, wearing a lot less. While they were residents and crashed in the on-call room in the middle of their shifts, the doctors changed in front of each other constantly. There was no time for modesty, and no energy. So, he told himself, it couldn't be her apparel.

Elliot supposed the factor really disturbing him was how . . . apprehensive . . . Deb seemed. Apprehensive wasn't like her. Deborah Brody was the most confident woman Elliot knew. She walked into every situation—classroom, operating room, conference room—as if she had the support of an Army behind her. Deborah didn't walk, she strode. Deborah didn't ask, she informed. Except tonight, her every sentence sounded like a question, and her every gesture came with an uncertain twitch of the lips, followed by a glance over her shoulder, as if seeking consent. She was acting, Elliot realized with a start, as if the Army she'd always counted on had abandoned her. Which was also when he realized what—or who—the phantom forces had been. And how desperately he wished he were now able to fill that role for her.

Which was the silliest wish of all, really. The

sooner Elliot cleared his mind of it, the better. He had no right to be thinking such a thing.

So, in his newly born crusade to distract himself, as well as her, with the illusion of normalcy, Elliot's on-going chatter stuck to the most mundane, routine details. In his campaign to be truly boring, he even began telling Deborah about the latest meeting of the hospital Budget Committee, which he chaired.

Warming up gradually to the topic, she warned, "I don't want to hear that they're cutting back on my department. We're underfunded as it is." When Elliot didn't disavow her allegation fast enough, Deborah accused, "They're thinking about it, aren't they?"

Just last week, Elliot had been musing how Deb was destined to ask him about this sooner or later, and how he truly, truly didn't want to talk about it. On the other hand, this minute, it was the safest topic he could think of, and so Elliot happily plunged right in. "Well, the overall hospital budget for next year—"

"I knew it." Deborah smacked the deck of cards she was holding against her palm. "I saw the writing on the wall when they cut me last year. The extra money, they're giving it to Morelli, right?"

Elliot winced. "Not all of it."

"But, what, about seventy-five percent of it?"

"Eighty-five."

"Terrific." She leaned back into the couch, her arms crossed. "The son of a bitch. Did he do his standard song-and-dance? Pour more of my money into his AIDS unit, or he goes back to screaming, 'institutional homophobia' to the press?"

"It's a persuasive song-and-dance. Kills 'em every time."

"Institutional homophobia." Deborah shook her head. "The man isn't even gay."

"Doesn't matter. Morelli's got his eye on the Nobel Prize for Medicine, and he figures a cure for AIDS is his best chance. If a few lives get saved along the way, well, call it a bonus. Guy's like something out of an Ayn Rand novel—what's good for him is bound to be good for society. Although, publicly, he claims he's asking only for his fair share of the hospital budget, and that we big, bad homophobes aren't giving it to him for personal reasons."

"I don't mind Morelli getting his fair share," Deb said. "I mind him getting *my* fair share." She guessed, "If they're cutting my budget, they have got to be cutting yours, right? I know there are idiots on the Board who still don't see why we need a regular *and* a Pediatric Trauma Unit. Accidents kill eight thousand kids a year—that's more than polio wiped out at its peak. And, still, nobody cares. We still have to stand in line for funding behind every trendy epidemic of the week."

Choosing his words with painfully exquisite care, Elliot faked concern with getting a jack of hearts to balance, as he asked, "Did you mean what you told the Committee?"

"Absolutely. If they cut my budget any more, I'm leaving."

Elliot said, "I see."

"Although"—the combat drained out of Deb like the final spurt of water from a garden hose—"right now, my job is the only thing I've got left."

Elliot swallowed hard. "You've got me."

"I know." Her answer was quick, simple, a throwaway. Her mind was obviously somewhere else.

He asked, "Are you going in to work tomorrow?"

"I've got to." She rubbed her face with one hand, leaving red streaks along the sallow of her skin. "I scheduled the Chan girl's tumor for tomorrow afternoon. I can't postpone it. Her folks are already on the edge. Another day of waiting will kill them."

"Are you sure you're up to it?"

In lieu of an answer, Deborah picked up a card in each hand, and, with rock-steady arms, balanced both atop their construction without toppling it. A surgeon to the end.

Elliot clapped softly, looking at his watch as he did so. He said, "In that case, I better get going." He stood up.

"No." It wasn't a statement. It was a plea. The exclamation escaped Deborah's lips without her giving it permission.

She was instantly guilty about it, covering her mouth with one hand, and casting her eyes downward. Elliot's heart crumpled.

"I'm sorry." Deborah took a deep breath, swallowed hard, and attempted to offer a brave front, a deed made even more poignant by her valiant struggle to keep up the pretense. "I wasn't thinking. You have early-morning rounds tomorrow, don't you? And here I've kept you—I'm sorry. I wasn't thinking."

"It's okay."

"No, it isn't. You're going to be dead on your feet tomorrow, and it'll be my fault."

Elliot planted both hands on his hips. "Listen to me, Brody. If you were drowning and I had to swim out to rescue you, I'd end up dead on my feet, too. But that doesn't mean I wouldn't do it."

She smiled wryly. "Why, Dr. Elliot, I had no inkling you were such a poet underneath that white coat."

Elliot made sure his tone matched hers exactly—wry for wry—when he told her honestly, "You inspire me, Dr. Brody."

She actually smiled at that, standing up also, and

stretching. She said, "It really is too late for you to drive all the way home. You'll barely get there before you have to turn around again and go to the hospital. You might as well stay here."

It was an offer he'd taken her up on, for geographic reasons, dozens of times. Both when Max was home, and when he was away on business. Deborah liked to say they were adults, they didn't need a chaperon. Besides, why was it permissible for her and Elliot to be alone at her home during the daytime, but not at night? Surely, anything they could do under cover of darkness, they could do just as well—if they really wanted to—with the blinds closed, in the middle of the day.

Still, Elliot felt the urge to balk. "Won't it look—"

"I don't give a damn." Deborah had no more strength left, not for arguing, not for putting up a happy front, not for caring. She was running on empty. "I know what I said earlier about not giving people ammunition to malign Max, and I know how important you think our reputations are at the hospital. And I promise, tomorrow, I'll go right back to caring about that stuff, too. But, right now, I just can't face the thought of waking up to an empty house. Okay?"

Elliot said, "Okay."

Chapter Three

That night, Elliot slept in Max and Deb's guest room.

Although, *slept* was probably not the most accurate term, since that would have required actually, for some length of time, losing consciousness. Or, at the very least, closing his eyes.

To be honest, what Elliot did that night in Max and Deborah's guest room fit better under the classification of stalking.

Because, each time he'd almost willed himself to sleep, Elliot would think he heard a noise from Deb's room, and his nerves would spring awake, piercing his skin like hot needles. And he would lie hushed as he could, listening, trying to identify the sounds he'd just heard, and somehow use them to piece together a mosaic of how she was feeling.

Immediately after Deb first bid him good night, Elliot heard expected sounds. Drawers opening and closing, footsteps padding to the closet, then back. He imagined he could make out the swish of Deb drawing back her blanket, the muted click of her bedside lamp going on, the creak of a brand-new, multipound book being opened. Almost an hour crawled by before Elliot envisaged he heard the book being shut, the light clicking off. During that sixty minutes, it took all of Elliot's resolve to prevent himself from getting up and going next door, knocking hesitantly, asking if there was anything he could do, if there was anything she needed.

Unfortunately, Elliot knew what she needed.

And it wasn't him.

But that didn't keep him from worrying about her.

After the lights went out, he listened for another hour to the creaks and gripes of her mattress, as Deb tossed from side to side. Staring at the wall between them, Elliot, out of forlorn futility, and the illusory whim that, with no genuine options, this just might do the trick, cautiously brushed the tips of his fingers against the wall, willing with all of his might for Deborah to find an ounce of peace, if only for tonight. They could worry about the rest of her life later.

He felt like a fool, especially when he fancied he could sense the warmth of his skin permeating through layers of wood, wrapping Deb in a sort of protective cocoon to keep her safe until morning.

Nevertheless, a few minutes later, the anxious coughing of her mattress stopped, and she seemed to have fallen asleep.

Elliot stayed awake for another hour, just to make certain she was okay. Then, as he was finally about to confer himself a brief respite from the watch, Elliot heard a sound he knew for a fact did not portend a good omen.

The mattress gasped, the light went back on, and her feet hit the floor. The closet door opened. Followed by a swish, a thump, and the hiss of something heavy being dragged against the carpet.

Elliot sat up with a start, rubbing his eyes. He hopped out of bed, already halfway to the door, before he remembered to throw on a robe over the pajama bottoms he'd gone to bed in—another beauty of being a doctor, he always had an overnight case in the trunk of his car, in case he got stuck late at the hospital.

It took Elliot only half a second to sprint down the hall from his room to hers. And a good five minutes to decide what he should do next. If Deb had wanted something from him, she would have come and gotten him. She certainly wouldn't have been shy about it. As residents, they'd felt no scruples about striding into the on-call room, shaking the other awake, and hissing, "Get up and help me." And Deborah certainly never hesitated to beep him when she needed him—whether it was the middle of the night or not.

So, why should this be any different?

Because, Elliot knew, it just was.

Tightening his palm resolutely into a fist, Elliot knocked on her bedroom door. He tried to make it sound like a question.

Unfortunately, he got no answer.

He knocked again, more insistent this time.

Still nothing.

Finally, Elliot looked up and down the hallway, as if to make sure no one was watching, and, tightening the sash of his bathrobe, turned the knob, and walked on in.

He found the walk-in closet door wide open, its

lightbulb on a chain glowing bright. Deborah crouched on the floor, a cardboard box from their television set in front of her, Max's clothes hanging haphazardly off their hangers, or scattered all around her in a pile of silk, cashmere, and cotton. Her hair was pulled back with a plastic, green-balled rubber band more appropriate to a seven-year-old. Deborah was barefoot, and wearing a lavender nightgown held up by a pair of wispy spaghetti straps, and featuring a single layer of lace to represent the bustline.

She didn't look up when he walked in. And she replied to his puzzled, "What's going on?" with a frenzied, "I need to get this stuff packed up."

"What for?"

"I want to take it to Goodwill, before I go to the hospital tomorrow. I never realized how much stuff Max had. A lot of it is still in very good condition, practically new. I'm sure they'll be able to charge a good price, make a nice profit, don't you think?" Deb stopped abruptly, like a horse suddenly jerked back by its bit. She didn't look at Elliot as she asked, sounding more like she was musing to herself, "Unless there's something here that you want . . . Is there anything of Max's that you want, Elliot?"

For a moment, he thought she was joking. That she was teasing him, or testing him, or just trying to drive him insane. But one glance at Deb told Elliot she didn't have the time for any of that now. And so he managed to keep his voice level as he assured her, "No. Thanks. Nothing."

She continued with her packing, as if he hadn't spoken.

"Brody." Elliot sunk to his knees, facing her, despite the fact that she still refused to glance up. "Brody, you know, you don't need—you don't have to do this, now."

"I do." Her head bobbed independently of her

arms, as, like some crazed assembly-line worker, she folded up sweater after shirt after tie after slacks, only to let them flop open again as soon as she tossed each item into the TV box. "I do. I've got to get this done by tomorrow morning."

"It can wait," he insisted. Then, when logic failed, Elliot deliberately adopted his most patronizing tone to instruct, "I tell you what, you go back to bed now, and, tomorrow morning, I'll help you. We'll get done much faster with the two of us working. How about that? Isn't that a better idea?"

He knew what he was doing. Even in the depth of despair, Dr. Deborah Brody was not about to let anybody patronize her. She suffered enough of that growing up with Mr. Peter Gordon.

His plan worked like a charm.

Halting her maniacal folding, Deb slowly raised her head, one eyebrow elevated as well. She said, "Cute, Elliot."

He spread out his arms—just a touch smugly—and grinned. "What can I say? I'm good."

Deborah surveyed the mess she'd managed to make, and, out of the blue, asked, "Have you ever swallowed a watermelon whole?"

"Can't say that I have."

She smiled faintly. "That's what it feels like, you know. I can't breathe in, I can't breathe out. Any move I make, I feel it, like being suffocated from the inside out. I hoped if I could just engross myself, I could make it go away. Not forever. I wouldn't want to make it go away forever. That would be wrong. That would be like making . . . that would be like losing . . ."

"Max?"

"Yes." Her gratitude at being understood—and not judged—even while rambling was visible in the relief drawn across Deb's face. "But I thought if I could occupy myself for a little bit . . . It'll be good to get back to work. Good to get out of this house. You know, the last three days cooped up here . . . I don't think I've ever spent three days straight here. . . . I need new carpeting."

"Something in a fluorescent green shag would be nice."

He'd almost made her laugh. Yet, the split second before she succumbed, Deborah's hand automatically flew to her throat, and she massaged it absently, like a cramped muscle. He assumed the watermelon was making another appearance.

"Thank you," she said simply. Still on her knees, Deborah leaned forward, balancing on her elbows, her face now only inches from his. "Thank God for you, Elliot. You're saving my life."

He didn't know how to respond to that. "Thank you" seemed somehow lacking. Besides, she'd already said it. He didn't want to be redundant. What he wanted to be was helpful. Hell, who was he kidding? What he wanted to be was goddamn heroic. He wanted to utter just the perfect thought, phrase, thing, and make all of Deborah's troubles disappear.

She'd claimed he was saving her life, but Elliot suspected Deb was only being kind. Because he knew he hadn't done everything he could to comfort her. Sure, he'd rambled and babbled and joked. But as a doctor, Elliot knew that the best salve came not from words, but from human contact. Since the night he saw her on the front porch, looking so young and small and lost, wrapped in Max's oversize shirt, Elliot had suppressed the urge to pull her into his arms and hold her until even she could believe that Elliot would give his life to protect her from the world.

But despite all his poetic—albeit silent—

proclamations, Elliot refrained. Except for his catching her around the waist at the cemetery—a spur-of-the-moment impulse . . . emotional triage—every single time Deborah had reached out to him, when she rested her hand along his knee, when she took both his hands in hers, he'd done everything he could think of to politely, but awfully quickly, untangle himself. Because it was awkward.

No, scratch that. Because, it was awkward for *Elliot*.

Deb needed him, and he was too busy stressing about his own issues—while, at the same time, fancying himself her rescuer—to give her what she really craved. Rather than only what he felt comfortable providing.

So, instead of replying to Deb's as yet unwarranted gratitude, Elliot decided to earn it. Ignoring his own uneasiness, he reached forward his right arm and, with utmost tenderness, stroked his palm along her cheek.

The serene smile that lit her face the moment he did once and for all confirmed the rightness of Elliot's gesture. She'd been starving for someone—no, not someone, for a friend—to stop treating her like she was made of glass, and to reach out to her.

Closing her eyes, Deb tilted her head a fraction of an inch, resting her cheek against his hand—all but falling into it, and finally allowing some of the tension in her bones to drain out. He felt the agitated energy vibrating off her skin like physical heat, felt the trembling he suspected lurked right beneath the tranquil mask she donned for the public subside somewhat. Her pulse hammered directly below his thumb, and, after a time, even that appeared to settle into an upper-range normalcy.

Her relief was palpable, and, for the first time since

this tragedy began, Elliot actually allowed himself to think that, while he might not be absolutely healing the problem, at least he was not causing any more harm. At this point, just fulfilling part of the Hippocratic Oath felt good enough for him.

Eyes still closed, Deborah sleepily rubbed her cheek against Elliot's hand, drawing strength from it. Then, once again turning her head a barely perceptible distance, she brushed her lips along his palm.

And softly kissed it.

The electric current that shot down his arm and directly into his heart spurred it into immediate double time. Inside his head, Elliot all but jumped out of his skin. In reality, he realized he couldn't move. Because that same electric shock proved anything but unpleasant.

He pulled her closer, until they were face-to-face, breathing the same air. She didn't open her eyes. But she also didn't draw back when Elliot, no longer able to distinguish right from wrong, good from bad, need from want, allowed himself the indulgence of consummating what she started.

He grazed Deb's mouth with his own. So briefly, it could hardly be judged a taste. Except that it was more than that. It was a piece of music building, a floodgate opening, a confirmation of why specifically Elliot had been so reluctant to take her in his arms in the first place. Because, he knew, without a shadow of a doubt, that, once he did so, he would never be able to let her go.

Their second kiss lasted longer. Elliot briefly caught Deb's lower lip between both of his, sucking on it ever so slightly. She swayed against him. He thought he detected a faint tremble in response.

But she had yet to open her eyes, to look at him, to credit what was happening.

The next time their mouths met, she parted her lips for him, allowing Elliot's tongue free rein to explore her from the inside out, to taste her and to nuzzle her and to caress her. Her hands remained staunchly by her sides, but her body shifted, just a hint, yet it was enough, toward him. Elliot cradled Deb's face between his palms, marveling at the velvet of her skin at the same time as he attempted to breathe her in, to encircle her, to possess her.

He couldn't remember how they got from sitting on the floor to the bed. You never could, in dreams, and that's what this was. He felt positive of it. Why else would both be stirring as if asleep, languid and dreamy, terrified that any sudden gesture would shatter the spell and force them to look at the situation under the austere light of day, instead of wrapped in the bluish hue of twilight.

Deb's nightgown came off, one spaghetti strap at a time. Like a spectral presence hovering on the periphery, Elliot watched himself, slowly and gently and with infinite care, slide off Deborah's nightgown until it wafted to her waist. She opened her eyes then. She looked at him. Only for an instant before glancing away again. But in that instant, Elliot assured himself he'd spotted a touch of bewilderment in the hazel hues, along with a touch of wonder.

But no regret.

And, certainly, no edict to stop.

Because he would have, if she asked him to. At least, that's what Elliot preferred to think.

Fortunately, he never had to find out.

He buried his face in the crook of her neck, tenderly kissing her there. He cupped one of her breasts in his hand, stroking the nipple with his thumb until Elliot felt it harden and reach out to him, encouraging him to continue, to go further. His own clothes melted away in the moment it took him to lower Deb onto the bed, lying down beside her, studying every inch of her with his eyes, as hungrily as he ached to with his hands and mouth. How had he ever missed seeing how beautiful she was?

Certainly, Elliot, after his initial assessment of her as nothing special some twenty years ago, had grown to realize that Deb was rather pretty, in an understated, wholesome, intellectual sort of way. Could it be that he'd been looking at her for so long, he actually missed her transformation from a reasonably attractive girl to a woman the sight of whom now took his breath away?

He freed her hair from its clasp, tangling his fingers in it, bringing it to his face, breathing her in. He kissed the hollow of her throat, smiling when he felt her pulse quicken in response, and gradually traced a path down her body, stopping to wrap his tongue around her right nipple, nibbling and sucking and teasing, until, like a miracle, he detected Deb's hand, lightly but unmistakably, resting on the back of his head, urging him to hurry, to take all of her, to please, please go on.

Elliot did as she bade, continuing to nuzzle her breast while slipping his hand between her legs, caressing her there in rhythm with the throb of his mouth. Her body responded to him where her spirit could not. She simmered beneath his touch, wet and bubbling and hungry. She wanted him. If Elliot still nursed any doubts to that effect, they were assuaged in the way Deb's thighs tightened around his palm, and the way she pressed herself against him, and in the contented sigh that escaped her lips the moment he followed her silent beseeching and slid one finger inside of her, allowing Deb to impale herself against him.

But it wasn't enough.

It should have been, but it wasn't.

Elliot needed her to look at him. Really look at him, and not just for a second before sinking back into that silent realm where, despite her eager response to his touch, Elliot still suspected she couldn't be reached. Before they went any further, Elliot needed to believe, thoroughly and wholeheartedly and without a shadow of a doubt, that Deborah was making love to him.

To Elliot.

That he wasn't a stand-in.

Or worse.

Ignoring her barely muffled groan of disappointment, he raised his head from her breast, and, on his elbows, hefted himself upward till they were face-to-face. Elliot rubbed his cheek against hers, thinking that he wouldn't survive if she answered incorrectly, but needing to ask. Needing to know.

"Who am I?" Elliot whispered, his breath warm along her ear. "Who am I, Deb?"

She stiffened, the furrow between her brows deepening, a touch of newly found rose fading from her cheeks as, with excruciating slowness, Deb opened her eyes. It took her a moment to locate him, to focus totally. A moment that lasted an eternity, and also ended much too quickly. Deborah peered up at Elliot as if seeing him for the first time. The hazel of her pupils swirled a murky brown and green so that, no matter how hard he strained, he couldn't make out anything concrete on the inside.

He got his wish. She was looking at him.

And looking at him.

And looking at him.

Her expression didn't change. It didn't even waver.

She looked at him harder and longer than she ever had before.

And then, she understood.

"Elliot." There was no hesitation in her voice, no confusion, no lethargy. "Elliot." The hand that had been resting on his head now pulled him closer, and, in the lifetime before Deborah's mouth found his, she repeated, "You're Elliot."

He couldn't hold back any longer. He planted his knee between her thighs, and she opened herself to him, allowing Elliot to slide inside her with quenching ease and a groan of relief two decades in the making. Deborah arched her back, raising her hips to meet him halfway and, despite Elliot's sincere intention to take it easy, to let her set the pace, the passion triggered by her desire drove him to thrust deeper and deeper and deeper within her, blood hammering primal against his skull until the only sounds he could still make out were his own heartbeat, and Deb's maddening moans of pleasure.

He craved to remember each one of them, to capture them inside him so he could return again and again to relive how he was able to rouse her, to thrill her, to satisfy her, and so Elliot covered her mouth with his, hoping to make every one of her dulcet cries a part of him. He couldn't remember the last time it had felt this good, this *right,* with a woman. To be honest, right now, Elliot couldn't remember any other women at all.

Deb wrapped her legs around his hips, the fingernails of one hand raking against his back, the fingers of the other tangling in his chest hair, tugging just hard enough to rouse his every muscle to attention. Chest to chest, their hearts beat in perfect sync.

It was getting harder and harder for Elliot to bridle himself from exploding, yet he was determined to gratify her first. Elliot wanted to watch her. He wanted to look down and watch as Deborah shattered, and know it was something he was able to do for her. He wanted to feel her tremble and hear her cry out. He wanted to hear her cry out his name.

Deb's knees dug into his hips as she bucked against him, the flush from her face covering the rest of her in a warm, rosy hue that almost succeeded in driving Elliot over the edge.

And yet, he held back.

Until, looking up at him, Deborah's eyes locked with his, and, with new conviction, she repeated, "You're Elliot."

His world erupted, sensation battling sensation for dominance, with Elliot emerging as the only true winner. Beneath him, he felt his outburst triggering Deb's own as she shuddered and clung to him and bit down on her lower lip to keep from crying out, an exertion that failed, and, instead, produced the sweetest sound Elliot knew he would ever hear.

His name, as a sigh.

They lay, silent and side by side, for the period it took their hearts to settle and their muscles to stop trembling with pure, exhilarated exhaustion.

Then, without warning, Elliot leapt out of Deb's bed, reaching for his rumpled clothes, and hurriedly yanking back on everything he'd discarded in an equal hurry, earlier.

Deborah pushed herself to a sitting position. She watched him dress. She did not say a word. She watched the way it was now *his* turn to avoid *her* gaze.

"You know, you didn't commit any crime, Elliot. It isn't necessary to flee the scene."

He turned his head and swallowed hard. Then he continued dressing.

"Say something," Deb suggested. Her suggestion echoed with the definite aura of a plea. "Say anything."

He tightened the sash of his bathrobe. He said, "I think I've done enough improvising for one night, don't you?"

He left.

Deborah didn't call after him. She didn't budge. It was only when she heard Elliot's car screech out of the driveway and out of hearing range that Deb covered her face with both hands, and, for the first time in three days, finally cried.

Chapter Four

The next morning, Deb woke up slowly, almost painfully, pretty certain that she didn't want to, but less certain as to the reason why. Her head felt as if, overnight, a team of trolls had come along with their axes and tunneled a series of intricate, airless caves directly behind her eyes. Her throat rasped dry and hoarse. She had to cough several times just to draw breath, then blow her nose for good measure. By the time Deb stumbled in front of the bathroom mirror, she trembled at the idea of sneaking a peek at her reflection. Gathering her courage, Deb did so anyway.

And got the shock of her life.

Because, she looked . . . absolutely the same.

She looked the way she did every morning. Eyes a

touch puffy, face a little blotchy, lips a tad dry, hair a lot mussed.

Yet, Dr. Deborah Brody, in no shape, form, or permutation *felt* even vaguely the same. She felt as if her life had been stolen out from under her, warped and mangled and twisted up like a children's party balloon, then handed back to her without explanation.

Max. Elliot.

Their two names echoed in her head with such resonance, they triggered visual hallucinations, where their two faces floated in front of her like the disembodied witches in *Macbeth*.

Elliot. Max.

Max. Elliot.

She didn't know where to look first.

Where to grieve first.

In less than a week, she'd lost them both.

The look on Elliot's face as he tore out of her bedroom gnawed Deborah's soul. It broke her heart. And, the worst part was, she didn't even fully understand why. All Deb knew was that she could not stand it.

She couldn't let twenty years of friendship go down the drain because, for one night, they'd lost their heads and done something utterly inappropriate.

Last night, she'd thought she would wait until she got to the hospital to talk to Elliot. After all, there was no sense making a bigger deal of the . . . situation . . . than it deserved, by breaking their traditional routine. But, now, when even the air around her seemed to be humming with the tension of something left incomplete, Deb suddenly couldn't bear to put it off for another minute. The sooner she and Elliot got matters settled, the sooner their lives could get back to normal. And, right now, Deborah craved normalcy as desperately as, a few hours earlier, she'd craved for someone to put his arms around her and reassure her that the world was not yet coming to a horrifying, unequivocal end.

Which, in retrospect, was how she'd found herself entangled in this damn mess in the first place.

While mentally giving herself a series of terribly satisfying kicks, she meant to reach for her hairbrush. Instead, Deb found the fingers of her right hand curling around the telephone on her bedside table, while her left ones dialed Elliot's office number so quickly, Deb could barely keep up with the sequence. They dialed so quickly, the sudden ringing on the other end caught Deborah by surprise. As did the fact that Elliot's assistant, Helen, was the one to pick it up. Helen usually answered all of Elliot's calls on his general line. But Deb had dialed his private number.

"Dr. Elliot's office." The clicking and rustling in the background suggested Helen was simultaneously chatting, typing, filing, stapling, collating, and—if Deb knew Helen—watering the many plants kept to "cheer up the place."

"Helen?" Deb cleared her throat. "Helen, it's Deborah Brody. Is Elliot—is Elliot available?"

"Actually, Dr. Brody, Dr. Elliot told me you might be calling, and he wanted me to tell you he's got a very crowded schedule this morning, and he'll speak to you later, alright?"

Of course, it was alright. Why shouldn't it be alright? Deb couldn't expect Elliot to drop everything and be available for her slightest whims. He was a very busy man. He was a doctor. He had lives to save. Of course, it was alright.

Damn you, Elliot.

It wasn't alright.

Deborah reached for her hairbrush, and attacked

her hair with all the pent-up frustration she'd re-strained herself from dumping on poor, innocent, effi-cient Helen. By the time Deb finished grooming, she thought it was a miracle she had a fleece of hair still growing from her head.

Driving to the hospital, she couldn't seem to select a street speed. On the one hand, Deb wanted to get there as soon as she could. She needed to talk to Elliot, and she wanted to get it over with as soon as possible. On the other hand, she wasn't precisely looking for-ward to it. So far, in her head, Deb had engaged in sev-eral possible conversations with Elliot. And a large percentage of them were not exactly pleasant. If reality was going to turn out like her invention, then Deborah preferred to delay the inevitable for as long as she thought she could get away with.

As a result, she alternately speeded and stalled down the L.A. freeways, a factor that pissed off every driver around her. Eventually, both too soon and too late, she got where she was going. The sight of the hos-pital looming around the corner grasped Deborah's lungs and, for ample measure, twisted the air out of them. Instinctively, Deb's eyes swept to the ninth-floor window of Elliot's office. The shades were drawn.

She made it to the door of her own office, resting one hand on the knob, before changing her mind. Then, turning decisively in the opposite direction, still wearing her coat and carrying her briefcase, she strode down the gleaming white hallway toward Elliot.

She knocked on his door.

Deb never knocked on his door.

Deb usually just walked right on in.

She knocked again.

Then she walked in.

"Good morning, Dr. Brody." As Deb had pre-dicted, Helen sat in the reception area, simultaneously filing and word processing. Two of her phone lines blinked red, on hold. The door to Elliot's private office stood closed.

"Good morning, Helen."

"Dr. Brody." Elliot's multitasking assistant effortlessly slipped yet another task into her repertoire. She looked up to greet Deb, all the while continuing to file, collate, and staple. "I'm terribly sorry about your loss."

"Thank you." Deborah swallowed hard, and, without meaning to, took an infinitesimal step back, as if trying to dodge the truth. Because for a split second there, she'd managed to forget.

To forget about Max.

The awareness struck Deborah with two separate sensations at once. Guilt. So much guilt, it almost made her double over. How could she have forgotten Max? Only a couple of hours ago, she had felt convinced that the pain would never stop, that she would drag it around behind her like that rock some mythological character spent eternity pushing up some cliff. Yet, for the moment, she had forgotten him.

Because she had been so busy worrying about losing Elliot, the grief over losing Max had momentarily been blocked. And, for that, in a way, she was grateful.

And even more guilty.

What kind of woman could feel grateful for forgetting her late husband—even if it was only for a moment, and probably a normal, self-protective, psychological block, besides? What kind of woman would let worry over losing some friend push aside the grief she obviously felt over losing her husband?

What kind of a monster was she?

Deb wanted to flee.

She wanted to get away from here, away from Elliot, away from what her anxiety over losing him had turned her into.

And yet, she needed to stay.

Matters would only get worse if she didn't.

Deb asked, "Is Dr. Elliot available?"

Helen shook her head. "No, not yet. I'm sorry."

"Is he with a patient?" Deb gestured toward the closed door to Elliot's office.

"No. But he told me he absolutely couldn't be disturbed this morning, except for an emergency. Is this an emergency, Doctor?"

Yes.

She considered losing her mind an emergency but instead said, "No, I'll try him again, later," and walked out.

She sighed, shifted her briefcase from underneath one arm to the other, and went to cure some kids. That was what the hospital was paying her to do, after all. So far, it was the one aspect of her existence Deb had yet to screw up. At least, when it came to curing kids, she knew what she was doing.

Three hours later, she was done.

The tumor removal she'd scheduled for that morning went off so well, even her anesthesiologist complimented Deb on it, adding how impressed she was with Deb's being able to place aside her personal tragedy and concentrate on the procedure.

Deb wished she could tell her the truth, she wished she could confess her personal motto: "Work is easy. Life is hard."

What was more, work was an escape from life.

However temporary.

But instead, she merely smiled her thanks, stripped off her scrubs, reassured her patient's distressed parents in the waiting room, and dictated postop care instructions to the recovery-room nurse. Then she went to page Elliot.

And waited for him to call her back.

When her phone finally rang, Deborah leapt on it, snatching up the receiver, and asking, "Elliot?" despite the reality that there were also about three hundred other people that it could be.

"No, Dr. Brody, I am sorry. It's Helen, again."

Deborah liked Helen, she really did. Except that, right now, she felt a mad urge to staple the assistant's mouth shut.

"Dr. Elliot wanted me to tell you he's still unavailable. If you need a consult, however, he said he could—"

"No." Deb dug her thumbnail into her forehead, drawing blood right at the base of her hairline, then guiltily brushing her bangs down to obscure the pierce. "That's alright, I can manage. Thank you. Again. I'm sorry I bothered you. And Dr. Elliot."

"No problem, Dr. Brody. I'll let him know you called."

Somehow, Deb suspected Elliot already knew as much.

She glanced at her watch, wondering how it could only be lunchtime. Hadn't she been at this for, like, an eternity?

If only she could figure out what *this* was.

Deborah told herself she would give Elliot an hour, then try again. She took advantage of the sixty minutes downtime to take a second look at the test results Jeff Greenwood had shoved under her nose minutes before . . . before.

Though she'd meant what she said then, everything looked fine from the neurological standpoint, she had been somewhat distracted. The concern that she might have, God forbid, missed something key, had nagged at her conscience since she tore out of the emergency room four days ago. She was glad for the second chance to analyze the EEG at length, and even more glad when a thorough, hour-long inspection confirmed her initial diagnosis. The little boy had not suffered a head trauma.

Although, Deb *was* starting to wonder if the same thing could be said about her. There was sound evidence to the contrary.

She'd never acted like this in her life.

She didn't even know if she was doing it right.

She only knew that everything she'd done so far felt wrong.

Precisely sixty minutes after she hung up with Helen, Deborah pushed herself back from her desk, took a deep breath, and, forgoing traditional communication devices like phones and pagers, decided to try a more radical approach. Face-to-face communication.

She took the elevator to the Pediatric Trauma Center, stepping gingerly through the swinging doors, lest she accidently interrupt a crisis in progress. Fortunately, the unit stood calm. A few of the nurses were filling out paperwork. Jeff Greenwood was leaning across the reception window, reaching for a pen.

Elliot was nowhere to be seen.

"Dr. Greenwood," Deb called, figuring she might as well close two wounds with one suture, as long as she was here.

He actually jumped at the sound of her voice.

Deb winced. For some reason, it simply wasn't as much fun to frighten the residents as it used to be.

"Dr. Brody." Jeff patted down his pockets, as if looking for homework he'd previously announced lost to a ravenous dog. "Hello. Hi. I—It's good to have you back."

"Thank you." She deliberately spoke softly, the way she did to her ill patients. Residents were such fragile little things, after all. "Dr. Greenwood, I'm glad I ran into you today. I owe you an apology for the other afternoon. I had no right speaking to you the way that I did. My only excuse is, I was—"

"Oh, no. I understand. Totally. I mean, I heard about—"

"Yes." Deb crossed her arms, defensively, across her chest. "Well, I apologize in any case. It won't happen again."

"Oh. Alright."

"How is your boy doing, by the way?"

"He's fine. It turned out to be just shock. You were right."

Deborah smiled faintly, hoping her consequent question didn't sound odd, and yet, suspecting it would. Even to her own ears, her voice rang phony, overly solicitous, foreign. She asked Jeff, "Is Dr. Elliot around?"

"No, actually, he's not. We had some downtime, so he said he was going to the gym for a quick workout."

The hospital had a gym in the basement for staff members who never found the time to visit a commercial establishment. Between on-call rooms, the cafeteria, and a gym complete with showers, Max used to joke that Deb had no reason to ever leave the building and come home.

At least, Deb hoped he'd been joking.

All of a sudden, it didn't really feel all that funny.

She thanked Jeff for the information, and headed downstairs. She felt kind of silly, entering the gym still dressed in the gray skirt, beige blouse, and white lab coat she saw patients in, while everyone else in the place was wearing sweats, shorts, and T-shirts. But any and all fashion awkwardness was quickly displaced by pure terror the moment Deb set eyes on Elliot.

He sat on the rowing machine, dressed in indigo shorts, white socks and sneakers, and a black sweatshirt, YALE printed in block letters across the front, both sleeves cut off. His hands gripped the oars with such intensity, they raised the veins on the back of his hands like a topical relief map. With every jerk of the machine, the muscles in his upper arms contracted and sent parallel trickles of perspiration to drip off his skin and leave shadowy splatters on the lime carpet below him.

Last night, Elliot had held Deb so tenderly within those same arms. She'd felt safe, protected, sound. So, why was it only now that she finally noticed just how powerful those arms really were. And how good Elliot looked in that cutoff sweatshirt that Deborah had only seen him in a hundred times. Not to mention the way the tendons in his thighs tensed with every forward lunge.

Elliot always boasted about how much he worked out. Deb now wondered why she never encouraged him more in the endeavor. The results were certainly not unpleasant.

"Elliot!" She took a hesitant step forward.

Elliot didn't turn his head. He simply rowed faster. At this rate, he was in fine form to break the time barrier, and rescue the *Titanic* survivors.

"Elliot," Deb repeated, this time standing at the foot of his high-tech machine. The only way he could now avoid looking at her would be if he looked straight down.

So he looked straight down.

"Elliot." She rested one hand on the speedometer, or whatever you called it when the vehicle in question wasn't going anyplace. "I—please . . . What's wrong, Elliot?"

Sweat slid down his face. Elliot wiped his cheek against the shoulder of his shirt.

"What makes you think anything is wrong?" he asked between puffs of air.

"You are not rowing merrily down the stream."

He grunted. Educated at Yale and UCSF, and the man grunted.

"Talk to me," Deb requested.

He shook his head. "I'm a little busy here, Brody."

She could see that.

And, under normal circumstances, she would even have honored it. But Elliot had been "busy" a little too much this day. And her patience was approaching the breaking point about as swiftly as Elliot was rowing.

So, Deb did what any rational, mature, intelligent woman would do under these circumstances. She slipped off her shoe and, with a brisk jab, stabbed it inside the rotary wheel regulating Elliot's paddles.

It jammed instantly, the jolt sending Elliot sprawling off his seat and onto the floor.

Without a word of explanation, Deb wrenched loose her shoe, noting that cracks in the leather did not make for an attractive, or even grunge, look. She slipped the shoe back on her foot. It offered a rather nice breeze now.

She said, "Land, ho, Doctor."

For a moment, there, Deb thought she actually had him. Elliot scrambled off the floor, lunging forward until his face was inches from hers, his mouth open, tongue and lips ready to form the first syllables of "What the hell are you doing?" or "Are you out of your damn mind?" or . . . it didn't really matter. As long as Elliot said *something* to her.

He was standing so close, the heat he'd worked up in the last hour radiated off his skin like a sunlamp. Deb could feel it seep in through her clothes like smoke, wrapping its tendrils around her limbs, boring into her pores. Her every breath embedded it further.

He hadn't looked at her since last night.

He didn't look at her now.

Just when it seemed he couldn't avoid making eye contact with her, Elliot looked away, over her shoulder and at the chin-up bar some three feet behind her. His eyes seized upon it like it was just the life preserver he'd been searching for, after being so unceremoniously dumped overboard. He responded to it like to some homing beacon. Elliot brushed by Deb, taking great care to ensure that not even a string of his clothing inadvertently whisked along hers. He didn't even say "Excuse me."

Deb counted to ten. Knowing that if she didn't, she ran the risk of making a fool of herself in front of some ten colleagues. Then, she turned on her heel and strode toward Elliot on the chin-up bar. He was bobbing up and down in rhythm as even as his rowing had been. She craned her neck for a better look.

"Elliot"—Deb tried a different tack—"Elliot, please." No belligerence or challenge or confrontation in her voice, now. Just a heartfelt plea.

Her earlier pugnacity, her demand that he speak to her, had apparently served only to make Elliot angrier. But the minute Deb let that drop and appealed to him the way she'd always appealed to him—as a friend, Elliot's cadence of chin-ups slowed to one last reluctant bob. As if suddenly running out of steam, he loosened the tension in his upper arms, carefully lowering himself until his feet tapped along the floor—though he did still keep his fingers wrapped around the bar over his head. He wasn't quite ready to let go of his life preserver, all at once.

"What do you want from me, Brody?" His words were aggressive, but the tone almost as pleading as hers.

She melted on the spot. Whatever anger Deb had carried into the gym as the result of Elliot's blowing her off all day, whatever anger had prompted her to destroy her shoe—and, most likely, an innocent piece of exercise equipment—all of it was vaporized by the vulnerability of Elliot's query.

She told him the truth. "I want to talk to you. Please. I *need* to talk to you. Otherwise, I'm afraid I'll lose my mind."

He sighed. He let his arms fall slowly to his side. He said, "I'll go get changed."

He must have done it in record time, too, because Deborah had barely gotten back to her office to wait for him, before Elliot was knocking on her door. Ruefully, she realized that in the past twenty-four hours they'd done more cordial knocking on each other's doors than in all twenty previous years combined.

"Come in," Deb said.

He'd obviously hurried to get to her. That was a good sign . . . wasn't it? He'd showered and dressed so quickly, Elliot was still tying his tie as he pushed open her office door with his elbow, and the edges of his hair lay a touch damp, moistening the back of his shirt collar, sticking the starched material to his neck.

"I'm here," he said, adding that final tug to his tie, as if getting ready for inspection. "What can I do for you, Brody?"

She told him the truth. "I need you to tell me why you're so angry with me."

For a split second, she was afraid he would offer her another smooth denial, like back at the rowing machine. But Elliot had never been the overly predictable type. He stuck both hands in his pockets, squeezing visible fists, and, for the first time since he walked into her bedroom a lifetime ago, looked Deb in the eye. He said, "I'm not angry with you. I swear it on my patients' lives. I am not angry with you."

"But you are angry?"

"Yes," he admitted after a pause.

"With who?"

He swallowed hard. "With me."

"What?" She'd been prepared for a myriad of answers. Except that one. "Why? Whatever for?"

He cocked his head to one side, as if unsure whether Deborah really didn't understand, or was just toying with him. He asked, "Are you serious?" Convinced that, yes, as a matter of fact, she was, Elliot sputtered, "Brody, forgive me, but I seriously doubt my conduct last night would rank too high on anyone's Top Ten List of Proper Behavior After a Funeral."

She didn't know whether to laugh or cry, and so settled for neither. Softly, Deb said, "It takes two to tango, Elliot."

He rolled his eyes, as if her answer was entirely what he'd been expecting her to say. He rebounded with his own, equally as prepared answer. "Under normal circumstances, maybe. But last night, the circumstances were most certainly not normal. You were upset. You didn't know what you were doing. You were counting on me to keep matters under control. And I had no right letting them get so out of hand."

"We were both upset," she reminded. "And, frankly, Elliot, if anyone is to blame for what happened, it's me."

"You?"

"Yes, me. I was the one who begged you to stay the night. I was the one so terrified of what the next hour would bring that I was ready to cling to anyone and anything who could promise me even a brief respite from the pain. You were just being a friend."

"Tell that to Max," Elliot snapped, then, instantly, looked like he wished he could swallow his tongue.

"Max?" Deborah asked. "Is that what's really bothering you? Our betraying Max?"

Another pause, even longer this time. Then, he said, "Yes."

"Well, in that case, we didn't."

"How do you figure?"

"Max is dead, Elliot. He's gone. Technically, I wasn't even unfaithful to him."

"Great," Elliot said. "As long as we get the Seal of Approval from *Webster's Dictionary*."

"Don't do this, Elliot," Deb begged. "Don't do this to me."

"What am I doing?" He looked so genuinely bewildered, the last remnants of Deb's resentment faded away, replaced by grief over the uncomfortable situation she'd put him in.

Her voice barely above a whisper, Deb asked him the greatest favor, yet. "Don't you leave me, too."

The fists he'd been clenching and unclenching in his pockets abruptly ceased mid-spasm. Elliot slowly raised his head, eyes opening wide, his lower lip unsticking from his upper with just the slightest of shock. "Leave you?" he repeated.

The tears Deb once had been unable to get started now proved equally unstoppable. She pressed her fingertips along her eyelids, as if that could somehow stem their flow. Bad idea.

Fighting to keep her voice steady, she explained, "I've lost Max. That's a fact nothing can change. But, if I lose you, too—Because of this one, damn, inadvertent moment of weakness, I don't know what I'll do. I need a friend now, Elliot. I need that more than I've ever needed anything in my life. And all I've felt since the moment you skulked out of my bed like some criminal on the lam, was you pulling further and further away from me. I don't know if I can deal with that right now. I need your friendship so much, I don't even have words to describe it. It's like, your friendship is the solitary thing keeping me tethered to this world. I can't believe I might lose it, because you feel guilty over something so—" Her voice cracked, and Deb took advantage of that opportunity to snatch a tissue from her desk and scrub viciously at her eyes, angry at herself for making a scene.

Angry at herself for having precipitated this crisis in the first place. Angry, and desperate.

Desperate to save the situation the only way she could think of, Deb blurted, "How about we forget about it? We can forget about it. If you and I making lo—if what happened between us is going to cause this roadblock in our friendship, then let's just forget about it. There will be no reason for you to feel guilty because nothing happened. And, if you don't feel guilty, there'll be no reason for you to avoid me. Please, Elliot. Please say we can put this dumb mistake behind us, and just go on like before."

He was looking at her again. Looking at her the way Elliot had just before he grabbed his clothes and disappeared.

Like he wanted her to say something more.

Only problem was, Deborah had no idea what that might be.

She'd already said everything she needed to. Hell, right now, she was terrified she'd said more than she needed to. Her single consolation was that every word was the God's honest truth.

"Elliot?" She made his name into a question.

He had to know how badly she needed an answer.

And yet, he refused to give her one.

But, then again, maybe she got what she was looking for, after all, when, in lieu of a verbal response,

Elliot simply turned on his heel and, wordlessly, walked out the door.

My, Elliot pondered on his way back to his office, it certainly did do wonders for a man's ego to be informed he was utterly . . . forgettable.

Well, how else was he supposed to interpret Brody's assertion that "We can forget about it?"

Deb was ready to forget about *him*.

Elliot only wished he could say the same about her.

Despite Deb's assurance that he wasn't a criminal and thus had no need to flee the scene, Elliot, nevertheless, felt worse than a thief or even a murderer. He felt like a first-class bastard.

Because, despite the bone-crunching guilt he felt wringing his soul like a relentless vise, what really incinerated Elliot was the guilt he . . . didn't feel.

He hated himself for taking advantage of Brody at a time when she was obviously incapable of thinking straight. He hated himself for betraying Max's trust in them. He hated himself for the gossip he risked triggering at the hospital, and the subsequent damage to both their careers. But for twenty years, Elliot had dreamed of making love to Deborah Brody. And, last night, he had.

For that, Elliot wasn't sorry.

And, for that, he hated himself most of all.

That's why he hadn't been able to meet Deb's eyes. Not in her bedroom. Not at the gym. Just the sound of her voice calling his name nearly tore Elliot's gut open. She knew. After twenty years of Elliot twisting himself inside-out to keep his genuine feelings for her a secret, Deb now knew everything.

Or, at least, that's what he presumed.

After all, how could Deb not know? Hadn't he made himself oh-so-very-very-clear last night?

He hadn't meant to. God knew, he hadn't meant to. And, even if he had, he certainly hadn't meant to do it in that manner, and certainly not at that juncture. But as that other popular cliché asserted—no one could unring a bell. What was done was done. After twenty years of hiding it, Elliot had finally, albeit inadvertently, allowed Deb to see how he really felt about her.

Whether accidentally, or accidentally on purpose, the die was cast, Deb knew that Elliot loved her, and they couldn't go back to how things were before.

Or, could they?

Deb certainly seemed to be leaning in that direction.

She wanted to act like nothing had happened between them. Elliot ultimately clued in on that right around the time she told him, "I want to act like nothing happened between us."

The worst of it was, she genuinely seemed to mean it.

Deb seemed to believe their making love meant nothing.

This was the problem.

Because Elliot thought it meant everything.

Naturally, if Elliot had been given an option in advance, he would not—not!—have chosen to reveal his feelings for Brody the night of Max's funeral. That, after all, wasn't just disrespectful. It was . . . tacky.

But now that the truth was out, Elliot thought they should at least discuss it. Deal with it. Hell, would it be asking too much to *acknowledge* it?

Apparently so.

Because Deb, obviously, just wanted to sweep the entire night under the rug.

And Elliot's feelings with it.

He was pretty sure she wasn't doing it on purpose. Deb wasn't trying to deliberately hurt him. That wasn't at all like the woman who, only yesterday, had nearly solicited herself into exhaustion, fussing to make sure everyone else was comfortable on the worst day of her own life. Yet, she had hurt him. So deeply, Elliot doubted he'd ever be able to catch his breath again.

He'd walked out of her office without a word, because Elliot truly didn't know how to react to her proposition. Frankly, he didn't know if he could do as she asked. Just forget about last night, and crawl back into the same cocoon of denial he'd already spent two decades burrowed in, the one where he pretended that all he wanted from Deborah Brody was to be "just friends." Granted, it had gotten comfortable in that cocoon after all this time. He'd decorated the place. The post office knew where to deliver his mail. But "comfortable" didn't actually mean he liked it there.

Elliot had walked out of Brody's office without a word because he was terrified that, if he did speak, he'd say something he could never take back. Not that he even knew what that might be. His every impulse screamed for Elliot to protect himself and get as far away from this already painful, potentially excruciating situation as humanly possible. To just walk away from it.

To just walk away from her.

From Deb.

Yeah.

Uh-ha.

Right.

Like Elliot could really do that.

Like, after Deb had stood in front of him, trying so valiantly not to cry, begging him to please, please not let their . . . mistake . . . ruin their friendship, begging him not to leave her, too; like, after all that, Elliot could just shrug and proffer a "Sorry, babe, don't feel like it. You're on your own."

Hell, Elliot would quicker break his Hippocratic Oath.

Deb needed him.

She needed him to be there for her during the most difficult period of her life. And she needed him to be there on her terms, not his. That meant going along with her. That meant forcing himself to forget how amazing she'd felt in his arms, how sweet she'd tasted, and how badly he needed her, too.

Elliot looked at his watch. Somehow, his musing— along with two emergencies—had swallowed the bulk of the afternoon. It was almost seven hours since Deborah had cornered him in the gym. And asked the biggest favor of his life.

He took a deep breath. He walked down the hall to her office.

He found Francie. Who told him Deb had already gone home.

Okay. Not a problem. Elliot could deal with that.

He knew where Deb lived. He could go there.

Even if *there* was the last place Elliot wanted to go again.

He drove slowly.

The lights were out at Deb's house. Elliot couldn't help it. He felt relieved. She wasn't home.

Yet odds were good, she'd be back sometime.

Elliot had already gone the avoidance route that morning. He thought putting off seeing Brody as long as possible would make her inevitable rejection—he'd told himself it was inevitable so the better to brace himself, but, deep down . . . oh, the hell with it—he thought that putting off seeing her as long as possible would make Brody's inevitable rejection hurt less.

Yeah. That was a good plan. That really worked well.

Time to change tactics.

Better to get matters over with quickly.

Better tear the Band-Aid off with one, quick *riiiiiip*.

Elliot pulled his Lexus into Deb's driveway, then reconsidered—for some reason, he didn't like the idea of her seeing it as she returned—and rolled back several feet into the street, away from the light. The clandestine position made him feel better. And it made him feel worse. What was he, a stalker?

Settling down to wait for Deb to come home, Elliot couldn't help letting his glance wander, quite casually, up to the second floor of Deb's house. Up to her bedroom window.

Site of their utterly forgettable encounter.

Okay. Elliot ran both hands through his hair and took a deep breath. He was obsessing. This much, he knew. He was a doctor, after all. And speaking from a purely psychiatric standpoint—he'd done a six-week rotation, that made him an expert in the field—how exactly had Elliot expected a woman who'd lost her husband only four days ago to respond to his shameful seduction of her? Did he expect her to be pleased? Appreciative? Charmed?

Elliot should've been grateful she didn't press rape charges.

Of course, Brody wanted to forget anything had ever happened. How could he blame her? Just because Elliot had spent twenty years wondering, and dreaming, that didn't mean Deb had ever seen him as anything more than what she always said he was—her best friend. Where the hell did Elliot get off blaming her for that? And where the hell did he get off blaming her for not wanting to alter their relationship? Especially now? God, what kind of a bastard was he?

Well, Elliot thought, they were about to get an answer to that question. Deb's car pulled quietly into the driveway. She got out and headed toward the front stoop of her house.

Elliot did the same.

He called her name.

Softly, determined not to frighten or upset her.

Yet, despite his best efforts, Deb still whipped around as if trapped in the crosshairs of some rifle. Startled, she didn't say anything. She merely froze in place, her fingers lightly stroking the hand rail paralleling the steps.

"Brody. Wait a second." Elliot jogged up the drive.

She didn't move. She just stared at him as if Elliot were a stranger. He opened his mouth, ready with a prepared speech, then, just as abruptly, shut it, tongue doing a somersault in mid-blurt as he noticed Deb looking . . . different.

He raised one hand, palm up, half-pointing. "What—"

Deb's own hand flew, self-consciously, up to her neck, fingers twisting around a lock of hair that was now about a foot shorter than it had been that morning. "Oh," she said. "This."

She'd had long hair for as long as he'd known her. Chestnut, and waist length, and pinned back off her face into either a bun, or a sensible ponytail clip. She'd never even taken it down for social occasions, just altered the style to something more fancy, like a French twist or a cascade.

Now, though, her stylist had trimmed Deb's hair to shoulder length, so that, instead of being tucked neatly behind her ears, it framed her face in supple, clement layers. Instead of it all being one length, he'd added bangs with just the faintest of flips. The new style accentuated Deb's features, highlighting the flair of her cheekbones, the hazel of her eyes, the softness of her mouth. It did not scream the sort of forbidding professionalism the hospital preferred in their female doctors.

But, then again, they weren't exactly at the hospital right now, were they?

He felt he should offer a compliment, but the words made it only as far as his throat, sticking to the palate of Elliot's mouth. He did, however, manage to pry out the most obvious question.

"Why?" Elliot asked.

Brody shrugged, fingers mindlessly kneading the locks of hair in question. She confessed, "I don't know. I just felt like I needed some kind of change. There was nothing for me to do at home, so I got in my car and drove. Next thing I know, I'm driving on Melrose Avenue. And next thing I know after that . . ." Deb smiled weakly, going for a joke. "Is impulsive styling a sign of Dissociative Disorder, do you think?"

Actually, Elliot had a pretty reliable idea of what impulsive styling was most likely a symptom of, but he kept the diagnosis to himself. Instead, he took another stab at the compliment that had stymied him earlier. He said, "You look great, Brody."

"Thanks," Deb said so softly, Elliot had to focus all of his attention on her, just to make out the word.

As if he weren't already doing that anyway.

She looked over his shoulder, halfheartedly searching for the Lexus she knew Elliot usually parked in her driveway, but one that, on this evening, was nowhere to be seen. Brows still knitted somewhat in confusion, Deb asked, "What are you doing here, Elliot?"

That was a fair question. Not on any other day, but certainly today. After the way he'd behaved in her office, Deborah had probably wondered whether she'd ever see him again. He'd acted like a jackass. His best friend in the world comes to him, aching and vulnerable and begging him to be there for her when she needed him the most, and Elliot—who'd once appraised himself a pretty acceptable guy, all things considered—had just walked out on her without a word, choosing to perpetrate his own, personal hissy-fit. A pretty acceptable guy? Ha!

He craved to make it up to her. But Elliot just didn't know what to say. Rather than giving her a straight—or honest—answer, Elliot reached into his sport jacket pocket, pulling out a deck of cards some pharmaceutical salesman had left in his office. He placed the deck on his open palm, and held it out to Deb, like a universal peace offering.

He smiled. The smile was genuine. He offered, "Best two out of three?"

For a moment, Deb stood so still, Elliot wondered if she'd heard him. Her expression didn't change. The only movement was the wisps of her hair tickling the edges of her face.

Then, like the sun finally popping out from behind the smog, Brody's lips parted into a smile of what Elliot hoped was genuine pleasure. She reached forward, taking the cards Elliot offered, her fingers brushing his ever so slightly as she shifted the deck from his palm to hers. She raised the cards to her face, tapping them lightly against her chin. Above them, her eyes glimmered a meadowy hazel. Softly, she said, "Thank you, Elliot."

His lungs sagged like exhausted bagpipes, as Elliot finally released the breath he hadn't even realized he was holding.

Picking up on his lighter mood, Brody took a step to the side, turned toward her front door, and asked, "Do you want to come in?"

His lungs shriveled again.

No. Not yet. He wasn't quite ready to go that far, yet. He gave her the cards to show that he was willing to be there for her. But not in that house. Not tonight.

Not as long as his true feelings were still so raw and exposed, it took all of his concentration just to keep them under wraps.

"I have a better idea." He improvised. "How about letting me take you out to dinner? I mean, I *know* you haven't got any food in the house. Right, Brody? And leftover casseroles don't count. No one really eats those. They're strictly decorative."

Deb squared her shoulders. Once, Elliot had thought he could read every one of her gestures like an impeccable lab report. But, right now, he hadn't the vaguest idea what her body language meant.

Deb nodded, turning away from her porch.

She said, "Okay, friend. Let's give this a shot."

Chapter Five

Even as she followed Elliot down the street to his Lexus, the cards he'd given her tucked in her palm, Deb still couldn't shake the suspicion that life was not yet quite as normal as Elliot would like her to believe.

On the surface, she got what she wanted. Elliot was willing to go along, to pretend, not to spoil their friendship. Elliot was willing to just let life relapse to the way it once was, without any flashbacks to the previous night.

At least, that's what he claimed.

But they'd been driving in his car for nearly two miles, and Elliot had yet to say anything. He kept his eyes locked on the road, one hand on the wheel, the other tapping absently in rhythm to the classic rock-

and-roll on the radio. Jimi Hendrix. Pink Floyd. Eric Clapton.

Hoping to trigger a conversation—any conversation, as long as it filled up the silences left between his drumming, Deb teased, "Ever listen to any music written in this century, Doctor?"

Elliot smiled. Without looking at her, he did turn the volume down a notch. "Are you perhaps suggesting that my taste in music is less than cutting-edge? I'll have you know, Dr. Brody, that I was the first person in my high school to listen to Led Zeppelin. And this was back in 1971."

"Impressive," she concurred. "Only problem is, you're *still* listening to Led Zeppelin."

Another smile. Stiffer this time. "If it ain't broke . . ."

Deb sighed. *Amen to that.*

Another minute of silence stretched into an interminable lifetime. The pressure built up like G force. Deb expected her ears to start popping at any moment. They couldn't go on like this.

Floundering about for something benign yet articulate, Deborah offered, "I got a note from Caryn. She sent her condolences."

"Caryn?" Elliot's eyebrow went up.

Deb chuckled and shook her head. "Remember, Caryn? The woman you lived with for—what was it?—over three years?"

"Oh. My Caryn." Elliot sounded genuinely interested when he asked, "How's she doing?"

"Great. She's living in San Diego. Married to a lawyer. She has a little girl."

"That's great." Elliot pulled his car into the parking lot of a restaurant Deb had never heard of. "I'm glad for her. Caryn did always want to get married."

Deb slid out of the car, shutting the door pointedly

behind her to remind, "Caryn always wanted to marry *you*."

Elliot shrugged, locking all four doors with a lone key flick. "Maybe. But she knew where I stood. I was straight with her from the start."

He had been. From the day Caryn first moved in—an act she initiated—Elliot made it clear he wasn't interested in marriage. Deb remembered asking Max why he thought that was.

Her late husband, without looking up from the papers he'd been sifting through, calmly explained, "Elliot will get married as soon as he stops dating women who all share a common flaw."

"Which is?"

"They aren't you."

She'd laughed it off then. She'd told herself he was kidding. And she made sure never to bring up the subject again.

Deborah and Elliot walked, side by side, into the restaurant. Side by side, but taking great care not to touch. Not even when Deb made a wrong turn did Elliot do the automatic thing and reach for her elbow to steer her in the appropriate direction. He simply called, "Brody," and pointed toward the well-hidden entrance.

Inside, the main dining room proved rather tight, with tables positioned so close together, you could eat from your neighbor's plate without altering your fork's trajectory. And any intimate conversation was out of the question. Although—on the brighter side—it was terribly convenient to ask for a package of sugar from the next table. In addition, the room was extremely well lit. None of that pesky, romantic ambiance for this place. Deb could have performed on-site surgery.

Gauging her reaction, Elliot assured, "The food is fabulous, though. Trust me."

"Oh, I do." She squeezed into the seat they'd been escorted to, and, looking around, said, "It's odd. This place isn't too far from my house, but I've never been here before."

"I know," Elliot said.

Something in his tone—she couldn't quite put her finger on what, but it was enough to get her attention—compelled Brody to look up at him, questioning. "What do you mean?"

He explained, "I picked this place on purpose. I wanted to take you somewhere where there wouldn't be any memories."

"Oh." Terrified that she might commence crying again—and in this place that could mean drowning the customers sitting on either side of her—Deb squeezed her fists as hard as she could, trying to focus on something, on anything, except on the automatic thought that had leapt into her mind the moment she'd walked in—that this place looked like fun, she had to remember to tell Max about it, so they could give it a try.

It wasn't until Elliot mentioned no memories that she'd remembered Max was gone. And remembering was just like hearing it again, for the first time.

Deb squeezed her fists so hard, and for so long, she dug the curved edges of her wedding and engagement rings deep enough into her skin to draw blood.

"Be careful, Brody." Elliot's half-shouted warning was purely professional, and his response was equally instinctive, as, at the first sign of her injury, he reached for Deb's hand, hurrying to remove the rings for a better look at the damage.

"No!" Her own response was equally instinctive. She snatched her hand out of his grip, hiding it under the table. "Don't. I'm okay. It's nothing."

"How about letting a doctor see about that?"

"I said, it's okay." It didn't matter how light-hearted Elliot was being, it didn't matter how strangely the two couples on either side were gawking at them. The single thing that mattered was that Deborah refused to take either ring off her hand.

Which didn't even make sense, since it wasn't like Deb was one of those women who swore that, once put on, the jewelry would never leave her hand. Deb took her rings off all the time. As a rule, she took both her rings off when she performed surgery, and even for certain complicated examinations. She had no hang-ups about it.

At least, she'd thought she had no hang-ups about it.

Until now.

Thankfully, Elliot understood.

He saw the panic in her eyes, and he understood. Slowly and carefully, as if dealing with an injured animal, he drew back his own hands, resting them on the table, faceup, in surrender.

"It's okay," he said. "I won't take the rings off. Just let me look at the cut." He smiled. "I am a trauma surgeon, you may recall. It would be unconstitutional to keep me from a trauma."

Deb laughed. She thought she'd forgotten how, but strangely enough, she laughed. It wasn't exactly a sound of glee, but then again, it wasn't a sob, either.

Progress was progress, even when it came in baby steps.

Hesitantly, Deb returned her hand to the table, inching it in Elliot's direction like a reticent worm.

He took it in the style with which it was offered, balancing Deborah's fingers gently between both of his palms. He nudged her rings up barely an inch, taking great care to ensure their staying on, and prodding the parallel cuts expertly and dispassionately.

Deb wished she could say the same from her end of the table.

She'd never guessed a slither of blood dripping from between her fourth and middle finger and circling her knuckle in a ragged crescent could qualify as a sensual experience. She'd sliced the skin between her fingers down to the bone. Her hand throbbed all the way up to her shoulder, and the open wound itself burned. But all of those sensations proved secondary to the massage of Elliot's palm cradling hers, and the way his fingers worked so efficiently to stop her bleeding.

He dipped a spotless, cloth napkin in his glass of water, and dabbed at the trickling blood, pressing down hard, applying direct pressure just like they taught them in basic first aid.

Deb winced.

Elliot promptly apologized, then promised, "You've been a very good patient. You can have a balloon when I'm done."

She said, "I can't believe I was so stupid."

"Accidents happen. If they didn't, I'd be out of business." He was using his doctor voice. Calm, confident, reassuring. His doctor voice always put anxious patients and parents at ease. Why, then, was Deb feeling herself growing more and more agitated?

She fought the urge to bolt. After the way she'd acted about the rings, jumping up and fleeing the restaurant would only confirm her new, deranged status. That wasn't precisely the image a doctor in danger of losing her entire department usually shot for.

Speaking of which . . . Deb tore her sensory apparatus away from the congenial way Elliot's hands felt against hers, and forced them to focus on tangible, serious—safe—topics. Swallowing hard, she asked, "So. What's the word from the Budget Committee?"

Checking to see that the bleeding had stopped before tightly bandaging her fingers, Elliot didn't look up, but he did sigh and shake his head ruefully. "Morelli's getting to them. I can see it every time I look around the Committee. Nobody wants to be accused of being politically incorrect."

"They'd rather let small children die?"

"Small children don't vote."

He was done with her hand. But Deb had yet to remove it from his grip. Instead, she griped, "My department can't operate on the budget they're proposing. Neither can yours. You require the same special pediatric equipment I do. Did you explain this to them?"

"I've explained it. I've written it. I've computer generated colorful charts and graphs. Next week, I'm having it delivered by singing telegram. In a bunny suit."

"Have you threatened to quit?" Deb offered brightly. "It did absolutely nothing for me."

Now, it was Elliot's turn to laugh. He stroked her palm with his thumb, seemingly without being aware he was doing it. He said, "You know, you could still try playing that card when the butchered budget gets handed down from the mountain, January second."

"Do you think I could at least get a chance to speak my piece before the Committee makes its final allocation?"

"I'll arrange it," he said. "Does next week work for you?"

"Next week is fine." Deb smiled. "You really are amazing, you know that? My hero."

He tried for a flourishing, gallant bow. A tricky proposition while sitting down. He ended up bobbing his head, and elbowing two of their dinner companions in the ribs.

And letting go of Brody's hand in the process. The skin where his fingers once rested felt suddenly cold.

But, at least, the tongue-tied silence that plagued them all during the ride to the restaurant was, thankfully, nowhere to be found on the drive back. From the time they pulled out of the parking lot, to roughly a dozen blocks before Deb's house, she and Elliot chatted as easily and as comfortably as they always had.

Deb told him, "By the way, I finally got around to apologizing to young Dr. Greenwood this morning."

"I bet that shocked the hell out of him. You do know that the residents think you eat crushed glass for breakfast?"

"Hey, Dr. I-Was-a-Jock-in-High-School, you try standing a foot shorter than most of your students and getting their attention. As long as they're scared to death of me, they listen."

"Ah," Elliot said. "Education the Dr. Roca way."

Deb raised a warning finger. "I would like to point out, I've never slashed anybody."

Dr. Jude Roca supervised UCSF's medical students through basic surgery. Once, in the middle of a routine appendectomy, Roca asked to be passed a scalpel. Brody did as ordered, but, just as she was handing him the instrument, Roca abruptly moved his hand, resulting in Deb's accidently slicing the palm of his rubber glove. Dr. Roca responded by grabbing the scalpel away, and, as an example to other students who might be tempted to repeat such a mistake, maliciously slashed the back of Deb's hand, drawing blood.

She didn't utter a word. She didn't so much as make a sound. Brody simply stood there and accepted the reprimand as yet another humiliation in that never-ending series of endurance tests that made up the joy that was medical school. Elliot, however, acting on obvious instinct, because no one who actually thought their act through would ever have summoned the guts to commit it, took a step forward and, eyes burning cobalt blue above his lime surgical mask, slapped Dr. Roca's arm with such force, the scalpel flew out of his hand, shooting across the room and bouncing, loudly, off the wall.

Her hero. Even then.

Funny, Deb had never thought about it that way before. She'd just assumed he was being a friend. That, if their situations were reversed, she'd do the same for him. That it didn't mean anything. Not then. Not now.

Elliot said, "So, I take it young Dr. Greenwood survived your apology without hemorrhaging?"

"I was quite humble. I even impressed myself. Besides"—she wrinkled her face—"he had a point. He was right. I was wrong."

"I'll alert the media."

Deb figured she'd let him have that last dig without comment. Because Elliot was right as well. Deborah Brody did have a touch of . . . fascination . . . with being correct.

Deb smiled. Elliot smiled back, and winked before turning his eyes back to the road. For the remaining six blocks leading up to Deb's house, they rode in radio-accompanied silence. But unlike the pall that had struck them earlier, this silence felt comfortable. It felt . . . safe.

Exhaling for what felt like the first time in nearly a week, Deb allowed her head to fall backward until it lolled against the plush rest beneath her neck. She uncrossed her arms, resting them in her lap, thumb mindlessly rolling back and forth along the now healing cut on her fourth finger. She stared at the vinyl covering the roof of Elliot's car, counting the orderly stitching along its perimeter, and feeling somehow co-cooned, protected. As if all the turmoil reality had to offer was banned from seeping in, like fog, past the fine bodywork of Elliot's pride-and-joy Lexus. As if the vaguely tinted windows were her armor. The high-tech dashboard an early warning system. The headlights and high-beams repelling swords. And the man at the wheel, a guardian angel.

Funny how that thought didn't petrify Deborah the same way her earlier image of him as her hero had.

She had always thought of Elliot as her guardian angel. Ever since that day with Dr. Roca, Deb had gone about her life with the certain knowledge that Elliot would never let anything grave happen to her. Elliot would never let her down.

And, no matter how badly he may have been beating himself up over their slip the other night, Deb knew he hadn't yet.

As the car entered her driveway, Deb cringed at the thought of going inside, despite her exhaustion.

It looked so cold, so dark, so lonely, from the outside. Not a single light was on. Not even the big one over the porch. Max always used to turn that one on, if he came home before Deb did.

Max always came home before Deb did.

Only now did she realize that he must have always seen their house like this. Every night, her husband went in, alone, and made their home warm and inviting. For her.

Why had she never noticed it before? Why had she never said anything about it? Why had she never thanked him?

"Keep going." The command blasted out of Deb's mouth and bounced around the interior of the car for a good split second, before she realized she was the one who'd issued the order. Her voice sounded harsh, like a bark. Deb deliberately modified it to, this time, ask, rather than dictate. "Please, Elliot. I—Do you think you could drive around? Just for a couple more minutes? I can't seem to—I can't—I—"

Elliot didn't say a word. He merely met Deb's eyes, nodded, and obediently whipped his car around with such speed, her house seemed to disappear at the snap of his fingers.

He asked, "Where would you like to go?"

"It doesn't matter. I—just, not home."

"Okay," Elliot said. Then, softly, added, "It's going to be okay, Brody."

She turned her head. The crushed velvet of his headrest rubbed against her cheek like a caress. Deborah whispered, "Everyone keeps telling me that. Why is it you're the only one I believe?"

"Oh, that's easy." He shrugged and signaled a left turn. "I'm a doctor. I ooze solace."

Deb couldn't help it. She smiled. "Yeah. That must be it."

"And because"—he sat up straighter, no longer a Sunday driver out for a casual jaunt, but a man with a mission—"I put my money where my mouth is."

"Meaning."

"Sit back, Brody," he said. "I'll take care of everything."

As a rule, she wasn't very good at that sort of thing. She'd never been very good at handing over the reins to anything, much less her life, to another person. Max had—jokingly, she hoped—once asked Deb whether she'd prefer changing the wedding vows from "Love, Honor, and Obey," to "Love, Honor, and Lead."

Her entire conscious life, Deb had been unable to conceive of a situation capable of changing her attitude toward favoring self-reliance at all costs. Heck, she'd been unable to conceive of a situation even capable of making her *want* to change her attitude.

And not that Elliot did. Not exactly, anyway.

She didn't so much change her attitude, as she temporarily . . . tabled it. She didn't forget it, she overlooked it. She didn't suppress it, she . . . Well, actually, she rationalized it, that's what she did. But, damn it all, Deb just didn't have the strength to fight anyone—not Elliot, not her own standards—anymore. Not now.

She did, however, find the energy to remind Elliot—lest he grow overly cocky—"You've caught me at a very weak moment, here, you do know that, my friend."

"Already noted on your chart."

"Where are you taking me, Elliot?"

He said, "Where do I take all of my wounded patients? To the recovery room, of course."

And Dr. James Elliot's notion of an ideal recovery room, if Deb's eyes were to be believed, was apparently the L.A. International Airport Domestic Departures. He'd parked his car in one of many, multicolored, multileveled garages, and fingers firmly on Deb's elbow, proceeded to guide her up two escalators, into an elevator, around a corner, and past a half-dozen souvenir carts, duty-free shops, and Pizza Huts. She followed him, because she'd said she would, and because, in spite of everything, she was damn curious.

At long last, Elliot stopped in front of the electronic board announcing imminent departures for all airlines. He slipped his Gold Card out of his wallet, and used it to point first at Deb, then up at the screen.

"Pick," he said.

Deb cocked her head to one side. "Uhm . . . I'll take 'What the hell is going on here?' for two hundred, Alex."

Elliot said, "I hear that Hawaii is beautiful this time of the year. Same with Florida, Texas . . . Guam . . ."

"You're out of your mind," she said.

He winked. "Old news."

"I can't go to Guam."

"What's wrong? Don't have the shots?"

"You're serious about this?"

"Well, no. Not really. I don't think Guam requires shots."

"You really expect me to drop everything and jet off across the country at a moment's notice? How do you expect me to do that, Elliot? I've got a full patient load tomorrow."

"You do not. You have no surgeries scheduled till the end of the week. And by the way, professional medical opinion here, you couldn't operate with that cut on your hand, anyway. You need to give it time to heal. *You* need time to heal."

"Still, I have other—"

"Your only other patients tomorrow are a postoperative checkup, which any resident could do, a new patient looking for a third opinion to a diagnosis you've already told the parents, over the phone, that you agree with, and you're due for a vacation from the emergency-room rotation—which, by the way, even if you weren't, I know people. I can pull some strings."

"How do you know my schedu—Francie has a big mouth."

"Francie is worried about you, too. She agreed with me. It was one thing for you to come in and do the procedure today. That couldn't wait. Everything else can. Indefinitely."

"Oh, so now you're getting rid of me, indefinitely."

"You need to get your head together, Brody."

"My head is fine."

"Your head is not fine." He didn't raise his voice, or shift his stance an iota. But everything about Elliot subtly shifted into wall-breaking mode, just the same.

"Elliot, I—" She couldn't fight him. Not while she

felt so at loose ends. The best Deb could do, under the circumstances, was throw herself on the mercy of the court. "I . . . can't."

Fortunately, mercy happened to be what Dr. Elliot excelled at. He softened instantly, turning to face her, and clutching both of Deb's shoulders with his hands.

"Why not, Brody?" he asked gently. "It will do you good."

"I don't want it to do me good." She hadn't realized she was telling him the truth, until she heard her own words bouncing off the sterile, beige airport walls. "Don't you understand, Elliot? I don't want to feel better. I want—I want to—"

"Pay a penance?"

"Yes." He did have a knack for cutting right to the heart of what Deb was feeling. Even when she herself didn't know she was feeling it. "Yes, I want to pay a penance. I want to hurt."

"Good God, why?"

"Because. It wouldn't be fair, otherwise. Why should I feel better, why should I ever feel better again, when Max is *dead*?" She spat the last word, as if trying to expel its meaning, too.

"I don't know," Elliot said. No platitudes, no clichés, no empty consolation or advice; just raw, painful, unpleasant truth. "You're right," he said. "It's not fair."

"I can't do this to him." In her mind, Deborah thought she'd calmed down enough to be speaking sense. But once she heard what she was actually saying, she realized what a pipe dream that was. She babbled, "I can't—I can't . . . leave him behind . . . like this."

"Then take him with you." So simple, and yet so complicated.

"What? What do you mean? How?"

"That's up to you. Brody, listen to me. I'm not

telling you to get on a plane and fly to wherever United flies at this time of night, to get *away* from Max. I'm telling you to get on the plane, to get away from everything that could *distract* you from Max."

"A shame I didn't think of that before he died," Deb snapped. "He might have appreciated it then."

"So, take advantage of the opportunity now."

"It's too late."

"For him, maybe. But not for you."

"You're trying to get rid of me." Deb let her shoulders slip out of his grip, arms falling to her sides. "Is it because we—"

"No!" The cool facade slipped, just a little. He readjusted it between the *n* and the *o*, though. "I'm trying to help you."

She believed him. No matter what, Deb always believed Elliot.

"Where should I go?" she asked, for the first time sounding as lost as she actually felt, and no longer caring who knew it.

"Anywhere you want."

"I—I don't have any clothes, or—"

"Buy whatever you need when you get to wherever you're going. I'll take care of the hospital stuff, and Francie said she'd handle the rest. She'll clean all those moldering casseroles out of your refrigerator. Forget about what's back here. Just turn around, go up to that counter, and buy a one-way ticket somewhere—anywhere. Disappear for a while. It'll do you good."

"But how long—"

"As long as it takes."

"To do what?"

"To say good-bye."

*   *   *

Deb did as Elliot told her.

She bought her ticket. She got on a plane. She went nowhere.

Well, technically, that wasn't true. Deb didn't go nowhere. She went somewhere. A dozen somewheres, as a matter of fact. Deb went lots of places. She just didn't get anywhere.

For close to a month, she just rode planes.

She came to the airport, she looked at the departures board, she picked the first jet with an empty seat heading out, she bought a ticket, and she went. To Sacramento, to Chicago, to Houston, to Miami, to Charleston. She barely stayed in one city long enough to chew a meal and wash her hair and toss and turn for a few hours at the local Hilton, or Sheraton, or Marriot, or whatever was closest, before she was back at the airport, booking her next flight. She liked being up in the air. She liked the discomfort of the worn cushions on the hard, metallic seats. She liked the arid air that dried the skin around her lips and inside her nose. She liked the ice-cold portions of alleged beef, or chicken, or pasta slipped in front of her day after day after day, followed by diluted coffee and the same old magazines. She liked that, up in the air, she had nothing to distract her. Because the last thing Deb wanted was for anything even vaguely recalling serenity or comfort to distract her from coolly, methodically, ruthlessly cataloging each unforgivable sin she'd committed against Max, since the day they'd met.

And so, for over a month, she winged her way to nowhere. And she remembered everything.

She remembered the late hours she kept, and the special occasions she missed, and the promises she broke, and the children she convinced Max not to have. She remembered every emergency that kept her away from home, and every out-of-town conference that

took precedence over her husband, and all the nights
she crashed in the on-call room, because she was just
too tired—no, too *lazy*—to make the two-mile trip
back to Max's bed.

With every tidbit she forced herself to remember
and relive, Deb's temper both plummeted and buoyed.
She hoarded each condemned morsel like Silas Marner
at a particularly avaricious hour, and she wallowed in
it. She breathed it. She *was* it.

It was only when Deb's individual heartbeat was
like a whip lashing mea culpa across her conscience,
when every blink of an eye brought a guilty wince and
any inadvertent glimpse of herself in a stray mirror
caused Deb to want to spit at her own image, did she
feel properly ready to book a flight home.

Home, of course, wasn't home.

Rather, home was not the house she and Max had
shared.

Home, Robert Frost wrote, was the place that,
when you turned up there, had to take you in. Deb felt
certain that if she made the mistake of stopping first at
the home she and Max had once shared, the structure
would vomit her out as disgustedly as a good stomach
pump. That's why her first stop was West Valley Hospital. Elliot's office, to be precise. The greeting Deb received there was a smile. A happy-to-see-you smile.
She was home.

And, once home, Deb told Elliot everything.

Dutifully, she read him her litany of sins, taking a
reverse pleasure in the self-flagellation. The more pain
she shoveled onto herself, the more appropriate she
judged her grief. Nevertheless, no matter how dreadful
she felt, Deb was sure it wasn't enough. A good wife

would be in more pain. A good wife would suffer more. Deb may have failed Max in life, but she was damned if she would fail him in death, as well.

As they sat on a green, wooden bench across the street from the hospital in the middle of the afternoon, one hand tightening their jackets around themselves at the collars to hold back L.A.'s version of an autumn chill, the other ones raised to shield their eyes from the sun, Elliot listened, quietly and thoughtfully and patiently, to every word Deb uttered.

When she, at long last, came up for air, he asked, "Finished?"

She nodded, weak and winded.

"What a bunch of bullshit," Elliot said.

Deb blanched.

Yet, on some level, she'd been expecting as much. Leave it to Elliot to see through her, to realize that, no matter how much she honestly and genuinely grieved for Max, it still wasn't sufficient. A good wife would have done better, a good wife would have—

"You were a great wife to Max. What exactly are you hoping to prove, by pretending you weren't?"

Deb turned her head to look directly at Elliot, wincing from the sun that burned into her eyes. "Weren't you listening to me? Didn't you hear what I said? Everything I did to him?"

"What about everything you did for him?" Elliot crossed his arms. "What about your not even applying for that internship in Europe we both know you would have gotten back in eighty-four, because you didn't want to ask Max to move from San Francisco? What about you taking the red-eye after four days straight in the OR to fly to Chicago to watch him pick up that award he got a few years back?"

Oh, that . . . Deb shrugged, dismissive. "So, once

every couple of years, I remembered to put his needs before my own. Big deal." She waved Elliot's words away. "Max did that on a regular basis."

"What about how, every cocktail party I ever saw you two at, you'd stand right next to Max, one hand on his arm, looking up at him adoringly, as those boring friends of his went on and on and on about bonding with some stock, or vice versa. Don't tell me you found the conversation scintillating?"

Deb shrugged, again. "Max hated that kind of stuff. But he needed to do it. For his career. I just tagged along to keep him company. It was no big deal."

Elliot reminded, "I never saw the two of you in the same room, without you touching him in some way. You either had your hand in his, or your hand was massaging the curve of his spine, or rubbing his neck, or on his knee, if he was sitting down. It didn't matter how many other people were milling around you, or if you were in a conversation; a part of you was always looking to the side, looking for Max, making sure that he was okay."

Deb didn't say a word. That—despite her long, excruciating trip down memory lane—that she'd forgotten.

Elliot said, "The toast you made at your twentieth anniversary party—You said that Max was the reason you were you. No. You said that Max was the reason you *were*—period. You said, if it hadn't been for Maxwell Brody, there would be no Dr. Deborah Brody. You said he was your strength, your faith, your anchor, and your wings. You stood up, you raised your glass, and you looked at him like he was the only man in the room. Like he was the only man in the world." Elliot said, "Believe me, Brody, a man can live for a long time on a tribute like that from the woman he loves. It makes up for a hell of a lot of missed dinners and undarned socks."

She didn't believe him. Deb felt certain he was saying those nice things only to make her feel better. Elliot was like that.

She appreciated his gesture, really, she did. But she didn't feel convinced. And she must not have looked it, either, because, after a long moment of staring at her expectantly, Elliot sighed, shook his head, and, although she initially didn't understand why, began to describe to her a conversation he'd had with her father, of all people, the afternoon of Max's funeral.

Deb listened carefully. She allowed the words to sink in, one by one, like medicinal drops slithering down the inside of an IV.

When Elliot was finished, she said, "Oh."

And then Deborah Brody started to cry for her husband, and for her marriage. For the last time.

The world kept turning.

Deb had forgotten it had a tendency to do that. Four weeks hopping from plane to plane had turned each day into a monotonous carbon copy of the previous one, and it was easy to pretend that, for the time being, time had cordially agreed to stand still.

But time had not stood still.

Her first day back at the hospital, Deb had a three-foot stack of cases to go through, not to mention appointments every hour on the hour, and a dozen surgeries needing to be scheduled ASAP. She dove back into the fray with an enthusiasm bordering on giddiness, glad for the return to routine. But work wasn't the only routine she returned to.

Both honoring their pledge of a month earlier to

pretend that all was hunky and dory and back to normal, Deb and Elliot went back to their long-standing routine of casual chats in the hallways, and sporadic lunches in the cafeteria, and frequent consults in their respective offices. The only thing they had yet to do—despite the cards he'd offered her the night they went out to dinner—was build another edifice. Or cross the threshold to Deb's house.

They met exclusively in public, now, and spoke exclusively of public matters. Patients, budgets, politics, interesting articles in the *New England Journal of Medicine*. For close to two months, they stayed doggedly neutral. How's-everything-oh-fine-did-you-hear-what-Morelli-is-up-to-now-with-our-poor-manhandled-budget neutral. It was a system that worked for both of them.

Or, to be honest, it was a system that worked for neither of them. Which, in a way, was sort of the same thing.

It was a system that worked for both of them, as long as both remembered it was in place.

One day, early in December, Deb forgot.

It was a minor slip, hardly worth mentioning. Or noticing. Or commenting on. Except that, these days, when it came to Elliot and Brody, there was no such thing as a minor slip.

They were walking out of the hospital at the end of the day, on their way to the staff parking garage. Earlier that morning, Deb's car had suffered a cerebral hemorrhage—she knew you were supposed to change the oil when the light told you to, it was the details on how that she was fuzzy on—and Elliot had volunteered to chauffeur her to the place she'd had it towed. As usual—at least, lately—they were walking side by side, careful to ensure that daylight could be seen between them at all times, that not so much as the sleeves of their jackets were within whisper-distance of brushing against each other, and that their eyes were constantly moving—the better to avoid inadvertent contact. It was a tough trick to pull off while waiting for the elevator, where the safe choices for not looking at each other narrowed down to looking straight ahead, looking up at the ceiling, or looking down at one's eternally fascinating shoes. Faced with such scintillating options, Elliot chose straight ahead, settling his eyes on a light blue, photocopied flyer inviting the hospital's medical students and doctors to a lecture discussing the latest in placebo research. He read the notice through twice, before turning to Deb and asking, in all seeming seriousness, "If you're doing research on placebos, what do you give the Control Group?"

For a moment, he actually had her. Elliot's tone and demeanor were so solemn, Deb was actually halfway to answering, "Well, you'd give them the drugs, obviou—" before she got the joke, and burst out laughing.

She laughed so hard that she all but doubled over, and tears came to her eyes. She had to wipe her cheeks with one hand, while, with the other, she instinctively reached out to steady herself, brushing her fingers against the back of Elliot's palm.

That's where she made her crucial mistake.

He wasn't prepared for it. He hadn't braced himself. And so Elliot stiffened at her touch, his own smile melting away like oil paint on a heated canvas.

He didn't pull away, of course. James Elliot was too much of a gentleman to pull away when a lady needed his support. But he might as well have.

Deb felt his sense of betrayal, his sense of . . . disappointment . . . in her. As if he'd expected better from her.

As if she'd let him down.

*   *   *

It took Deb the bulk of their ultrafun evening at the auto mechanic's to regain her equilibrium. She let Elliot do all the talking there. Not, she told herself, because she was subscribing to the cliché that men knew more about cars than women did. That, after all, would be a stereotype.

She did it because Elliot—fanatic Lexus owner— knew more about cars than she did. That was a fact.

She let him do all the talking with the mechanic, and she stayed out of his way, disappearing into the waiting area with a two-year-old issue of *Newsweek*. If she held the issue just right, Elliot didn't even have to see her face while he listened to the mechanic explain what she'd done to her car, and how much it would cost her to fix it—or while Elliot patiently explained why she, in fact, would be paying exactly half that, because the mechanic was, in Elliot's words, "full of it."

Brody told herself that this cowardly hiding on her part was for the best, so Elliot wouldn't think she was breathing down his neck. Or something like that.

He did appear to appreciate her effort. After his half-hour haggle with the mechanic—during which Deb didn't so much as risk making eye contact with Elliot by ducking out even furtively from behind the magazine—he came out in better spirits. By the time he was driving Deb home, Elliot apparently felt revitalized enough to risk making another joke, or at least to speak to her again—without fear of unpleasant consequences.

Elliot indicated the infinite road stretching out in front of them and nostalgically recalled, "I drove down this exact highway twenty years ago after I graduated UCSF and got the residency here. Piled every piece of junk I owned in the trunk of my car, and simply took off. I was so psyched to get here. I looked at the horizon and I thought I could see my perfect, brilliant future unscrolling before me like a magic carpet. I knew exactly what I wanted. I knew how to obtain it. I knew precisely where I was going."

"Yes," Deb reflected. "I remember you from twenty years ago. If only we could have boosted your ego just a touch more—"

"I'd have been utterly intolerable."

"Oh, I don't know. Most of us hotshot medical students could have given you a run for your money in the ego sweepstakes. That's what happens when you tell thirty high-IQ twentysomethings they're the best of the best, then hand them a tray of tools and urge, 'Go ahead, cut into that poor guy's chest. He won't mind. Haven't you heard? You're all gods-in-training.' "

Elliot shook his head. "Twenty years ago, driving along this freeway, I was certain I knew exactly where I was going. But you know what I just realized a second ago?" Elliot pointed out a sign trumpeting a town even the census takers didn't know existed. "I'm lost. I, god-in-training, have no idea where I'm going."

"That's a little too James Joyce for me, Elliot." Deb peered out the window into the dark. They'd needed a Thomas Guide to find their way to the towing place. She figured they'd need one to come back, too. "Are we really lost?"

"I am." Elliot sighed. "But you look like you're doing okay and comfortable over there on your side."

Now, what the hell was that supposed to mean, Brody wondered. The question had come out of the blue, and yet, seemed so pointed. She did her best to keep with the spirit of things. Softly, she reminded Elliot, "We're traveling together, friend, remember? If you're lost, I'm lost."

His eyebrow twitched. Abruptly, he pulled over to a shoulder of the road. The suddenness made Deb lurch forward against her seat belt, then snap back into her seat. Her head spun.

Elliot said, "In that case, we're definitely lost, Brody."

She didn't reply. She didn't know how to.

Elliot said, "I never, ever intended for things to get out of hand like this."

Elliot sat across the elbow-rest from her. As columns of cars zoomed by them, their headlights slapped against his face, plunging it into oscillating masks of light and dark. The flickering strobe effect made reading his expression virtually impossible. Somehow, Elliot was managing to look simultaneously two decades older, and as young as an inexperienced teenager. Brody tried analyzing his body language, hoping it might present a better clue as to what it was Elliot really *was* trying to tell her. But she would have had better luck using a microscope to analyze the secrets of the moon.

Body-language-wise, Elliot was, and forever had been, utterly unreadable. Professionally, the attribute was invaluable. Parents waiting to learn if their child would live or die, for some strange reason, did prefer their diagnosis to be delivered by an unruffled, imperturbable, *cool* physician. And if a man like Elliot could ever be characterized by any single word, *cool* would fit the bill best. Deb had known him for twenty years, and yet there were still entire chunks of his life and psyche she'd never been able to access. On many occasions, she'd no idea what he was thinking. Or feeling.

Like, say, right now, for instance.

Right now, Elliot sat, both feet off the pedals, facing her. His left elbow rested on the steering wheel, the right on his knee. His shoulder leaned, rather casually, into his seat. All he needed to complete the Bogart-esque, I-don't-stick-my-neck-out-for-nobody-because-I'm-so-cool picture was a wafting cigarette. Why then, despite all appearances, could Deborah not shake the idea that the air around them was practically vibrating with tension?

Maybe it was because, in twenty years, Elliot had never looked harder at Deborah than he was doing that very moment.

No, that wasn't true. Elliot had looked at her that hard once before. Three months ago, to be precise.

He'd been looking for an answer then.

He was looking for an answer now.

It certainly would help a lot if Deb knew the question.

She wanted to look away. There was nowhere for her to look.

He was everywhere. Brody couldn't take even a shallow breath, without tasting his presence. It crackled on her tongue.

Elliot repeated, "I didn't mean for things to happen the way that they did."

"You mean, tonight? At the elevator? Please, that was—it was my—I didn't—"

"I mean all of it, Brody. Everything, starting with the day Max died, right up until . . . until this. I never meant for this—this conversation, even—to happen."

Deborah shook her head. She'd prayed they might be past all this. "I told you, Elliot, it doesn't matter. We can—"

"No." It was the tone he used on residents who carried their hypothetical debates into the dangerous arena. It was the tone he used on administrators who tried to convince him they perceived the needs of his department more sufficiently than he did. It was the tone that left no doubt Dr. Elliot could, and would, not be budged. "Listen to me, Brody. Let me finish what I have to say."

Deb swallowed hard and nodded mutely.

Elliot relaxed. If relaxation could be qualified by the vein that had been throbbing in quadruple time at the base of his throat beginning to throb in double time.

He offered, "Contrary to what my behavior the night of Max's wake may have suggested, I do understand the concept of propriety. Of waiting a . . . reasonable . . . amount of time after a man's death before moving in on his wife. I also understand that, in most cultures, three days does not constitute a reasonable amount of time. Neither does three months."

Deb said nothing.

He asserted, "Nevertheless, it happened. For whatever reason, under God-only-knows-how-extenuating circumstances, you and I made love, three months ago. That's a fact. Wishing differently won't make it go away. And here's something else you probably don't care to hear." Elliot looked down, briefly, at his hands. He'd been squeezing his right wrist so painfully between his left thumb and the inside of his palm, he might have been taking his pulse. Or trying to stop it. He looked back up at Deb. Calmly, Elliot said, "I don't want it to go away. I don't want to forget it. I don't want to pretend it never happened."

Deb did not recall consciously making the sound of awareness. She did not instruct her brain to formulate a response, she did not authorize her lips and tongue to form the vowel. The reaction came directly from her gut, bypassing the brain and any other organs she once thought so integral to communication. It squeezed out of her, like the *pop* of a soda can opening. "Oh."

The visceral reply seemed to please Elliot.

He said, "The whole time you were gone, and then, the last two months since you've been back, I've really been giving this matter a lot of thought. I know *you* want us to forget that anything ever happened. But do you think that maybe, for just a minute, I might have a say in voicing what I want?"

Deb swallowed hard. She knew the only answer to his question had to be yes. It was the only decent answer, the only equitable answer, the only fair and just and compassionate answer. To say no would be to reveal herself as heartless and self-centered and selfish and petty. Elliot would never know how much Deb ached to answer no. But Deb could no more do that than she could have stopped herself from fussing over the guests at Max's funeral, at her own expense. It just wasn't her style.

So, what she said was, "Of course, Elliot, I never meant to shut you out. And, if I did, I'm sorry. Tell me, please, what is it that you want?"

"What I want, Brody, what I really want, is not to forget that night, but to—to . . . build on it. I know this is way too early, and, please, believe me, I never would have brought it up so soon, if it hadn't been for what happened between us. I don't mean to pressure you. And, I can wait as long as you need. God knows, I think I've shown how I can wait. But I would like to know this much: Do you think you and I could ever have a future together?"

Chapter Six

Three months.

Give or take.

He'd kept his vow for, give or take, three months.

Was it just a few months ago that Elliot had sat in his office, vowing to do whatever Brody needed to make her comfortable, his own feelings be damned? Sure looked like him. Sounded like him, too. He'd even meant it. At the time. Of course, three months later...

Oh, yeah. Elliot had hero written all over him, now.

There was no pretty way to put it. He'd cracked. Crumbled. Blew it big-time. He just wished he regretted it more.

He hadn't planned for anything to turn out this way. Though, twenty years ago, he hadn't planned on falling in love with another man's wife, either. And he certainly had never planned on letting her know about it.

If Max hadn't died, Elliot felt confident he would have kept things as they were until both Elliot and Brody were too old to do anything about them. Furthermore, if he and Deb hadn't made love, Elliot felt confident he would have kept his improper feelings to himself until an appropriate period of time had passed. And, if Brody hadn't been so damn adamant about ignoring what happened—for one month, for two, for three—he felt confident he would never have been struck by this compulsion to press the issue.

In the end, though, Elliot asked Brody whether she thought they might have a future together for one reason, and one selfish reason only: He really, really wanted to hear her answer.

Brody, however, really, really wanted to slip under the dashboard and disappear from the face of the planet. At least, that's what she looked like as soon as the question was out of his mouth.

Elliot was a doctor. He viewed everything through medicine-coated glasses. Clinically, dispassionately, he noted the increase in Deb's respiration, the pallor—instantly replaced by blush—of her cheeks, the dilation of her pupils, the tightening of the muscles at the base of her neck, the tremor in her hands. Lights wincing off her diamond ring bounced around the interior of his car like a trapped Tinkerbell.

Diagnosis: She wanted to disappear.

Deb opened her mouth to speak, but no sound came out. The tip of her tongue peeked out from between her teeth, then darted back inside, a furtive mole. She pursed her lips, virtually swallowing them in the process, and nervously flexed her left hand.

She exhaled. She said, "Remember how, when we

were in school, spending all those hours together cramming for finals, remember the stories people spread about us?"

"I remember that they weren't true," Elliot said.

She smiled faintly, but the doctor in Elliot recognized it as the reflexive reaction of a person who actually didn't know how to respond.

Deb said, "What I remember is what those rumors did to Max."

"Max?" He'd been expecting the name to come up, but not in this context. "Max never said anything—"

"Max never said anything." Deborah took a pause. "To you." Another pause. "He didn't say much to me, either."

"That's good."

"At first."

"At first," Elliot repeated, noncommittal.

"Max knew how much going to UCSF meant to me, he knew how much excelling at UCSF meant to me. He didn't want to do anything that might jeopardize that. So, when he heard the early whispers about you and me, he didn't mention it. For my sake. He told me later, he was afraid it might make me self-conscious. That I would spend so much time worrying about how things looked and what people might be thinking, that it would interfere with my work."

Softly, Elliot said, "That sounds like Max."

"The only reason he finally mentioned even having heard the rumors to me, was because he wanted me to be cognizant of what people were saying, in case it affected my chances for landing the residency I wanted. He thought I should know everything I had been surreptitiously accused of, so I could fight it, if need be."

"Was that all he said on the subject?" Nervous and

eager to hear the answer for so many reasons, Elliot didn't even know where to begin cataloging and qualifying them all.

"Yes." Brody nodded, the gesture somehow transmuting into a shake of her head, mid-movement. "No. He also told me he didn't believe a word of what was being said, and that I shouldn't think of changing my behavior based on somebody else's bilious attacks. He told me to hold my head high. And that he would do the same."

For a moment, it seemed like there was nothing more to say on the subject. Except for one little problem. Despite having talked for a good ten minutes straight, Deborah had yet to answer Elliot's initial question. And, well, he really would have liked her to.

"Brody," he began tentatively. She cut him off.

Deb said, "I'm getting to it."

That was the problem with knowing somebody for twenty years, he decided. They could read your mind.

It was the problem with knowing somebody for twenty years—and the blessing.

"For twenty years, Max didn't say anything about us. Granted, we lived in two different cities for the eight years after finishing med school, but you'd be amazed how people still talked." She was crying without tears now, holding them back so she could force out what she wanted to say without stuttering. Her whole body trembled from the Herculean effort of it all. It made Elliot want to reach out, and wrap her in his arms. It made him want to tell her that it was okay, that she didn't have to do this anymore, she'd didn't have to shred herself open for his sake, or anybody's. Except, he knew the display would not be appreciated. Because Deb was a woman on a mission.

She said, "Do you think people gave Max credit for taking the high road? Do you think they said, 'There goes a wonderful man and wonderful husband who loves and trusts his wife and doesn't choose to wallow in the mud just because others would like him to'?"

"From the tone of your voice, Brody, I'm going to guess the answer is no?"

She snorted, bitterly. "The answer is—most certainly, no. The same bastards who loved to gossip about you and me sliced Max no slack, either. Our esteemed, upright colleagues at this fine institution, you should have heard what they said about him. They called him a dupe, and a fool. An ostrich with his head stuck in the sand. They said he couldn't see what was right in front of his face, that he was blind. A cuckold. They called Max—Max! one of the most clear-eyed, brilliant men I ever knew—they called him a cuckold. And they laughed at him. Not just behind his back, but in front of his face, whenever he was brave enough to accompany me to a hospital function. Like he was this dirty joke. I know you must have heard at least some of it. Because, Max certainly did."

He had to admit she was right, but added, "I guess I always hoped he'd managed to avoid it. He never acted like—"

"That was for me. He was a gentleman, and, for me, he chose to rise above it. He never acted like he heard a word. Elliot"—Deb looked him in the eye for the first time since eternity began—"I will not give those bastards who hovered around the edges of my marriage like drooling vultures the satisfaction of having the last laugh at Max's expense."

His expression must have broadcast Elliot's confusion, because Deb elaborated, "If those scandalmongers at the hospital found out about us—the night of the funeral, I mean—just what conclusions do you think it would lead them to draw about Max?"

He saw where she was going. He saw where she was going, and he detested it with every muscle in his being. Unfortunately, he also couldn't tell her she was totally wrong.

She said, "I will not, not, under any circumstances, give them even a second of self-righteous enjoyment, thinking they were right about us all along, thinking they were right about Max. My husband is dead, Elliot. And, God help me, I know I contributed—however inadvertently—to his humiliation while he was alive. I am going to make sure he has his dignity now. I will not, for so much as a minute, do, or say, or suggest anything that might present him in a less than positive light. I owe him that much, at least. Don't you think? Don't you agree that I—*we,* owe him that much?"

Elliot swallowed hard. A little harder, and he suspected he could have easily imploded from the inside out. Elliot swallowed hard. He said, "We do."

Elliot expected the ride back to Deb's house to be quiet, like it had been that first night, when she'd begged him not to take her home—not yet. Much to his surprise, however, this evening, Deb seemed downright talkative, giddy almost, during the half an hour it took them to figure out where precisely they were, and how they could get out of there as soon as possible. As they maneuvered their way along Los Angeles' labyrinth of freeways, the sight of a stretch limo with a quartet of drunken and howling teens sticking their torsos out of the sunroof, turned the conversation to, of all things, high-school proms.

Deb brought the subject up first. She asked Elliot about his, forcing him to admit that the night was barely more than a hazy fog buried somewhere deep in the I-don't-want-to-remember part of his mind. Why was she so interested?

Brody said, "Probably because I never got to go to mine. It's such a major rite of youthful passage. I feel like I missed out on a piece of Americana."

Elliot raised an eyebrow. "I refuse to believe no guy asked you to the prom."

"Never got a chance." She explained, "I graduated high school a semester before everybody else, in January. And then I got early admission to the University of Chicago, so . . ."

"No prom."

"No prom." More academically curious than regretful, Deborah reflected. "Now that I think about it, I missed a hell of a lot of those pesky rites of passage. Never had a high-school graduation. Never even had a college one."

"Really? Why not?"

"Max and I got married two weeks after I graduated. My family didn't want to make the trip to Chicago twice."

"Hm," Elliot said.

She offered, "Know what else I never did?"

"What?"

"I never dated."

"I beg your pardon?" Elliot tried for a laugh, but the sound never quite left his throat. "Did Max order you from a catalog?"

Deb said, "I mean, I never dated continually—like you."

"Hm," Elliot said.

"Sure, I dated a lot in high school. But, that's high school. Then, my first year in college, I was only seventeen. Scared a lot of guys off. Something about transporting minors over state lines, and statutory rape laws. Sophomore year, I met Max. And that was it. We went steady—do people still use that word?—for three years, and then we got married."

"Point, game, set, match," Elliot said.

"Exactly."

He wanted to ask if she regretted it. He wanted to ask if she ever wondered what she'd missed.

If she ever wondered whom she'd missed.

"Brody!" Elliot stood at one end of the hospital's eggshell-colored corridor, calling to Deb, beckoning her with one hand. "Come over here. I want you to meet my new girlfriend."

She hurried down the hall, stopping beside Elliot as he knelt beside a crib-shaped bed in Pediatric ICU, and tenderly stroked the wavy head of a coffee-colored two-year-old lying immobile and wrapped from the armpits down in white bandages. The little girl beamed up at him, and Elliot returned the expression. He said, "This is Miss Tammy Baldwin. She is a very brave young lady. Tammy had a little accident, but she is going to be just fine. I promised her that."

Deb didn't need to look at Tammy's chart to know the girl had suffered third-degree burns over most of her body. She recognized the dressings. Instead, Deb smiled brightly, and said, "How do you do, Miss Tammy." She teased Elliot, "Quite the lady-killer, aren't you, Doc? Got her eating out of the palm of your hand."

"What can I say?" He shrugged. "I'm irresistible."

Deb turned her head to look at him.

But didn't say a word.

They bid their good-byes to Tammy and exited

the ICU, heading toward the elevator and the meeting Elliot scheduled for Deb with the Budget Committee. Neither said anything about the other night. Neither admitted to themselves they were even thinking about it.

Instead, as they rode the elevator, Deb chatted as animatedly as she had earlier in his car. And loudly enough to drown out the Muzak. She said, "Oh, you'll never guess who came to see me this morning. Jeff Greenwood. Guess what he wanted?"

"He is filing a complaint charging you with cruel and inhuman treatment of a resident?"

"Stranger than that. He's putting in a request to train under me for a specialty in pediatric neurosurgery."

"Whoa!" Elliot's eyebrows emphasized the verbal punctuation. "I would have thought a silver-spoon kid like that would settle on a nice, high-paying, easy specialty. Like dermatology, or, I don't know, sports medicine."

"Jeff says that's why he wants to do pediatric neurosurgery. To prove he isn't some dilettante just marking time until he cashes in on dear old dad's inheritance."

"You going to take him on?"

"Who am I to stop someone from picking a specialty to settle an old family score?"

"How *is* your father these days, Brody?"

"Fine and dandy, thank you. He sends his best to you."

"So Greenwood wants to train with you?" Elliot grinned. "What a brave lad. Granted, he picked the best hands in this business to learn from. But. Still. Brave lad."

"I'll be gentle with him," Deborah promised, tongue firmly in cheek. Then, turning serious, sighed. "That is, if I'm still here by the end of the year."

Elliot opened the door to the conference room occupied by the Budget Committee, and gestured, Sir Galahad–like, for Deb to walk in ahead of him. He said, "Let's find out."

She was dealing with idiots.

No. Worse. Bureaucratic idiots.

Deb saw she was banging her head against a brick wall when the head of the Committee noted, "I've looked over your proposed budget for next year, Dr. Brody, and, I must confess, I fail to understand why you've requested specially designed and manufactured equipment. Why not employ what's already in stock?"

Deb sighed. She went through this every year. Why was it so troublesome for pencil-pushers to understand that children were not adults. They were, for one thing, smaller. Their miniature bodies weren't compatible with standard equipment. To be fully effective, Deb needed miniature needles, miniature IVs, miniature drills.

The Committee head queried, "Couldn't you find a more economic way to acquire your supplies?"

"Well," Deb proposed, tongue this time all but protruding from her cheek. "I suppose I could dash down to the hardware store and pick up that Black & Decker they've got on sale."

It was a five-member Committee. Only Elliot smiled. And even he did it solely with his eyes. For the remainder of their allotted forty-five minutes, Brody and four of the Committee members—with Dr. Elliot abstaining—went back and forth over a string of facts they'd already gone back and forth over a dozen times before. She was being humored, not listened to.

Deb did not enjoy being humored.

It sounded too much like being patronized.

She put up with it as long as she could—a half hour

longer than Deb usually put up with being patronized. Then, forty-three minutes into this exercise in futility, Deb exploded.

For the record, she exploded in the peerless style of Deborah Brody. She did not shout, she did not square her shoulders, and she did not throw objects.

On the contrary, now that the threshold of no return had been crossed, Deb visibly relaxed. The previously rigid muscles in her jaw and forehead loosened. Both hands relaxed by her sides. She lowered her voice, forcing everyone in the room to lean forward in their chairs and pay close attention to her for the first time in God only knew how long, to make out each perfectly enunciated word.

Brody informed them, "This is unacceptable. You are hindering my performing my duties to the best of my ability. You are risking the lives of children because you're afraid of someone branding you with that ultimate California damnation—political incorrectness. I will not endanger my patients for this. And I will not—not!—work like this. If I don't receive at least two million dollars more than you have allocated me out of this current budget, I will leave. And I will take the million-plus dollars a year that I bill for this hospital with me. This is not a threat, gentlemen. This is a fact. For those of you who presumed I was bluffing before—hell, maybe I was. But that was then. These days, I'm not in the mood for bluffs. Never play chicken with a reckless woman, boys." Deb smiled grimly. "I got nothing more to lose."

'Twas the night before Christmas and, as far as Deb could see, her life was in a major holding pattern.

Professionally, the Budget Committee had developed a case of Jungian collective unconsciousness. The apportionment was due on the second of January, but so far, Elliot reported they had yet to reach a consensus. This was a Committee that took twenty minutes to settle on a take-out Chinese place. They'd only had nine months to come up with the budget. And a yea-or-nay verdict on the rest of Deb's professional life.

Then, of course, there was Deb's personal life.

Deb did not have a personal life.

What Deb had was a personal mess.

Had she given any advance thought to sleeping with Elliot, she still never could have predicted the outcome. She never would have guessed that their encounter that one regrettable time would prompt Elliot to fall in love with her.

He'd said as much—though not in those exact words—to her that evening they spent cozily parked along a freeway on-ramp. Not that Deb believed him.

She didn't think Elliot was lying, exactly. She just thought he was confused. She didn't blame him. Elliot was her friend. He cared about her. He wanted to make things better for her. It—his hinted-at, romantic claim, that is—was a perfectly natural, terribly sweet impulse. But it wasn't love.

Which wasn't to say she didn't believe Elliot loved her. She just knew he wasn't in love with her. It was the sex that confused everything. As sex was wont to do.

The key problem, as Deb saw it, stemmed from Elliot's staying a bachelor for too long. Well, that, and his being a fundamentally nice person. The dichotomy rarely mixed. In the twenty years Deb knew him, Elliot had gone through an abundant series of affairs and romantic relationships. Caryn was the longest and, presumably, the most meaningful, since she actually made it into Elliot's house for longer than one weekend. But all in all, Deb had long ago stopped trying to keep a tally of his women. And she'd often wondered how a basically decent man like Elliot could justify such a promiscuous existence. Then, she figured it out. Whichever woman he was with, no matter for how lengthy or how brief a duration, Elliot must have persuaded himself that he was in love. It made perfect sense, balancing his character against his lifestyle. Elliot convinced himself he was in love with the women he slept with.

And now, he'd done the same with Deb.

She didn't blame him. It was Elliot's preferred way of living with himself, and not feeling like a villain.

She just wished he'd forget about it.

She'd tried her best to reassure him it was okay. She didn't blame him, or judge him, or think that he'd taken advantage of her. She told him so over and over again. But he wasn't listening.

Not that Elliot had uttered so little as a word on the subject in the three weeks since he first asked her to contemplate a future for the two of them. But Deb still felt . . . something.

It emanated from him, as if riding the coattails of that wonderful, brisk aftershave that was as much a part of Deb's sensory recollection of Elliot as those crinkles at the corners of his eyes when he smiled, or the soothing sound of his voice. Or the way his hand felt on her cheek that night almost four months ago.

Right before she lost her mind.

Okay . . . New train of thought, please.

She'd been reflecting on Elliot. Not herself. Elliot and the reality that, despite his contention to the contrary, she still felt a distance between them. And she didn't know how to make it stop.

There was something fundamentally depressing about Christmas in the Children's Trauma Ward of a hospital. All the ornaments and tinsel in the world couldn't cover the casts, and the IV poles, and the breathing tubes. Or the sense of hope for a better new year.

Deb figured she could use some of that.

It was going to be her first working Christmas. She typically got the evening and day off; the hospital tried to be accommodating with married staff. Elliot clocked in every year. He was also in charge of the ward party and he took the position seriously.

Most people—men, in particular—when handed the chore of organizing a Christmas celebration for the under-eighteen group, after a probable hem, haw, and protest, would typically settle for a small plastic tree, a couple of plastic streamers, and, maybe, if feeling particularly magnanimous, some plastic ornaments.

Dr. James Elliot did not do plastic.

To begin with, his tree was authentic. And ten feet tall. It smelled of outside. At a site reeking of disinfectant, outside was an important concept to reinforce. Elliot had the tree erected in the playroom, where the floor was covered in sparkle-dusted cotton, to simulate snow. Most of his California patients weren't too sure what the real stuff looked and felt like, so the non-melting aspect of it didn't really bother them. The week leading up to the party, Elliot charmed the nurses into organizing all the kids to cut snowflakes out of white construction paper, and now every effort hung by fishing wire from the ceiling. There were old, bulbous pillows for snowman building. A chair dressed up as Santa Claus, and so, perfect for lap sitting. The walls were covered in butcher paper, and plates of crayons lay strategically around the room because, as a kid, Elliot remembered being chastised for drawing on the walls. He told Brody he figured Christmas ought to be the day to indulge all sorts of whims and forbidden impulses. Holiday music jingled through the sound system, and homemade baked goods—sugarless for diabetic patients—contributed even more to stifling the smell of Lysol and gauze. But Elliot's pièce de résistance truly came in the ornaments. No bargain plastic here. Elliot not only ordered two dozen glass balls in a rainbow of colors, he had each engraved with the frosted calligraphy of every child's name.

Seeing for the first time wonders she'd only heard about all the previous years, Deb closed her gawking mouth long enough to tell Elliot, "I think you missed your calling, Doc."

He shrugged, and, offhandedly, reminded, "I know what it's like to spend Christmas locked up in here, too."

Despite the blatant lack of self-pity in Elliot's voice, there was still something innately sad about his statement. Impulsively, Deb reached for and squeezed his hand, her fingers slipping between his with an ease and naturalness that seemed to startle them both. Elliot's chin jerked upward. Granted, it was only a quarter of an inch but, for a master of cool self-control like Elliot, the minor spasm qualified as a major jolt. He turned to face Deb, eyes first straying downward to where their connected hands gently swayed back and forth, fused and intact, then up to meet her eyes. She assumed her instinct would be to look away, but Deb met Elliot's gaze head-on. Standing half a foot shorter than him, she had to crane her neck for a better view. It forced her breath to curdle in her throat like a melting square of toffee. His thumb brushed her thumb, ever so slightly, between Deb's life and love lines. The tip of his nail scraped her skin. It was the single, concrete sensation still left in the room. Everything else fell away like the false-front sets of a play.

This was not good.

Yes, it was.

If they were living in a movie, Deb thought, the moment would inevitably be broken by a child or a nurse or a particularly prompt and festive parent walking in to disturb them.

But rather than being interrupted by the clichéd contrivance of an interloper, Deb and Elliot took a beat to swallow and digest where he was, where she was, where they were. And then, as if responding to a dog whistle only they could hear, Deb and Elliot slowly drifted apart. Their hands disconnecting first, then their eyes, and, finally, their minds. There was nothing wrenching about the separation, nothing jerking, nothing painful or harsh.

Only comfortable. Safe. Soft.

The expected festive parents arrived a few minutes later.

Didn't matter by that point.

Stepping aside to allow Elliot to fulfill his hosting duties, Deb quietly tried to blend into the background. She watched him go around from child to child, from parent to sibling, from nurse to resident, taking time to make everyone feel welcome and special. It was curious, really. On the one hand, Elliot was a generally taciturn, private person. On the other, he could quite easily be the life of any party. When he wanted to be.

A social renaissance man. Deb smiled wistfully at the image.

Factoring in that a majority of the patients had an eight PM bedtime, at seven on the dot, Elliot announced that it was time for his present to the ward. Deb had heard about this. Apparently, it was an annual event, something the regular staff looked forward to all year. Elliot called it "a spoonful of my own medicine."

Once a year, as his gift to kids forced to spend their holiday healing, Elliot declared it open season on . . .

himself. Armed with noisemakers, foam paddles, toy hammers, chilled stethoscopes, and tongue depressors, Elliot's patients got to "let him have it," and torture the good doctor to their hearts' content. It was payback time for all those painful blood tests and scary MRIs and medicines that made you throw up and other yucky procedures.

The kids really got into it.

One little boy stuck a pipette in Elliot's ear and demanded, "Does that hurt?" all the while giggling with glee. A little girl kept handing him cup after cup of pink water to force down, while intoning, "Just a little more, or the X-rayer won't work right."

Even little Tammy Baldwin, barely able to move and in obvious pain from her burns, sported the biggest grin ever as, ignoring the tools she'd been provided with, she pummeled away at Elliot's thigh with her tiny fists. And giggled.

"He really is terrific with the children, isn't he?" A woman crept up to Deb, a plastic cup of punch in her right hand. Her name tag read GABLE. Same as the little boy whose test results Jeff Greenwood passed on to Deb the day the world crumbled. No. That wasn't right. It was the day *Deb's* world crumbled. She had to remember that. There was a whole, big world out there that didn't give a damn about her, and her problems. It was a comforting feeling.

Deb nodded to Mrs. Gable, concurring, "Elliot has a knack. So many doctors just go through the motions. He really cares."

"Do you and Dr. Elliot have children of your own?"

It was a question Deb was used to. People expected pediatric physicians to have children. She just wasn't used to Elliot being included as part of the equation. "I'm sorry, what?"

The deer-in-the-headlights confused look on her face obviously suggested to Mrs. Gable that she'd blurted out a faux pas. It prompted the woman to stammer and backpedal. "Oh, I—I thought . . . I saw your wedding ring, and I saw the way you were talking to Dr. Elliot earlier, you two seemed so—I guess, I just assumed—"

"It's alright." Mrs. Gable wasn't the first to make such an error. It just never bothered Deb before.

Actually, considering how her chest was contracting with such force Deb expected her eardrums to shatter and her limbs to fly off from the air pressure, *bother* was probably too gentle of a word.

"Would you excuse me, please," Deb entreated Mrs. Gable. She could barely hear her own voice above the hum in her head.

The drone continued all the way down the hall to Deb's office. It only intensified once she sat behind her desk. It may have been a minute, it may have been an hour—she couldn't tell anymore—but all Deb knew was that the instant she absolutely, positively couldn't take it anymore, she looked up to find Elliot standing in her doorway.

Deb's posture radiated a single, wordless plea: Help me.

She didn't say it. But Elliot heard it just the same.

He stepped into her office. He held out his hand.

He said, "Always."

Chapter Seven

E lliot." Deb chose her words with precise care. "We seem to be in—now, correct me if I'm wrong, but . . . a karaoke bar?"

He held open the door for her. "Excellent diagnosis, Doctor."

But not a very difficult one. The premises Elliot led her to consisted of a room that may have stretched half a block in length, but was also about as wide as a normal hospital corridor. Mirrors mounted along both walls attempted to beget the illusion of depth. They failed in that respect, but did succeed in causing patrons to regularly bump into the walls while searching for an exit. Round wooden tables teetered in a serpentine pattern parallel to the bar that took up most of the left wall. Three smaller tables pushed together made a banquet one. At the very north end of the hallway-masquerading-as-an-establishment—next to the bath-room—was the stage, complete with two microphones mounted on poles, and a television monitor broadcast-ing the same lyrics as were currently flashing across the half-dozen other monitors bolted precariously above customers' heads. The customers themselves were a standard L.A. blend of shirts and ties, halter-tops and roller-blades, bleached denim and mascara, steroids and black leather.

To Deb's experienced eye, the mixture spoke of only one thing. "Elliot," she said, "we seem to be in a—now, correct me if I'm wrong, yet again—a gay karaoke bar."

He took her by the hand and pushed their way toward an empty table through a pair of heartily boogying men each wearing a nose ring—with a single foot-long chain connecting them. He blinked in feigned innocence and asked, "What makes you think so, Brody?"

On cue, every TV monitor vibrated with the pul-sating beat of the Village People extolling the benefits of Navy life.

Deb and Elliot burst out laughing. She sat down, patting her purse close to her body, just in case. Elliot followed suit, first gesturing over her shoulder to the bartender, and signaling for the waitress to bring them two beers.

"You come here often, Sailor?" Deb yelled to be heard over the noise.

He paid the waitress for their beers, handed one to Deb, and shouted back, "Whenever I need cheer-ing up."

To illustrate the merriment available, he pointed

out a man dressed up as Shirley Temple, complete with pinafore and ringlets, waiting patiently by the edge of the stage for his turn to perform Madonna's "Like a Virgin."

Deb twisted the cap off her beer, took a cautious sip, made a face, and, deciding there was nothing critically toxic in the brew, sipped again. She asked, "You need cheering up tonight?"

Elliot shook his head, and, gently, clicked his bottle against hers. His eyes met Deb's. He said, "I figured you might." Then, "You looked like you were drowning."

Deb shrugged. Not because his observation was not true, but because she was afraid of letting him know just how often she felt that way. After all, even Elliot with an overdeveloped Galahad-complex had to grow weary of perpetually throwing out the life preserver to her. The last thing Deb wanted was to exhaust him into washing his hands of her.

Elliot asked, "And how may I interpret that shrug?"

"Well." She managed to draw out the meaningless conversation-staller into a handful of equally meaningless syllables. "If you were really my friend you could elect to interpret it as—'All is going along swimmingly, and how are you this evening, Dr. Elliot?' "

He set his beer bottle down on the table, his thumbs tapping along the curve of the neck, his nail drawing a three-dimensional geometric pattern in the condensation. He cleared his throat. He said, "I am really your friend, Brody. If I wasn't, *then* I'd humor you."

Deb went for the joke. "In that case, do you think you could try being a little worse of a friend?"

"No," Elliot said.

She sighed, trying to pump a last ounce of humor

into a setup Elliot was obviously choosing to take quite seriously, by making it an exaggerated, cartoon-style sigh, complete with a rueful shake of the head, and a roll of the eyes.

No dice.

Elliot asked, "What happened with Mrs. Gable?"

Deb shrugged. If she knew how to squirm, she would have done that, too. She admitted, "Mrs. Gable asked if I had any children."

"What business is that of hers?"

"She didn't mean anything by it. And she's not the first one to ask. I mean, you and I, we work with kids. People wonder why we don't have any of our own."

Just like Deb wondered if Elliot noticed her adding him to the equation. She hadn't meant to do it. It just came out. Probably because it pertained to the truth, and Elliot did have the nasty knack of prompting her to be honest. As soon as she blurted out the words, though, Deb wished she could take them back.

Lucky for her Elliot interpreted her inadvertent *we* as the universal, rather than identity-specific, variety. He nodded thoughtfully. "Yeah, it's true. I get that all the time, too."

"As part of the why-isn't-a-phenomenal-guy-like-you-married package?" Deb teased. Not that this was a subject she particularly wanted to discuss, either. But it deflected the conversation away from her, which was, after all, Deb's first priority.

"Sometimes as part of the package, sometimes as a stand-alone intrusion. Depends."

"What do you tell them?"

"Depends," Elliot repeated.

"On what?"

"On how I feel, that particular day, about complete strangers butting into my personal business."

His well-covered, but nevertheless visible, spurt of

anger surprised Deb. Mostly because Elliot very, very rarely got angry. She'd never realized how strongly he felt about the subject. And so she wasn't certain how to react.

He said, "If I'm feeling particularly magnanimous, I simply grunt and change the subject. If I'm feeling less magnanimous, I slice the buttinsky in half. Sans scalpel."

"Well," Deb pointed out, mischievously. "I just butted into your personal business. What do you feel like doing to me?"

Elliot cocked his head to one side, raising an eyebrow. He warned, "Don't go there, Brody."

He was kidding. Of course, he was kidding.

He had to be kidding.

Why, then, did Deb feel like he was not kidding?

She shivered. Over a hundred people stuffed into a non-air-conditioned room the size of a freight elevator, and Deb shivered. It didn't make any sense. Especially considering the fact that, at the same time, she felt a bead of sweat trickling down her neck and settling between her breasts like a damp question mark.

"So why did Mrs. Gable asking you something you've been asked a hundred times before upset you so much, this time?"

Deb sighed. She'd been trying to figure out that one herself. And, unfortunately, she had.

Deb explained, "Because, this time, I actually listened to the question. I heard it. Not just in my head. In here." She tapped the area of her chest where typical women grew a maternally leaning heart. "You know why Max and I never had kids? Because I didn't want them. Because *I* was too busy with my career. I wanted to be Chief of Pediatric Neurosurgery. I wanted to be the big shot. And a family would have just slowed me down."

"That's true," Elliot said. "It would have."

"So the hell what?" Her outburst frightened Deb as much as it did Elliot. She felt like the sentiment had been forcibly wrenched out of her mouth with a stomach pump. "I mean, really, so the hell what? I am Chief of Pediatric Neurosurgery. Well, whoop-dee-doo! Considering the way Morelli has been gunning for me, that probably won't last too long. Come the new year and new budget, my precious career is going to spill down the drain. And then what will I have left? I used to think that, even if I lost the work—not that I ever seriously believed that would happen—I would still have my marriage. I would still have Max. Talk about stupidly taking things for granted. Do you realize that, if I have to quit, I won't have anything—not a damn thing—to call my own?"

Elliot didn't say a word.

Deb raged, "It's all my fault. I was the one who said no to children. Maybe if I hadn't, maybe if I'd had a family, I wouldn't be sitting here, now, alone."

Elliot didn't move a muscle.

He waited for Deb to hear herself.

But she was too busy talking.

So the moment that should have been occupied with her apology, was, instead, filled by a thirtysomething man with a briefcase in one hand and a drink in the other, stopping to curiously exclaim, "Dr. Elliot?"

Elliot's chin bobbed up automatically, and, like the forever-prepared trauma-care doctor he'd been trained to be, he half-rose out of his seat, looking for the emergency.

"I thought that was you." Briefcase Man pushed his way past several bar patrons to reach Elliot and Deb's table. He stretched out his hand, shaking Elliot's, and reassured, "I'm sure you don't remember me. I'm Luke Hughes. We met, oh, I guess it's been over fifteen years ago, now." To Deb, Luke Hughes explained, "All those Thanksgivings ago, my partner, Brian, sliced his index finger clean off trying to cut the turkey. We grabbed it and rushed over to the nearest emergency room, where, can you believe it?—well, I guess we shouldn't have been surprised, this was the mid-1980s and everyone was still squeamish, but I thought they still had to obey the Hippocratic Oath . . . anyway, soon as they found out Brian was HIV positive, nobody at the hospital would have anything to do with us. Brian is sitting there, bleeding like a fountain, and we're getting the runaround. If it wasn't for Dr. Elliot—"

"I'd been called down for a consult on a hurt child that came in earlier," Elliot explained.

"I don't know what would have happened if it weren't for Dr. Elliot. He came right on in, and told the nurses and those, what do you call them? Interns? He told them, 'Gloves, people. Has no one here heard of gloves?' And then he stitched Brian right up."

Deb smiled. She could so clearly see Elliot in action. And she could so clearly see him stepping into a quagmire no one else would dare touch.

"I remember that," Elliot said softly. He asked Luke Hughes, "How is Brian, now?"

A deep breath. "He's gone. He died about six years ago."

The words were directed at Elliot. But Deb experienced each sound like a tree trunk smashing through her chest. She'd been a doctor for sixteen years. She'd been present at dozens of deaths, and been told about hundreds more. Yet, never before had the idea affected her so deeply. For the first time in her otherwise overdiplomaed and decorated career, she understood what her professor must have meant when he lectured about empathy. His key mantra had been, "Never tell a patient or their family, 'I know how you feel.' Because, until you've been through it, you don't."

Right now, Deb knew exactly how Luke Hughes felt.

Especially when, as he was telling Elliot about Brian's death, his eyes, ever so briefly but guiltily, snuck toward the bar, where another young man in a three-piece suit stood, waving him over.

Elliot nodded sympathetically, indicating he'd expected Luke's answer, and asked, "What about you?"

"I'm alright." Luke shrugged. "God only knows why, but, I'm alright. No symptoms."

"That's wonderful!" Elliot may have stayed cool on negative issues, but when he was truly happy about something, there was no mistaking his sincerity. "That's really good news."

"Thank you. And, well, anyway, I just wanted to come by and say hi. It was good seeing you again, Dr. Elliot." Luke melted back into the throng—and toward his friend at the bar.

Deb watched him go. Indicating the departing figure with a nudge of her head, she asked, "Does Morelli know about this?"

Elliot turned around in his seat from where he'd been smiling at the sight of Luke and his new friend embracing each other, and, spirits buoyed, returned his attention to Deborah. In reply to her inquiry, he shrugged, indifferent, and finished his beer, tilting his head back to suck the last drop from the bottle. "Why should he? Morelli's got nothing to do with it."

"If he knew, it would sure put a crimp in his Dr.-Elliot-is-a-horrible-homophobe campaign."

Elliot's lips crinkled to the side in a signal of disregard. "You know, Brody, it's frightening how little I care what Morelli thinks of me. Besides, it's not me he has a problem with, per se. He's just in a snit because I keep fighting his resolution to take money from our department and sacrifice it down the impotent black hole that is his. The man's got the most inefficient unit at the hospital. Not only is he asking for more money than the rest of us are getting, he doesn't even know how to use it properly. That's what I object to. In case you're wondering where I stand on AIDS, let me clear it up: I'm against it. I hope and pray that they will find a cure. Just as hard as I hope and pray that they will find a cure for cancer, and diabetes, and heart disease, and spina bifida, and cystic fibrosis, and sickle-cell anemia, and Tay-Sachs, and—"

"Point made, Doc." She held up her hand, bidding him to stop before the list got morbidly depressing. "And, by the way, Elliot, please remember, you never have to justify yourself to me. I, more than anybody, know what an immense heart you've got. I know you're doing what you believe is best for every patient at the hospital. But, you *are* the only little Indian left standing between Morelli and a blank check. I'm afraid he'll do—and say—anything to get you out of the way."

Elliot rubbed his hands together, palms turning pink from the friction. "Then, I say, let him try."

It wasn't his confidence necessarily that impressed Deb—they were doctors, after all, they'd been trained to consider themselves deities—but, rather, Elliot's calm before what most would have judged a serious problem. As far back as Deb could recall—and this was going sixteen, twenty years back in time—he'd been the epitome of composure. Nothing rattled Elliot.

Even when, on paper, it should have.

Matching Day, 1984.

She'd almost kissed him that time. It took sixteen years for Deb to admit it, but everything being relative, she guessed it was a tiny sin to confess now, and so she was finally ready to do it.

Sixteen years ago, she'd almost kissed Elliot. As far as Deb was concerned, that had been something worth losing a few ounces of cool over. Personally, she'd thought her head would burst.

When their house of cards crumbled, Deb's blood pressure went with it. She felt lightning rip through her skull, scour past her lungs, and smash against her abdomen with such force, her legs shook for weeks. Her skin burned as if scoured. Her throat tied itself into a knot, and her brain went feral, turning, cannibal-style, on itself, a cornucopia of thoughts and doubts and emotions pulsating madly, trying to blast free.

On the other hand, sixteen years ago, Elliot had looked ready to light up a casual cigarette.

Coolly, he watched their cards collapse, and, without missing a beat, finished his original thought. Elliot told Deb, "Max must be thinking I've kidnapped you, Brody."

Max. Deb remembered Max. She remembered him now, and she certainly remembered him back then.

She was married to the man, for Christ's sake, of course, she remembered him. Just . . . Not . . . Not that very minute.

Was that really so awful?

Deb thought so.

She loved Max. How could she forget him? Even for a second?

The mere possibility had scared Deb as straight as any public-service documentary. Scared straight. Forever.

Then, Elliot said, "It's going to take a lot more than that to shove me out of the running."

Deb blinked.

My, oh, my, but it was confusing to live in two time zones simultaneously. For a minute there, she'd been both forty-one and twenty-five years old. And she'd sat there with two Elliots, now and then. And with two Maxes.

Elliot was right. She *was* drowning.

But she couldn't let him see it.

He'd already seen so much more than she ever meant him to.

She swallowed hard. She said, "Oh. You mean Morelli."

"Yes, of course, Morelli. Who did you think I meant?" Elliot leaned forward, solicitous. "Are you okay? You look pale."

She felt crimson. She wasn't sure which was worse.

"Do me a favor, Brody, okay?" Elliot rested his elbow along the back of his chair. "Stop beating yourself up."

"I am not—"

"Yes, you are. You are. The night Max died, you were ready to believe your lack of culinary finesse was responsible. Now, you've latched on to another lame explana—"

"It's not the same."

"I know." The strident tone softened a touch. "I know. But I wish you'd stop being so hard on yourself. You didn't have kids. You made a choice. There's nothing wrong with that. Look through your files. Make a list of the hundreds of children who are alive today because of your choice to become a neurosurgeon instead of a mother. How the hell can you feel guilty in the face of that?"

Deb crossed her arms. She tapped her tongue against her upper lip. She said, "Amazingly enough, I can."

He smiled. "You're an incredible woman, Dr. Brody."

"I'm an incredible *surgeon*. But as a woman . . ."

"You"—Elliot's eyes darkened—"are an incredible woman. Go with me on this one, alright?"

She'd seen Elliot's game face before. It was the face he put on when handed an exam by a professor notorious for never giving an *A*. It was the face he put on when told to forget a patient some other doctor considered impossible to save. It was the face he put on when he had no intention of taking no for an answer.

Not even from God.

So, what chance did Deb have?

She nodded without realizing it, and her lips formed a single word. "Al-alright."

"Good girl." His appreciative smile reminded Deb of a sunbeam bursting through the clouds. No wonder people constantly asked why Elliot wasn't married. The man wasn't just smart, kind, fun, great with kids, and professionally successful. He was also . . . cute.

When the hell, exactly, had Elliot become cute?

And how much longer before he gave it a rest?

Deb needed him to give it a rest.

And she needed a distraction.

Now.

So she told Elliot, "Sing."

"I beg your pardon?" His smile didn't so much fade, as shift. His dimples deepened.

Dimples. Not a good thing.

Dimples were even cuter than all the stuff that came before.

More firmly this time, Deb repeated, "Sing."

"Now, Brody? Here?"

"It's a karaoke bar. What else did you bring me here to do?"

"I brought you here," Elliot reminded, "to cheer you up."

"Your singing would cheer me up," she insisted. "In fact, I'd wager it would make me downright giddy."

In other words, she really needed Elliot to get up and sing.

Now would be nice.

"Go," she said. "Look, I'll even pick a song for you." Deb quickly scanned the song list offered, like a menu, at every table. She smiled when the most obvious title caught her eye, and flipped the sheet over, pointing to it with her index finger. "There," she said. "How can you resist that?"

Curious, Elliot slowly lowered his head, still unsure exactly how to react to Deb's oddball suggestion, and so playing it safe with a generic, cool demeanor. He obligingly read the song title.

Dionne Warwick. "That's What Friends Are For."

Elliot smiled. There were yet more dimples.

Deb was learning not to mind those so much.

"Brody," he pointed out, "we have a tiny problem. I don't know this song."

"That's why they put those nice, block letters on the screen."

"Ah . . ." Elliot nodded sagely.

"Go," she urged. "Sing."

Elliot sighed and shook his head ruefully, already half-turned in the direction of the stage. "Your wish is my command."

"That's good to know."

He had to stand in line for his turn, stance wide, both hands on hips, lips crinkled in amusement at what he'd been talked into doing, eyes circling the room in the typical time-passing manner, with only a periodic lock with Deb. They grinned at each other in the sort of giddy cheer that always preceded making a complete fool out of oneself, but neither had the guts to hold the look for more than random seconds at a time.

When Elliot finally got called to step onstage, he made a big show out of clearing his throat, and warming up his Elvis hip-swivel. He may have been preparing to make an idiot of himself in front of some one hundred people, but as soon as the music began, Deb felt as if they were the only two in the room. It wasn't quite that part in *West Side Story* where Tony sees Maria and every other overage teen at the dance turns into a colorful, blinking light.

But it was certainly something.

The first few notes took Elliot visibly by surprise. He'd been expecting something upbeat and chirpy, ergo, the practice hip-thrusts. He hadn't been prepared for a ballad. To be honest, Deb had kind of forgotten how sensually the song oozed, too.

Elliot looked at the printed words on the screen, and cleared his throat. This time, he didn't seem to be kidding.

For a moment, Deb thought he was about to put up his hands in a *T,* and, like back at the ice rink, call a time-out. He certainly looked like that's what he wanted to do. His eyes darted from side to side, like a sick child who can't decide whether to bite or kick her doctor first. He looked so uncomfortable, a guilt-stricken Deb felt halfway tempted to call the whole thing off. She pressed her palms against the table, ready to stand up, and tell him he didn't have to do this. That it was a bad idea.

But then, Elliot put on his game face.

Deb's impulse to stand fizzled.

It didn't matter what she said, now. Elliot was determined to go through with this. And it no longer had anything to do with her needling him. It had to do with . . . something else.

"And I . . ." Elliot stepped into the first beat of a song as if he had been practicing it with a Broadway mentor for weeks. But that was Elliot in the proverbial nutshell. Once he made up his mind to do something, he did it well. Always.

"Never thought I'd feel this way/And as far as I'm concerned/I'm glad I got the chance to say . . ." Elliot really did have a very pleasant voice. Deb had heard it year after year in the Christmas carols he led his patients in on the days leading up to his party, but she had never really listened before. There was a masculine quality to it she couldn't quite distinguish, a faint raspiness, a catch that disturbed the perfect-pitch baritone just enough to make it almost unbearably endearing.

The man sounded good.

And Deb wasn't the only one who thought so. The same assembly that, earlier, had sung along with the Shirley Temple impersonator, and fluttered their arms to spell out YMCA, now stopped—or at least, slowed down—what they were doing and turned around to listen, enthralled not so much by the quality of singing, but by the same undescribable quality that had first mesmerized Deb.

There was a word for it.

Sincerity.

Elliot may have hit a few flats on the transition notes. But there was no denying he meant every syllable coming from his mouth. In fact, the way Elliot sounded, it was easy to believe the words were not printed in "little, block letters on the screen," but were spilling genuinely from his heart.

Deb hadn't counted on that.

She also hadn't counted on the next line of the song.

She'd thought she remembered it well enough.

She'd thought it was safe. But, the eighties were a long time ago, and her memory proved not quite as infallible as she'd hoped.

Glancing up at the screen, Deb saw the next line turning blue a second before Elliot did, while he was still concentrating on the previous sentiment. But there, in all its digital glory, was the subsequent declaration: "That I do believe I love you . . ."

Deb saw the precise moment when Elliot's eyes narrowed on the line, prior to his singing it out loud. Elliot's eyes met Deb's. In them, she saw a question. And a defiance. Game face.

She wanted to call the whole endeavor off. She wanted to tell him to stop. She wanted to beg him to stop.

But she could do nothing. She couldn't even move. She could only listen.

"That I do believe I love you . . ."

Why hadn't the world stopped turning? Deb had felt certain it would. Or, maybe, she'd just been hoping for it. At this moment, annihilation of the human race was the most optimistic scenario she could think of. And still Elliot kept singing. He didn't even have the courtesy to stop looking her way. For the whole rest of the song, he kept looking at her. Not apologetic, not ashamed, not even reluctant. Defiant.

She felt mortified. Mortified, and guilt-ridden, and self-conscious, and angry. And so thrilled, Deb could barely stay in her chair. No other man had ever looked at her like that.

Her brain sort of fizzled into a puddle and sloshed around her skull like a forgotten Eskimo Pie on a summertime sidewalk.

When Elliot finished, there was a moment where nobody clapped. It seemed that nobody even breathed. The karaoke-bar clientele was used to camp and whooping it up in appreciation. They weren't used to . . . sincerity, and so weren't quite sure how to react.

Elliot took advantage of the silence.

Resting his microphone on the stool set up for that purpose, he strode off the stage, reaching Deb's table much quicker than she could have guessed possible. He looked down at her. She looked up at him. And then he kissed her.

That's when the applause finally began.

Elliot's mouth cupped hers, his tongue first caressing, then parting her lips. And Deb responded. She didn't have any choice. Especially when the warmth of Elliot's breath permeated her throat and lungs like sizzling steam. Especially when she could taste him all the way to the tips of her toes and fingers, so that both tingled and rang and throbbed to near explosion.

She thought she'd be the one to break the kiss. But Elliot beat her to the punch. He moved his head back an inch. Yet, their lips stayed as close as his had earlier to the microphone, and they generated, she was willing to bet, an equal electrical charge.

Under cover of applause, Elliot smiled lazily, and whispered, "Merry Christmas, Brody."

Chapter Eight

The worst part about Christmas, Deb decided, was that New Year's Eve sprang itself upon you a mere six days later.

She'd never been a big Christmas person. Christmas was a kids' holiday, and, as she'd clearly established earlier, Deb didn't have any of those. New Year's Eve, on the other hand, was a grown-ups' celebration. Deborah Brody was born a grown-up.

For the past eight years, she and Max had spent their night at the hospital's Fund-Raising Ball, a phenomenon built on the premise that twenty hours a day wasn't enough time to see their coworkers, and maybe they'd like to make it an even twenty-four, albeit, this time, in formal wear. Which was alright with Deb. Her favorite part was the formal wear.

She liked dressing up. After sixteen years of going to work in a white lab coat, with an occasional digression into the scrub-blue that was all the rage in operating rooms, Deborah figured she earned her once-a-year extravagance. Except this year. This year, Deb's abominable deportment hadn't earned her anything, short of a one-way trip straight to Hell.

Four months ago, denial-born-of-self-preservation had made it possible for Deb to pretend she and Elliot had done nothing wrong. Not on purpose, anyway. But, the day before the dawn of the actual new millennium, Deborah Brody experienced an enlightenment. It smacked her somewhere between Elliot's uttering, "Merry Christmas," and "Brody."

The enlightenment was this: She was not a good person.

Which was a nice way of saying that she was a bad one.

Elliot's kiss made every nerve in her body shake off its dust, and snap to attention. Her clothes suddenly felt too constrictive. She crossed her legs, then uncrossed them, then crossed them again. The kiss had turned her on.

Bad, Deb. Very bad.

Equally bad was Elliot's role in all this. Instead of pushing or pressing his advantage, or any of those other sins the magazines were always accusing evil men of doing, Elliot . . . hung loose. Did people still use that expression?

In more common parlance, Elliot didn't do anything. He kissed her, he wished her a Merry Christmas, and then he sat down next to Deb, grinned, and ordered another beer.

Six days later, Deb was still wondering whether she'd imagined the whole encounter. But then the sense memories would kick in, her temperature would jump-start, her breakfast would do a little break-dance in her stomach, her breath would catch, and Deb would realize that, no, God help her, no, she hadn't imagined a thing.

She'd thought it would be tough to face Elliot after the night they'd spent together. But, for some reason, this was harder. Deb suspected it was because, that first night, she knew she'd been out of her mind. No such convenient excuse this time around.

Not that Elliot was asking for one. Or offering.

His mind appeared to be in a different space entirely, as he asked Deb, "You need a ride to the Grovel-a-Thon, tonight?"

They'd met by accident, in the elevator—Deb wearing scrubs, Elliot in his white coat. Everything perfectly proper.

"I'm not going," Deb said.

"Oh, sure." Elliot smiled. "Brody, I know you. You had your dress picked out last Labor Day."

"Last Labor Day, I had a date." *And a life.*

"So, come with Janine and me."

Janine was a respiratory therapist Elliot had been dating on and off for nearly six months. Deb wished she could say the girl was a teenybopper bubblehead who snapped her gum and giggled in Valley-Speak. Unfortunately, though Janine was barely thirty, and a blonde to boot, she was also a graduate of Vassar, whose hobbies included astronomy and symphony composition on her computer. That was the problem with Elliot: He never found idiots attractive.

"I have no interest," Deb snapped, "in dating Janine."

"I'm sure you don't. But I don't want you—"

She bristled. "Would you stop worrying about me,

Elliot. It's really starting to get on my nerves. I don't need a keeper. I'll be perfectly fine staying home, watching Dick Clark drop a ball in Times Square."

"Wait a second. I was only—"

The elevator doors opened. It wasn't Deb's floor. She stepped out anyway.

Unlike Deb, Elliot hated dressing up. Sometimes, he thought he became a doctor because the job came with a uniform. It didn't matter that, as far back as the junior prom, random women had been telling him he was born to wear tuxedos, that they made him look dapper, elegant, sophisticated. They still made his neck itch. As far as Elliot could discern, the only challenge to formal wear was learning how to tie a tie. Elliot could fasten a ripped intestine with one hand. The bow tie had long ago lost its intrigue.

The only reason Elliot kept showing up at this New Year's Eve shindig year after year was because it was a command performance. The hospital liked to parade its top doctors in front of its top financial contributors. Like trained seals. So, in the interest of his patients, Elliot had spent the past year diligently learning to balance a ball atop his nose.

The man who patented the exhibition, Morelli, was, by the time Elliot arrived at the Gala, already off in some corner, barking his loudest for a gaggle of overdressed philanthropists. Morelli spied Elliot looking at them, and grinned broadly. Then he put one arm around each of the self-dubbed good samaritans, and led them out of Elliot's sight-line.

"The gentleman doesn't like you." Janine strolled up behind Elliot, a drink in each hand. She rested her chin on his shoulder, breasts pressing against his back, handing Elliot his cocktail at the same time as she took a sip of hers.

"Hm," Elliot said.

Six couples down from them stood a woman Elliot had never seen before. Her hair was cut in the exact same style as Brody's. The ends caressed the nape of her neck, back and forth, in a beat as hypnotic as windshield wipers.

Janine said, "I hear he's going around telling people he's got you backed into a corner on next year's budget."

"Hm."

The woman wore a backless dress. Brody was too conservative for such a fashion. Last year, she'd shown up in a crushed maroon velvet: floor-length, high-necked, shoulderless, with long sleeves. It didn't reveal nearly as much as the gold-lamé backless currently before him. But while Elliot was already bored with the gold, the velvet still glimmered in his memory, especially the way it tapered down Brody's arms, adding a balletic grace to her every gesture.

Janine said, "Morelli looks smug enough to start coughing up canary feathers."

"Hm."

"I hear he snacked on Tweety Bird before coming over."

"Hm."

"I 'tawt I 'taw a Puttytat eyeing him suspiciously earlier."

Elliot said, "You know, just because I'm not snapping back the repartee, my dear, doesn't mean I can't hear what you're saying."

Janine dropped her arms and sauntered around to block Elliot's view of anyone but herself. "I was beginning to wonder."

"Hm."

Janine gave up. "I'm going to get another drink. I'd ask if you wanted anything, but—" She glanced over her shoulder at the woman who'd mesmerized Elliot, and instantly noted the resemblance. "What would be the point?"

Elliot wasn't an idiot. A huge part of his profession hinged on being a proficient observer, and so he could see what had just happened between him and Janine. He could see it. He only wished he cared more.

And he wished he cared a little less about how mad Brody had appeared to be at him, earlier this afternoon. That, he didn't understand at all.

It would have made sense for her to be furious with him right after the stunt he pulled Christmas Day at the karaoke bar. That anger, Elliot would have deserved. Even if, in court, he would've felt no qualms about pleading temporary insanity as his defense.

How many times in his career had Elliot stood in front of a contrite parent who'd just pushed their toddler down the stairs, or smacked them into a coma, and listened to them swear, "I don't know what came over me." Elliot didn't buy the justification then, and he didn't buy it now. He did, however, feel the urge to borrow it.

Elliot had no idea what came over him somewhere in the middle of the apocryphal "That's What Friends Are For."

Oh, hell. Yes, he did.

What came over him was the urge to stop playing the nice guy. He may not have made a habit of acting the bastard in his various romantic relationships. But nonetheless, his given first name was James. Not Patsy.

There was just so much even he could take.

Deb had looked so lost that day in the karaoke

bar. So lost, and so broken, and so miserable. And so beautiful.

He hadn't been able to help himself, that's all there was to it. And he was sorry immediately—almost immediately afterward. So sorry that, as soon as he felt the cold chill of reason return to his body—well, first, it returned to his brain, his body took a while longer—in any case, as soon as that damned, cold chill of reason returned, Elliot felt so sorry about his behavior that he, instinctively, withdrew to the stance Brody had so often told him she preferred. The one where they both pretended nothing had ever happened. And nothing ever would. He thought it would make her happy. She did not seem happy on the elevator.

Which made for a rather interesting point. Maybe Elliot had been wrong all his life. Maybe, GPA to the contrary, maybe he really was an idiot. Maybe he hadn't the slightest clue what was really going on.

Elliot needed to find Janine.

Half an hour before midnight, Deb had yet to figure out the appeal of Dick Clark. Everyone said he looked ageless. Deb just thought he looked plastic. And not too skilled at distracting her from the depressing reality that, for the first time since she was a teenager, Deb was spending New Year's Eve alone, dressed in an extralarge T-shirt, and watching television. Bad television.

She supposed she could just go to bed. But considering that, since the day Max died, Deb had found it impossible to fall asleep earlier than a few minutes before dawn, she doubted the plan would work on this particular night, of all nights.

She decided her current loneliness was Elliot's

fault. She'd gotten accustomed to picking up the phone anytime, day or night, and counting on hearing his voice. When she knew that wasn't a possibility, it made her unpleasantly anxious.

She supposed she could still page him now. She doubted Elliot would appreciate her paging him, now. And she knew for sure that Caryn . . . no, Janine—hell, was it her job to keep track of Elliot's women?—wouldn't.

So, instead, Deb hallucinated the doorbell ringing.

She must have been hallucinating because there was no reason for her doorbell to be ringing at twenty minutes to midnight.

She was hallucinating again. This time, more insistently.

What the heck? She might as well play along and hallucinate opening the door.

Suddenly, Cary Grant was standing on her porch.

Well, alright, maybe not the actual movie star. He was dead, after all, and Deb hadn't gone that far over the deep end, yet.

Cary Grant, in the flesh, might not have been standing on her front porch. But Elliot, in a black tuxedo and white dress shirt, hands in his pockets, weight back on his heels, head cocked to the side as he peered up at her through half-mast lids, was damn close.

Why was it that every time Elliot drew out of her sight, she seemed to forget just how attractive he was, so that, over and over again, it came like a revelation, hijacking her breath, and her reason and her sanity?

"Hi, there," Elliot said.

"Good evening." Her voice sounded queer. Deb hadn't the slightest idea why she was sounding this way. She knew only that she was. She winced internally.

"Can I come in?" Elliot asked, yet made no move to actually do so. Dressed in his Cary Grant finery, he hovered cautiously along her porch, as light on his feet as a lion poised to spring forward—or back—depending on the provocation.

And Deb, as much to her surprise as his, apparently was in the mood to be provocative. "Where's Janine?" she asked.

After two decades of soothing grieving relatives and petrified patients, Elliot had earned his master's degree in Neutral Facial Expressions. His features didn't flicker. So Deb had no idea how he might feel about her asking so bluntly.

His voice wasn't exactly brimming with helpful nuance either, when Elliot calmly informed her, "When last I beheld her, Janine was busy helping the piano player tickle his ivories."

"I beg your pardon?"

"Turned out the evening's piano player was an old friend of hers. They had a lot of catching up to do—duet-style, no trios, they were quite clear about that. Don't worry. I made certain she wouldn't end up alone on New Year's Eve."

Of course, he had. Deb didn't doubt it for a minute. It was an action so in character, she didn't know whether to laugh or cry. Of course, Elliot would not abandon Janine without making sure she was taken care of. He was, if nothing else, a gentleman.

Unfortunately for Deb, though, the more time passed, the more she realized that he was also much, much more than simply that.

She tried a joke. When all else failed, Deb always tried a joke. Not that the technique ever worked out, but, at least, she could show that it was well-honed. Deb teased, "And then you raced right over to do the same favor for me?"

"No. I raced right over to do the same favor for me." Elliot repeated, "Let me come in, Brody."

He hadn't altered the timbre of his voice. He hadn't moved a muscle in his body. Yet, somehow, the atmosphere encasing him had grown tentacles, soft, persuasive, probing, insistent tentacles.

She stepped aside, and opened the door as wide as it went.

Elliot smiled, crossing the threshold with such confidence and boldness, Deb was ready to hand him the keys to the place.

He crossed into the living room, staring at the television for a good moment before observing, "This is moronic."

"It's either this, or infommercials on the other channels."

Elliot reached for the remote, flicking around so quickly, her TV began to look like a broken string of film. "I don't know about you, Brody, but I can never hear enough about Ginsu knives."

He was standing less than two feet away, and still there was this hula hoop between them. They couldn't see it, but they could feel it pressing against their ribs, setting parameters. The hoop locked them into an illusory orbit that neither dared cross. Like electrons circling the nucleus.

She was really getting sick of it.

Staying mad at Elliot certainly took a lot of energy.

Especially when she had to exhaust so much of it struggling to remember why it was she felt mad at him—because he'd pushed her too hard this time around, or not enough?

Deb wanted to tell him that she was sick of all this, that the last month had been hell, that she wanted to hit the reset button and start all over again. Friendship came with an undo key, didn't it? She wanted to tell him how scared she was that the uncertainty between them might lead to the two growing further apart, until Deb lost Elliot forever, and how that was the single thing she knew she would never survive.

Deb wanted to tell Elliot how badly she wished they could just go back to the way things were before. But, instead, all she could manage to ask was, "You hungry, Elliot?"

He didn't stop flipping channels with the remote to point out, "If I were, this is not the first place I'd come for relief. Don't tell me you've started keeping food in the house."

"Well, no," Deb admitted. "But I have memorized the numbers of seven more take-out places."

"Bringing your grand total to, what? Four thousand and two?"

"I've got the Valley covered. Hollywood's next."

Elliot grinned. "Where do you think you'll find a restaurant that's open on New Year's Eve?"

Deb gave the question some thought, eventually suggesting, "A kosher deli?"

"That's true. Their New Year is in the fall."

"An Indian place?"

"Also true. The Hindu New Year, I believe, falls in the month of Kartika."

"Or Muslims-R-Us? Their calendar is based on cycles of the moon, so the whole year is shorter."

"Okay, Brody, we know you went to college, quit showing off."

"Look who's talking. The Hindu New Year falls in the month of," Deb teasingly imitated him, breaking the word into syllables, "Kar-ti-ka? Now, who's showing off?"

"I went through a Hindu phase in med school."

"I know," Deb reminded softly. "I was there."

For a split second, she thought she'd uttered the

wrong thing, and driven the fluctuating temperature in the room to polar levels. But Elliot took no overt notice. Instead, he queried, "So, your inquiry into the state of my hunger was what? Statistical?"

"No. It was"—she paused, then grinned with the satisfaction of making up a brand-new word on the spot—"it was host-istical."

Elliot shook his head, clucked his tongue, and sighed. "You know what you are, young lady? You, Brody, are a tease."

The fictitious thermometer that only Deb seemed aware of took on cartoon characteristics as the silver mercury inside it suddenly turned red and shot straight up, shattering the rounded tip. Deb's throat went dry. "W-what do you mean?" she stammered.

"A tease," he repeated, head bobbing with new-found conviction. "You draw attention to, and thus inflame, my desires, all the while knowing you have no intention of satisfying them."

She understood that he was teasing her. Which by no means prevented her internal organs from melting into puddles, her skin from prickling like flower buds at first spring, and a funnel of a tornado from sucking every lucid thought out of her head.

"Why ask if I'm hungry, Brody, if you've got no food in the house, and no means of getting any in the immediate future?"

Well, what do you know? Of course, he's been kidding.

Why, then, weren't her symptoms subsiding?

Strictly on automatic pilot, Deb defended, "I have food in the house. Granted, none of it happens to be in an edible state, but I do have ingredients. I think. Consider it a dinner . . . kit."

Elliot laughed. Just like Deb hoped he would. She thought if he laughed, it would cut through the tension and trigger the reset key. When Elliot laughed, his eyes crinkled and sang through every shade in the azure spectrum, while both his dimples deepened.

Oh, yeah. Her plan worked *real* well, there.

He said, "A kit, huh? Well, okay. We are surgeons. Between the two of us, we should be able to construct a sandwich."

"A sandwich, huh? Uhm . . . what goes into that, exactly?"

Elliot half-turned toward the kitchen, and held out his hand to Deb, inviting, "Let's find out."

His fingers were powerful, muscular, and randomly dotted with long-healed scars from assorted scalpel nicks. The veins under his skin throbbed in inviolate unison, furrowing under the harsh hockey calluses on his palms.

His hand felt cool when Deb slipped hers inside his grip. Or, maybe, it just felt cool when compared to the heat of her own skin.

"Wow," Deb said. "You're good."

Elliot raised an eyebrow. "I haven't done anything, yet."

"*Au contraire*," Deb pointed out. "Unlike me, you walked into the kitchen, and recognized it immediately."

"Now, for my next trick . . ." Elliot opened the refrigerator with a flourish. And dropped Deb's hand in the process. "Uh-oh."

"What?"

"Brody." He glanced at her over his shoulder. "I'm afraid we have hit the wall of my expertise."

"Bull," she said. "I know you. There is not a task on earth that, once you put your mind to it, you fail to execute perfectly. You are a bachelor, my friend. And, as everybody knows, bachelors love to impress women with their culinary expertise. So, 'fess up, Doc, you're like some five-star gourmet chef, right?"

"There you have it, folks." Elliot turned around, closed the refrigerator door behind him, and leaned against it, crossing both arms for good measure. "Indisputable proof that you, Brody, spent the past twenty years married, and not out there in the cold, cruel dating world. That 'impressing women with your culinary expertise' nonsense is a women's magazine fantasy. You want the real scoop on bachelor tricks for picking up chicks? Listen close." He lowered his voice to a conspiratorial whisper, and ducked his head so that his face hovered inches from Deb's. "You want to know why I never learned to cook? It was a conscious choice. See, women prefer to feel they're helping you out, that they're making your life better. At least, that's the cover story. Personally, I think they like to make you wholly dependent on them. It offers them an apparition of assurance, believing that you'll never stray, for fear of starving to death. Now, if I learned to cook, I would end up stealing that security blanket away from some perfectly decent young woman. And, you know me, Brody, I'm too nice of a guy to ever do that. . . ."

Deb listened to his entire speech. She chewed on his words. She slapped his arm, and said, "You are so full of it, Elliot."

"Yes." He sighed. Then, straightening up, quickly kissed Deb on the nose before turning his attention back to the fridge. "But I'm also cute as a button. That helps like you wouldn't believe."

Actually, Deb thought, he'd probably be surprised by how much she believed it.

Opening the refrigerator door for the second time in as many minutes, Elliot proceeded to peer deeply at the ingredients, as if sheer intensity could force the stray items lolling lonely on the shelves to magically combine themselves into a foodlike substance.

He stared so hard and so long, Deb quipped,

"Yeah, that's the problem with these things. They have to be watched constantly."

"One more crack out of you, Brody, and somebody'll be starting the new year hungry."

"It doesn't matter how I start the new year," Deb disclosed. "I just want the old one to end."

She'd been shooting for flip, but Elliot heard the swallowed sorrow underneath. Without turning to look at her, he cautiously asked, "Has it gotten any better, Brody? Any easier?"

"Sometimes." Deb didn't even realize she felt that way, until the word was out of her mouth. Elliot's truth-curse strikes again. She elaborated, "Sometimes, I go entire hours without feeling like the ground's been snatched out from under me. Those hours, though, are usually at work. Put a scalpel in my hand, and I am steady as that rock the Pilgrims landed on. But let me open the mailbox and see some stupid flyer addressed to Mr. Max Brody, and I can barely grip the envelope. I expect it to be him when the telephone rings. And I see him. I'll be sitting here, at the table, and, out of the corner of my eye, I'll see him pass. I'll even hear his footsteps on the stairs, and I'll think, 'Oh, Max is going to work.' I turn around to wish him a nice day. And I feel like such a fool. . . ." Deb took a moment to collect herself, before reiterating, "I want this year to be over, Elliot. I want it more than I ever wanted anything in my life. I just want to stop hurting, and, the way I see it, time's really the only thing capable of making that happen. I want to go to bed tonight, and wake up tomorrow morning to learn that six months have passed and I can breathe again without feeling my heart rip in two. I want it to be next year. And, at the same time, I am so petrified of midnight, I'd be happy if it never came. Because, I'm leaving him behind, Elliot. No matter how slowly and painfully, I am moving on. And

I'm leaving Max behind. How can I do that to him? How can I *want* to do that to him?"

"Brody—"

"No." Deb slashed the air with her left arm, palm up, like a window washer. "Don't, Elliot. Don't you dare say a word."

"I was just going to point out that—"

"I said, don't! Damn it. Don't give me one of your patented, pacifying platitudes."

"Very well alliterated."

"Every time I come crying to you about the latest tragedy in my life, you're always so reasonable about it, so logical, so damn *supportive*, I can't help but feel cheered up."

"And this is a problem, because . . ."

"It's a problem because . . . because . . ." Deb gulped. "Because, every time your pep talk wears off, and I go back to feeling rotten again, I think I've let you down."

Slam went the fridge again. For this one, Elliot had to turn around. "What!?"

"You work so hard to pull me out of my funks and make me feel better about myself. Whenever I slip and get depressed or anxious, I can't help thinking I've disappointed you."

"That's ridiculous."

"It's how I feel. Oh, hell, Elliot, I'm just trying to do the right thing for everyone. I am trying as hard as I know how not to let anybody down, and, every time I turn around, I screw up."

"Not true." He wasn't arguing with her, just stating a fact.

Deb was about to defend her claim when, from the other room, the sound of a half million drunk people cheering a ball dropping in Times Square seized her attention.

The breath in her throat turned to razor-sharp icicles as any other thought fled her mind at the speed of sound. "Oh, God," Deb covered her mouth with her palms, fingers rubbing the bridge of her nose, thumbs propped against her neck. "It's New Year's. . . ."

"Don't," Elliot commanded, his doctor voice unquestionably on. "Don't do this, Brody. Don't think."

"Oh, come on, Elliot." She made a face, waving his words away with a dismissive hand. "I'm not one of your kids."

"I said, don't think." His tone grew more authoritative. Any protest Deb may have been planning to launch, crashed on the pad.

"Let your mind go blank," he commanded, voice dropping to that same soothing, hypnotic murmur she'd seen him wave a thousand times to distract a patient from a shot or some other painful procedure. "Don't think about anything. Don't feel anything. Stop focusing on yourself. Focus *outside* yourself."

"Elliot . . ."

"The moon." Elliot's fingers firmly squeezed Deb's shoulders, sending electric pressure to reverberate throughout her body at the same time as he turned her around so that, instead of watching him, she was looking out the kitchen window, into the night. "Look at the moon. Focus on it. Concentrate. Let go of yourself, and hold on to the moon. See how the light sort of shimmers around it, like a halo. Notice the shape, and the texture, and the way its craters are laid out. If you look hard enough, you start to see a pattern. See if you can make it out. See if you can conquer the moon."

His hands lingered on her shoulders, gently kneading in rhythm with every word, until the cramped knots in her neck were throbbing and pulsating in unison. He wasn't touching her anywhere else, and yet

Deb could sense him along every cell in her body. His voice permeated her mind, weaving and caressing her soul, as balletic as smoke. If Elliot's intention had been to distract her from the vicious crossroads of midnight, he'd certainly achieved his goal.

Which was a problem all of its own.

Because while Elliot surely intended for her contemplation of the moon to serve as an adequate distraction, when Deb looked where he directed, the only image to seize her focus was the image of the two of them reflected in her kitchen window.

Against the dim glass, they looked like one body. Their limbs grew one out of the other. Their forms fit together so seamlessly, it was impossible to tell where one ended and the other began.

Elliot's chin, ever so slightly, brushed the back of her head. No flesh-on-flesh contact, just a few wisps of hair serving as the conduit of sensation. Hair wasn't supposed to possess the capacity to feel. Deb's hair did.

She didn't dare look at him directly. But the window made it safe. If she met Elliot's eyes in their reflection in the window, it would be alright. It wouldn't be her, and it wouldn't be him. The people in the window were like the negatives of a photograph, ghostly visages who merely looked like the two of them. Ghostly visages, free of corporeal concerns.

Deb raised her gaze slowly, feeling as if she were pulling it up from the depths of her toes. She may have been only lifting her eyes, but she felt like a Greek mythological figure rolling a boulder up a cliff. Her shoulders tightened, driving Elliot's fingers even deeper into her skin. It burned as if scorched.

Elliot lowered his head. His tongue found the tip of her ear, flicking against it, like a question. She didn't pull away. She didn't move. She watched the reflection.

Emboldened, Elliot's lips traced the counter of her left ear, his tongue burrowing inside her as if the flesh and bone there were merely a technicality. His breath was warm, and as penetrating as a stream of heat through an ice sculpture. She leaned toward him instinctively. She didn't decide to do so, she just did it. His hand slipped up her neck, cradling Deb's face as if Elliot expected her to slip away at any moment.

She didn't remember turning around, but at some juncture Deb must have done so because, all of a sudden, they were face-to-face, and Elliot was kissing her forehead, moving from right to left so languidly and carefully, he might have owned all the time in the world. He kissed her eyelids. He kissed the curves of her cheekbones, and the slope of her nose, and the outline of her jaw. She felt rooted to the spot. She felt like she was floating.

She gasped, and so her mouth was ajar by the time Elliot, at long last, found it. His tongue slipped in naturally, and utterly unobtrusively. It looked for hers, stroking first one side, then the other, before turning its attention to the inside of her lower lip. Deb inhaled Elliot, pulling him in closer.

He obeyed, arms moving to encircle her, his hands rubbing her back, fingers dancing up and down her spine, and up to that sensitive spot at the base of her neck. He crushed her against him, showing Deb how perfectly they snapped together, all the while continuing to toy with her mouth, her tongue, her lips.

Her own hands rested on Elliot's hips, and, through the custom smoothness of a tailored tuxedo, she felt him pressing against her stomach, hard and eager and famished.

Had he wanted her this hungrily the other night? Deb couldn't remember. The passionate details of four months ago had long been encrusted with the guilt and recrimination and chaos that followed in its wake. They were all Deb had allowed herself to remember.

And, even as Elliot's kiss made her want to melt against him and into him and through him like rain drenching a parched field—they were all Deb could think about now.

Chapter Nine

Elliot felt Deb pull away.

Mentally, at first. One moment, her soul was intertwined with his. The next, there was only barren air.

Only then did she physically pull away. She didn't jerk, she didn't wrench, she barely even moved. Nevertheless, one minute she was there snug in his arms and the next, even though her body still was, Deb wasn't. He couldn't explain it. He could only feel it.

The cold.

The winter cold.

Elliot was the one who dropped his arms. Elliot was the one who reluctantly took a step back. And still, both knew it was Deb who had gone away.

"Why?" Elliot asked softly. She was looking straight into his eyes, looking straight into his soul, and still, he had no inkling what she was thinking. Or feeling. Or needing.

They stood at arm's length. And miles apart.

Elliot expected Deb to be timid, apologetic, uncertain. Yet, her voice was strong, confident even, as she reminded him, "I told you before, Elliot. No. I can't do this. I won't do this."

"Because of Max." It wasn't a question.

"Because of Max." It was an answer.

"Max is dead."

"Yes."

"You think he would mind us—"

"You don't?"

"Alright." Elliot winced. "Max would mind."

She actually looked grateful for his agreement.

"But, then again, so what?" Elliot wasn't sure what Brody had expected him to say. He was pretty sure she hadn't been expecting that. And, when she refrained from following up, Elliot seized the gauntlet. "Brody?"

"What?" It was a word bitten off at the quick. It was a word suggesting Deb wasn't in the mood to be messed with.

"Would you say I'm a generally decent fellow?"

"You're a prince among men, Elliot."

For the record, *he* was in no mood to be messed with, either. Voice level, Elliot repeated, "Would you say I'm a generally decent fellow, Dr. Brody?"

She shrugged, but didn't allow her gaze to stutter or slink away, guiltily. "You're okay."

"Thank you." Elliot turned his back on her. He walked to the kitchen doorway, pausing there for a moment before slowly pivoting, and crossing his arms. "Am I the sort of fellow to go after another man's wife, Brody?"

She knew what answer he was waiting for, she

knew exactly how Elliot expected her to answer. It was inevitable, after all, that her knowing him as long and as well as she did, there could be only one truthful answer to his question.

"Yes," Deb said.

He raised a probing eyebrow, head cocking just a smidgen.

"When you set your mind on getting something, Elliot, even God—much less some insignificant flesh-and-blood husband—scurries out of the way."

He smiled at that, just like Deb had hoped he would. That was yet another of Elliot's honorable qualities. He never failed to recognize when another was correct and he was wrong, no matter what personal consequences avalanched atop him as a result.

Not that, a split second later, he didn't counter with a fresh way of looking at the circumstance and tilting the scale of reality in his direction. Elliot rephrased, "Am I the sort of fellow to go after another man's wife, Brody, when she doesn't want me to?"

Now, *there* was blood of a whole different Rh factor. Like a computer screen-saver blinking and flashing through all its psychedelic possibilities simultaneously, a host of images and sounds and sensations assaulted Deb from every side. She espied Elliot twenty years ago and right now and all the years in between. She watched him on the first day of medical school, the James Dean mystery man, who, rumor had it, earned his tuition by driving a nitroglycerine truck or roping cattle, or posing for a nude "Ice Boys" calendar. When asked directly, Elliot only smiled in that enigmatic way Deb once would have sworn he practiced in front of a mirror, and offered, "All of the above."

She watched him on their morning before Matching Day, and the afternoon they said good-bye—casually, just a wave and a shouted promise to keep in touch—when Elliot drove down to L.A. In the space of a solitary breath, Deb watched Elliot grow and mature and acquire those traces of gray in his hair, the ones that he brushed so unself-consciously with the palm of his hand, when really deep in thought. She watched Elliot, and she watched herself. Herself and Elliot. All those years.

Then, as quickly as the memories scrolled to the surface, Deb swallowed them down, holding her breath for good measure. A long time ago, she'd learned there was a difference between hearing, and listening. It was a shame that the act of seeing didn't come with two such pithy verbs. She could have used them right now, to name the choice Deb wasn't even aware of herself making.

She swallowed every memory, until not a trace of a picture or a realization was left. That's how she was able to sound utterly and genuinely impassive when, in answer to Elliot's "Am I the sort of fellow to go after another man's wife, Brody, when she doesn't want me to?" Deb definitively replied, "No."

She couldn't tell if he was pleased or disappointed with her judgment. She couldn't tell which she was, either.

It didn't really matter, though. Elliot knew exactly what he meant to say next, no matter what Deb's answer would have been.

"Brody," he reminded softly, "you're not married anymore."

And it was her turn to ask, "So what?"

Another pause. Then, "Are you serious?"

"Are you?"

"Yes." Deb imagined she could literally see Elliot shrugging off his defenses, his issues, his buffers, as he stood in front of her, simultaneously more vulnerable and more powerful than she had ever seen him. "Yes,

Brody. I am serious. About you. About me. About the two of us."

"The two of us," she repeated slowly.

"The two of us." Elliot stepped forward, taking both of Deb's hands in his, rubbing his fingers against her palms in rhythm with his words. "We can do it, we can make it work. At the very least, we can give it a shot. We're not kids anymore, Brody."

"My," Deb blurted out the initial thought that sprung to her mind, aware that it was likely inappropriate, and equally aware that she could think of no other way to respond. "You're certainly full of insights about the obvious, tonight, Dr. Elliot."

"Can it."

Elliot may have instinctively bent over backward when it came to behaving courteously, especially where women were concerned. But he was nobody's fool. And he was nobody's doormat.

"Give it a rest, Brody. We're about twenty years past playing coy games. And it doesn't flatter you."

She observed, "I know we're not kids anymore. What I fail to grasp is why you felt a need to make note of it."

"Because. Time isn't infinite. You, of all people, should be aware of that. I don't want to waste any more time, Brody."

"Meaning?"

"Meaning . . ." he trailed off, changing directions in the space of a breath. Elliot dropped his arms to his sides. He stuffed his hands in his pockets, and looked, first down at the floor, then up at the ceiling. He sighed. "I've been listening to you, you know. I don't want you thinking I haven't, because I have. Very closely. I hear what you're saying, when you talk about not wanting to ruin Max's reputation posthumously. I understand that people will talk. I understand that they'll assume all sort of things about us, and I understand that in some idiotic eyes, Max will end up looking the cuckold. If you think I want that, you're mistaken. I liked your husband. He was a good person. I know that's not a very specific adjective, but, in my eyes, it's the highest compliment I know how to pay. He was a good man. And he put up with a lot for us. I'm grateful. But not at the expense of my own life."

Deb said, "That's your choice, Elliot. You make the decisions about your own fate. Kindly extend me the same courtesy."

"Do you think we need to wait a longer period of time?" Elliot asked. "Because I agree with you, four months is not a very long time, at all, and, if you think we should wait—a year, eighteen months, I'm willing to do that. I understand you care about everything looking proper. I would never push you in that respect."

"That's not it. I mean, yes, it is, but it doesn't matter how long we wait, Elliot. It would still be wrong. I won't do this to Max. Can't you understand? This is the least I owe him."

"You're giving up your life for him?"

"He practically gave up his, for me."

"You're making a mistake."

"I don't think so."

"You're making a mistake, Brody, for all the wrong reasons."

"You're wrong."

"I'm right. Max loved you. While he was alive, he swallowed whatever decidedly nonwarm, nonfuzzy feelings he harbored about me, because he wanted to see you happy. Why is it you assume your husband's stance would change now that he's gone?"

He had her there. Over a barrel, under a table, and anywhere else one could pin somebody. For the first time since their night together sparked this interminable debate, Deb honestly didn't know what to say in response. "He just would," wasn't exactly the pithy response forensics champions dreamed of, after all.

Deb was still trying to untangle her way out of the argument-winning hand Elliot had so skillfully dealt himself, when, from out of nowhere, he hit her with a full-house.

Coolly and calmly he apprised Deb, "I think it's time you stopped hiding behind your husband."

She would have answered him. She wanted to answer him. Hell, from the way the fine hairs on her arms stood up, the way her back arched, the way her toes curled and her chest lurched forward and her tongue pressed against her teeth, Deb felt pretty sure she was about to answer him. And it would have been a good answer, too.

Except for one thing.

At the moment, she stood a little, teeny-tiny bit short on words. Or more precisely, on *apt* words.

Elliot continued. "This isn't about Max. Maybe it started out that way, but your road hit a turnpike weeks ago. I'm forty-three years old. Believe it or not, I have been dumped, once or twice or a half-dozen times, in my life. It didn't kill me then, and, in my professional opinion, it won't kill me now. You don't want to give me a chance? That's fine. But at least have the courtesy to tell me, honestly, why, if for no other reason than because Max deserves better than to be used in such a fashion."

She laughed. It was an odd reaction for an odd situation, and for an even odder reason. But Deb laughed.

Damn, Elliot was good.

He was wasting his time with this doctor nonsense. Obviously, the law was his intuitive profession. Who else but a lawyer would prove so adept at using her own arguments and defenses and excuses against her? Deb was so delighted by his rhetoric, she wanted to hug him. And slug him.

Elliot acknowledged her laughter with a smile of his own. He broke the serious mold that, just a second earlier, seemed as stuck to his face as a funeral shroud on an Egyptian mummy, to ask almost rhetorically, "I am good, aren't I?"

"You're good." Deb felt no qualms about articulating out loud what she'd only thought earlier.

"Think this might be why folks don't like arguing with me?"

"A definite possibility, yes."

"Thanks for the accolades." He pressed, "But do you think I could have an answer to my original question, now?"

He'd asked, "You don't want to give me a chance? That's fine. But at least have the courtesy to tell me, honestly, why."

Deb said, "You're the one hitting verbal bull's-eyes all night. Maybe you should be doing the talking for both of us."

"Alright." He visibly brightened at the prospect. "How about this?" Elliot rubbed his hands one against the other, then raised his arms, palms up, like a magician depicting having nothing up his sleeve. As he made each point, he curved a corresponding finger on each hand in illustration. "One: The sight of me prompts vomiting, fever, and/or a rash. Two: You're in the middle of a hot, sizzling affair on the Internet. Three: Max merely faked his death and the two of you are plotting to swindle the IRS and assume new lives in Tahiti. Four: You're becoming a nun. Or five . . ." With only pinkies left, Elliot dropped his hands, yet the gesture in no way made him look defeated. He met Deb's eyes. He guessed, "Five: My silliness aside, you know that you could never love me as anything more than a friend. But, as a friend, you also have no desire to shatter my heart. By invoking Max, you're trying to let me down gently."

Elliot would never know how easy it would have been for Deb to agree with him. She'd asked him to put the words in her mouth, and Elliot delivered the tastiest dish ever. What a shame it dissolved to slime the minute Deb's conscience tried to swallow a bite.

She couldn't lie to him. Even when he provided the lie, Deb still couldn't even mutely nod her head in approval.

So, she told him the truth. "Elliot?"

"Yes?"

"The sight of you does not prompt vomiting, fever, or a rash."

"I'll note it on your chart."

"But you're right. I am hiding behind Max."

Elliot's eyes widened, and his mouth opened, ready to respond.

Deb cut him off. "I mean, I'm not making anything up. I really do think we owe Max something, and I really don't want his reputation sullied, and I hate, hate the idea of people thinking . . . oh, hell, I'm just repeating myself, now. This is stupid. We're not in a soap opera. We don't need to restate the same truth, ad nauseam. You already know what I hate the idea of people thinking."

"Yes," Elliot said. "And believe me, Brody, I do understand."

"I know you do. That's why you deserve the whole truth, not just the part that makes me comfortable. I am trying to let you down gently, Elliot. But not for the reasons you think. Max is a small part of it. The truth is—the truth is . . . I'm scared."

"Scared?" The concern on his face was as intense

and heartfelt as the day he stood on her porch, awkwardly asking if there was anything he could do for Deb. "Of me? You're scared of me?"

"No . . . Uhm, yes."

"That wasn't multiple choice, Brody."

He could still make her smile. No matter what the situation, Elliot could still make Deb smile, like no one else on earth. She loved him for that. She'd always loved him for that.

"I'm terrified of losing you, Elliot."

"Like you lost Max?"

"Yes . . . Uhm, no."

"Okay, maybe I'm wrong. Maybe this *is* a multiple-choice test. Did I miss a memo?"

There he went again, making her smile. How in the world was Deb supposed to explain to him now that it was precisely for this reason that she would never allow herself to view him as anything more than a friend?

She mused, "I suppose I am a little gun-shy. The thought of loving somebody and losing them again the way I lost Max—I never considered it, but my God, I don't know if I could survive that."

Elliot tapped his chest with his fist. "I'm a wholly healthy fellow. Feel free to peruse my medical records."

She couldn't let him distract her. She had to keep talking. She had to make her point before he made her laugh again and forget her every objection. And so she pressed on, mentally covering her ears with both hands to insist, "But there is something I know for a fact I could never, ever survive. And that's losing you."

"But you wouldn't lose—"

"I'm not talking about your dying. I'm talking about things not working out between us. . . . Romantically . . ." It was the first time she'd said the word in the context of relative possibility—a possibility denied, but a possibility just the same. She wasn't prepared for the reaction it provoked in her. For a split second, Deb could look down the road at next week, and next month, and next year. She saw, as clearly as if on a television set, the life that was waiting for her, the life she could easily have just by saying the word. The life they could both have.

Deb changed the channel.

Elliot asked, more intellectually curious than offended, "Why do you assume things wouldn't work out between us. Romantically?" From the pause he took after that last word, Deb guessed it must have snuck up on him, too.

"Things happen," Deb said. "Couples break up."

"And some couples stay together. Look at you and Max. You guys beat the odds. In spite of ... everything."

"You don't understand, Elliot. I need you too much. Do you realize that there are days when I wake up, and, for the life of me, I cannot feel *anything*. It's the strangest sensation, being empty, being hollow. I close my eyes, and I think, now I'll just float away. There's nothing to keep me here. And if I float away, there won't be any more pain. Because, there's always pain. Even when I don't feel anything, I feel pain. I know that doesn't make sense, except that the pain is no longer a sensation. It's become an extra appendage, like growing another arm. There are days when floating away sounds like the finest recourse. I'm ready to do it. And then I stop. Because I remember you. You're here. You'd care if I disappeared. I don't want to leave you. You make me smile."

"But that's what I want, Brody." Elliot's hands trembled as he held them palms up, not pleading exactly, more like ... offering. "I want to make you smile. I want to make you smile every minute of every day of the rest of your life. I want to make you happy."

"You do." She clutched his fingers between hers,

shaking them a little, like tiny slaps to awaken a medicated patient. "The way things stand between us right now, you make me very happy. That's why I'm scared to change anything."

"We could make things better, Brody."

"We could. But we also risk making them worse." She shook her head. "Damn it, Elliot, I would've thought you'd be the last person I'd need to convince that, sometimes, romantic relationships don't work out. They end. Usually badly. And people end up going their separate ways, never to see each other again."

"You would be referring to the women I've dated in the past?"

"All seven thousand of them, yes."

Elliot smiled. In spite of everything, it warmed Deb's heart that she also had the power to make *him* smile.

"It would be different with us," he promised.

"Maybe. I don't know. But Elliot, I am in no shape to risk finding out. See, I can handle losing you as a lover. But I know I would never survive losing you as a friend."

Then, "Okay, Brody," Elliot said, voice husky, and tired, and resigned. "I understand. And I'll make sure to act appropriately."

Deb swallowed hard. She said, "Oh."

She was thrilled.

Before she left for work, Deb made a mental note to keep reminding herself of that fact. When a mere mental note proved inadequate, she pulled out her appointment book, and, feeling like the fool-of-all-seasons, drew a happy face under the date. Deborah Brody was *thrilled*. See?

She did feel relieved. Deb didn't need visual aids to

tell her that. She was glad everything was finally out in the open. Maybe now everything could return to normal. Deb pulled out her calendar again, and made a—physical, this time—note to check how many times she'd wished for *that* in the last four months.

But all in all, Deb was satisfied with how she and Elliot had left things the night before last. Matters might not have exactly turned out for the very, very best they could have. But, then again, she had avoided their turning out the very, very worst. And Deb was a lot more scared of the latter, than of a lifetime without the former.

The former, she was used to.

The former was what they called reality.

So what if, last night as she lay in bed, she'd periodically felt the echo of Elliot's fingers as they caressed the back of her neck, or the ghost of his mouth nuzzling hers, his tongue moist and warm and sensually slick against her teeth. That didn't mean much. Deb never claimed she wasn't physically attracted to the man. Oh, alright on that, too, she had. Once or twice. Or seven thousand.

But that was a long time ago. Things were different then. And besides, she was over it. Nowadays, Deb felt no qualms about admitting that she was physically attracted to Elliot.

She just didn't intend to do anything about it, that's all.

Just because the memory of the way he'd looked at her, even through a reflection, made Deb's stomach release a swarm of bees to hum their way up her chest and down her thighs until her knees sent up a query asking how much longer they might be required to remain standing, didn't mean Deb wanted to risk losing something a great deal more precious in exchange for feeling like that again.

Or all of the time.

Or for the rest of her life.

After all, wobbly knees were the last condition she needed to strike her in the middle of performing surgery.

Alone in the elevator on the way to her office, Deb smiled to herself. There. Now she had two reasons for not getting involved with Elliot.

She felt better. And, what was more, she felt . . . secure.

It had been a very long time since she'd felt that way. Ever since Max's death, Deb had walked around tentative about each step she took, convinced that every subsequent one would prove the one during which the earth would permanently crumble beneath her feet. She answered every phone call expecting the news to be terrible. She pondered every X ray and CAT scan devoid of her old conviction that, whatever was wrong, Deb would be able to fix it.

January first of the new year marked the first time since the first week of September that Deb could honestly say she felt like her old self again. Secure, confident, brave, ready.

And she owed it all to Elliot.

Deb no longer feared the earth crumbling because she knew its most important ingredient, her and Elliot's alliance, was no longer in jeopardy. Elliot would continue to be there for her. He would be her rock, and her anchor. He would continue to be her friend. She would not lose him, now.

Deb hadn't even realized how big of a weight her fear of this potential deprivation was, until it skidded off her shoulders and made an ever-so-satisfying crash on the metaphorical floor.

She felt ten pounds lighter. She felt ten years younger.

For the first time since that vicious week in September, Deb felt . . . released.

If she knew how to whistle, Deb probably would have been doing so as she strode into her office.

Jeff Greenwood certainly put an end to that plan.

Her protégé was leaning over her desk, a ballpoint pen in one hand, a yellow Post-it note in the other. When he heard her come in, he dropped the pen, crumpled the note, and, snatching a faxed sheaf of papers from the in-pile on her desk, spun around, his arm outstretched so that the papers all but brushed her nose.

"What are you going to do about this?" Jeff demanded.

Deb ducked instinctively, and walked around Jeff, dropping her briefcase into her chair, and peeling off her coat, as she pointed out, "*This*, being?"

"Didn't you get your copy faxed at home?"

"I don't have a fax at home. I fail to see progress in using a telephone to send a letter."

"This is not a letter." Jeff rained the fax onto Deb's desk, and angrily shifted his weight from foot to foot—pacing without actually getting anywhere. "This—this—this is a travesty!"

"Calm yourself, Doctor." Deb had no idea what he was talking about, but she had yet to encounter a situation in which the edict to calm down was not apropos. "What does the fax say?"

Jeff waited for Deb to pick it up and start reading the first word, before impatience got the better of him, and he blurted out, "It's the new hospital budget report."

Yes, she could see that. Deb skimmed the columns upon columns of numbers, looking for the ones that pertained to her, but once again, Jeff just couldn't wait.

"They went ahead and did it, Dr. Brody. Those

bastards sliced two million dollars from the Pediatric Neurosurgery budget. Jesus, they've barely left us enough to pay for Band-Aids."

She heard Jeff's tirade, and, a moment later, Deb even found the paragraph confirming and enumerating what he was saying. But she still couldn't believe it. Despite all of her pleas, despite all of her reports and memos and test results and statistics, the hospital Board, in their infinite wisdom, had still decided to all but obliterate her department.

What were they thinking, that her kids should wait until they were eighteen to seek medical treatment?

"Did you know this was coming?" Jeff's voice sang disbelief.

Shell-shocked, Deb could only shake her head side to side.

"What about Dr. Elliot, did he say anything—"

"Not a word." Deb slowly raised her head, staring not so much at Jeff, as through him. "Elliot didn't tell me anything of this nature was about to happen."

"You'd think, knowing about it in advance, he could, at least, have warned you."

"He said he would." That empty, hollow feeling was sneaking up on Deb again. It started in her gut and slithered up her spine like a serpent around a tree. "Jeff, when did the Budget Committee sign off on this final draft?"

"Oh, I heard they were still making changes right up till this morning, when it was due. See right there, the secretary who typed it up put down this morning's date."

Elliot had promised to tell Deb as soon as the Committee made its final decision about her department. The fact that he hadn't done so New Year's Eve suggested to Deborah that, as late as that night, her budget was still more or less intact. This recent—what did Jeff call it?—travesty? must have been among the last-minute changes typed up that morning. It could only have happened if the holdouts against cutting her funding had, all of a sudden and for no particular reason, changed their votes.

And, as far as Deb was aware, the solitary holdout previously standing between the Budget Committee and her involuntary expulsion from the hospital was . . . Elliot.

Chapter Ten

Speeding down the hall to Elliot's office, Deb heard the *rat-a-tat* of her heels along the floor, but she still refused to believe her feet ever touched the ground. She was that mad.

But not so mad that, when she got to the doors of Elliot's office, Deb didn't pause to ask his assistant, Helen, whether the doctor might be in with a patient.

He was.

Damn. That was just like Elliot. Never there when you needed to yell at him. Deb felt loath to turn on her heel and bluster out of the room, only to return at a later time. Righteous indignation did harbor a tragically short shelf life. It was hopeless to stay steamed when one needed to call first for an appointment.

So, Deb waited.

She could have sat down in one of the chairs Elliot set out in the room designated specifically for that purpose.

But she preferred not to.

Again, that righteous indignation thing.

So, Deb waited.

And, as she waited, she went over and over again, in her head, the rivulet of reasons that had brought her to this agitated state.

Elliot had betrayed her.

There could be no other explanation.

Sometime between New Year's Eve 2000 and January 2, 2001, the man she considered her very best friend in the world had signed his name to a document effectively voiding Deb's life.

Well, alright, perhaps she was getting a smidgen melodramatic, here. Elliot hadn't exactly signed a warrant to put her head on the chopping block. The problem was, he might as well have. Deb's job was the only constant still left in her life. It was the one thing she'd been able to hold on to as, piece by piece, her entire existence crumbled into unrecognizable chaos. Deb was no longer a wife, and, at times, she'd wondered if she could even still be considered a functioning human being. But through it all, she'd remained a doctor. A pediatric neurosurgeon at the best facility for her specialty in the country. It was her identity. It was her rock, when even Elliot seemed ready to surrender the job. And now, she was being forced to let it go.

Elliot was aware of Deb's ultimatum to the Budget Committee. They'd discussed it numerous times. He knew she had threatened to quit if they stuck her with an unmanageable operating budget, and he also knew that she meant to go through with her vow. Deb had too much pride to back down. She had to resign. Or lose face.

For months, Elliot had been the sole obstacle in the Budget Committee's slashing and burning its way through her department. All he had to do was hold on for another day, and the crisis would have passed. Deb could have gotten her money. Deb could have kept her job. Deb could have stayed at the hospital.

But sometime between New Year's Eve 2000 and January 2, 2001, the man she considered her very best friend in the world had decided that wasn't such a great idea.

And so he sold Deb down the river.

She thought she knew why.

The door to Elliot's office opened, and a seven-year-old boy in a wheelchair, both legs in heavy casts, appeared in the waiting area. His chair was being pushed by a woman Deb presumed was the child's mother, but as he twisted around in his seat, legs pointed one way, torso and head another, it wasn't his mother he addressed, but Elliot, still standing, all but invisible, in the depths of his office. "See, Dr. Elliot, The Flash, he's the fastest man in the world. But, Superman can fly. So, I'm not sure who's really the fastest, because, you know, they do different stuff, and—"

"Say good-bye to Dr. Elliot, Sasha," the mother instructed, but with her tone of exasperation was also mixed the continuing wonder that this child who once might have been given up for dead was able to chatter on in such a fashion.

"Good-bye, Dr. Elliot," the boy echoed obediently, then picked up right where he'd left off. "They do different stuff so I guess you'd have to have a race or something to figure it out."

"I'll see you next week, Sasha." Elliot's voice boomed from the other room, as reassuring and comforting as ever. Was it only this morning that Deb had bought into that reassurance as eagerly as little Sasha and his mother had now?

She waited for the boy to wheel comfortably out of earshot—she was furious, after all, not suddenly oblivious to professional courtesy—before reprising her zoom into Elliot's office.

He was sitting behind his desk, chuckling at a pair of comic books lovingly sealed inside plastic covers, and obviously donated in return for services rendered. Elliot glanced up, surprised to see her. He made a move to stand up, but Deb thrust out her hand and, with the force of one word, pushed him back down in his chair.

She ordered, "Explain."

He cocked his head to one side, trying to decide whether to go with befuddled or amused for his dominant emotion. "Direct object, please, Doctor?"

If she had bothered to think ahead, Deb might have remembered to bring the offending fax with her. She could have crumpled it into a ball and hurled it at his face. Failing that, she could have at least thought to tuck the paperwork inside a manila file. Those suckers were pretty aerodynamic, too.

As things stood, though, the only thing Deb really had handy to throw was her shoe. But she'd already ruined one pair trying to attract Elliot's attention. She wasn't exactly Imelda Marcos.

She said, "Graph this sentence, Elliot. Verb equals Explain. You equals Implied. Direct object equals My Department Is Losing Its Budget."

"Oh." Elliot's focus finally forsook The Flash. "That."

"That."

He scratched his ear sheepishly. "You never check your office fax. I was hoping I had a little more time before you found out."

"Unfortunately for you, Jeff Greenwood is a regular Alexander Graham Bell."

"I'm sorry," Elliot said. "Let me explain."

He wasn't denying it.

Until the confirmation trickled so casually out of his mouth, Deb hadn't realized just how much she'd been expecting him to deny it. Or how much she wanted him to.

"Explain?" Deb repeated numbly. Her heart beat so loudly, all they needed was a DJ and it could be set to a rap beat. "You think you can explain this?"

"It's complicated, Brody." Elliot leaned back in his chair, crossing one leg over the other, and raising one pedagogical hand to make a point. He looked every inch the erudite educator, coming down from the mountain to sprinkle his wisdom among the peasants. It was a pose reminiscent of every professor they painfully endured in medical school. It was a pose that pushed Deb over the edge.

He looked so damn smug, so damn full of himself, so damn sure that, as soon as she heard whatever excuse he'd earlier concocted, she would swallow it as gullibly as she had all of his other lies.

Like the ones about his being Deb's friend.

Like the ones about his caring for her.

"Alright, Elliot." Deb crossed her arms, chin bobbing up and down as feverishly as Howdy Doody's in his heyday. "Explain it to me. Explain to me how your damn male ego was so ticked off at my turning you down the other night, that you decided to get back at me by ruining the last shred of security and satisfaction I still possessed in my life."

Her words pinned him, like daggers thrown from a distance, to his chair. He looked like he wanted to lean forward, but the sheer weight of her accusation was acting like a cement blanket, so that only his head slowly submerged an inch downward. He must have been raising his eyebrows at the same time, because, from where Deb was standing, it looked like Elliot's jaw, chin, mouth, nose, and eyes lowered, while his brows remained in the same spot.

She spat, "What's the matter, Doc? Seeing me, day in and day out here at the hospital, each time, being forced to remember that I had the effrontery to say 'no, thank you,' to the great Dr. James Elliot—was that more than your vanity could handle? Is that why you decided to get rid of the problem by getting rid of me?"

Elliot didn't say anything. He just stared at Deb as if he'd never seen her before, and wasn't sure if he ever wanted to, again.

She wished he would answer. Even the lie of a denial would be welcome at this point. The silence was siphoning Deb's anger like a slowly collapsing bicycle tire. And she didn't want to lose her anger. She needed it. To keep from bursting into tears.

So, Deb kept talking, her mouth running a race to stay ahead of her gradually moistening eyes, and, ergo, utter humiliation.

She charged, "You promised me you would keep the Committee from cutting my budget. You knew how important it was to me. You knew that, even though I made the threat, the last thing I wanted was to lose this job. I love this job. This job is my life, damn it. I trusted you. I put my fate in your hands, and you screwed me over royally. And for what? A fleeting moment of retaliation? Are you really that insecure, Elliot? Are you really that petty?"

"I don't know." His voice was dead and hollow. "We've known each other for twenty years. You tell me."

It wasn't like Elliot to surrender without a fight.

When he felt that he was right and the other person wrong, Elliot could go for days, debating, and arguing, and asserting his position. Seven years ago, despite three other doctors diagnosing his patient with Attention Deficit Disorder, Elliot kept on digging and testing and consulting every medical book seemingly ever published to determine that an obscure allergy was actually the cause of the problem. He dealt with every aspect of his life like that. In hockey, Elliot spent more minutes in the penalty box than on the ice, arguing with the referee. He flunked a Russian Literature class at Yale, because Elliot insisted on arguing, daily, with his professor over there being only one allegedly correct way to decode Dostoyevsky's *Crime and Punishment.* The professor failed Elliot not because his work was bad, but because the professor didn't agree with Elliot's interpretations. Naturally, Elliot fought the mark all the way up to the Dean's office, and, naturally, in the end, he got his way—an *A.* Elliot always got his way. Because Elliot fought for it.

The only time Elliot declined to fight was when he knew he was wrong.

As Deb stood in front of him, accusing Elliot of machinations that a few hours ago she would have never dreamed him capable of, Elliot declined to fight back.

Now, she really was going to cry.

"How could you do this to me?" Her prodigious vocabulary and otherwise celebrated communications skills deserted Deb precisely when she needed them to build a sturdy wall for her to hide behind.

"I don't know," Elliot repeated. All of a sudden, he seemed not to know a hell of a lot.

"Did you think you could get away with it?" Somewhere, there had to be a reasonable explanation for all this. And, since Elliot seemed in no hurry to provide it, Deb would have to go spelunking for it, herself. "Did you think maybe I wouldn't figure it out?"

If one could sigh with one's body, rather than only with one's throat, then that was what Elliot did. He stopped fighting against the concrete blanket pinning him down, and, instead, seemed to give in to it—all but snuggling, resigned, underneath the covers. He proposed, "Maybe I was hoping you would never be able to imagine me capable of such a thing."

Well, at least that was some kind of answer, albeit not a very good or comforting one. Deb asked, "That's what you were counting on to save you? My being too stupid to put three and four together and come up with a prime-number suspect?"

"Yes," Elliot said. "Alright. That was it."

This was not like him. This was not the Elliot Deb knew.

But, then again, under the circumstances, she was compelled to wonder whether she ever really knew him at all.

She gave it her last, best shot, fully aware that, if it went wild and failed to hit its target, all would be lost. Not that all probably wasn't already lost, but what the hell, it was never too late to become a practicing optimist, was it?

"Why aren't you defending yourself, Elliot?"

He stood up, white lab coat hanging loose over the kelly green shirt and silk tie. He rested both hands on the edge of his desk. He leaned forward, supporting much of his weight along his athletic arms. He said, "Because, Brody, I'm a doctor. I know the meaning of, and the difference between, 'curable' and 'terminal.' I fight only for the 'curables.' As long as there's even a fraction of a chance of success, I will break my own back to fix a problem. Sometimes, though, the injury is too critical. The wound too deep. There is nothing anyone can do. In cases like that, I refuse to prolong the misery. You want me to defend myself to you—or is it, for you? You want me to put on a little show of contrition, or regret or—What would be the point? You've made up your mind. You've got it all figured out. And you are the precocious one, after all."

He was making fun of her. Somewhere, amid the metaphors and the medical philosophy of James Elliot, he was making fun of her.

"So, that's all you've got to say for yourself?"

"Yes." He crossed his arms.

Well, okay. That was pretty clear and to the point.

Except that it wasn't.

Deb had come flying into Elliot's office psyched to listen to him deny and explain and cajole and wheedle and charm. She'd been prepared for that, prepared for the assumption that it would take her hours, days, maybe even weeks to wear him down to a point where he could be willing to admit—much less explain—his actions.

She figured closure would come when Elliot acquiesced.

Well, here he was. Acquiescing.

Meanwhile, Deb didn't feel even a little bit . . . closed.

Surely, Elliot had prepared some measly, piddling, premature baby of an excuse. Surely, his whole, entire defense couldn't have been propped on the wing-and-a-prayer hope that she'd never figure out who cast the vote that pushed her out of the hospital.

Unless he'd been hit by a large bus or popped a small blood vessel in his head overnight, Elliot was *not* that stupid.

But, then again, she was not dealing with Elliot the doctor and reasonable human being, here. She was dealing with Elliot—Man Rejected. God only knew how much cranial damage that could do.

At this point, Deb was ready to accept it even if Elliot told her his voting to cut her budget had to do with hospital politics, or a deal he'd made to bolster his own department, or even that his astrologist read it in his coffee grounds.

Deb was so desperate, she was ready to accept any excuse.

Except the confirmation that his reason for kiboshing her life was personal.

"Elliot," she began, but at that moment, an echo piped in.

"Dr. Elliot." Helen stepped into the room, clutching a file in one hand, and a pen in the other. "I need you to—oh"—her gaze fell on Deb—"I'm sorry. I didn't realize you were still in your meeting. I'll come back later."

"No. That's alright." Elliot stepped to the side, and walked around his desk, reaching for the file and pen, turning his back on Deb to sign it. He said, "Dr. Brody and I are through."

Thank *God,* Deb took the hint and left.

If she hadn't, Dr. Brody, Neurosurgeon, would have witnessed a display even her profession hadn't prepared her for. She would have seen Elliot's entire cranium split apart from the sheer force of keeping his anger inside and in check.

After Deb left, Elliot did no more than sit at his desk and, rather aimlessly, sift through the piles of paperwork that tended to accumulate there. Technically, he didn't actually explode. He simply felt like he might. Any fucking minute now.

Naturally, this was not the first time in his life that Elliot had stood unjustly accused. People accused him of unjust things all the time.

When he was still driving that nitro truck, his supervisor liked to accuse the "college boy" of thinking he was better than everybody else. That accusation, thankfully, was put to bed with a bone-crunching, bruise-swelling, blood-letting fistfight in the bowels of a late-night parking lot.

Elliot suspected a similar approach might not work here.

In medical school, Elliot was periodically accused of cheating by professors who didn't trust his string of one-hundred-percent quizzes. As an intern, he'd been accused of second-guessing doctors, and, horror of all horrors, sometimes listening to a nurse's or a pharmacist's input over an MD's. That accusation was put to rest when Elliot was able to prove that he had listened to the attending physicians—he just chose to decode their words rather unorthodoxly. He'd been accused by a few girlfriends of cheating on them. He'd been accused of cheating on his taxes, and he'd been accused of cheating on the hockey rink.

But this . . . this!

Just who the hell did Deb think she was?

Well, alright. So, she was the most enchanting, fascinating, brilliant, alluring, desirable woman he'd ever met.

But Deb didn't have to know he felt that way.

And, even if she did, that still didn't give her carte blanche to treat him in such a manner.

Elliot understood, the minute he grudgingly signed his consent to trimming her budget, that Deb would be incensed. And she would have every right to be. Especially after Elliot had promised her that he would fight tooth and nail and, when that didn't work, fist and knee, to keep the worst from happening. Elliot knew precisely how much her job meant to Deb. He saw it in her eyes, in the way they started to sparkle the moment she turned the corner and first saw their high-rise building. Elliot knew that sparkle. He'd felt it more than once in his own eyes. Whenever his personal life was in what he liked to euphemistically call an "ailing arc," the hospital became his lifeline, his salvation. So—to reiterate—Elliot understood exactly how Deb felt. He wouldn't have ripped her safety net away from her, for anything in the universe. He would have sooner fallen on a rusty scalpel. Not exactly Sir Galahad and his puddle, but the noble concept was the same.

That's why, even as he was sweeping through the double *L*'s in signing his name—thanks to an end-run political maneuver thrown at him, ipso facto, by Morelli and Company at six on the morning the budget was due—Elliot was already formulating a plan to get around this, and keep not only Deb's department open, but also keep her in place as Chief of Pediatric Neurosurgery.

He'd hoped to get to Deb and tell her about the last-minute change of plans before she heard about the budget cuts, but his appointment with Sasha took longer than Elliot counted on—when a boy who, eighteen months earlier, was suffering from such severe aphasia that he couldn't identify a cat or a muffin or an airplane, now wanted to spend an extra half an hour extolling the virtues of Superman versus The Flash, who was Elliot to stop him?

He wasn't surprised when Deb burst, respirating fire, into his office. That's why Elliot had barely reacted. He figured he'd let her get the rant out of her system—there was nothing folks hated more than being cut off mid-rant, and, besides, if Elliot tried to interrupt her righteous indignation, it would have taken him twice as long to deliver the same amount of information. Elliot did not play at shouting matches. It didn't go with his "cool" image.

So, politely, he'd waited for her to finish.

Only, by the time Deb did finish, Elliot, for the first time that he could remember, didn't have a single word he wanted to say.

She'd shocked him into silence. No one—not parents, not teachers, not girlfriends, not patients—had ever done *that* before. The moment he heard her words, the ones accusing him . . . accusing *him* of . . . Elliot refused to repeat them. Not even to himself. A few more repetitions and his aphasia would be worse than Sasha's.

The moment he heard her words, the moisture on Elliot's skin chilled, covering him with a layer of frost. He felt like the Tin Man from *The Wizard of Oz,* or a victim of Batman's archenemy, Mr. Freeze—encased in ice, and immobile. As a doctor, Elliot knew about the phenomenon of your heart skipping a beat. But he hadn't realized that it could also keep beating, and yet truly be stopped, just the same.

It wasn't that Elliot didn't want to say anything to Deb. He simply, physically, couldn't. He was paralyzed. He was numb. He was . . . dead. The fact that he kept on apparently moving and talking afterward was merely a postmortem, utterly instinctive, series of muscle contractions.

This was not a broken heart. Elliot had experienced broken hearts before. Broken hearts clawed at your chest and scraped your lungs and pureed your brain. Broken hearts hurt.

This didn't hurt. This wasn't heartache. This was the abyss.

This was falling off a cliff, and falling so long that, after a while, you stopped feeling scared, and just didn't care anymore.

This was infinity.

Elliot supposed he hadn't made the circumstances any better by declining to defend himself. He knew Deb must have interpreted it as a sign of admitted guilt. She, better than anyone, knew how he liked to dig his heels in and debate the life out of any important issue. When Elliot didn't fight back, Deb must have thought he had nothing to fight back with. Which was true, in a way. While he did possess the words, what he lacked was the motivation.

He hadn't previously imagined it possible, but the minute Deb thought him capable of such treacherous behavior was the minute he stopped caring what she thought of him.

If, after twenty years of friendship, Deb could even imagine him doing anything—especially deliberately— to hurt her, then, obviously, all twenty of their years had been for nothing.

This was Hell.

What a shame Elliot didn't have time to stick around and see the satanic sights. To the right of him was an open office door, beckoning future, scheduled patients, and yet-to-be emergencies. To the left of him, was a phone ringing loudly enough to wake the dead.

Elliot snatched up the receiver, answering with a snarl of his name. While he listened, he reached for the comic books Sasha had left behind, and opened a desk drawer into which to tuck them for safekeeping. The first thing he saw, glaring at him from the open drawer, was a deck of playing cards.

Elliot sat down. He tucked the receiver between his chin and neck. Then, very slowly, emphatically, and dispassionately, Elliot proceeded to rip each card in the deck into confetti.

Deb had a deck of cards, too.

That night, after she couldn't fall asleep, and after two mugs of warm milk, three TV infommercials, and a really lousy mystery novel, Deb got up and grabbed a deck of cards. She meant to play solitaire.

The only problem was, she didn't know how.

Forty-one years old, and she'd never really been alone.

She didn't even know any card games like Poker or Twenty-one or Old Maid. Her mother never let her kids play. She thought that led to gambling. As a result, the only thing Deb knew how to do with cards was build houses. And only because Elliot had taught her, back in medical school.

Twenty years later and lacking options, she set down two cards on her coffee table. And started building.

Deb figured—if years of English courses insisting on poetic symbolism for every gesture were to be believed—that it would be harder to build a house of cards, alone.

It was actually easier. You had more control, more balance, and no second set of hands to get in the way. She also figured, all things considered, that her house was destined to collapse from its own weight, before she even started on the second floor.

Four floors, and she was still going strong.

So much for symbolism.

So much for all sorts of things Deb had once believed in.

Friendship, loyalty, trust.

And one more thing.

Deb once believed that, as soon as someone hurt

you, you were entitled to cut them entirely out of your life. Stop caring about them, stop thinking about them. Make them invisible, an un-person. At least, that's how it always worked before. Whenever anyone hurt Deb before, she would shut her heart and her mind, so that, in her world, they no longer existed. And, as everybody knew—someone who no longer existed could hardly possess the power to hurt you, now, could he? It was an effective system for making any and all pain go away. Except for this time. Except for Elliot.

No matter how hard she tried to exorcise him from her psyche, he continued to cling to the outskirts of her consciousness, like a shadow ingrained into cement after a nuclear blast.

No matter how hard she tried not to care about Elliot, and, by extension, not to care about what he'd done to her, Deb couldn't do it. She couldn't be indifferent to the man.

She could only be furious. Which was very disturbing.

Because, as long as Deb could still feel fury toward Elliot, that meant she was still open to feeling . . . anything.

Chapter Eleven

Nothing happened.

Nothing dramatic, anyway.

Deb had kind of been expecting drama.

Nothing Shakespearean, or Brechtian, or even Aaron-Spellingish. But, nevertheless, some kind of tangible evidence of her life having spiraled quickly and painfully down the proverbial gutter *should* have happened.

Deb needed the evidence. Granted, she anticipated it hurting like hell. But, still, considering how things had been going, she needed proof that she wasn't losing her mind and imagining things. She needed proof that this wasn't some horrible nightmare she could still wake up from any morning. Elliot had actually betrayed her. The world actually had come to a crashing halt.

Deb wasn't sure what she expected to happen the first time she and Elliot ran into each other again at the hospital, though their running into each other was inevitable. It was a large hospital. But not that large. On the one hand, Deb wished that it would go on indefinitely. Avoidance and denial were unquestionably viable and successful strategies for handling a calamity. On the other hand, there was much to be said for the bite-the-bullet-and-get-it-over-with approach. And Deb really, really wanted to get it over with.

Partly because she was impatient to test out her own behavior under fire, as it were.

But mostly because she was dying of curiosity, wondering how Elliot intended to handle it.

Deb figured there were two directions he could run with this. There was Fire, and there was Ice.

Fire would be Elliot in attack mode. He was good at that, Deb had seen it. She'd seen him lash into other doctors—especially ones who didn't agree with him—with the force of a defibrillator and the precision of a laser. He had a knack for looking through people, X-raying their weaknesses and insecurities, and then using those weaknesses and insecurities against them with such finesse, it was sometimes impossible to discern the lancet coming, until it was sticking out a back or chest. Precisely because he was so good at decimation, Elliot rarely, rarely, very rarely, wielded his talent. Unlike a bully, Elliot knew exactly the impression he could have on others, if he chose to. So he kept the faculty tightly reined in, and only to be brought out under extreme circumstances.

Deb wondered if he'd consider this an extreme circumstance.

He really had no right to. Deb was the victim, after all, not Elliot. She had certainly not gone gunning for him unprovoked.

Unless, of course, Elliot considered her figuring out what he had done and refusing to listen to any excuses a provocation.

She tried to see the situation through his eyes—if only to anticipate how he might retaliate, but found it nearly impossible. Over and over again, Deb kept coming back to the same premise. The man she was dealing with today was not the same man she had known for twenty years. This was a different Elliot. This was an Elliot she'd never previously encountered—one whom she'd rejected not as a friend, but as a man.

Deb was a doctor. She knew about hormones. They did strange things to people. One had only to look at the strangeness they'd driven her to the night of Max's funeral, for conclusive proof of the fact. And she supposed that hormones—along with pride and machismo and honor—could have driven the Elliot she thought she knew to act in a way she never could have imagined him capable of. That didn't mean she had to like it. Or accept it. Or forgive it.

Deb didn't think she could ever forgive it. And that's the part that broke her heart.

Here she had explained, so painstakingly, to Elliot that the reason she was turning him down romantically was because Deb felt too afraid of losing him as a friend—and look what happened.

She lost him anyway.

And, hell, she didn't even get sex in the bargain.

All that effort. All that denial. And she lost him anyway.

Driving to work the next morning, Deb found herself dreading the sight of the hospital—a sight that, quite recently, had been the only one capable of cheering her up. She dreaded the sight of the hospital because she was dreading facing Elliot's Fire.

But even more than that, she was dreading facing his Ice.

Elliot enraged was upsetting. Elliot cold could kill you.

Because Elliot cold could make you doubt your own existence.

His notion of the silent treatment took the orthodox approach, and multiplied it. Elliot wasn't satisfied simply to stop speaking to you, or ignoring your phone calls, or passing you in the hall without a greeting or acknowledgment. When Elliot cut you out of his life, you all but started to shimmer like a prebeam *Star Trek* character, right before you became invisible. Facing Elliot while he indulged in deep-freeze mode meant becoming an un-person.

Naturally, he was the one Deb had learned her own un-person technique from. Although, compared to the master, she was a mere novice. And, as she'd determined last night, a lousy one, at that.

When Deb stepped out of the fourth-floor elevator and spotted Elliot, a resident on either side, striding toward her, expounding on some fine point of Pediatric Trauma Care, Deb's initial impulse was to duck back inside, to keep out of his way, and avoid getting doused with either hail or a firestorm. But, on the other hand, she was curious how he would choose to handle their new malignity.

As Elliot drew closer, Deb braced herself for a blow. Sort of like she imagined plane-crash victims braced themselves in the last moment. She prayed the instant of impact would never come, and she prayed to get it over with as quickly as possible.

At last, and sooner than she was prepared for, it happened.

Nothing happened.

Elliot and Deb came face-to-face.

They couldn't help it. It was either come face-to-face with Elliot, or with the elevator, and his pushing the call button just as she was making up her mind made the latter escape impossible.

Elliot and Deb came face-to-face.

And nothing happened.

He didn't berate her. He didn't mock her. He didn't question her professional judgment, and he didn't let rip with one of those sly asides he was so good at— the ones that seemed benign on the surface, but cut straight to the sinew just beneath it.

He didn't say much of anything.

So. It was to be Ice, after all.

Well, she'd been expecting as much.

She'd been wishing it wouldn't come to this, but she'd been expecting him to erase her from the universe.

Except that, he looked at her.

Not through her. At her.

Elliot looked right at Deb. And he smiled.

He smiled, and he bobbed his head as courteously as an English gentleman at high tea. "Good morning, Dr. Brody."

Not a letter out of place, not a note out of the ordinary, not a suggestion that, less than twenty-four hours earlier, they'd been to Hell, back, and all the pit stops in between.

"Excuse us, please."

He rested his hand on her elbow. Even through the silk of her jacket, she could feel how cool his fingers were. How dry, and how steady. In comparison, the simple touch of his palm sent a shudder through her body worthy of a convulsion.

With minimal exertion, Elliot whisked her aside. He gestured for the residents to accompany him inside the elevator. He pushed the button for his floor. He settled at the head of the elevator, and turned to face Deb, his stance wide, his hands behind his back.

He smiled.

The doors closed.

Deb felt like a fool, standing rooted to the spot just outside the elevator. But even though her knees, spine, and tongue were—slowly but surely—returning to a state of normalcy, she still lacked enough moral mettle to actually budge.

He didn't care.

How else was Deb supposed to interpret this— this—this ... slight ... of Elliot's?

Elliot didn't care.

He didn't even think she was worth the effort of retaliation.

The awareness jump-started the vortex in Deb's chest, leaving her feeling as hollow as a test tube. How could she have meant so little to Elliot, that the end of their friendship didn't even prompt him to mourn its passing?

She comprehended that it was a touch twisted, standing here, upset because he hadn't done either of the things she had earlier been so upset by the prospect of him doing. Considering the *Wizard of Oz* yellow brick road her life had taken lately, it seemed perfectly in character.

How could Elliot be acting so nonchalant, like nothing was out of the ordinary? Why wasn't he acting as if he, too, had stayed up all night, mourning?

Instead, Elliot was acting as if he'd slept better than he had in years. Was that an actual spring in his step that she spotted? She knew for a fact he was freshly shaven. And Elliot shaved that fastidiously only when he had plenty of spare time in the morning. And when he was in a particularly excellent mood.

Why the hell was he in such an excellent mood?

Deb hadn't the slightest idea.

All she knew was, it certainly didn't help hers any.

And Deb's mood failed to improve when, inside her office, she passed the morning, for the fifth time in as many days, staring at an X ray of ten-year-old Bethany Kawahara's brain. Bethany had a tumor. An ugly, carnivorous one, that, for the life of her, Deb could not think of a way to remove, without also blinding the child in the process. Of course, to keep Bethany from going blind, Deb could always not operate. In that case, Bethany would die.

Deb didn't turn around when she heard her office door opening. She merely nodded absently to recognize Jeff Greenwood's greeting.

He joined Deb in contemplating Bethany's X rays, and, after a moment, sighed. "Anything?"

His voice was so pleading, it made Deb wonder whether Jeff thought Deb could twitch her nose and make everything better, if only she could be convinced to really want it so.

Well, she had news for him. If that were the case, Deb would have been doing a hell of a lot more twitching the last month and a half. And, especially, the last day and a half.

Deb shook her head, and pointed to the trouble spot. "See right there? The capsule is attached to both branches. It's got to be a blunt dissection. No other way."

"Have you told the parents?"

She laughed at herself, but all that came out was bitterness. "I told them. They took a couple of days to think about it, consulted with other specialists, and, finally, they gave me permission to go ahead and blind their child. And then they asked me to be the one to tell Bethany. But I'm too chicken. I keep putting it off. I keep hoping maybe I might see something, some other way to—"

"Have you?"

"Not yet."

Jeff visibly deflated. Tough. Deb didn't have time today to deal with Bethany, *and* Elliot, *and* Jeff's diminishing image of her as Neurosurgical Superwoman. The sooner her little protégé faced reality, the better off he'd be.

How was that for a bit of "physician, heal thyself," wisdom?

Jeff asked, "When's the surgery scheduled for?"

"Tomorrow afternoon."

"And then?"

"And then I call in the shrinks, and the specialists from the School for the Blind. My job ends when the incision heals."

"No. I mean, what happens when you're done with the patients you've already got scheduled? Will you really leave the hospital?"

Well, now. In her obsession with learning how Elliot intended to handle their schism—and her subsequent, complete confusion—Deb had totally forgotten what prompted their dispute in the first place. *Gee, Jeff, thanks. Thanks for reminding me that not only am I now friendless, I am also jobless.*

Deb said, "I have to. I cannot operate on the money they've delegated me. It would be a disservice to my patients."

If Elliot were there, he would, inevitably, have taken a light jab at her self-importance by prompting, "And, of course, your ego has nothing at all to do with this." Deb would have elbowed him in the ribs, they both would have chortled, and, if the company around them were particularly stuffy, they both would have worked very hard to stifle their chortles.

Deb didn't really feel like chortling now.

Jeff said, "That's too bad."

Unless he could now read her mind, or Deb had slipped into the habit of thinking out loud, she presumed he was not referring to her chortle-free state.

"Your feeling you have to quit, I mean. It's a real loss for the hospital, and, well, frankly, from a selfish standpoint, I was really looking forward to doing my residency under you."

When in doubt, Deb, as always, darted for the joke. "Come up with an extra two million dollars, kid, and I'm all yours."

"Really?" The serious manner in which he enunciated the word suggested to Deb that Jeff wasn't being facetious.

"You got an extra two million lying around?"

"Actually. Sort of. Yes."

"Resident salaries must have greatly gone up since I graduated from medical school."

"Oh, no." Jeff smiled self-consciously. "I'm still making—what does it average out to?—like, a dollar-fifty an hour, same as anyone else."

"So, where did the two million figure come from?"

"My family, Dr. Brody, they, uhm"—Jeff searched for the most tactful way to put it—"they earn a little more than that."

"For instance?"

"Two million dollars is half the interest off my trust fund."

"Ah."

"You can see why I don't like letting that get around."

"Yes. Your colleagues find out, they might make you spring for the whole pizza."

"That trust-fund money, I don't have any access to it. It's all in my father's control."

"But you think if you asked . . ."

"I think I could get him to consider it a worthy investment on my behalf. Doing a pediatric neurosurgery residency under you will be great for my career. My father may not have understood why anyone would go into medicine over investment banking, but key words like 'great for my career,' he should be able to comprehend."

This was too good. This was too easy, too convenient. There had to be a catch, or some problem Deb was overlooking.

Oh, wait. Here came one, now.

Deb said, "Conflict of interest."

"What?"

"If your family donates the money to keep my department open, and then people like, oh, say, Dr. Morelli, find out I picked you for my residency, it could come off like a conflict of interest."

"But you selected me for the residency three weeks ago."

"I know that. You know that. But, Ethics could—"

He offered, "What if my father makes the donation anonymously? He has a whole foundation for doing just that. He believes giving money publicly is tacky."

"I can live with that opinion," Deb said.

She would have smiled, too. If funding her department weren't the least of her worries, these days.

After Jeff left to call 1-800-MILLION (or two), Deb continued staring at Bethany's X rays, eventually deciding that, while they were not able to thoroughly exorcise the thought of Elliot from her mind, they made a nice background against which to dwell on him.

Deb knew she should be getting over it. But she couldn't get over it. She could not, no matter how hard she tried, get over the fact that she and Elliot were finished. And that he seemed happy about it. Well, maybe *happy* wasn't the accurate word, but, at the very least, unconcerned.

If Elliot had Fired, or even Iced her, she would have been sad and hurt and angry. But she would at least know that he'd cared enough to do his very worst. She would have had a confirmation and a validation of her own feelings. She would have had closure.

Granted, you couldn't call closure at three AM and ask it to talk you through a panic attack.

But it was still better than nothing.

Which was what Deb had now.

Nothing.

No husband. No family. No job.

No best friend.

And a patient she was scheduled to mutilate in twenty-four hours.

She needed Elliot.

And that was the worst of it.

She didn't just need Elliot's presence, or his company, or his proximity. She needed his help. Desperately.

Elliot was great with patients and parents. Only last week, she could have gone to him, and he would have helped her figure out what she had to say to Bethany, and how she should prepare both her and her overwhelmed parents for the upcoming trauma. As an added bonus, he would even convince Deb to feel, if not okay about what she needed to do, at least, not as rotten.

She needed him so much now.

She couldn't imagine how she was supposed to get through this procedure without him.

She would have to get through this procedure without him.

And, sooner or later, she'd have to accept that she would have to get through the rest of her life without him, too.

The next day, knowing it would take her forever to get ready for surgery, Deb began dressing an hour before she actually needed to make the first incision. And then she scrubbed so slowly, the soap had time to congeal on her arms into a white film, before she got around to listlessly rinsing it off.

She didn't want to go in there. She didn't want to go into the operating theater, and blind a little girl. And yet, she knew she had no choice. Bethany was ready. Deb had explained, as best she could without Elliot to provide the script, what was going to happen. Bethany had cried and cried. Her parents had cried and cried. Deb had wanted to cry, as well. Only she hadn't bothered. Because she knew there was no one left to comfort her.

In the operating room, she would be surrounded by nurses, and an anesthesiologist, and Jeff Greenwood to assist. And still, she would be all alone.

Oh, hell, why should the operating room be any different from the rest of her life.

Last night, she'd sat in her house, reading a novel, and not retaining a word of it. Because she was waiting for the phone to ring. She was waiting for Elliot to call.

And say anything.

He could yell at her. He could argue with her. He could do what he did best and try convincing her that she'd misunderstood, that he wasn't to blame for what had happened. That the obstacle was all in Deb's head. She was the guilty party, he the innocent.

He could have done anything, and she would have been grateful.

Because she would have had evidence there was still a being in the universe who cared whether or not she existed.

Elliot didn't call.

Not last night, not this morning, not even during the hour when she was putting on her scrubs, and tying back her hair.

And she'd left her cell phone on, just in case.

It really was over. *They* really were over.

She'd turned Elliot down, and he'd decided to break off all contact with her—skewering Deb professionally in the process.

Deep down, hadn't she always known this would happen? Hadn't she been expecting it, kind of, sort of, since the first day?

She thought she'd done everything to avoid it, to maintain his friendship without ever letting things get more involved than that.

Well, alright, perhaps there was that one thing she could have done, or, rather, not done. She could have not slept with him the night of Max's funeral. But she'd already said she was sorry. God, was she sorry. She was so far on the other side of sorry, she couldn't even see it anymore.

Two hours into surgery, Deb's worst fears came to light. The tumor was tangled up in Bethany's optical nerves. There was no way to slice around. She'd have to cut through. No options. No choices. No escape.

Deb couldn't do it.

For the first time in her neurosurgical career, Deb raised her scalpel, brought it up to the position of incision, and she couldn't do it. It wasn't that her hands started to tremble. The time that happened, Deb would know it was time to retire. The tremble was on the inside. She felt her breath catch and she felt her mind rebel.

She put down the scalpel. She swallowed hard.

There was a secondary procedure that needed to be performed on Bethany, in addition to the actual tumor removal. Deb had planned to delegate it to Jeff, after she was finished with the main chore. But there was no reason not to get the secondary procedure out of the way first.

Deb gave her surgical team detailed instructions on what she wanted done. They all had performed identical procedures, unsupervised, over a dozen times, and Jeff, especially, had shown a knack for the precise work necessary. So Deborah felt no qualms telling them, "I'll be right back."

The gloves were off her hands and in the trash as soon as Deb stepped through the swinging door separating the OR from the wash area. But she didn't stop there. Without bothering to change her bloodstained surgical scrubs, Deb walked out of the operating room, into the hallway, and didn't stop until she hit the Doctors' Lounge.

No one was there.

Deb opened the miniature refrigerator at the foot of the faded mahogany couch, and reached for an apple-juice box. She peeled off the plastic straw, and stuck it through the silver perforation on top with such force, she nearly slit the bottom.

Eyes fastened so fiercely on the wall she expected to melt its paint off, Deb planted herself in the turquoise, leather armchair, and gravely sipped her apple juice until she'd reduced the tip of the straw to powder with her teeth.

She had to go back into the operating room.

She couldn't go back into the operating room.

Because for the first time in her life, Dr. Deborah

Brody no longer felt all-powerful, or all-knowing, or all-capable.

She no longer felt invincible.

In a normal person, that was a sign of a nondelusional, nonpsychotic personality.

But it was absolute death for a surgeon.

Surgeons had to go into the operating room not only believing that they knew better than Fate, but that, when push came to shove, they could out-wrestle Fate. It was the single way any of them found the guts to pick up a scalpel and coolly and methodically slice open another human being's brain or heart. Without that conviction of superiority, a surgeon would never have the guts to proceed.

She'd end up running out of the operating room, hiding in the Doctors' Lounge, and drowning herself in apple juice.

Damn Elliot.

This was all his fault.

Deb wasn't sure how exactly, but she knew that it was.

And it helped having someone to blame it on.

He'd shattered her confidence.

By acting so utterly out of character, by letting Deb down so royally, and by refusing to respond to their estrangement in either of his traditional patterns, Elliot had shattered Deb's confidence in her ability to judge reality.

A week ago, she could have sworn that the Elliot she knew and loved for twenty years would never abandon her just when she needed him most, that he would never deliberately sabotage her happiness, and that, in case of an argument between them, he would move earth and Heaven to set things right again.

Showed how much she knew.

Obviously, all these years, Deb had overestimated

both Elliot and their friendship. The realization made
her wonder if maybe, all these years, she'd been over-
estimating her own proficiency, as well. What if Deb
Brody wasn't nearly as precocious as she'd lulled herself into believing?

What if she wasn't as good a doctor, as good a surgeon as she thought? What if another physician could
take one look at Bethany Kawahara's X rays, and, right
away, notice a solution Deb missed? What if Deb was
about to blind a little girl for nothing?

Every nerve in Deb's body screamed for her to
leap out of the chair, and hightail her way to Elliot's office. Elliot always knew what to say when she worked
herself up into these states. Elliot would be able to fix
everything.

Except that Elliot no longer gave a damn about her.

She realized it the moment he brushed by her on
the way to the elevator. If Elliot regretted, even a little
bit, what he'd done, and what they'd lost in the
process, he would have never have acted in that way. If
Elliot cared, and if Elliot wanted to repair their friendship, then Elliot would have been hostile to her—or
Elliot would have been frigid to her. That was his way.
That was how he dealt with things. When Elliot cared,
Elliot reacted.

But what the hell did she know?

Deb didn't even know enough not to have her crisis of confidence on a day when she would be forced to
deal with it alone.

Deb wasn't used to dealing with things alone.

For twenty years, she'd had someone. From school
reports to oral presentations to brain surgeries, she'd
had someone. Someone to look at her work with fresh
eyes, someone to offer her a unique perspective, someone to check her own stupidity. Oh, sure, Max had
tried to help out, and, quite often, he had. But in the

end, she couldn't be satisfied until another specialist had looked over her work, and given her the thumbs-up sign.

So, for twenty years, she'd had a friend.

My, but she'd enjoyed that.

And, my, oh, my, had she taken it for granted.

She had to go back into the operating room.

She couldn't go back into the operating room.

When she heard the door open behind her, Deb didn't bother to turn around. She was in no mood for mechanical conversation. But, when she heard who it was that walked in, she froze.

Deb knew what Elliot's footsteps sounded like as surely as she knew the rhythm of her own heartbeat.

She continued staring at the wall. There was no more juice left in the wax-coated box, but Deb refused to let go of the straw between her lips. She ran her tongue nervously around its chewed-up plastic ridges, and feigned frighteningly intense concentration on the task of sucking liquid no longer there.

She heard Elliot walk up to the back of her chair. He stopped half a foot before his legs would have brushed against it. Then he stood there. Silent, except for the even keel of his breathing.

Deb wished she could say the same about hers. Her own breath seemed to have gotten tightly wedged somewhere between her ribs and her throat. She heard Elliot move. But considering she was still ever so busy staring at the wall, Deb had no idea if he was moving to leave, or to straighten his tie, or to pick up a magazine.

She felt Elliot's hand on her shoulder. His fingers rested on her tightest, sorest muscle, his thumb grazing her collarbone, his wrist pressed along the base of her neck. It took all of her self-control to keep from springing, like an anxious cat, at his touch. Except that she wouldn't have been springing away. She would have been springing toward him.

Elliot squeezed Deb's shoulder. And that one silent gesture magically managed to convey all his understanding, all his empathy, all his sympathy, all his faith, and all his support. No Vitamin B shot—hell, no blood transfusion, could ever have infused Deb with so much renewed vigor.

Yet, still, she couldn't move.

And so, for a long moment, they did nothing but remain as they were, Elliot's hand on Deb's shoulder, his pulse pounding smoothly against her carotid artery, until Deb's heart, without her noticing it, picked up the rhythm and proceeded to beat in sync with his.

She felt his strength, his confidence, his competence, with every beat. As far as she could tell, it was the solitary thing keeping her grounded to reality. As far as she could tell, it *was* her solitary reality.

She needed more. At least, a part of her did. Deb couldn't remember consciously giving the order, but all at once, her hand raised independently, and, like an earthquake survivor attempting to claw her way out of the rubble, wrapped around Elliot's wrist. She needed to feel the solidity, the reality of it. She needed to know that he was really there, that she hadn't imagined him. And that she hadn't imagined what his coming here like this meant.

She pushed her luck too far.

Elliot allowed her barely a second of holding on, barely a second of comfort, before he, politely but firmly, extricated himself from her grasp. He still didn't say a word. But Deb could hear the familiar footsteps head for the door. And she could feel the air that had once been so warm between them growing colder.

She wanted to call out his name.

She knew she could never take such a risk.

And so, instead, without turning around, her voice as dead as she'd been feeling all morning, Deb said, to no one in particular, "If I go back into that operating room, a little girl will be blind for the rest of her life."

The footsteps stopped. Even though she had already heard the door open partway, the footsteps stopped.

"If you don't go back into that room," he reminded gently, "a little girl will have no life."

Chapter Twelve

It wasn't as if Elliot ever had a choice about coming.

He'd been aware of Bethany's surgery for weeks, and he knew how much Deb was dreading it. In another lifetime, he would have expected to talk her through it, to be there for her, to support her, and, hopefully, help her feel better about the inevitable.

But that was a lifetime the last twenty-four hours had so thoroughly erased, it left Elliot wondering whether he had simply imagined the whole thing. The person he'd thought Brody was, was gone. It felt like a death. Worse, it felt like a betrayal. Yet, if there was one thing the doctor in him knew, it was that, even after death, certain impulses survived. He'd performed too many autopsies on cadavers who suddenly twitched an arm or a leg or an eyelid, to doubt that truth.

It was the same with him. His feelings for Deb may have died, his affection for the woman he thought she was may have atrophied, but the instinct to take care of her and to protect her still beat harder than ever. It didn't matter that the simple thought of her filled him with an empty, barren, yet excruciatingly painful dread. It didn't matter that he knew the best way to protect himself from further attacks would be to stay as far away from Deborah Brody as possible. Deb needed him. And, like salmon following a biological urge to swim upstream, he felt compelled to be there for her.

Of course, even Elliot's biological urges had their limits—though not the night that Max died, but that was neither here nor there at the moment. He'd followed Brody into the Doctors' Lounge because he suspected she would need a little extra support to force herself back into the operating room. He'd rested his hand on her shoulder and squeezed it just hard enough to, hopefully, return at least a fraction of the confidence he knew she'd lost. He wanted to reassure her. The last thing he wanted to do was talk to her.

Because talking would, eventually, lead them back to the pus-dripping wound at the center of this cataclysm: Brody's conviction that he had deliberately, and vengefully, set out to annihilate her career, and, by extension, her life.

It didn't matter that, if they talked long enough, Elliot felt pretty confident he could bring Brody around to seeing things from his point of view. That was no longer the point. The point was that a woman he'd loved for twenty years had, for much longer than the split second, actually believed him capable of such behavior. That was the injury. That was the mortal wound.

Bringing the subject up again, even for the exclusive cause of Elliot vindicating his name, would mean articulating the accusation again and again and again, until Deb believed him. Elliot couldn't do that. He could hear those words again. But not from Deb.

But Elliot also couldn't just keep walking for the door. Not when he so clearly heard Deb crying out for his help.

He told her, "If you don't go back into that room, a little girl will have no life," because it was the truth, and because it was what Deb desperately needed to hear. But it was the maximum that Elliot could give. He waited until he'd made sure his words had sunk in, that Brody was once again ready to pick up a scalpel.

And then, he left.

He should have known he wouldn't be getting away that easily.

Bethany Kawahara's surgery lasted four and a half hours. Five minutes after that, Elliot looked up through the open door of his office, to find Deb standing there, looking at him.

She was still wearing her blue scrubs, the front now stained with smears of blood. Her hair was pulled off her face in a makeshift ponytail. Surgical scrubs came with no pockets, so she had no place to stick her hands. They hung listlessly by her sides. Then, when she spotted Elliot looking at her, Brody raised both to chest level, using one thumbnail to flick beneath the other. Her cheeks flushed pink with the exhaustion of a lengthy and difficult surgery. Perspiration dabbed Brody's forehead, dripping low enough to clump her eyelashes. He could see the red ridge on her nose, where her surgical mask had dug in and left a crease.

She looked absolutely beautiful.

She looked so beautiful, she made him want to glance away.

Because Elliot couldn't do this again.

He couldn't allow himself to get sucked in a second—third, fourth, hell, bazillionth time. He couldn't allow himself to fall in love all over again. He couldn't allow himself to risk a repeat performance of the kind of pain one thoughtless remark on her part had already seared him with.

He realized that Brody didn't understand where he was coming from. Elliot wasn't mad. Elliot was hurt. If he was mad, Elliot would have wanted to get back at her. But, hurt, he just wanted to avoid her. And the best way he could conceive of to do that was to ... neutralize ... their relationship. Giving her either his Fire or Ice treatment would have been the antithesis of his intentions. Elliot did not want to intensify their affiliation. He wanted to nullify it. That was why, when he looked up from behind his desk to catch her standing there, looking lost and candid and grateful and so ... reconciliatory, Elliot had no choice but to shuffle his papers and feign fantastic interest in a year-old article from the *New England Journal of Medicine,* while he inquired politely, "Is there something I can do for you, Dr. Brody?"

He missed seeing the reaction on Deb's face. All he heard was her sharp intake of breath, almost like a sob, and, when he finally did dare to look up, she was gone.

Elliot wished he could blame her. But, for days afterward, the only person he could think of to blame was himself.

Maybe if he'd been more honest with Brody in the last twenty years, maybe then she would have known him well enough so that she never could have accused him of betraying her. Maybe if he'd let her see some of what he was really thinking and feeling, she would have been incapable of pouncing on such a catastrophic conclusion.

It was all Elliot's fault. He was the one lacking the guts to be honest with Deb. He was the one too skittish to take a chance. How could he blame Brody for not knowing him well enough, when it was Elliot who'd never given her the chance to do so?

Driving that nitroglycerine truck the summer between junior and senior year of college had once made Elliot feel so brave. Ten years ago, operating on a child trapped under a ready-to-collapse bridge embankment made him feel brave. Balancing a beating human heart in his hand made him feel brave. Hell, even charging the net with its goalie three times his size made Elliot feel brave. Was it his fault that, in the middle of all that surface bravery, he'd somehow failed to notice that he was, in fact, a coward?

Elliot should have told Deb. Twenty years ago, he should have been straight with her. Surely, if Deb understood how much and for how long he'd adored her, she never would have thought . . . Except that— how could she not know? How could Deb not know how he felt about her? *After all these years, how could she not have known?*

Deb couldn't deny the truth any longer: Not only did Elliot not care enough about Deb to get wrathful with her, he didn't even care enough to thoroughly ignore her.

But, then again, "ignore" did seem to be the universe's choice for dealing with Deborah Brody these days. Elliot may have been the worst of it, but, in addition, her effort to drum up private funding to keep her department open was going absolutely nowhere. So far, not even Jeff's father had so much as returned a phone call. And she was running out of time. Deb had threatened to quit if her budget was cut. Her budget was now officially cut. It had been officially cut for over a week now. If she waited any longer to turn in her indignant resignation, the hospital Board, with her luck, would probably forget what she was protesting.

Deb could see no way out of this. She would have to quit.

And she'd have to send a congratulatory card to Elliot.

Telling him he'd won.

Everyone on the Children's Trauma Staff was assigned a beeper. And everyone on the Children's Trauma Staff knew that when they got a 911-1 page, that meant: Get down to the ER, ASAP—We got a bad one. Elliot found out just how bad, as soon as he sprinted into the emergency room and got a report from the EMTs. Fourteen-year-old boy. Drive-by shooting. Unconscious. No pulse.

The boy, dark-haired, slender, with skin the color of tea, had been shot less than eight minutes earlier, and already there was no pulse. To Elliot that meant only one thing: Cardiac Tamponade. A bullet had penetrated the heart, filling the tough membrane around it with blood, and preventing the heart from beating.

Fortunately, Cardiac Tamponade could be corrected. Through heart surgery.

Unfortunately, they were nowhere near an operating room.

"We'll move him," a scrub nurse suggested, already reaching for the gurney.

It was the most practical solution. If they got the boy to an operating room, they could, most likely, still save him. That is, assuming he didn't die along the way. Three minutes of travel time could be dreadfully long when you didn't have a pulse.

But doing anything else was too big of a risk.

On the other hand, hadn't Elliot just passed the last several days ruminating over what not taking risks had already cost him?

He didn't remember consciously making the decision to throw caution to the wind. All Elliot knew was, if he let them take the boy to an operating room, they could lose him.

And Elliot refused to lose him.

"No." Elliot held up both his hands, signaling for a pair of gloves to be slipped on him. "No time. We'll do it here."

"Dr. Elliot—" The protest was almost instantaneous.

But if they didn't have three minutes to waste wheeling him down the hall to an OR, they certainly didn't have three minutes to waste arguing about it.

"Start a cutdown," he ordered one nurse, meaning for her to find the largest available vein, puncture it, suture around, and begin a transfusion. To the one who just finished putting on his gloves, he barked, "CPR." To the scrub nurse, he called, "Open a thoracic tray," and, soon as she had, he reached for the thoracic scalpel. It was a large-blade instrument, solid enough to slice through flesh, ribs, and muscle. Which was precisely what they needed to perform heart surgery—down and dirty, guerrilla-style, right in the ER. Hardly the preferred way to do it or, for that matter, the AMA-approved way.

But, sometimes, it was the only way.

"No." As soon as she saw what Elliot was about to attempt, the nurse he'd directed to begin a cutdown stepped away from the table. "No, Dr. Elliot. You can't."

Elliot jerked forward, as if wearing a seat belt in a suddenly stopped car. He was a doctor. He wasn't used to his orders being treated like suggestions. Or worse, requests.

She said, "You haven't even anesthetized the patient."

Elliot looked down at the boy on his table, his chest heaving erratically, his breaths harsh and irregular.

"The patient is unconscious, Ursula." He pointed to the heart monitor, with its glowering flatline of activity. "For all intents and purposes, the patient is already dead. Now, I don't know about you, but I'd like to prevent that becoming a permanent condition."

"The patient is not dead." To her credit, Ursula refused to cower under a doctor's censure. With twenty years of emergency-room experience, she took her position as her patient's advocate very seriously. "But what you're about to do will kill him."

"Not necessarily."

Her spine hardened. "I won't do this, Dr. Elliot. I will not follow your orders on this."

"Fine." Now was not the time for ego trips. They were losing priceless seconds. Which meant heartbeats. Which meant oxygen to the brain. Elliot turned to the nurse he'd previously asked to do the CPR, and ordered, "Finish the cutdown."

The girl, not as experienced as Ursula, and thus more prone to wilting like a flower before authority, hesitated. She looked from Ursula to Elliot, unsure. And useless.

"Jesus Christ, I've got a dying boy here." Elliot glanced from face to face, wondering when exactly he'd lost control of the situation, and guessing it probably happened right around the time Dr. Elliot began behaving out of character. Right around the time Dr. Elliot decided to stop playing it safe and go for broke. They all probably thought he'd lost his mind. No one trusted him. Not to the point where they would risk being named a codefendant in a malpractice suit, anyway. No one was going to help him. He saw it in their eyes. Five emergency-room nurses and two residents stood rooted to the spot, too frightened to take a risk.

He couldn't really blame them. A week earlier, Elliot would have agreed with their assessment. What he was about to do *was* damn risky. He shouldn't even have been trying it.

Except that there was a life at stake. And Elliot just wasn't in the mood to sign a death certificate, today.

He looked from face to face, desperately searching for a crack or a sign that at least one person was even wavering. He could do this procedure with only one other body to help him.

But he couldn't do it alone.

"I'll do it."

The voice didn't come from any of the faces glaring at him so censoriously. For a moment, Elliot even wondered if he'd imagined it. But if he had, why had he imagined the volunteering voice to sound so much like Brody?

He hadn't heard her come in. But it made sense. Brody was a member of the Trauma Staff, too. She was always called if head injury was a possibility.

Without giving Elliot a chance to accept or refuse her offer, Deb kicked off her shoes to facilitate quick movement, and, in the same gesture, hurriedly yanked off both her wedding and engagement rings. The diamond on the second one wouldn't fit under a surgical glove. She searched around for a safe place to deposit them, but, realizing that time was of the essence, and that the congregated personages in the room were still too stunned to do the humane thing and, at the very least, step forward and take the jewelry off her hands, Deb, impatient and momentarily indifferent, just flung them aside. The clatter of two gold bands hitting the sterile Formica got lost in the general din.

As soon as she had her gloves on, Deb swiftly and efficiently completed the cutdown he'd asked for, making sure the patient would have plenty of blood coursing through him, even as Elliot bore down on the thoracic scalpel and bluntly cut through the fat between his patient's fifth and sixth ribs.

"I'll intubate," Deb offered. She didn't even wait for Elliot to nod in agreement, before proceeding to press rhythmically on the center of the boy's chest, above where Elliot had cut.

Sweat pouring down his forehead—and people wanted to know why he spent so much time at the gym; surgery was damn hard work—Elliot sliced through layer after layer of muscle, until his knife perforated the chest cavity. Blood poured out like from a homemade volcano. It stained the gurney, and dripped down onto the floor. Deb's feet, protected only by stockings, turned bright red.

Elliot continued probing the wound with a gloved finger, but it still wasn't wide enough for his purposes. He opened his mouth to ask for a retractor, but before the first letter was even out of his mouth, Deb had not only provided him with the instrument, she'd also found a pair of heavy-gauge shears, and began snipping the initial incision open wider. He hadn't told her exactly what he intended to do, but, magically, Deb seemed to know without being asked. With impeccable precision, she sliced open the rest of the pericardium just wide enough for Elliot to, gratefully, slip in his fingers and wrap them around the soft, quivering heart muscle.

Rummaging blind, Elliot felt his way up the heart muscle until he'd located the bullet's entrance wound. Gritting his teeth, he covered the entrance wound firmly with his thumb, then repeated the process, locating the exit wound and covering it tightly with his middle finger, to keep any more blood from draining out.

Beneath his hand, the heart muscle contracted.

"We've got a pulse," Deb said.

"Marvelous." It wasn't quite yet time to relax, but Elliot did allow himself the luxury of a single joke. "Now, all we've got to do is sew me into this patient, and we've got us a healthy boy."

With half of Elliot's arm still inside his chest, the teen an ID check revealed to be named Adrian Pharsi, was finally wheeled down the hall to the operating room, where a cardiac surgeon took one look at Doctors Elliot and Brody's handiwork, and let out only a level whistle. He might have been impressed, he might have been appalled. Heck, he might even have been both.

Brody didn't accompany Elliot. She figured the sight of one blood-drenched surgeon was alarming enough to the patients. They didn't really need to see two.

She squished when she walked. Her feet were so soaked, Deb hadn't bothered to put on her shoes, holding them in one hand and away from her body as she gingerly hurried down the hall, toward the Doctors' Changing Room. Her white coat had managed to protect her lemon-colored silk blouse and ebony knee-length skirt only in that it had absorbed the initial blood splatter. But performing heart surgery, triage-style, was hardly the recipe for safeguarding your wardrobe. Enough crimson liquid had soaked through to render both garments more or less dust-rag worthy. At the start of her career, Deb had done silly things like try taking her clothes to the local dry cleaner. But she got tired of them looking at her like they thought she performed taxidermy on the living during her free time. It might not have been cheaper to junk the entire outfit, but it was better for Deb's peace of mind.

Because her job came with the periodic, unexpected bath in blood—or worse—Deb always kept a spare blouse, skirt, shoes, pantyhose, and underwear at the hospital. Every doctor had a locker in the Changing Room. They did, however, have to bring their own locks. The administration told them to think of it like a health club. Deb, though, thought it was very high school.

She scurried inside the Changing Room, pleased that she hadn't bumped into any tiny, impressionable patients along the way—or their less tiny, but equally impressionable parents. Although it technically wasn't true, there was just something about the sight of their surgeon dripping blood head to toe that didn't fill folks with confidence.

Thankfully, when she made it in, Deb was the Changing Room's only occupant. Although they'd never admit it, fellow doctors—especially nonsurgeons—didn't exactly relish the sight of her drenched, either. *Wimps.*

Deb stripped off her lab coat, followed by the blouse, skirt, and pantyhose that had definitely seen better days. She tossed the loosely bound bundle in the trash. Her colleagues would just have to deal with the smell until the janitor crew got there. Grabbing the bottles of shampoo and liquid soap she kept on the top shelf of her locker for just such occasions, Deb headed for the shower.

Unlike the health club they were all supposed to pretend this was, the showers in the Doctors' Changing Room were coed. There was a reason for it, though.

A combination of parsimony and sexism.

Up until fifteen years earlier, there simply weren't enough female surgeons to warrant their getting their own showers. Those women foolish enough to choose surgery as a career and then have the bad judgment to need a shower afterward were told to use the Nurses' Changing Room. This, for women surgeons, was an issue.

A big issue.

Doctors did not change—they didn't do anything besides work—in the same space as nurses. Snobbery was alive and well in the medical profession. It was just sexism they wanted to stamp out.

To make their point, women surgeons insisted on using the same showers as the men. Until they got showers of their own, that is. Unfortunately, Valley Hospital, as Deb well knew, was rather tight with its budget. Each year, they somehow never managed to find the resources for a female Doctors' Changing Room. And so, the alleged health club also became a coed college dorm.

Deb honestly didn't mind. Her conviction was, if you needed a shower after surgery, modesty was the furthest concern from your mind. Besides, they were all doctors. The odds of anyone sporting something none of them had ever seen before were awfully slim.

She let the shower spray wash over her, closing her eyes, and wallowing in the soothing, white noise. She scrubbed her hair with extra fervor, scouring to expunge the smell of blood that otherwise clung to her.

She remained submerged beneath the scalding spray for as long as she dared. There was something so sheltering about the shower. It gave Deb the illusion of time standing still. Nobody could get to her. Nobody could harm her. She was in her own world.

The blast of frigid air that came with opening the door at the conclusion of her shower always cured her of that fantasy rather quickly.

Eyes still swimming in soap, Deb fumbled for the white terrycloth towel the hospital did, at least, deign to provide them with. Her fingers bore into the fluffy warmth, and she pulled it toward her. It didn't pull as if sliding off a metallic rack. It pulled like someone was handing it to her.

Deb opened her eyes. The shampoo she'd missed exorcising in the rinse cycle burned them like lye. She squinted and winced, and raised a palm to rub her lids raw. But that did not, in any way, prevent her from realizing that it was Elliot doing the honors.

He'd obviously come to the Changing Room with goals identical to Deb's. After all, Elliot had been the one who, fifteen minutes earlier, thrust his hand up a boy's chest to plug the bullet holes in his heart. Deb doubted a scrap of his suit was salvageable.

He'd already given up on his lab coat, shoes, and socks, and now stood in front of Deb, barefoot and dressed only in gray slacks and a white shirt. A white, unbuttoned shirt.

They'd been changing in the same places for years, and yet, she'd never noticed how flat his stomach was, or how the muscles there smiled with his every breath. She'd never noticed the way the straighter hairs around his nipples brushed the smooth, brown skin there like the petals of an autumn flower. She'd never noticed the sloping curve of his chest, or the way his collarbone punctuated his skin, or how all the velvet, salt-and-pepper hair of his chest liquefied into a triangle the farther down you went.

Which was probably why it took her an extra moment—once the initial cataloging was done—to notice that Elliot was standing in front of her wearing only slacks and an unbuttoned shirt, while Deb stood in front of *him* wearing absolutely nothing.

Elliot, on the other hand, didn't even notice that much.

He handed her a towel with an expression of complete, absolute neutrality. But it wasn't even the good kind of neutrality. The kind that suggested he was being courteous, or discreet.

This neutrality was indifferent.

Elliot looked at Deb the way he'd look at any other doctor he happened to catch exiting their shower, and decided to help out by handing them a towel. He didn't act as if he didn't see her so much as he acted not particularly impressed.

Now, why in hell should that piss her off?

Deb hadn't the slightest idea.

She knew only that, for twenty years, Elliot had looked at her a certain way. And now, he'd stopped.

And that pissed her off.

Royally.

Deb snatched the towel he offered, hoping that her furtive wrapping of it around her body might remind Elliot that, hello . . . she was naked, here.

But no such luck. Elliot merely took advantage of his newly freed hands to begin peeling off his own sticky shirt. Indicating the shower with a bob of his chin, he remarked, "Guess great minds think alike, don't they?"

Small talk.

Deb was doing her best to hold it together through the worst crisis in her life, and the man she'd thought she could trust with her soul was making small talk. Clichéd small talk, at that.

"Listen, Brody." Elliot balled his soiled shirt, the muscles in his shoulders straining against the skin like lengths of sturdy rope as he threw it, blindly, into the hamper behind him. The shirt went in. Of course, it went in. The universe was out to get Brody these days. For Elliot, it was practically bending over backward. "I wanted to—"

"What?" She snapped his sentence in half with her teeth as brutally as a steel trap on a bunny-rabbit's foot. "You wanted to what? Gloat? Whistle, 'I told you so'? I'm not surprised. You got your wish, didn't you, Elliot? I haven't been able to come up with the money to keep my department running, so I'm quitting. Is this the lesson you wanted me to learn? That women who say no to James Elliot are condemned to live out their lives sitting alone in their houses, watching the dust accumulate, wondering where exactly it was they took that wrong turn? Well, I guess I'm lucky. I know exactly where I took my wrong turn. I trusted *you*. And now I get to pay the price." She took a deep breath, having exhausted the last one practically to the asphyxiation point. "Was that it, Elliot? Was that what you wanted to tell me?"

He hadn't budged during her tirade. Except to slip his right hand into his pants pocket, and stand there, staring at Deb like some frozen-mid-pose *GQ* model. He let her finish. Of course, Elliot let her finish. Why should he bother to interrupt Brody and beat her up, when she was doing such a good job of it herself?

And so he let her finish.

Only when it became obvious that Deb had run out of words and breath, did he continue with the action he'd started while she was just winding up. Elliot reached into his pocket. His hand came out fisted. He opened his hand and there, on Elliot's palm, lay Deb's engagement and wedding rings. A little bloody, but none the worse for wear.

He picked up Deb's left hand, and, with an act almost surgical in its precision, slipped both back onto her fourth finger.

Chapter Thirteen

The first time a man put a ring on Deb's finger, she hadn't trembled. She was twenty-one years old, and proud that, already, even before medical school, she could keep her hand so steady.

Her left hand, however, made up for it, now.

It trembled so viciously, she fancied she could make out the joints under her skin knocking together like Halloween skeletons.

And the one clutching the towel around her torso wasn't doing all that great, either.

What the hell did Elliot think he was doing?

Was he trying to mock her? Unsettle her? Provoke a reaction out of her?

It had to mean something. Men didn't go about

sliding wedding bands on Deb's left fourth finger every day of the week.

She searched Elliot's eyes, his face, his demeanor for a clue as to what, in heaven's name, was going on here.

She found nothing save a gentleman doing as he said, playing Lost-and-Found Guy, and returning a piece of misplaced property to its rightful owner.

It didn't make any sense.

A few days earlier, he'd been lobbying her for a chance at a romantic future together. And now, here he stood, her hand in his, a wedding ring sparkling between them, and Elliot was acting like this was a scenario he relived three, four times a week.

Well, then again, maybe he did. After all, as Deb had just so recently discovered, she didn't know the man nearly as well as she once thought she did.

But, nevertheless, this was still very, very weird.

How could Elliot not think this was weird?

After all, Deb wasn't asking for him to commence humming "The Wedding March," or even "The Wedding Song." She wasn't asking him to fall to both knees and propose, and she wasn't asking him to burst into tears and beg her forgiveness for pummeling her life. Well, that last one wouldn't be so terrible, but . . .

She wasn't asking Elliot to really do anything, except, maybe, for a split second, concede that something abhorrent had happened, and, in fact, was still happening, between them.

That's what was really driving her insane. This position of Elliot's that all was harmonious. All was not harmonious, damn it. Deb hadn't slept a stretch of more than four hours a night for the last nine days. She'd lost five pounds and counting, and her nails—this was the worst part—her nails looked long and lovely.

Deb was so upset lately, she couldn't even muster the enthusiasm to chew on them. Another week of this angst, and she might be forced to get a manicure.

How could Elliot fail to acknowledge that he was driving her to a manicure?

She wondered if he expected her to respond in some way to his weird gesture? He probably did. Elliot never did anything without a purpose, and then a subpurpose beneath that, just to keep things interesting. He was waiting to gauge her reaction.

Well, Deb would show him.

Two could play at harmony. In fact, if they got all musically technical about it, didn't harmony—*Webster's Dictionary* speaking—necessitate two players?

Oh, boy, was she clever.

Never let it be said intelligence didn't get you anywhere.

Like in a hell of a lot of trouble.

Copying the apathetic tone he'd rolled out Deb's way when she came by to try and thank him for helping her survive through little Bethany's surgery, Deb politely inquired, "Is there something I can do for you, Dr. Elliot?"

If those words stabbed at his heart with even a third of the intensity they'd employed to rip out hers, Deb would consider the day—and the barb—a success. She wanted Elliot to know what that kind of cold dismissal felt like. No. She *needed* Elliot to know what that kind of cold dismissal felt like.

But since when did the Heavens care about her needs?

Instead of being hurt or offended, Elliot smiled at her words.

The bastard actually smiled.

Dimples, and all.

Both of them.

He smiled, he shrugged, and he shook his head, letting go of Deb's hand in the process. It fell limply to her side, slapping her thigh with a muted thump that echoed off the tile walls.

"No, thanks. I'm good." He stepped around Deb, turned on the shower, and proceeded to strip off his soiled shirt.

Leftover, bloody fingerprints glowed smeared on his back and neck. They were daubed so haphazardly, that, for a passing second, Deb thought she perceived the outline of fingers moving sensuously along his skin, stroking and caressing and digging in with the raw force of complete abandon.

It was obviously an optical illusion. But just to be on the safe side, before the complete second passed, Deb did.

Right through the door that led out of the Changing Room.

Even though she'd promised herself that the day Adrian Pharsi was admitted was to have been the day she formally submitted her letter of resignation to the Board, Deb, well ... flaked.

She told herself she had reasons for doing it. Good reasons. It had been a hell of a day, for one thing. Deb may have been a surgeon with fifteen years' experience opening up people's brains, but it wasn't every day she helped open up a person's chest—in five minutes, and with no anesthesia or even a nurse to distribute instruments. Her adrenaline levels had shot through the roof. It took a while to come down from a high like that.

Not that Elliot hadn't done his very best to help her there.

It took her two days to recover from the shower escapade.

Or so Deb told herself.

She told herself Elliot's shock to her system was the reason she kept putting off delivering her resignation. And not because she passed hours by the phone, waiting for one of the sources she'd groveled to, to come up with the two million dollars Deb needed to keep her department going.

The morning when she decided she couldn't put the inevitable off any longer, Deb awoke like a patient after anesthesia. Groggy, cranky, and weary.

She asked for a meeting with the hospital Board—if she had to go out, Deb intended to go out with a lot of style, and an equal amount of pounding the table with her fist.

She got referred to the Chief of Staff. Another good sign.

Not only was the Board willing to let her go without protest, they weren't particularly interested in anything she had to rant. They figured they'd let Dr. Wylie handle it. Dr. Wylie, the Board believed, was good with their staff; especially those high-strung, prima-donna surgeons. He'd take care of the Dr. Brody problem.

He did.

Before she even got a chance to open her mouth, Dr. Wylie said, "Don't."

Deb said, "What?"

Dr. Wylie said, "You don't have to quit."

Deb said, "Oh, yes, I do."

"It isn't necessary."

"It is. I swore that if the Committee didn't—"

"The Committee didn't," Dr. Wylie agreed. He tapped an azure folder lying closed on his desk. "Someone else did."

Now was a great time for Deb to show off all her precocious verbosity. She said, "Huh?"

"Yesterday afternoon, Dr. Brody, I received a donation of two million dollars, earmarked exclusively for your department. It's what you wanted, isn't it? No need for you to resign, now."

She came close to offering another, "Huh?" Instead, Deb managed to stammer out, "W-who? Who donated the money?"

"I'm afraid I can't say." Dr. Wylie crossed his arms, as if hugging the folder to his chest. "The benefactor prefers it that way. They fear inciting a conflict-of-interest accusation."

Conflict of interest. Deb smiled. Greenwood's father finally decided to come through.

God, rich people did like their drama, didn't they? Could he have waited any later to stop her twisting in the wind?

Not that any of it mattered now. She had her key two million. She had her department back. She had her job. She had her life.

Take that, Elliot.

The day called for gloating.

It wasn't written into her appointment calendar, but Deb felt the urge to do so, nonetheless.

And gloating wouldn't nearly be as much fun to just anyone.

"Elliot!" She called his name—heck, she practically sang it—when Deb spied him standing by the nurses' desk at the end of the hall. He looked up, noted that it had been Deb who'd called to him, and promptly returned to signing the stack of papers in front of him. He stood with one hip pressed against the nurses' station, his elbow propped on top of it, for balance. He scribbled quickly, and dispassionately, and with, visibly, half a mind somewhere else.

Deb decided to check if she could coax it back to the here and now. *Now.*

Resting her own elbow atop the nurses' station, Deb stood face-to-face with Elliot. "I'm still here," she said.

Elliot nodded absentmindedly. "Sondheim song."

As she'd so succinctly queried earlier, "Huh?" She was trying to tell him that his plot to drive her out of the hospital and out of his life had failed, and Elliot was playing *Name That Tune?*

Deb reiterated, "I'm telling you I'm not going."

"Jennifer Holliday."

"Wonder why?"

"Fleetwood Mac."

"Jesus Christ, Elliot." On a good day, Deb wasn't the most patient person in the world. And this wasn't a good day. "Can't you just let it be?"

"Beatles." He finished writing, neatly replaced the cap back on his pen, tucked it inside his jacket pocket, set the file he'd just signed in its appropriate spot, and straightened up. "Excuse me, Dr. Brody."

He walked away without ever once having looked at her.

Deb's mouth dropped open, generating a circle as wide as her eyes. Who did—What the—Just who did that man think he was?

Dr. James Elliot? Who the hell was Dr. James Elliot? Where did he think he got the license to treat people like this?

Deb had earned her gloat, fair and square, and he wasn't even allowing her to indulge.

It was bad manners.

It was bad judgment.

Damn it to hell, it was bad . . . sportsmanship.

Incensed into that ruby, fiery realm of fury beyond

words, Deb impulsively reached for the file Elliot had just completed signing. She wanted to see for herself what was so important the eminent Dr. Elliot couldn't spare even a moment for her triumphant crowing.

Mind still on her own self-righteousness, Deb opened the file.

And found Tammy Baldwin's death certificate.

The little girl from the Christmas party.

The one with the third-degree burns. The one whom Elliot had called his girlfriend. The one he'd promised she'd get better.

Stunned, Deb skimmed the chart beneath the death certificate. Tammy appeared to be recovering nicely, Elliot had even made a note about sending her home by Valentine's Day. But, then, an infection settled in her lungs. And no antibiotic proved powerful enough to fight it. She'd died less than two hours ago.

Less than two hours before Deb decided to make a spectacle of herself. In front of Elliot.

Elliot, who, in spite of his immense professional skills, had never really gotten the hang of losing patients. Especially those he'd gotten to know.

"Oh, God." The whimper bubbled from Deb's throat without her being aware it even wanted to. "Elliot . . ."

She took off down the hall after him.

He wasn't in his office.

Deb hadn't really expected him to be, but, to be thorough, she took a perfunctory peek. When asked, Helen replied she didn't know where Dr. Elliot was, either.

But that was alright. Because Deb did.

She took the elevator to the roof. Actually, she took it even farther, up to the helipad. Unless they had an emergency patient coming in, the school yard–size stretch of cement where the helicopter landed was usually empty.

Which made it perfect for roller-blading.

That is, if your demarcation of "perfect" was a bumpy surface thirty stories up in the air, and no guard rails along the edges.

Elliot liked it just fine.

He came up there to think. And to tear around on his roller-blades at God-only-knew how many kilometers an hour, body-checking invisible opponents— like God, Death, and Fate—into the boards.

Elliot was always challenging those three to a duel.

She knew from past experience that, when Elliot got like this, there would be no catching up to him. Deb didn't have the strength to run in never-ending circles, trying to keep up on foot while he sped up on wheels. And she doubted that even flying off the edge of the building could break Elliot's stride.

So, when she got to the roof and confirmed her hunch—he was there, alright, roller-blades on, sport jacket off, sleeves rolled up, tie flapping in the wind behind him, knees bent, arms pumping by his sides, breath coming fast and hard, face grim—Deb picked a nice, sunny spot, and waited for him to skate by.

The first time he rushed past, creating a gust of wind to join the one already tugging at her hair and lab coat, Deb simply called out, "I'm sorry."

The second time he wheeled by she pleaded, "I didn't know."

And, the third: "What can I do to help?"

He didn't look in her direction at any time.

But, at least, he didn't invoke song titles, either.

Instead, Elliot continued skating his furious laps, right leg crossing over left in a perpetual motion that, Deb presumed, could be rather pacifying when the rest of the world was running every-which-way-but-sane.

"Talk to me, Elliot," she suggested the next time he skidded into hearing range, wincing inwardly from how closely that echoed her "Say something. Say anything," the night of Max's funeral.

"I'm a good listener," she offered on the next lap, knowing it was technically not true. Elliot was a much better listener than she was, but she figured now was as good a time as any for her to return twenty years of similar favors on his part.

"Alright, so maybe I'm not so terrific. But it beats falling off the roof," was her rationalization the time after that.

Elliot smiled.

It couldn't exactly have been called a grin, and maybe the sun shining in her eyes did cause Deb to hallucinate, but for a moment there, it actually looked like Elliot smiled.

A few laps later, he let the arms he'd been pumping like someone trying to squeeze water from a stone drift to his sides. He continued to skate, but it seemed to Deb he slowed down some. She was either getting through to him, or Elliot was beginning to feel his age. Marathon demon-exorcising laps were one thing at twenty-three. Quite another at forty-three.

The next time he skated by her, Elliot didn't exactly skid to a stop, but he slowed down enough and narrowed his orbit enough so that he was now circling around Deb. Within hearing range.

She said, "I went over Tammy's chart. You did everything you could for her."

His breath came out in painful gasps, chest heaving with every inhalation, and rattling his shoulders with it. Still Elliot kept moving. As long as he kept moving, there was still a likelihood he could outrun whatever it was that was chasing him.

Elliot sighed. The sheer depth of the action seeming to drain his body of every last oxygen molecule. He might have been asleep, or deep in thought. Then, unexpectedly, his head jerked up, and he pushed off so hard with his left skate, Deb worried he was about to go over the edge. In more ways than one. He kept circling her.

She could think of nothing productive to say. All Deb cared about now was keeping Elliot's attention focused on anything other than the edge of the roof. So, she repeated, "I *am* sorry, Elliot."

It took another lap before he said, "Accepted."

She'd missed him.

The thought should by no means have been a surprise, and yet it walloped Deb from behind, with all the force of one. She, Deb, had missed Elliot. She'd missed . . . them.

She wondered if Elliot did.

She wondered if he'd expected to, when he decided to destroy their friendship. She wondered if he ever regretted it now?

Because, in a way, that was all Deb wanted from him.

Sometime during her six nightly hours of tossing and turning, Deb had come to the astonishing conclusion that what infuriated her most was not so much what Elliot did to her—although she wasn't quite ready to play priest and unequivocally exonerate that little slipup, either—but how he seemed thoroughly indifferent to the plan's consequences. If Elliot would just give her some sign that he was sorry about what his revenge—warranted though it may have seemed in his head—had done to their friendship, well, maybe she could then see clear to forgiving him, to wiping their slate clean, to starting again.

Because, vexed as she perpetually seemed to be these days, Deb also really, truly did want that.

Because, vexed as she perpetually seemed to be these days, no matter how hard she tried, Deb couldn't seem to find the energy to hate Elliot. She still cared about him too much.

And she wanted her friend back. She wanted everything back to the way it was for twenty years. Exactly the way that it was.

No variations, or last-minute adjustments.

Well, maybe a few adjustments . . .

But they didn't have to decide on those now.

All they had to do now was somehow, magically, reconnect.

Both had to let go of their anger, Elliot's for her rejecting him, and Deb's for his machinations.

They had to become friends again.

"Elliot," she began.

And then, she stopped. Because, really, that was all she had. Deb had kind of been hoping Elliot would pick up the slack.

He said, "It shouldn't have happened."

He meant Tammy. But he was right, across the board.

Deb nodded. "No. It shouldn't have."

"I thought I had it all under control."

"I know. But, lately, I've begun to suspect that maybe that's an illusion people like us have to learn to give up."

"Or go crazy?"

"Exactly."

Elliot crossed his arms, the skating circle around Deb growing tighter and tighter. Like a noose.

Or an embrace.

"And how, exactly, does one do that?"

"Give up illusions?" Deb shrugged. "Hey, I came up with the overall concept. You work out the details."

It was getting very disconcerting, trying to keep up with him. Deb could turn her head only so far, before Elliot disappeared from sight behind her head. And, because his velocity refused to remain constant, she could never predict when he might pop up again in her peripheral vision. It was like trying to track smoke.

He came up behind her. Deb heard the scraping of the wheels finally coming to a permanent stop.

She could feel Elliot as acutely now as she had days earlier, when he came up to stand behind her in the Doctors' Lounge. For better or for worse, Deb suspected that she could perpetually feel Elliot, no matter where he was, or how far away from her.

"But, don't you find"—his breath kissed the back of her neck—"that illusions are often the very things that make it possible for us to keep plugging away at reality?"

Roller-blades added a further inch to his height. Deb wasn't used to hearing Elliot's voice coming from so far above her. That must have been why his words disoriented her so.

Yeah, Deb. That was precisely it.

She said, "You mean, like us having to think we're invincible, or we'd never be able to pick up a scalpel?"

"Maybe." Even the wind couldn't distort the melancholy in his utterance. "Or, maybe, I'm just talking about good, old-fashioned, generic-prescription hope."

"Hope?"

"We have to hope that somehow, someday, someway, eventually, we'll score what we really want out of life. Or else, what's the point of continuing to beat our heads against the wall?"

This from the man who'd once told her, "I keep hitting my head against the wall, until the wall breaks."

"So"—in light of anything better to say, Deb fell back on a medical-school, theoretical, otherwise known as the three AM game of *What If?*—"would you rather die never having achieved your dreams, but still clinging to the hope that they might happen? Or having realized and accepted the futility of one dream, and given it up in time to achieve another, lesser one, not to mention build a little character to boot?"

"You know what I would prefer?" Elliot said following a pause. "I would prefer not to have any more character-building experiences. Character-building experiences are what people settle for when they can't obtain what they want. I, Brody, would rather just get what I want."

"But wouldn't that require knowing exactly what you want?"

"That"—Elliot's voice sucked sensuously along each syllable—"has never been a problem for me."

If she hadn't heard the purr of his roller-blades, Deb would have never known that Elliot moved. She would have simply watched him materialize before her, like an angel, or a devil, or some odd offspring of the pair. He would have simply appeared, more windblown than usual, taller than usual, but as determined as always.

The minute Elliot's eyes locked on to Deb's, she knew she had no chance of breaking free. And so she didn't bother.

Deb knew what Elliot wanted. She wanted it, too.

And, since Elliot refused to rest until he got what he wanted, Deb didn't fight it when, dipping his head an extra inch to make up for the height discrepancy, he, purposefully and wholly, and oh, so knowingly, seized her mouth with his.

Chapter Fourteen

---

*T*his is a mistake, Elliot thought.

He should not be kissing Brody.

Not now, not ever. He had too much to lose.

Like his mind. Again.

It would have been so easy to keep going, though.

Not even easy. Instinctive.

He presumed he had remembered every tang, every texture, every scent, every tremble of the way she tasted, felt, smelled, and moved in his arms. And beneath his tongue. And against his chest.

He was wrong.

Sense memories may have proven almost sufficient at two AM—alone. But the 3-D, Technicolor, You-Are-There Panorama presently erupting inside, and outside, and around him did, most succinctly, drive home the point that . . . uh . . . no . . . this way was better.

She tasted like a wish granted. Elliot knew no other way to describe it.

She tasted like a miracle.

And she didn't feel so bad, either.

Standing an inch more below him than usual, Brody had to tilt her head all the way back, in order to kiss him. The pose left her at a vulnerable angle, making it necessary for her to lean against Elliot for balance. Her right hand rested atop his chest, fingers digging in hard enough so that he could feel their imprint through his clothes on his skin. Her left hand rested on his hip, also for balance, also a wonderment.

Also a very bad idea.

He couldn't let Brody do this to him, again. He couldn't let her suck him in like this, a second time. It didn't matter that, technically, Elliot had initiated their kiss. She'd been the one who'd made him *want* to initiate it.

Elliot had already lost his heart to her once, and, God knew, she, most likely, still owned it. But that captivation had opened the door to a pain more savage and lethal than even a doctor could have imagined. Deb may have still cradled his heart, but he would die before he let her have his head, as well.

It was a very good thing that Elliot was on wheels.

Because he doubted he could have forced himself to extricate from her embrace, on his own power.

Luckily, while balancing atop roller-blades, all it took was a slight shift of his weight—so subtle that his mind was able to fool his body up until the conclusive minute—and Elliot promptly rolled out of the danger zone.

Out of Brody's arms.

She seemed rather surprised by that.

For a second, Deb actually remained as she was, embracing the shadow of wind where Elliot had once been. It made for a peculiar picture. For that split second when Deb still stood, clasping his ghost, Elliot got the chance to see from the side something he usually saw only from within. He, too, got the chance to face a shadow.

His own.

He saw the way Deb held him. He saw the way her body seemed to turn toward him, like a flower toward the light. He saw the slight smile playing around her lips, and the way her eyes blazed.

He saw a lot of things that made Elliot ache to do that weight shift again, and roll right back into Brody's arms.

Luckily, the roller-blades had a brake in the back.

Elliot dug his heel into the ground with such force, he would not have been surprised to see a divot rip the concrete.

The shadow moment passed.

Like a light switch being flicked off, Deb dropped her arms to their sides, then, displeased, plopped them militarily on her hips. She straightened her spine. The smile disappeared.

She asked Elliot, "What just happened?"

Elliot said, "Leave."

"Huh?"

"Leave me alone," Elliot repeated.

"Why?" The arms from her hips migrated to cross against Deb's chest. "What's going on here, Elliot?"

What was the matter with this girl? Had forty-one years of brilliance and achievement rendered her incapable of recognizing rejection when she saw it? Elliot judged himself darn brilliant and full of achievements, too. But he could certainly recognize rejection when it bit him. Elliot had had twenty years of Deb's performing an in-home, in-office, and anywhere else they happened to be demonstration of it for him. He practically had a PhD in the subject.

"I'm asking you to leave, Brody, that's what's going on."

"Why?" She wasn't doing a hysterical woman bit. She sounded genuinely curious. Like a research scientist.

"Because," Elliot said. "I want to be by myself."

"What about . . ." She waved her hand across the space where his ghost had earlier looked so happy. Across the space where every neuron in Elliot's body was screaming with the reminder, he could be very happy again. All it would take was a push of the wheel.

Bad idea.

Very, very bad idea, Elliot.

He said, "What? You're the only one allowed to slip up and do something meaningless to dull the pain of a really bad day?"

That counter was a work of art. A painstakingly worded retort sculpted to make Brody flee and stop taunting him with that satanic way she had of just being herself.

There was only one problem.

Deb hadn't read the stage directions.

She didn't know she was supposed to flee.

Instead, she observed, "Nice one, Elliot. Now, tell me what's really going on here."

Did Elliot say satanic? He meant she was more than that. She was the damn anti-Christ, herself.

What did she want from him? Did she want him to dissolve into a puddle at her feet? Was that what she needed to be happy?

It wasn't enough that she had wholly gutted him on the inside, she needed to see the results of that on the outside, as well?

Well, it would be a warm day in San Francisco before Elliot ever broke enough to give her that satisfaction.

"Alright, then," he said. "I'll leave."

And proceeded to skate his way toward the roof's door. That part went relatively smoothly. Clunking down the successive steps while still wearing roller-blades, however, proved a problem. His exit was not, to put it charitably, graceful.

But it was lifesaving.

Alright. Now, Deb was mad.

All that stuff that came before? Kids' stuff.

Displeasure. Annoyance. Irritation. Vexation.

But not anger.

Oh, no.

Only now did Deb know what real anger was.

And she'd tried her best not to get angry. When Elliot first went schizoid on her, she'd kept her cool. She'd tried to give him the benefit of the doubt. She'd tried to understand.

There was nothing to understand.

James Elliot was a bastard.

That, after twenty years, Deb finally understood.

She'd been trying to be amicable. Trying to say, "I'm sorry," about poor, little Tammy, and, under the circumstances, about Deb's pummeling her recent good news in Elliot's face. Not that she was necessarily sorry about that latter one, she just might have chosen a more apropos moment to gloat.

But after the way Elliot treated her earlier, all bets were off. No more apologetic, no more sympathetic, no more . . . nice. Why was Deb killing herself trying to be nice to a man who'd schemed to destroy her career? Why was she killing herself trying to be nice to a man who could kiss her one minute, then dismiss her the next? Why was she killing herself trying to be nice to a man who didn't give a hiccough of a damn about breaking her heart?

Because he was the same man who, a few days earlier, made it possible for Deb to go back into the operating room.

Because he was the same man who, the night of Max's funeral, came to her home, and kept Deb from losing her mind.

Because he was the same man who, the morning before Matching Day, made Deb feel worthwhile.

Because she may have been hating Elliot for a few weeks. But she had loved him for twenty years.

And old habits died hard.

Especially when you didn't really want them to.

Deb may have wanted to hate Elliot.

But, damn, if she didn't still love him.

And God, this all seriously sucked.

Why was Elliot doing this to her?

And how could Deb best make him pay for it?

Opportunity walked through Deb's door, wearing a black Chanel suit, and a matching hat, purse, shoes, and gloves. It came in the form of a raven-haired woman, about Deb's age, but with a sense of imperial style that Deb, despite all her fondness for dressing up, could never hope to duplicate. The woman was so perfectly arranged and put together, Deb's first impulse was to genuflect. She fought it successfully, and settled for looking up from her desk, and her paperwork, to ask, "Can I help you?"

"I am Nadia Pharsi." Withdrawn languidly from the glove, her bronze, outstretched hand was impeccably manicured, and her—Deb guessed—Iranian accent drawled equally polished.

"Adrian's mother," Deb guessed.

"Adrian is my son, yes. May I speak with you about him, Dr. Brody?"

"Well." Deb glanced up at her clock. She didn't have another appointment scheduled for fifteen minutes, but . . . "I'd be happy to speak with you, Mrs. Pharsi. Except that I'm not Adrian's primary physician. I'm a neurosurgeon, and his injuries aren't—"

"You were in the emergency room when he was brought in?"

"Yes."

"You helped Dr. Elliot perform his procedure?"

Oh. Suddenly, Deb was hearing the word *malpractice* echoing in her ears. The song did not have a great beat, and it was not easy to dance to. This was not good news.

Nevertheless, Deb was a professional. She stood by her work.

She said, "Yes."

"I am told that you and Dr. Elliot sliced Adrian's chest open, and Dr. Elliot plugged up the holes in his heart with his fingers?"

"More or less."

"This is not a conventional procedure."

"No."

"Other doctors would have taken Adrian to the operating room, and performed the surgery there?"

"Under normal circumstances that would have been the best way to go, yes. But your son's heart had stopped beating. Adrian was barely breathing. He was seconds away from brain-dead. The three minutes it would have taken us to transfer him might just as easily have been the three minutes that killed him."

"So, the nurse that drew up the complaint against Dr. Elliot, the one who says he took an unnecessary risk treating my son, she is wrong?"

"What nurse?" Deb asked, although, as soon as she did, she guessed she already knew that answer. There was only one nurse it could be. Ursula covering her own tracks. What Deb did not know, however, was "What complaint?"

"There is to be an inquiry by a hospital committee on Friday, to discuss Dr. Elliot's performance with my son. I have been asked to come speak to them, and I am willing to do this. But, first, I need to understand exactly what happened with Adrian. Please, Dr. Brody, tell me what is your opinion of Dr. Elliot's actions."

Deb would have learned about it sooner or later, anyway. Dr. Wylie wanted her to make an appearance and answer some questions—very informally, of course. This was a casual inquiry not a license hearing. Not yet, anyway.

Wylie said, "I realize that this might be troublesome for you. Your relationship with Dr. Elliot goes back further than your relationship with this hospital. Still, you do understand that we are obliged to investigate every complaint."

Even, Deb supposed, when that complaint stemmed from a nurse so afraid of being censured herself—doctors did not take kindly to being told no under any circumstances, much less critical ones—that she decided to launch a preemptive strike against Elliot and file a complaint criticizing his behavior, before he had the chance to do the same about her. It was a sound strategy, if also an obvious one.

Deb told Wylie, "Oh, I understand completely. You don't have to worry about me. I know exactly what I need to do about this."

Deb supposed that modesty would have dictated her swearing she wasn't used to opportunities tumbling into her lap like this. But that would have been a lie.

Deb was born precocious. She was rather used to opportunities tumbling into her lap. Big, juicy ones, traditionally with rewards like "Full Scholarship" stamped across the front.

But, she had to admit, no "Full Scholarship" had ever made her feel this deep-down tingly.

It was finally her turn to demonstrate to Elliot what betrayal felt like. It was her turn to make him grasp the agony of watching the most meaningful thing in your life, your work, weave and dangle off the end of a precarious, worn thread. And to know that someone you once trusted with your life was responsible for the purgatory.

That last one was particularly important.

It was so important that, unable to catch him at the hospital, Deb drove all the way out to Elliot's condominium to discuss it.

He let her in, wearing a look combining surprise, resignation, and indifference. But that was merely Elliot's face. The rest of Elliot was wearing sneakers, indigo running shorts, a white T-shirt—and a dimple. The shirt, damp with sweat, stuck to his back, chest, and stomach. The left sneaker had a recently ripped hole in the sole, and the shorts had definitely been to the laundry more than once in their athletic lifetime. The dimple, on the other hand, barely looked winded. *It* looked like it could go on dimpling forever.

Not if Deb had anything to say about it.

She told Elliot, "I hear you're up a creek."

He shrugged. "Ursula."

Deb wondered if that was supposed to be a question, an answer, or both. In any case, she found it unsatisfying.

Deb had come to Elliot's like the Grinch, poised to spread angst wherever she went. Deb wasn't leaving until there was angst.

"Dr. Wylie asked me to answer a few questions at the inquiry."

Another shrug. "Logical. You were there."

Elliot smelled only slightly of sweat. The rest of it was the tart, wintergreen redolence of an antiperspirant working admirably hard to verify why that extra fifteen cents per ounce was worth the expense. It mixed with the sweat, to fill the room.

Or maybe just the part Deb was standing in.

All she knew was, whenever she moved, the scent followed her.

"Nervous?" Deb asked. She meant about the inquiry.

And about her testimony.

Elliot was not a witless man. He should be able to put seven and three together, and come up with revenge to the power of ten.

He didn't even bother to shrug this time.

He was too busy arranging his cool stance. Too busy looking as if he didn't have a concern in the world. Or a care.

If his running shorts came equipped with pockets, Elliot would have stuck his hands nonchalantly in them. So he did the next best thing. Wiping sweat off his forehead with one hand, he crossed to his kitchen, and, with his other one, opened the refrigerator door. He scanned its contents and reached for the orange-juice carton. Eschewing something as uncool as a glass, he drank it straight, then tossed the drained quart in the trash.

His easygoing body language said it all. Deb may have come by looking for angst, and, if she was honest with herself, itching for a fight. But Elliot had no intention of obliging.

God, but he was irritating.

And, God, did Deb wish she could be more like him.

She wished she could be that detached.

Or, at the very least, possess the energy to fake it.

Problem was, Deb had no more energy.

This struggle had drained *her* as thoroughly as Elliot had that orange-juice container. The only energy she seemed vaguely capable of summoning these days was anger. But, if Elliot refused to light the fuse, she alone couldn't unearth the incentive to go off.

Which was a greater calamity than it appeared on the surface. Because, since Max's death, Deb had noted her every feeling slowly shutting down, and atrophying like an unused muscle. The solitary emotions she found herself capable of generating were ones linked to Elliot. Good ones, at first. Lately, primarily bad ones. But they were genuine emotions, nonetheless, and Deb clung to them as vestiges of her humanity. Even the anger she felt for Elliot was better than feeling nothing at all. And, no matter how furious she grew with him, Deb never lost track of the comprehension that—for better or worse—he was the only person, place, or thing left on earth still capable of making Deborah Brody feel . . . something.

If she lost that, she truly would have nothing left.

"I'm sorry," Elliot said. He took a step toward Deb. He asked, "Did you want some juice, too?"

His face was a CD-ROM dictionary illustration of

the species *bland*. If he'd appeared vaguely malicious, or arrogant, or even obnoxious, Deb would have rejoiced. Because any one of those words would have been enough to spark the fading ember of emotion buried underneath all the scars life had slashed in her over the past few months. Any one of those words would have been welcome. But the utter indifference in his demeanor was more than Deb could bear.

She shook her head. Once, twice, then three times, clearing it at the same time as she struggled to regain her voice, and strip at least the most audible disappointment from her syllables.

"No, Elliot," she said softly, turning toward the door and an exit. "That's alright. There's nothing I want from you."

The night before she was scheduled to bear witness at Elliot's medical court-martial, Deb didn't even manage her customary four hours of sleep. As she stared at her face in the mirror prior to pulling out the big-gun cosmetics, Deb sternly lectured herself about the importance of catching at least that crucial half hour a night. The gloomy bags under her eyes only giggled in reply.

Oh, yes, this was going to be a lovely morning.

Especially when Deb walked into the boardroom and realized that, not only was Pain-in-the-Ass-Morelli a member of the five-doctor Committee sitting judgment on Elliot, but that Elliot, who'd already given his statement, was free to remain in the room while Deb answered her questions.

Somehow, in all the simulations she'd run in her head, Deb had never considered that possibility. She'd expected to testify in a vacuum, with everyone's face fuzzy, or, better yet, camouflaged by a blue dot, like on TV. And she'd certainly expected Elliot to be somewhere else entirely.

He sat at the far, narrow end of the oval table, dressed in a gray suit. Unlike Morelli, who perched on the edge of his chair, arms forward, fingertips digging into the table, and ready to pounce on the narrowest opportunity, Elliot reclined in his seat. Legs crossed, right elbow balanced on the armrest, the backs of his fingers propping up his chin, left palm splaying cool as could be atop his upraised knee, Elliot might have been listening to an intriguing discourse on a subject that bore no effect on him personally. Something like breast cancer, for instance. As a doctor, Elliot might have been intrigued to hear about mortality rates, but they didn't worry him like they did, say, Deb, whenever she went to a similar lecture.

He looked up when Deb came into the boardroom, and, while the greeting he offered her could never be regarded a smile, it wasn't quite a frown, either. It was, in fact, the typical hello-how-are-you-nice-to-see-you-again greeting prosaic to casual acquaintances, neighbors, and colleagues everywhere.

Deb could think of nothing to do but nod curtly in return.

She took a seat where indicated. It was at the center of the table. She couldn't see Elliot clearly, unless she made the effort to turn her head. But there was no way she could avoid the flash of his red tie from flickering in her peripheral vision.

Deb stated her name for the record even though everyone in the room recalled who she was. Only a few weeks earlier she'd paced in front of most of these same people, haggling for her funding.

The introductory questions were simple. A sort

of name, rank, and serial number of the medical kind. She barely had to meditate on her answers before stating the basic facts about Adrian Pharsi's condition and prognosis. She'd read his chart before arriving, and the facts were clear enough in her head to come automatically.

Not once did Deb glance in Elliot's direction. And she was fairly sure he wasn't looking at her.

Yet, she could still feel him.

The same way she'd felt him when he came up behind her prior to Bethany Kawahara's surgery. The same way she felt him standing behind her on roller-blades.

Despite the presence of five other doctors, plus a secretary, plus the accusing Ursula in their room, Deb imagined she could hear Elliot's breathing above all. The steady, rhythmic, unhurried pace could only belong to him. It permeated Deb's consciousness, burrowing in through her skin and wafting in as she inhaled, until it baptized her own respiration to the same beat.

After ten minutes of softballs, Dr. Wylie, in the same tone he'd employed for all the other queries, finally, but, without any fanfare, finally got around to the million-dollar question. Wylie asked, "Dr. Brody, in your opinion, were Dr. Elliot's actions with Adrian Pharsi reckless, and detrimental to the patient?"

She'd known this question was coming.

Hell, knowing this question was coming had been Deb's primary reason for booking a front row seat at his tar and feathering.

"Dr. Brody?" Wylie's "We're waiting" was implied in his tone.

Deb took a deep breath.

She arranged her thoughts.

She linked her hands together in front of her.

She looked down.

And saw her wedding and engagement rings staring up at her.

The night of Adrian Pharsi's shooting, Deb had gone home and scrubbed both of her rings. To get the blood off. Yet, no matter how hard she scrubbed, she couldn't as easily remove the memory of Elliot returning her rings, by slipping them back on her finger.

Elliot's breathing quickened. No one else heard it.

Then again, no one else had Elliot's breathing regulating theirs.

The second that Deb had glanced down and noted her rings, Elliot's breathing had quickened.

He remembered giving them back to her, too.

Now—Deb smiled inwardly—now, she bet he was nervous.

She squared her shoulders. She straightened her spine. She got ready, like George Lucas's empire, to strike back.

Elliot's recently quickened breathing caught in his throat.

Funny. Deb's was, for the first time since she'd entered the boardroom, doing quite nicely. Because, for the first time since she'd entered the boardroom, Deb knew exactly what she had to do.

Deb said, "Dr. James Elliot's treatment of Adrian Pharsi was unspeakably reckless. It was impetuous, it was hazardous, and it was certainly iconoclastic."

There were nine people total inside the room. Only eight were still breathing. Although, to be statistically accurate, Morelli was hyperventilating enough for two.

Deb did not turn her head. She did not look at Elliot.

She didn't have to.

She knew exactly what he looked like.

She would have bet the two million dollars Greenwood's family recently donated to her department that Elliot hadn't shifted a muscle since she'd begun speaking. He was still playing it cool.

But none of that mattered.

Waiting to hear what Deb would say, Elliot quit breathing.

It didn't matter how far back he leaned in his chair, or how neutrally he arranged his features. Elliot quit breathing. Elliot was no longer indifferent.

Elliot was no longer indifferent—to her.

Deb continued. "Performing heart surgery without anesthesia is not behavior that this hospital should encourage." She twisted her ring around her finger, so that the diamond now stared her directly in the eye. "Unless, of course, it is being performed by a surgeon of Dr. Elliot's skill and heroism, and when it's obviously the only procedure with even a prayer of saving the patient's life."

It's a good thing they were in a hospital.

Morelli almost swallowed his tongue.

Deb finally turned her head to look at Elliot. He'd shifted in his chair so that both of his elbows rested on the table, palms over each other, chin propped atop his hands. He stared at Deb so intensely, he might have been piercing her with a lance. He didn't look surprised. He didn't look grateful. He looked . . . puzzled.

In reply, Deb smiled enigmatically. At least, she hoped she was smiling enigmatically. Often, when she smiled enigmatically, it came off looking more heartburnish.

"This is preposterous." Morelli overcame both the throttled tongue and the hyperventilation to throw his hands up in the air, the right dismissing Deb, while the left rejected the rest of the universe. "Why are we even bothering to listen to this? Dr. Brody can't be objective in this matter. Not only are she and Dr. Elliot lifelong *friends*"—he made that last word sound as if "friends" was a capital offense—"but the primary reason she's supporting him here is because Dr. Elliot donated the two million dollars Dr. Brody needed to keep working at this hospital."

Chapter Fifteen

It was a good thing they were in a hospital.

Because Deb nearly swallowed her tongue.

Morelli had announced it so casually. She knew what that man sounded like when he was being deliberately perverse, and this had not been one of those times. He'd announced it casually because he assumed everybody in the room, Deb included, sat aware of the fact. He hadn't been aiming to hurt with the information itself, just his own interpretation of it.

Doubleheader, Morelli, Deb applauded. *Two birds, one stone.*

Her hands were shaking. Deb failed to notice it immediately, because the sensation was such a novel one. She might have never noticed it, if not for the anxious Teletype clicking of her nails along the hardwood tabletop.

She looked down at her hands. It was easier than looking anywhere else, and less dangerous. Deb looked down at her hands, and, guiltily, clamped one over the other, hoping to cover up her sin.

She would be required to look up sometime. For one thing, Dr. Wylie was telling her thank you, Doctor, and they were through with her, and Deb could go now. The way that he said that last one made it clear that Deb, in fact, *should* go now.

How could she leave the room without looking at Elliot?

But, then again, why should she want to?

Deborah Brody, after all, was a lot of things—actually, she was now aware that she was a lot more things, not all of them good, than she had once believed. But she hoped she was not a coward.

She'd made a mistake.

A terrible, horrible, selfish, nearly unforgivable mistake.

That she hoped would be forgiven.

But that couldn't happen until Deb apologized.

And she could think of no better time than now to commence the ceremonial groveling.

She looked at Elliot. She stood up, nodded a curt good-bye to the Board members, and she looked at Elliot.

He looked back with the last expression Deb ever expected from him. Elliot looked at her not with hatred, not with contempt, not with self-righteousness, and not with understanding.

He looked at her, with pity.

Elliot felt sorry for her.

Deb wasn't sure why that was.

But she was pretty sure she was terrified of finding out.

The old Deb would have planted herself in the hall outside the boardroom, waiting for Elliot to come out so that she could pounce on him. But even measuring with the world's most indulgent ruler, the old Deb had already caused enough trouble.

She did have to talk with Elliot. Very, very badly. But she also had to remember that, while she sat in her office, practically vibrating with nervous energy, guilt, and self-flagellation, Elliot was fighting for his professional life in front of some of the same men who, only a few weeks earlier, he'd been arm wrestling over the hospital's budget. And, when Elliot arm wrestled, he arm wrestled to win. Elliot didn't spot points, he didn't advance head starts, and, above all, Elliot did not suf-fer fools gladly. Consequently, very few of his fellow Committee members liked him. As long as they were equals battling over budgetary concerns, Elliot genuinely didn't care what they thought of him. Medicine, he liked to say, was not a popularity contest—"I'm a doctor, not a politician" was his *Star Trek* cribbed-self-definition. Technically, this was a lie. When he needed to be, Elliot was as good a politician as anybody. The difference between him and Morelli was Elliot plied his backroom shenanigans reluctantly, and for the benefit of his patients. Morelli did it with pleasure, and to help only himself.

Because Elliot held Morelli and all doctors like him in esteem so low that if you dropped a penny down that well you'd never hear it hit bottom, he didn't particularly care that those same doctors didn't respect, or even like, him in return. Previously, there was nothing they could do to hurt him.

Now, there was something they could do to hurt him.

Getting Elliot out of the way, Deb knew, would make a busload of Valley Hospital doctors terribly happy.

If Deb knew that, then Elliot, certainly, had to.

No matter how low-key Dr. Wylie tried to play it, the inquiry into Elliot's conduct was a very, very big deal. Deb understood it was a very, very big deal, and she was very, very worried about how it would affect Elliot and his future, and all that other stuff.

Nevertheless, Deb really needed Elliot to shove all that aside for a minute, and focus on her.

She knew how selfish she sounded.

Selfish, and childish, and avaricious, and foolish, and . . . and . . . damn it, she'd run out of self-hating words.

To summarize, though, Deb did realize how she was acting. And she figured the postmodern self-awareness made it a tiny bit okay.

Oh, hell, who was she kidding? Instead of making this crisis with the Board somehow easier for Elliot—God knew, he would have done the same for her if their situations were reversed—Deb was just complicating his life further.

She really should not have been doing that.

And she promised herself that she wouldn't be doing that.

Just as soon as she got this one, small hiccough of theirs all straightened out.

To her satisfaction.

The old Deb would have planted herself in the hall outside the boardroom, waiting for Elliot to come out so that she could pounce on him. The new Deb did no such thing. The new Deb spent the day in her office, seeing patients, returning phone calls, filling out paperwork. At seven PM, the new Deb called Helen to verify that Dr. Elliot had left for the evening. At seven-fifteen, the new Deb called Elliot's home and hung up when the machine clicked on. At seven-thirty, the new Deb drove to Elliot's condo, timing herself to arrive at the same time as he usually did from his jog.

The new Deb waited for Elliot outside his door.

The new Deb, she thought as she looked down the hallway for a place to sit, and acknowledged, once again, her own self-centered behavior, was still somehow looking a lot like the old one.

"There's nothing you can say." The words were out of Elliot's mouth the second he rounded the corner of his hallway and came into view, prompting Deb to assume she hadn't caught him by surprise and that he'd spotted her car outside, jogging up the stairs prepared.

Deb had been standing with her back against the wall, fingers tangling her purse strap. When she saw Elliot, she sprang forward like a fish jumping off a hot plate. It was not dignified. But dignity had long ago fallen down that same well as the previously mentioned penny. Now was not the time for dignity.

Except in Elliot's case. He seemed determined that dignity be maintained. Not for his sake. For hers.

Elliot stuck his key in the lock, and opened the front door of his condo. He told Deb, "There is nothing you might say to me that could make things alright between us. So, please, don't try. The last thing I want is for you to feel humiliated."

Boy, Deb thought, chivalry sure is different postmillennium.

Once, a chivalrous fellow fought duels for your honor. At the very least, he laid his cape across a mud puddle. In 2001, he very politely told you that you had no chance, so don't demean yourself by groveling, sweetheart.

It was pompous.

It was egotistical.

It was insulting.

It was sweet, as only Elliot could be.

He'd made up his mind. And, when Elliot made up his mind, he did not change it for anyone or anything. Mountains crumbled under the persistent trickle of water quicker than Elliot under any form of persuasion. At the conclusion of an argument with Elliot, his opponents reported symptoms of exhaustion, hoarseness, fever, rash, dementia, defeat, self-loathing, and, yes, humiliation.

Elliot simply wanted to protect Deb from all that.

Which had to mean that he still cared about her.

Deb drew her strength from the analysis, and promptly followed Elliot inside his condominium. Because, as long as he still cared about her, she felt convinced there was still time to avoid pulling the plug on them. Besides, Deb drove over with something to say.

And Deb was going to say it.

But, first, she said, "I'm sorry."

"Brody . . ."

"Not about that. I'll get to that, later. Believe me." Deb sighed. "I *will* get to that later. Right now, though, I'm sorry about barging in like this. I know you must have a million things on your mind. That hearing, today, it was brutal. I don't know where any of them get off treating you like that. Not a single one of them is half the doctor you are. This whole thing stinks, big-time. You need all your resources to fight it, and I'm pretty sure the last thing you need now is to be distracted by me." Deb took a deep breath. "So, just say the word, Elliot, and I'll leave."

He said, "Leave, Brody."

"Say another word."

He shook his head, as if he'd expected nothing else—since when had Deb ever put his needs ahead of hers, and why should she start, now?—and turned his back on her.

Her spirits plummeted. But she *had* made the initial offer.

It broke her heart. But she did as he asked. The new Deb was determined to, for a change, think about what Elliot wanted and needed. She squeezed her hands into tight fists, biting her tongue to keep from blurting out anything he might find inappropriate and retreated to the door.

Her hand was already on the knob, when she heard Elliot say, without turning around, "Wait."

She froze in place, not daring to move.

"You're just going to keep hounding me and hounding me, until you get out whatever piece it is you think you need to say to me, aren't you?"

"Uhm . . ." Deb hesitated. "No?"

He snorted. He still didn't turn around. But after a pause, he did say, "Alright. Just get it over with."

Her heart beat in double-time, and she felt pure adrenaline pumping through her veins like a drug.

He'd given her an opening. He'd given her a chance. He did not have to tell her that it would be her only one.

She resolved to run with it to the ends of the earth.

Deb rested her hand on Elliot's shoulder. Steam rose off from his skin and entwined itself around her fingers. He startled. Deb began, "I didn't know."

"There was no way you could have." He shrugged his shoulder, shaking her off like a rodent scurrying along his neck, and turned around to face her, to prevent further surprises.

She had her speech prepared, and she launched into it without any preliminaries, speaking briskly, lest Elliot change his mind and withdraw her dispensation to speak freely. Deb rambled, "Wylie told me the donor asked to remain anonymous for fear of conflict of interest, so I assumed Greenwood . . ."

"That's what I expected you to assume."

"Why didn't you tell me?"

"It's a conflict of interest for me as well. A piece of your department falls under my auspices. I didn't want it to look like I was playing favorites."

"Where did you get the money, Elliot? Two million dollars is a lot of money."

"Brody?" He sighed.

"Yes?"

"How much do I bill a year?"

"I don't know. A million-two, a million-three . . ."

"A million-six. I bill one-point-six million dollars a year, and have been doing so for roughly ten years, give or take cost of living. I don't fly planes, I don't do drugs, I don't have a wife who lives at the plastic surgeon's, and I don't have kids who ride horses, ice-skate, or attend private schools. Two million dollars is a manageable amount for me to save."

"And give away?"

"When necessary."

"I have another question."

"You always do, Brody."

"Why?"

"Why did I donate it?"

"Yes."

"Because I didn't want you losing your work, too."

"Like I'd already lost Max?"

"Yes."

"Like I'd already lost you?"

He didn't even take a second to think about it. "Yes."

"I'm sorry," she told him plainly. "I'm so sorry for what I said, and how I behaved."

"I believe you."

They might as well get it all out, now. "Why did you let them cut my budget?"

"Morelli did a runaround against me at the last minute. It was my fault, I didn't see it coming. He'd arranged it so the decision came to either cutting two million from your budget, or losing five million from my Pediatric ER. That would have ended up crippling too many juvenile specialties. I had to make the choice that would do the most good, or, at best, the least harm."

"You'd have explained it to me if I'd asked, wouldn't you?"

"I was planning to explain it to my whole department. You're not the only one who took a hit."

"But I am the only one you saved out of your own pocket."

"That's true."

Deb asked, "I lost you as soon as I accused you of betraying me, didn't I, Elliot?"

"Yes."

"I lost you even before I guessed that you were furious at me for rejecting you on New Year's Eve—it wasn't my guessing at the motive. It was the accusation, itself."

"Yes."

"Oh, God, I know you so well."

Elliot said, "That's what I used to think, too."

"I made a mistake."

"I know."

"I want to atone for it."

"Try a temple next Yom Kippur."

"No good, it won't help. I don't care about God forgiving me. I want you to forgive me, Elliot."

"I can't."

"Try."

"I won't."

"Damn it!" She felt as drained and exhausted as after an hour volley at the tennis net. "Why not?"

"Because I have no interest in being hurt by you, again."

Deb said, "I love you, Elliot."

"I used to think *that*, too."

"No." Deb crossed her arms, looking him right in the eye, and believing every word, every letter, every syllable, and every sound that came out of her mouth with every fiber of her soul. "I really love you, Elliot."

She let the proclamation hang in the air like a puff of silver smoke from a ten-dollar cigar. She let it hang there and dissipate slowly, seeping first into Elliot's tactile senses before beginning the inevitable climb to his brain. She watched the process the way one watched a spider spinning his web, fearful to budge or breathe too loudly, lest that throw him off rhythm.

The words sunk in one by one. There were only five of them—and the last was his name, so it probably scampered to the head of the line relatively promptly—but it was still taking Elliot an extralong time to convert the data.

He blinked finally. But, still, he didn't move. Or respond.

She waited.

He waited.

She waited some more.

Elliot said, "When?"

She'd been expecting a "What?" Alright, maybe a

"Why?" or a "How?" She had not been expecting a "When?"

"I love you, Elliot," Deb repeated, figuring that since she couldn't make out his question, she'd go with a sweeping truth, and see if that covered any stray bases. "I think I've known it for a while now. I think I knew it New Year's Eve. Heck, I think I knew it Christmas Eve. I couldn't admit it, yet, though. Not to you, not to me. I was too scared. But, hearing what you did for me, even after everything I—I had to admit it. I love you, Elliot. I love you the way that you wanted— the way that you *want* me to love you."

"So, let me get this straight." Elliot counted off wryly on his fingers. "December twenty-third, you didn't love me. Christmas Eve, you did. New Year's Eve, you loved me. Day after New Year's, you hated me. Today, you love me again. Have I got it all straight?" He asked, "What's the matter, Brody, pharmacy run out of Prozac?"

Voice soft, she said, "It wasn't quite like that, Elliot."

"Really? Did I miss a few more flip-flops along the way?"

"I never hated you. Even when I thought you'd betrayed me, I never—I think . . . the opposite of love isn't hate, Elliot. It's indifference. These last few weeks, I may have been furious with you. I may have, in my darker, more petty, moments, wanted to make you suffer as deeply as I was suffering. But, see, never, ever, was I indifferent to you."

"Oh, well, that's a relief."

"I think, even when I believed you'd betrayed me, I think I still loved you, even then. Because, no matter how hard I tried, I couldn't not care about you, one way or another."

"You think that, do you? And when might you know for sure?"

Deb pleaded, "You think this is easy for me to say to you? Do you know how much soul-searching it took before I could even say it to myself? My husband has been dead for six months, and I'm standing here, telling another man that I love him. Do you know how that tears at me? Do you know how that makes me feel? About myself? It destroys me. It makes me look at my reflection in the mirror, and want to claw that horrible woman's eyes out. It would have been very, very easy for me to keep quiet. To not risk making myself so vulnerable to you. I mean, you could not just reject me, you could tell everybody what I said. Hell, you could post it on the hospital bulletin board: Dr. Deborah Brody is garbage. That would certainly do wonders for my reputation. But I thought you deserved to hear the truth. You made a sacrifice for me. You put yourself on the line for me. The least you deserved was my making an equal gesture in return."

It was a long answer, and an honest one. And yet, ultimately, an unsatisfactory one. She could see the verdict on Elliot's face. He'd needed her to say something specific. And Deb had failed.

She knew that she'd failed. But for the life of her, she didn't know how to pull herself out of the morass.

She pleaded, "I thought this was what you wanted from me. You wanted me to love you. New Year's Eve, you said—"

"I know what I said."

"Then why not—"

"I don't need to be thrown a bone."

Deb blinked. The image was so comical, all she could think of to say was, "Well, you're not a cocker spaniel, so I'd think not."

He didn't even smile. That's when Deb knew this wasn't going to be pretty.

Elliot reasoned, "You need me. In twenty years, you've gotten used to having me around. For instance, need an organic chemistry tutor?—"

"I happen to have gotten an *A* in organic chem."

"Call Elliot. Need an escort to a movie your husband refuses to see? Call Elliot."

"I—"

"Need an ally on the Budget Committee? Need a lunch partner? Need someone to keep you from getting bored between patients? Call Elliot. I'm a jack-of-all-trades. You need me."

"I never claimed that I didn't."

"And you'd do anything to keep me around, performing all of my little services, wouldn't you? You'd do anything. Even tell me you love me."

Deb inhaled so sharply, she practically whistled.

God, but had she been on target with that earlier call. This was most definitely not pretty.

"You think I'm lying to you about how I feel?"

"I think you're desperate."

"So, I—you're basically calling me a hooker."

He considered her question from all angles, finally conceding, "Using the traditional definition? Then, well, I guess so, yes."

"So, I'm a whore who sleeps with a man rather than lose him as a friend? Sounds a trifle backward, don't you think?"

"I never said you were a good hooker, Brody."

"What if you're wrong?"

"And you're a better hooker than I gave you credit for? Oh, well, even surgeons aren't infallible."

"What if you're wrong, and I'm not trying to manipulate you? What if I'm telling the truth?"

He sighed. It was a sigh that came not from Elliot's

throat, not from his lungs, or even from his diaphragm, but from his soul. It was the darkest, saddest sigh Deb had ever heard.

He said, "Frankly, Brody, I don't have the heart to find out."

"You mean you don't have the guts?"

"Heart, guts, kidney, spleen, some internal organ."

Deb cocked her head to one side, and, looking Elliot right in the eye, she said, "I'm going to change your mind."

For the first time since she'd come in, Elliot smiled. It was a grim, little thing, but it was there. "You're going to change my mind?" Elliot asked.

"Yes," she informed him.

"Nobody changes my mind, Brody, except me."

She shrugged. "We'll see."

"We will?"

"And here's a start."

Deb raised her left hand, and, with a smooth, positive stroke, pulled off both her wedding and her engagement ring.

She picked up Elliot's arm, and plunked both into the center of his palm. She curled his fingers shut, so that he was clutching the rings, and said, "You hold on to these for me. I'm not going to need them for a while."

And, before he had the chance to ask what she thought she was doing and what her dramatic gesture was supposed to mean, Deb swept out of his condo.

She had to get home.

To plan her offensive.

Chapter Sixteen

As with all good of-
fensives, Deb began by taking stock of her obstacles.
And she knew that her biggest obstacle to making
Elliot believe the sincerity of her feelings for him was
the fact that she'd so recently come to comprehend
those feelings herself.

The little buggers kind of snuck up on her. When
she drove to Elliot's condo the evening following his
inquiry, she'd wanted only to apologize and thank
him, not play a round of *True Confessions*. She hadn't
known she was going to confess her love for him, until
the words pricked her tongue. She knew only that, despite its rash spontaneity, the confession was one hundred percent authentic.

She was in love with Elliot.

Not just as a friend, but as a man.

She knew it was improper and too soon.

She knew what total strangers would think, and what they would imply, and how horribly unfair this was to Max, and how detrimental this could be to both her and Elliot's careers.

But for the first time in months, the sum total of all those negatives could not outweigh the reality that Deb was honestly and truly and positively in love with her best friend.

She first knew it for sure at the inquiry, when hearing it was Elliot, who, despite her dreadful behavior, had been the one to save Deb's future almost made her swallow her tongue.

She'd known that she loved him for sure, then. But she must have known it for not-so-sure, for weeks prior. Why else would Deb have let Elliot kiss her at Christmas, and at New Year's? And why else had she fought him so diligently, all the days in between?

And all those years that came before?

Just briefly, Deb forced herself to entertain Elliot's charge: that she was so reluctant to lose his company as a friend, she was willing to make any claim to keep him from leaving. Deb forced herself to entertain the charge, because that was the choice way to arm herself against it. And because, if it was true, she wanted to nip this monstrosity in the bud, before it hurt Elliot further.

She gave the issue some serious thought, used up two decks of cards and constructed a lovely Renaissance palace on her coffee table, before freely decreeing that there was no monstrosity to be nipped. Deb loved Elliot. The feeling was heartfelt and unfeigned and not even a fraction manipulative. Well, unless your definition of manipulative included plotting strategies to make a man admit he felt the same way.

On the other hand, Deb was convinced Elliot felt the same way. So, it wasn't really manipulation. It was more like . . . like . . . it was more like therapy. Therapy was good for you.

Oh, God. Deb was forty-one years old, and, courtesy of this caravan of thought, she was sounding not a day over fourteen. What was she planning to do, hang out at his locker and then pretend to bump into Elliot accidently?

Actually. That wasn't such a bad idea.

Deb knew where his locker was. . . .

Elliot stood in front of it the next morning, peeling off the brown sport jacket he'd come to work dressed in, and shrugging on his white lab coat, getting ready to conduct rounds. Deb walked in quietly, hands in the pockets of her own lab coat, and stopped just to the side of him, watching.

Elliot didn't even need to turn around to notice her coming. She'd planned it that way. This was a friendly salutation, after all, not an ambush.

Elliot nodded. "Good morning."

His voice was soft, respectful, and utterly noncommittal.

Deb smiled in return. Like a cowboy taming a wild horse, she took the fact that he didn't flare his nostrils at her as a sign to scoot a tentative step forward.

Elliot hung up his sport jacket, neatly, inside his locker, taking extra care to tuck the sleeves just right, then made a few swipes with his hand across the front and back, brushing off lint specks only he, apparently, could see.

Deb took her hands out of her pockets and stretched them out in front of her, palms up, as the first step to placating an enemy was demonstrating your lack of deadly weapons.

She said, "You know, in all the excitement yesterday, I forgot to ask: What happened with the inquiry?"

He closed the locker door and leaned against it when he turned around to face her, unafraid.

Deb had to give the man credit. Whatever flaws he might have had—and there were flaws, no matter how much she loved him, Deb was aware the man was not a god; for one thing, he was stubborn as hell—nevertheless, one thing you could say for Elliot was that he wasn't a coward. Elliot faced everything head-on.

He said, "Hung jury. Not enough votes to censure me, but not enough to totally let me off the hook, either. Wylie decided there should be further follow-up, another round of questions. It wasn't quite what Morelli had in mind, but he's appeased for now."

"That bastard is out to get you," Deb said.

"He has been, ever since he found out that, when it comes to playing the press, I'm the hardest department head in this hospital to smear. Everyone else he gets to call bloodsucking leeches only in it for the profit, and the general public tends to agree. Hell, everyone's had a bad experience with a urologist or a gynecologist, or even a plain old pediatrician. But, children's trauma surgeon? We've got halos around our heads even Morelli can't knock off. Try as he might, my cute-as-a-button accident victims carry as much PR cachet as his AIDS victims." Bitterness seized Elliot's voice until his soft timbre had turned to acid. He spat, "Do you know how sick it makes me, pitting patient against patient in this vulgar grovel for sympathy? They're all suffering, they all deserve treatment. I don't want to close Morelli's AIDS ward. I stayed up night after night, trying to stretch our deficient hospital budget so everybody got their fair share. Do you realize how many alternate proposals I submitted? Seven. All of them with a very bountiful allocation for the AIDS ward. But that's not good enough for Morelli. I may not want to close his department, but he certainly wants to close mine. And, since there is no way you are ever going to win public support for condemning an ER for children, the easiest option is to get public support for condemning the ER's chief."

"You think he's going to use the incident with Adrian Pharsi?"

"He'd be a fool not to. I suspect average parents would feel a touch squeamish about bringing their baby to Valley Emergency, if they believed Dr. Elliot intended to rip the youngster's chest open with his bare hands. What do you think?"

"He's going to the press with this?"

"He already has. Check this morning's *L.A. Times*."

"I'm sorry, Elliot."

He shrugged, sighed grimly, and stared up into space.

Softly, she asked, "What can I do to help?"

"Nothing." It wasn't a rejection or a dismissal as much as it was a statement of unadulterated fact.

"I can't accept that," Deb said. "I won't accept it."

"Some battles can't be won, Brody."

"But all battles can be fought."

"To the death?"

"If necessary."

"Then what have you won?"

"Honor."

He smiled faintly. "And what might honor be, Madame Quixote?"

"The knowledge that you did everything you

could, gave everything you had, and never allowed even a single opportunity to slip through your fingers."

"That's nice," Elliot said. "Except that you're still dead."

He had a point. But Deb wasn't about to give up that easily. "Honor isn't about how you died. It's about how you lived."

"Suffering? Taking needless risks? Banging your head against a wall that would never, ever break? If you know there's no chance of winning, why not take the easy road and coast?"

"Honor," Deb repeated.

"Medical school crap," Elliot countered.

"What?"

"What you're spouting now, it's that damn medical school crap they indoctrinated us with, while we were sleep-deprived. All that jingoism about fighting the good fight, even in the face of certain defeat. You know why they tried to make us believe that? Because, in the end, we are all fighting certain defeat. Every last one of our patients is going to die. Someday, somehow, probably with some doctor by their side. There's nothing you or I can do about it."

"Does that mean we should stop trying to save them?"

"If keeping them alive would generate more pain than joy."

"Who are we to make that judgment?"

"We are the perfect ones to make that judgment. Because we are not emotionally involved. We can take a step back, assess the situation from a purely intellectual bend, and we can decide. That might be the choice way. After all, when has a person under duress from fear or guilt—or grief—ever made a good decision?"

"I did," Deb said simply, frankly. "When, in every crisis I ever suffered in my life, I turned to you."

Elliot had not been expecting such a swift flip from the land of the abstract to one of more tangible examples. He took a beat. And then he said, "Thank you for your offer. But I don't need any assistance from you."

The way he enunciated the words, so clearly and crisply, and as decisively and finally as a lawyer reciting closing arguments, Deb fully expected the concluding phrase out of his mouth to be, "I don't need any assistance from you. *Thank you.*" But the last word to come from Elliot's mouth before he left the room was, "Please."

It was the closest Elliot had ever come to begging.

He'd never had reason to exercise that skill before. Now he did. And, like the song said, Elliot wasn't too proud to beg.

Because he was begging for his life.

Or, at least, this thing that kind of, sort of, but not exactly looked like his life. Lately, it seemed he was living in a mirror image of what he'd always thought was his life, one where left was right, and up was down, and tall was short, and Brody wanted him.

Not just as a friend.

It was everything he'd ever dreamed of.

Problem was, Elliot didn't believe her.

Oh, he believed that Deb believed in what she was saying. He believed she was sincere. She wasn't lying to him.

Deliberately.

He just didn't believe Deb knew what the word truly meant.

How could a woman who so recently had accused him of trying to destroy her suddenly turn around and claim she was in love with him? It was not organically correct.

Deb was not in love with him. Deb was grateful to him. She was grateful, and she felt guilty about what she'd said, and, in an attempt to make it up to him, she'd impulsively offered Elliot the one thing she thought he'd always wanted.

So, alright, so maybe it was what he'd always wanted.

But not like this. This wasn't love.

This was . . . a peace offering.

Love was what Elliot felt. Love was what Elliot had felt for twenty years. Love didn't just spark one day, like the flick of a cigarette lighter. Love was something concrete and implacable like the sky. Deb claimed she realized she loved Elliot the instant she found out about the cash he'd donated. That part, Elliot believed. The part about her only commencing to love him, then. Because if Deb had loved Elliot before, she never would have been capable of denouncing him the way she did. A woman who loved him, could never even have imagined him capable of such treachery.

So, even accepted with utmost generosity, this love that Deb now claimed to feel for him was, what? A good forty-eight hours old?

Now, there was something concrete and implacable. There was something sturdy enough to risk crushing your heart on.

Because that was what Brody was asking him to do.

She was asking Elliot to forgive how she'd hurt him recently, and to overlook all those other slights from the less recent, and not so recent past, which she obviously judged not even significant enough to be mentioned, and to take a chance on being hurt again.

Not just hurt. Demolished. Devastated. Annihilated.

Was there a fool alive to whom this sounded like a good deal?

Elliot was supposed to drop everything to plunge into the arms of a woman who'd already proven her fickleness, as well as her gift for inflicting heartbreak, all because, forty-eight hours earlier, she'd come to the out-of-the-blue conclusion that she loved him?

And this was all even before he factored in the fact that Deb arrived at this conclusion at a moment in her life when what she'd assumed she knew for a fact—Elliot's treachery—was revealed as a falsehood. In the space of a few minutes, Deb's entire world turned upside down. Her world had a tendency to do that. And so, out of desperation and instinct and habit, she'd flailed about and grabbed on to the one solid she could always count on.

Elliot. Good old Elliot. Good old, dependable Elliot.

Good old, dependable Elliot was getting a trifle tired playing the part of a black rubber inner tube.

It was one thing for him to act as Deb's rock when she was his best friend, his soul mate in a world where people took better care of the bottoms of their shoes than the feelings of others. He'd been happy to be there for Brody, then. Happy to be there for all of it. Matching Day, and taking the Boards, and relocating to L.A. and becoming head of her department, and staying up all night building houses of cards, and Max's dying. Elliot had been happy to support her then, because, then, he'd thought he knew the woman in front of him. And he thought that she knew him.

She never knew him.

That was the tragedy.

He'd never let her know him.

So, now, how could she claim to love him? How could anybody love someone they didn't really know?

It was a self-feeding circle that returned to the same spot every single time.

Deb was mistaken. She was not in love with him.

Time would pass, and she would realize this sensation for what it genuinely was: a moment of panic, a moment of guilt, a moment of self-delusion. But not love. If it was love, it would have shown itself a long time ago.

Deb would realize the truth inevitably. She was far, far from a stupid woman. And Elliot was even further from a stupid man. He had no intention of buying into Brody's fantasy, only to have his heart decimated so mortally for a second time, no doctor could save him. Soon—very, very soon—Deb would understand where he was coming from. Unfortunately, however, Deb was currently taking her sweet time coming to this obviously inevitable realization.

As one day nudged another into the middle of March, Elliot found himself hard pressed to decide who was pouring more anxiety into his life—Morelli and his campaign to discredit Elliot, or Brody's resolve to save him from it.

Morelli got in the first shot. He made certain the *L.A. Times* knew the result—or lack thereof—of Elliot's inquiry, managing to make "inconclusive" sound as damning as a revoked license. Deb countered by ensuring that, bright and early the next morning, the *L.A. Times* received a hand-delivered declaration of support for Dr. Elliot, signed by the parents of three hundred and fifty children he'd treated over the years. When, at a follow-up inquiry, Morelli graphically described Elliot's "butchery" of Adrian Pharsi, repeating the phrase "oceans of blood" so many times, even Dr. Wylie suggested he lose the damn hyperbole, Brody exhibited Nadia Pharsi—whose polished, low-key statement managed to make Morelli sound like a foam-at-the-mouth lunatic in comparison.

After a day of deliberation, the second inquiry

concluded that Elliot's actions had been neither reckless nor damaging. The *L.A. Times*, however, somehow failed to publicize the development. Until Deb made sure they did.

She told Elliot, "Can't have people thinking negatively about the future Surgeon General, now, can we?"

He grinned, and, for the second time that minute, scrutinized with wonder the morning newspaper Deb had so proudly opened across his desk. "How'd you do this, Brody?"

"An old friend of Max's is on staff there. I just called and laid on the charm."

"You are good at that."

"It's about time you noticed."

Why was she doing this to him?

Well, alright, so that was a senseless question. Elliot knew exactly why she was doing this to him. Brody had been overly clear about her reasons for doing this to him. She had, in all fairness, even warned him to expect it.

But then, she went about it all in a most unexpected manner.

Without sounding sickeningly arrogant—he liked to save that for boasting over his professional exploits—Elliot felt he could freely say that, having been an arguably eligible bachelor for over twenty-eight years—he started playing the field like he meant it at fifteen—this was not the first time a woman had announced her intention to "land him," and then proceeded to fire every weapon in her arsenal to accomplish just that. Elliot had ample experience being pursued. It had started with giggling gum-chewers hanging around his locker in high school, doing little beyond giggling and chewing gum. It continued to college, where tipsy sorority girls used the half-keg of beer they'd just inhaled as an excuse to appear lost as they somehow—accidently, of course—found themselves under the covers of Elliot's bed, waiting for him.

In twenty-eight years, Elliot had been pursued by professional women and by blue-collar women, by colleagues and by the mothers of his patients, by women who threw themselves at him and by women who played hard to get—aggressively. He'd been pursued by seductive women and short women, thin women and blond women, Black women and jock women. All in all, it was an awfully good thing Elliot really liked women. In all their varieties.

But the only thing Elliot had never yet been was pursued by a woman as . . . classily . . . as he was now, by Brody.

He had to hand it to her. What dozens of women over the years had done casually or calculatedly, tempestuously or academically, Deborah Brody did with style.

She didn't throw herself at him, and neither did she play hard to get. Deb, simply, was.

She was there for Elliot, not only when he knew he needed her, but also when he didn't. Brody was his quiet champion behind the scenes, going to bat for him with Wylie and the *L.A. Times,* certain that, when the time was right, Elliot would learn of her endeavors, and equally content if he never found out. She declined to thrust her work in his face, or come up, tail wagging, like a puppy asking to be petted. Brody didn't demand praise or thank-yous, though she accepted both graciously and with a smile so radiant, Elliot felt the heat melting right through him, like laser through bone.

In the weeks during which they wrestled with Morelli, he found himself thanking Brody quite a bit. Which wasn't easy.

Not the actual "thank you" portion. Elliot had always been a believer in giving credit where and when it was due. He was one of the few surgeons known for taking time after any procedure to thank his team. It wasn't hard for him to say, "Thank you."

It was hard for him, when Deb was the recipient, to keep from doing more. Or, at least, wanting to.

Every time he heard about another rabbit she'd yanked out of a hat for him, like sending Adrian Pharsi's test results to the top three cardiac surgeons in the world and asking them how they would have handled the predicament, or getting Jeff Greenwood's family—who finally got around to returning a phone call—to make a very public donation to the Pediatric Emergency Room in implicit support of Elliot—every time he heard about another miracle Brody pulled off for him, Elliot wanted to do nothing less than wrap her in his arms and bury his face in the crook of her neck so she wouldn't see how close her actions came to moving him to tears.

That, Elliot understood, would not be a good thing.

He understood he had to fight the temptations.

He just wished Brody understood how hard that was.

Although, considering she did nothing to prevent the instinct from bubbling up in him on a habitual basis, Elliot suspected that she, most likely, already did.

He tried to keep things casual. Light. Friendly.

And unmistakably nonromantic.

When Deb brought him the *L.A. Times* reporting his vindication, Elliot managed to swallow his true emotions and instincts in favor of casually asking, "How in the world did you ever learn to be such a great friend, Brody?"

He put special emphasis on the second-to-last word.

Deb looked him up and down. She looked at the newspaper, and brushed her fingertip ever so gently against the edge. She looked back up at Elliot. Softly, she told him, "From you."

This was never going to be over.

Elliot realized the dismal truth of his frustrated statement when, gathering he'd lost the battle to declare Elliot a danger to society, Morelli reverted to type and proceeded to, while the press and public still gave even a fraction of a damn about James Elliot, once again paint him as a homophobe for fighting to prevent Morelli's AIDS unit from getting all the funds it annually demanded.

The accusation pissed Elliot off on a personal level, because, as Brody pointed out, the future Surgeon General of America did not need that kind of negative publicity. But what really pissed him off was when a protesting throng of ACT-UPers blocked the entry to his emergency room, thus delaying an ambulance carrying a little girl hit by a car.

That sort of nonsense, Elliot refused to stand for.

He treated the little girl, relieved that the majority of her injuries were superficial, just cuts, bumps, and bruises, and that Deb confirmed there was no brain damage. Elliot signed the papers to get her admitted to pediatrics. Then he went out to confront the protesters.

Which, in retrospect, was a mistake.

As Elliot told the policeman taking down his statement later, he didn't have too clear a chronology of what went down. Elliot stepped out to have a chat with the protesters, notifying them that they could hate him all they liked, but they had no right to block an entrance to the hospital. A bald guy with a megaphone told him they had the right to do anything they damn well felt like, and, to prove his point, when they heard the siren of another ambulance in the distance, he stepped in front of the emergency-room door, hands planted on his hips, lips curled into a sneer.

So Elliot hit him.

He would have liked to say he didn't hit him hard, but the fact was, he did. He hit him very hard.

And the fellow went down, also hard—molars rattling, nose bleeding, knuckles scraped from where his beloved megaphone rammed his hand into the gravel sidewalk.

Elliot helped the guy get up. After he examined the patient who'd come in on the ambulance and decreed him stabilized, Elliot even carefully bandaged the ACT-UPer's hand, and gave him an ice pack for his swollen nose.

But he did not, at any time, suggest that he was sorry.

The hospital, however, was very sorry. The hospital issued a formal apology to the victim, to ACT UP, and to the gay community, promising that they would take into consideration whether a doctor with Elliot's "attitude" should be allowed to practice on staff.

Politely, Elliot asked Dr. Wylie when exactly concern for his patients' speedy treatment became an unacceptable "attitude" for a physician at Valley Hospital.

Dr. Wylie told him to stuff it.

The publicity from the incident had been terrible, with ACT UP encouraging not only the gay community but everyone in Los Angeles to boycott the hospital.

For the first time in his life, Elliot actually believed that not only his dreams for a political future, but his entire career, had been permanently derailed. For the first time in his life, he actually spent one night sitting in his condo in a funk, listening to the phone ring, and the machine pick up.

Deb called. Twice. She said, "If you want to talk . . ."

He didn't.

Especially not to her.

Because Elliot knew, the state he was in, if he allowed Deb to say so much as one kind word to him, he would be lost for good.

And then, Deb saved him.

When news and television crews came to report on the ACT UP boycott of Valley Hospital, they were met not by a public relations flunky, not by an apologetic Dr. Elliot, but by Luke Hughes, a man who, with minimum melodrama, and consummate dignity, calmly told the tale of a Thanksgiving accident, an HIV-positive victim, and the one doctor who didn't hesitate to treat him.

Even Morelli had to cry "uncle," after that one.

But, nevertheless, this had to stop. Deb had to stop. Elliot couldn't take it anymore.

He had to tell her the truth.

He called her at home. A telephone meeting was much easier to deal with than face-to-face. She sounded so thrilled to hear from him, Elliot almost lost his resolve. But, then, he remembered.

And he knew what he had to do.

He said, "Thank you for finding Luke. It's funny, actually, but I'd forgotten all about that."

"We bumped into him. At the karaoke place. You remember?"

He remembered. Elliot remembered everything about that night. Including all the words to "That's What Friends Are For."

He told her, "You've got to stop this, Brody. You've got to stop acting like you and I had some spat, and you're trying to make it up to me by being extra nice."

She tried to sound blithe, but Elliot heard the tightness in Deb's tone. "You know a better way? I'm glad to take direction."

"I'm not mad at you," he said.

"Well, you sure could have fooled me."

"Just listen to me for a sec, Brody, alright?" Elliot sighed. "I am not mad at you. I wish I were. Because mad . . . mad burns hot and bright, and then mad goes away. Mad is easy to fix. But I'm not mad. I'm hurt. And hurt is forever."

A sharp intake of breath on the other end, like someone stuck Deb with a needle. No, not someone. Elliot. Elliot had hurt her. And, unfortunately, he wasn't done yet.

To save himself, he had to drive that needle in even deeper.

He said, "You broke my heart. You broke it in places I didn't even know it had nerves. I don't know how I managed to put it back together. Maybe I've got a little Humpty Dumpty in me. But in my professional opinion, that part simply can't take another blow. It wouldn't survive it."

"Elliot, I swear, I will never, ever jump to conclu—"

"It doesn't matter. The mortal damage has already been done. The fact that you could, even for a minute, think me capable of deliberately trying to hurt you, that says that you never really knew me. And, if you don't know me, you can't love me."

"But, I do. Elliot, please, let me—"

"You think you do. But, obviously, the man you think you love can't be me. You don't know me."

"Then give me the chance to know you."

"I can't do that. I have to protect myself."

"From me?"

"From the one person who can exterminate me with just a wrong look, or a wrong word."

"Hurting you is the last thing I want to do."

"You're doing it every day. Every day that you labor so hard to earn my forgiveness, you're hurting me. It kills me, having to push you away. Every time I do it, a portion of my soul dies."

"So, stop pushing me away."

"I have to."

"Elliot." Her voice had sunk to a murmur, and she clutched the receiver so tightly, Elliot heard the scrape of her fingernails on the plastic. "I love you."

He would have died to hear those words once. Now, Elliot died hearing them. "I love you, too," he whispered. And then, he said, "Good-bye, Brody."

She had no one to blame but herself.

Much as Deb would have liked to blame Elliot for the despair currently coursing through her body, she knew that the fault nestled securely in her lap. She'd hurt him. She'd made it so that Elliot couldn't trust her. She'd put him into this state of fear. And she couldn't blame him for being afraid. Only a masochist would open his heart for a second time to someone who'd so wickedly stomped it earlier. Elliot was no masochist.

Deb suspected that if she really put her mind to it, she could eventually wear him down. If she just kept on doing what she was doing, Elliot was destined to break. He knew that as well as she did. That's why he wanted Deb to stay away. Not because he would never fall victim for her again, but because Elliot knew just how close he teetered to already doing it.

Another woman might have judged his weakened state a victory, and gotten down to counting her unhatched chickens. But Deborah Brody was not just any woman. Deb loved Elliot. More importantly, she cared for him. And she owed him. Far too much to continue on torturing him in such a manner.

The man she loved had asked her to stop making him love her.

She would do her best to grant his final wish.

Deb thought, *Make note to self: The next time you decide to be so goddamn magnanimous, try not to do it during so tough a week.*

A week to the day after she hung up the phone, Elliot's "Good-bye, Brody" ringing in her ears and squeezing her heart, was Max's birthday. She had not been looking forward to it.

Somehow, his not being around on this one particular day felt worse than his not being around on Christmas, or New Year's Eve, or even Valentine's Day. Max being gone on his birthday underlined his passing with a permanent, black laundry-marker. He would have been turning forty-five. Now, he would never be forty-five.

That, Dr. Brody, was death in a nutshell.

On all the previous birthdays they'd spent together, Deb used to tease Max about being *so* much older than her. He would counter by noting what a lucky break she'd scored: By the time he died and left her a widow, she'd still have enough life left in her to kick up her geriatric heels on the cruise-ship and shuffleboard circuit. Once, they both found the image of Deb unleashing her competitive instincts on poor, defenseless, fellow senior citizens very funny.

Oddly enough, Deb did not find it very funny now.

She was all alone.

She never, ever expected to be all alone. And so she never prepared for the possibility.

Because—Deb didn't tell Max this—deep in her heart, as she giggled over the image of herself wearing orthopedic shoes and a hearing aid, stalking the shuffleboard circuit, she expected Elliot to be right there with her.

Come to think of it, Deb never actually informed Elliot of her plans for antiquity, either. It hadn't occurred to her to ask him how he might feel about a life of floating all-you-can-eat buffets. She'd simply assumed he would want what she wanted. She'd assumed he would follow her to the ends of the earth, no questions asked.

God, but she was a bitch.

No wonder Elliot was fed up with her. No wonder he wanted her to keep her distance and stop hurting him.

Now that Deb could finally gauge herself clearly, the question was no longer why had Elliot turned away from her, but why it took him so long to get around to it.

Heck, maybe she was wrong. Maybe he was more of a masochist than Deb had originally thought. After all, who was she to judge character? She couldn't even clearly assess the face that stared back at her every morning from the mirror.

How in the world had she ever thought herself a nice person?

She knew how. She did it not by believing the reflection in the mirror, but by believing the reflection in Elliot's eyes.

In Elliot's eyes, Deb was wonderful.

She'd wanted to believe it. And so she made herself believe it. Sort of a "Mirror, mirror, on the wall" thing. Problem was, she forgot to ask the mirror how he felt about the whole thing.

Well, at least it was a correctable oversight.

The more she thought about it, the more reasons Deb came up with to validate her choice to leave Elliot alone. To let him go.

For his sake.

After twenty years, it was about time she did something for his sake. Even if it meant her own life finally hit the bottom of Hell with a thump so noisy, it practically knocked Deb over.

The morning of what would have been Max's birthday, Deb spent two hours getting ready to go to the cemetery. Not because it was that hard to color-coordinate an all-black ensemble, but because she was giving new meaning to the word *stalling.*

She didn't want to go.

No, that wasn't true. She just didn't want to go alone.

There was nothing like standing in an open field: green lawn, gray headstones, and silence stretching out as far as any sense could see, hear, smell, touch, or taste, to drive home the point that yes, Dr. Brody, you are totally alone in the world.

Heck, why would she be stalling to get to that?

The doorbell rang.

She shuffled down the stairs, and opened the door, expecting a pesky salesman.

What she got, however, was Elliot.

Chapter Seventeen

E

ven as he was bidding Brody "good-bye" over the phone, Elliot knew this was all far from over.

Saying good-bye was the easy part. Any man with a tongue and vocal chords could pull that simple trick off without undue strain. Meaning good-bye, on the other hand, well, that was something else entirely.

Problem was, Elliot suspected he'd been Don Quixote in another life. A tricky escapade, seeing as how ol' Don was fictional. So, maybe he hadn't been Don Quixote. Maybe he'd been Galahad, or St. Francis, or, hell, even the Lone Ranger.

All Elliot knew for sure was, in his past life, he had to have been one of those noble, heroic, valiant morons.

How else to explain his compulsion—no, it was more than a compulsion, it was a biological drive—to rescue anyone and anything that crossed his path?

He would have thought becoming a doctor might have fulfilled that urge quite adequately.

Nope. No such luck there. Sure, he had needy damsels in distress tumbling out of his ears. Unfortunately, a majority of those damsels were under the age of eighteen. And, in this life, Elliot apparently needed more grown-up damsels to satisfy him.

Don Quixote enjoyed charging windmills with only a fruit bowl on his head for a helmet. Elliot didn't even have that fruit bowl. When he rang Deb's doorbell, he wore no armor at all.

She had to have been surprised when she first saw him through the peephole. But by the time Deb actually opened her door and surveyed him on her stoop, her features had composed into reserved civility. On the other hand, maybe Elliot was slicing himself too much credit. Considering everything else she had to juggle today, Elliot was probably the least and last of her concerns.

She was dressed all in black. Skirt, blouse, blazer, shoes. The single splash of color came from an ivory brooch pinned to her lapel, and matching earrings. She wore no other jewelry.

Elliot reached into his pocket, and wordlessly produced her engagement and wedding rings. Deb's sincere pleasure, her smile, spiced up her dour outfit more than any treasure chest of gems ever could.

She allowed Elliot to place the rings in the palm of her right hand, nudging both with her thumb to where she could grip them with her fingers. Flipping over her left hand, her fingers splayed and headed for the bands. She stopped short when her left fingernail clicked against the sparkling gold. She hesitated. She looked up at Elliot, and, eyes on him, deftly picked up the rings with her left fingers. She then slipped the pair onto the fourth finger of her . . . right hand. The widow's hand.

Finished, Deb held it in front of her, checking how both rings liked it on their new home. She wiggled her fingers, adjusting the fit. Then, satisfied, or, at least, resigned, she cocked her head to one side, and sighed.

Neither of them had yet said a word, until Deb asked, "Why?"

He said, "I thought you might need a little company, today."

"What I need, today, is a little lobotomy."

"You're in luck. I'm qualified to do those, too."

She cocked her head to one side. "I am a lucky girl, then."

Elliot asked, "Max's family coming?"

That had been his key worry. If the Brodys were driving down from the Bay Area to accompany Deb on this birthday pilgrimage to Max's grave, Elliot's presence would only make matters more anxious for Deb. And, seeing as how he was in full, raging-hero mode, that was the last thing Elliot wanted.

Deb shook her head. "This is private. Between him and me. We always celebrated his birthday, just the two of us. Would you believe it was the one day I always remembered to ask off from work, in advance?"

He hadn't known that. Deb had never mentioned it. Elliot wondered why. And then, he understood. Because it was something just between her and Max, and, just like there were things about her life at the hospital and Elliot that Max never knew about, so were there things about her life with Max that Elliot wasn't privy to. The realization made Elliot smile on the inside.

Because that was exactly how it should have been.

"Do you want me to leave, then?" Elliot half-pivoted toward his Lexus, hoping to indicate that such a request would be totally alright by him. He wouldn't get his feelings hurt.

But Deb said, "Don't you dare."

She drove them both to the cemetery. She didn't say very much. Which, under the circumstances, was good. And also, bad.

Elliot couldn't get over how ravishing she looked. Now that Brody's hair was short, she wore it down more often. It framed her face, grazing and caressing it, drawing Elliot's attention to every contour. The shorter hairstyle made her eyes look bigger, and drew out the brown in her hazel pupils. Before, Deb's eyes glistened of melted caramel, deep, rich, and sweet, with just a sprig of mint for flavor. Now, Elliot spied a pinwheel of shades. Ripened chestnut, sunshine bronze, burnished mahogany, and, even, in a certain light, a pinch of spicy ginger.

Quite an intoxicating libation, to be sure.

A shame Elliot had already committed to abstinence. He asked, "How have you been, Brody?"

"Terrible." No self-pity or plea for sympathy in the answer, just heartbreaking truth.

"I'm sorry."

"I know." Also, pure truth. "I miss you, Elliot."

It deserved a truth in return. He said, "I think I would be happier if you could hate me."

Brody pulled her car into the parking lot beside the cemetery. She turned off her ignition. She said, "Me, too."

Deb had a vague idea of exactly where Max was buried. She led Elliot in through the intricately coiled gates and down a series of paths—brows furrowed, lower lip getting a healthy chewing, head swiveling uncertainly every few feet.

She said, "It's this way . . . I think."

Trying to be helpful, and, yes, fine, perk up the mood, Elliot asked, "What does it look like?"

"Green lawn. Gray slab. Flowers."

"Shouldn't be too hard to find, then."

Deb smiled weakly.

Elliot felt like he'd discovered a cure for the common cold.

They walked another five minutes past unending waves of green lawns, gray slabs, and flowers in various stages of the life cycle. Everything smelled freshly mowed, yet there wasn't a working soul in sight.

"Here it is," Deb said.

Max's grave looked the same as all the others. His tombstone was a no-nonsense, gray rectangle, uncluttered by the flounces and abstract art of some other stones. MAXWELL DENNIS BRODY 1955–2000. "THANK YOU FOR HAVING BEEN."

Elliot read the epitaph out loud. He told Deb, "That's nice. The wording, I mean. I really like it."

She shrugged. "Best I could do."

Elliot said, "You always did the best you could for him."

She turned her head. She looked at Elliot for a beat, tongue pressed against her lips, eyes all but bulging from the pressure of a thought dying to express itself. She swallowed hard, and made it disappear. Deb turned back to the grave, getting down on her knees to pluck up the dying flowers left there during a previous visit. Indifferently wiping both soiled hands on her hundred-dollar skirt, she stood up to walk the few feet toward the nearest garbage can and throw them away, before laying down the crisp new arrangement she'd brought.

Elliot watched her go, noting how straight Deb kept her back, and understanding how hard she had to be straining to keep everything together. He'd already noted how her wearing no makeup had made Deb appear even paler than usual. He wanted so desperately to help her. But he could think of nothing more practical to offer than the ever-popular "Hey, look over there" distraction routine.

"Brody?"

"What?" She got back down on her knees, arranging the fresh flowers she'd brought from home at the base of the grave, shifting stem over stem as if in search of that perfect composition to make everything alright again.

"Can I ask you something?"

She tried putting the red roses on top, changed her mind, and shifted them to the side. "Hm."

It wasn't a yes. But, then again, it wasn't a no.

Elliot asked, "What did Max think of me? I mean, I knew him for over twenty years. And I don't think I ever really had a clear idea of what he thought of me."

"Max liked you." The bulk of her concentration was focused on a fistful of white lilies. Their yellow powder specked the sleeves of her black jacket, like bee pollen.

"How do you know that?"

"Didn't you get those Valentines he sent every year?"

The sarcasm was a symphony to Elliot's ears. As long as Brody was being a wiseass, this woman could be saved.

"Very funny," he said.

Deb sat back on her heels, knees nudging the dirt-edge of the grave, and contemplated the bouquet's composition from a visitor's distance. She cocked her head, and, raising one hand to shield her eyes from the sun, peered up at Elliot. Slowly, she offered, "Max respected you. And he was grateful to you. For being such a good friend to me. I know this. He told me this."

Elliot had initially posed the question only in an attempt to distract her. He'd never expected to be so affected by the answer. Max Brody respected him? Max was grateful to him? It was a lot to process. Frankly, Elliot would have settled for "Max tolerated you." To be honest, he'd been braced for "I had to regularly stop Max from putting out a contract on your life."

Deb asked, "How about you? In twenty years, I never heard you mention how you felt about Max."

"Guess he never got those Valentines *I* sent, either."

To her credit, Deb managed to muster up a fragile smile. She fingered a rose petal, the crushed-out red juice staining her skin. Softly she asked, "What did you think of my husband, Elliot?"

"I liked him." It was as perfunctory an initial reply as hers had been. And Deb knew it.

"Did you?" she asked.

"Yes." He nodded once. Then, when the truth of his statement—and the reason for it—settled inside Elliot's cerebellum, he nodded again, surprised, but newly sincere. And brave. The kind of brave that made you stupid. Elliot said, "I liked Max. He was decent. The most decent man I ever knew. And he was great to you. He made you happy. I could see it. So, how could I not like a man who made the woman I loved happy?"

It was only the second time he'd ever uttered that word out loud. The first time was on the phone with Deb, the night he'd told her good-bye—he thought—for good.

That night, the admission had been reluctant, made

from sheer weariness and exhaustion, and a desire to just put an end to this thing. That night, the admission had been a surrender, and a plea.

Now, it was simply a statement of fact.

One that hadn't been wrung out of him. One offered honestly, and of his free will.

It was, no more and no less, an inescapable truth.

And, because of that, he felt like it was the first time he'd every really said it.

Yup. This was exactly the kind of brave that made you stupid.

A month ago, Elliot would've predicted his slip of the tongue to send Brody scurrying. He would've expected her to act shocked, or flustered, or to pretend she hadn't heard a word. Then, a week ago, he supposed she would have been so thrilled to hear the words, she might have grinned, triumphantly, ear to ear, and kissed him, as happy about his declaration as she was about the fact that she'd finally made him admit it.

But, these days, Brody was too weary for such carrying on.

She heard Elliot's words. He could see the moment they struck her, because she did sway just a touch to the side, as if shaken by a stiff wind. Yet, overall, Deb remained impeccably composed. She didn't even drop the flower she'd been stroking. She laid it down, gently, in front of Max's headstone, smoothing down the petals with her fingers, and tucking the stem in with the rest of the flora, so that it wouldn't fly away.

She said, "This is not the proper place to discuss this."

"I couldn't agree more," Elliot said.

However, on the trip home, she clarified, "You were in love with me? While Max was still alive? Why didn't you tell me?"

"I did tell you," he reminded softly. "The night I asked you if you thought we might ever have a future together."

"No." Deb shook her head, utterly convinced of her position and damned if he was going to convince her otherwise. "You didn't tell me everything. You let me think your feelings for me appeared out of the blue the night after we first made love."

"You drew that conclusion yourself."

"You didn't correct me."

"What would have been the point?"

Deb repeated, "Why didn't you tell me?"

"Tell you what? That I loved you since the moment I saw you?"

"Because that would have been a lie," she pointed out. "The first moment you saw me, you thought I was an idiot."

"I was being poetic."

"Let's try honest, for a change."

"I never lied to you," Elliot insisted. "In twenty years, I have never lied to you."

"Oh, please. Even our tortured legal system recognizes omissions as lies."

Elliot shrugged. He said, "I've loved you for twenty years."

"Then why didn't you tell me?"

"Because." He had his answer prepared. He'd had twenty years to think about it, after all. "I would have lost you."

"You wouldn't have."

"I would. Think about it, Brody. If I'd told you how I felt twenty years ago, or five years ago, or even one damned year ago, what would have happened? The exact same thing that happened after we slept together last September. Only much worse. You think you felt guilty, then? How would you have felt if Max was still alive? If Max were still alive, how would you have felt about continuing to run into me at the hospital every day? How would you have felt about my coming by the house—and I would have had to keep coming by, or else Max would have wanted to know what was wrong, and you would have had to lie to him, and I know how that would have killed you. Do you see the can of worms my telling the truth would have opened? It wouldn't have done any good, only harm. The moment I confessed, our friendship would have been effectively over. And I didn't want to risk that. After all, as long as we were friends, I still had some part of you."

"And now?" Deb challenged. "After all the things we've said and done wrong this past month, now, what have we got?"

Elliot shrugged. "Just call us the poster-children for 'Damned if you do, and damned if you don't.' "

"Oh, hell," Deb said. "Why is irony entertaining only in an O. Henry short story?"

"Because, when he's poetic, it actually works."

"You know, sometimes in the middle of a long shift, I'll sneak into the lounge and watch whatever soap opera is on TV. I've watched a lot of different soaps over the years. And they're always having discussions like this. Only they never sound like this."

"Melodrama works better when O. Henry does it, too."

"I feel like we should be much more dramatic. Don't you feel like there should be more teeth-gnashing, or something? We're too polite. Too civilized."

"Okay." Elliot quoted her earlier edict, "I can get down and dirty, if you like." He challenged, "How about now you be honest, for a change."

No organ music swelled up to punctuate his declaration, and no camera pulled in for a close-up. But Elliot got his point across, just the same. "I may have lied to you for twenty years, but I'm sorry, Dr. Brody, no one is that fabulous an actor. You want me to believe that, for two decades, you didn't suspect a thing?"

"About you?"

"About us."

"I wouldn't allow myself to suspect anything." Deb bit her lip, focusing on the road as she attempted to arrange the thoughts jumbled in her head into some kind of coherent narrative he could understand.

Finally, she justified, "You want to know why I presumed your feelings for me started the night following Max's funeral? Because that made it okay. As long as I told myself that your feelings for me, and *my* feelings for *you,* began after we made love that night, then, I could continue to live with myself. If I, even for a day or an hour, or a moment, let myself recognize how long-standing your feelings for me truly were, then, well, I would have to admit that I felt the same way. Do you know how much you scared me, Elliot? The day I married Max, I was twenty-one years old, and certain that there was no other man in the world more perfect for me, save the one standing by my side at the altar. I met Max when I was eighteen. I was a virgin. I'd never even had a serious boyfriend before him. My friends and my mother told me I should live a little more, see what else was out there. But I was quite an arrogant little thing. Precocious, you remember. I was sure I didn't have to listen to them. I knew what I wanted. I knew Max was it. And then I met you. You made all my arrogance crumble away. Because, all of a sudden, I wasn't so sure anymore. Oh, I still loved Max. Max was a wonderful man, I still love him now, and, for the kind of life I wanted to live, and the kind of life he wanted to live, we were perfect for each other—probably more perfect than you and I would have been, back then. We were too much the same, after all. We wanted too much of the same things. But, I wasn't sure anymore. After I met you, I was never sure of anything, again."

Elliot didn't know what to say. The "I'm sorry" that slipped out of him, instinctively, felt terribly inadequate.

"You did nothing wrong."

"I could have gone easier on the dimples."

"Well, yes, that would have helped."

They exchanged smiles.

Deb said, "I was too stubborn. I couldn't admit that here I was, a married woman for a whole three weeks, and I was attracted to someone else. And so I ended up shortchanging you both."

"Sounds like you shortchanged yourself, too, Brody."

"But it was my fault. I'm the villain. If I'd only made up my mind; but, I was too selfish. I wanted it all. I couldn't bear giving up Max, so I end up hurting you. And I couldn't bear giving you up, so I hurt him. Then, after he died, I felt so guilty—"

"I understand."

"I was upset that night, yes. I was devastated. I felt alone and lost and so guilty that I couldn't save him. I needed comfort. Afterward, I told myself that was the sole reason I turned to you like that. But what if it wasn't? What if I was only using Max's death as an excuse to do something I'd wanted to do for twenty years? What kind of a monster does that make me?"

"What if I was only using Max's death as an excuse to do something I'd wanted, for twenty years, too? What does that make me?"

"It's not the same," Deb said calmly. Despite the

ascent of their conversation, she had yet to shed a tear. Her composure was almost eerie. "He wasn't your husband."

"No," Elliot agreed. "But I think I'm only just now starting to realize that he was my friend."

"He *was* your friend. He tried very hard to be," Deb agreed. "But, Elliot, it's still not the same."

"I know."

"I thought, maybe, I could make up for the way I wronged Max while he was still alive, by, after he died—"

"Being as pure as Caesar's wife?"

"More like Mother Teresa, Elizabeth the First, and the Virgin Mary rolled into one."

"Tall order."

"And I guess I blew that, pretty quick, too."

"Our one night was a slipup, Brody."

"Maybe. Maybe it was. And maybe the . . . extreme ways we both reacted afterward, maybe that was a mistake, too."

"You think?" Elliot raised an eyebrow, his lips twitching on one side, a dimple starting to form in his cheek.

"But, Elliot, see, right now, admitting that I loved you, that *wasn't* a mistake. For the first time in a long while, I'm sure of something, again."

Chapter Eighteen

Deb told Elliot, "It may have taken me twenty years to admit it just to my-self, but, once I told you I loved you, I knew it was the truest thing I'd ever said."

He stared out the window, tapping the glass with his fingers to the rhythm of "We Will Rock You," and politely inquired, "So, it's bye-bye Mother Teresa, Elizabeth the First, and Virgin Mary?"

"It wasn't easy, Elliot."

One look at Deb's face, and he wanted to kick himself for the flippancy. "I know." Elliot swallowed hard. "I'm sorry."

"I still think about Max. I think about him more now than I did when he was alive. Isn't it awful how I took him for granted? I got so used to him just being there, I didn't realize how big of a hole he'd leave behind. I didn't realize that, between the space he took up in my life, and the space you took up in my life, there really wasn't much of a life left."

"Oh, come on, Brody." Finally, an issue he could argue fair and square. "That's not true. You have your work."

"Work is not a life, Elliot. That's a lesson they forgot to teach us in medical school."

"Bullshit." Elliot snapped, "You save lives, Brody. What you do is as important and, arguably, more meaningful than any prosaic, picket-fence existence. I don't know if you've been watching too many detergent commercials, or what, but damn anyone who makes you feel guilty for finding your work fulfilling."

Deb pulled into her driveway, and climbed out of her car. As she closed the door on her side, she noted, "You know, it's funny. You're still defending me. Even to myself."

Elliot shrugged. "Old habits die hard."

"How about old feelings?"

The woman did know how to go straight for the jugular.

What did she want Elliot to say? Did she want him to say, no, old feelings actually died easily. For instance, since the day he hung up the phone on Deb, he hadn't thought of her once. He hadn't spent the last month imagining he heard her voice outside his door, or startling every time the phone rang, hoping and dreading that it would be her on the other end.

Or, did Brody want him to say yes? *Yes, old feelings do die hard. Yes, I'm still in such agony from loving you and losing you that I know I can never risk my heart in such a manner, again. That's why I can never be with you. And that's why I'm standing here, dying, wishing I were anywhere else, yet, unable to leave.*

Stuck between telling a patient that he either had six months or half a year left to live, Elliot said nothing. He shut his car door and followed Deb inside her house.

And, unable to respond to her question, he parried with one of his own. He asked, "What made you change your mind?"

She turned on the hallway light, and without pivoting to face him, requested clarification: "About?"

"Me."

Deb tossed her purse into the closet, and slipped out of her blazer. The blouse underneath was black, long-sleeved, and high-necked. And practically translucent. When she moved, shafts of ivory skin and curves winked at him. He imagined he could see her skin drinking in the fresh air, breathing with relief at the tough day's task finally being done and out of the way.

Elliot kept his sport coat on. No sense even pretending to be comfortable. Or, like Deb, relieved. No sense pretending that his toughest task of the day was anywhere near completion. The way he calculated the tables in his head, it was just now beginning.

Elliot took a seat in the armchair on the left side of Deb's couch. She watched him select it. Then, tactfully, Deb settled in the one on the right, a good two yards away. Deb slipped off her shoes, and tucked her legs under her. She rested both her elbows on the chair's right stuffed arm, and lowered her chin on top of her upraised palm. She rephrased, "You mean, what finally forced me to admit to myself that I have always loved you?"

The implied comfort of her unruffled body language surprised Elliot. Once, even the whisper of this subject propelled her into tension coiled enough to launch rockets. Now, however, Deb seemed wholly and totally comfortable in her own skin. Elliot envied her.

He reminded, "You said it was finding out that I donated your money. But, after twenty years of denial—it couldn't have been that simple, Brody."

"It wasn't. And it was."

"Oh. Thanks. That clears it all up."

She smiled. "I missed you, Elliot. The last few weeks when we haven't been speaking, I missed you more than I missed Max."

It was a huge admission, both for Deb to make and for Elliot to hear. But, true to form, tradition, and the way he happened to feel at that particular moment, Elliot sought to make it less so. "Understandable. I'm not dead. Subconsciously, you knew there was no chance of reconciling with him—Max, so you transferred your feelings. Knowing that I was still alive, and, therefore, at least theoretically, available for a reunion, that's why our estrangement bothered you more. It's a common psychological reaction."

"Well, well, well, now, would you look at that— six weeks on a psychiatric rotation fifteen years ago, and Dr. Elliot *is* the Jungian Collective Unconscious."

"Now, who's showing off her education?"

Deb stuck her tongue out at him, defending. "Don't you think I considered that option? I was on your same rotation, remember? I gave my motivations serious thought, before I decided that the reasons for my feelings didn't matter. Only facing them did. I realized I wanted you in my life. And then I did some math."

"Math," Elliot repeated.

"It was a most basic equation. You're my best friend, Elliot. You make me laugh, you make me think, you cheer me up, you boost my ego, you give me strength. You also have the cutest set of dimples in the known universe, and those biceps aren't bad, either. Every time you touch me, my skin crackles like I'm popping corn inside my veins. Put them all together, Doc, and they spell 'Love you.' "

"So, that's it?" Elliot asked. "A cute equation, some charged metaphors, and I'm supposed to believe you? I'm supposed to risk my sanity, to believe you?"

"I'm sorry, Elliot." The complacent Deb of a moment earlier was gone, replaced by one wrapped in sincere contriteness. "I am so sorry that I did this to you. I'm sorry for hurting you, and I am dreadfully, dreadfully sorry for killing your trust in me."

Slowly, Elliot said, "That moment in my office, when you said you believed I was out to destroy you— I have never felt anything like it before. It was like my own personal, in-house eclipse. I could actually feel my blood pressure fall. I felt it burrow into my shoes, like dead weight. It made me wonder if, overnight, the whole universe had shifted thirty degrees south. It didn't just break my heart. It broke my soul."

Deb bit down on her lower lip, and blinked hard, resolved not to cry. Voice hoarse, she whispered, "Tell me what to do, Elliot. Tell me what I can do to make it alright."

"I wish to God I knew."

She sat up, elbows digging into the chair's arm, body leaned forward, adding credence to what she was saying. "You do believe me, though, don't you? You believe me when I say that I love you?"

Elliot slowly shook his head from side to side. "I can't. I won't let myself."

"You still think I'm making it up? You still think I'm trying to trick you?"

"No. No, Brody, I never believed that. I think you are being sincere. Rather, I think that you think you're being sincere."

"Dr. Collective Unconscious doesn't think I know my own mind?"

"You didn't for twenty years. You just told me so, yourself. So, how can you be so sure you know it now?"

"That's what I get for being honest," Deb snorted. Then, her eyes lit up. Elliot could see the new thought forming in her head, layer by layer, like a card building. She obviously thought it was a darn clever thought, too. She grinned as she enunciated it.

"Elliot?" Deb began.

"What?" His tone was as cautious as a teenager creeping past his parents' bedroom after curfew.

"You said that you didn't believe I really loved you, because the feeling seemed to come out of the blue. You rationalized that a spontaneous combustion like that couldn't be real, that it had to be an impulsive reaction, destined to fade with time and clarity."

Damn, but he hated how closely that woman listened. Elliot could see where Brody was going with this. He scrambled frantically for ammunition to head her off at the pass with. But the trap was too well laid. And the trapper, too lovely.

Which was all even before the aforementioned lovely trapper zeroed in for the kill. Deb pointed out, "Now that I've admitted I've been in love with you for twenty years, how can you call my feelings impetuous?"

He stood up, he crossed his arms. He said, "I can call them anything I want. It's my neurosis."

Yes, it was true, that was the best Elliot had managed to come up with. He did have an excuse. It had been a long day.

"What are you so scared of, Elliot?"

Now that he'd stood up, he couldn't very well sit down, again. It would look too awkward, and too strange. If he sat down, again, he'd lose whatever illusion of power he'd entered this conversation with. Of course, now that Elliot was up, he found that he was also full of a nervous energy that refused to allow him to simply stand there and radiate his traditional, cool detachment. He pointedly aimed a finger in Deb's direction, as he tried to phrase his answer in terms Deb could understand. "What were you scared of, seven months ago?"

She didn't shirk back from the accusatory finger. She held her ground as noble and unbowed as a warrior princess. She asked, "You mean, besides the fact that my husband had just died, and I was all alone for the first time in my entire life?"

"Yes, Brody." He withdrew his hand, tucking it into the cross of arms against his chest. "Besides that."

"Damn." Deb flopped back in her chair, hands limp in her lap. She looked at him admiringly. "You are good."

He smiled. It was a lucky shot. But Deb didn't have to know that. It still counted, after all.

Before he had the chance to drive his victorious point home, she articulated his argument for him. "I was scared that any kind of romantic relationship would ruin our friendship."

"Well, that, my dear, is a nonexclusive fear."

"Problem is, our friendship is already ruined."

"Yes," he said. "And, I don't know about you, but I've had enough fun. This recent experience is not one I care to relive. Our friendship ending already nearly killed me. Take a minute to imagine what a romantic breakup might feel like."

"So, you're saying that we should just cut our losses and flee our separate ways?"

The word stuck in his windpipe like an undigested pebble. It scraped his insides and clogged up Elliot's throat. Still, it was a word that needed to see the light of day. For both their sakes.

Elliot said, "Yes."

"Coward," Deb spat back.

"Maybe. Or maybe, Brody, I'm just the only one who has given some serious thought to what's best. For both of us."

"Coward," Deb repeated.

Okay, if this was how she wanted to play it, Elliot could be as immature as the next guy. After all, enough women had accused him of suffering from Peter Pan Syndrome. If Deb wanted to engage in name-calling, the least Elliot could do was show her how silly she sounded. And get a couple of his own potshots in.

"Sticks and stones," he began, "may break my b—"

Deb picked up an ashtray off the coffee table, and hurled it at him, full force. "How's that?" she snapped.

Elliot caught it with one hand. The glass smacked against his palm, hard enough to sting. He turned it over a few times with his fingers, pondering the shape, structure, and manufacturer's mark on the bottom. Then, face and voice expressionless, he set the bauble back down on the table, and gently slid it in Deb's direction. He said, "I think you dropped something, Brody."

She laughed.

From fury to mirth on the edge of a second. The woman really did possess an amazing plethora of gifts.

The problem was, her laughter had no joy in it.

Just bitterness.

It took Elliot a moment to realize it wasn't directed at him.

"I did this," Deb said, between grim chuckles. "I did all of this. I created this mess. God!" She turned her head toward the sky, her cry cleaving out part roar, part moan. "What the hell is wrong with me? How could I have tried so hard to do the best thing for everyone, and have it all go so wrong?"

Her self-hate punctured Elliot's heart as easily as a needle through Styrofoam. He couldn't bear to see her like this.

"You had a little help in the mess-making department," Elliot reminded. "I was there, too."

"Oh, yeah, you were there. Grounding me, cheering me, helping me keep my head together when all around, people—including me—were losing theirs. Yeah, you're a real monster, Dr. Elliot."

Elliot smiled. He couldn't help it. Even dying in the depths of despair, Deborah Brody could still make him smile.

He knelt down in front of her. He looked up into Deb's eyes, and offered, "Maybe, if I'd been honest about how I felt from the start—"

She shook her head, stroking his hair with one hand, the way she might comfort a child. "I could have had my little malfunction sooner, and we could have stopped being friends earlier?"

He moved his head a fraction of an inch, not shaking her loose exactly, more like politely ducking, before her affectionate caress shattered the last of his self-restraint. He knew Deb wasn't doing it on purpose, her gesture hadn't been manipulative in any way.

But that didn't mean it hadn't pierced him, all the same.

Elliot said, "Honesty, twenty years ago, would have spared us both a lot of pain. We could have gone our separate ways, and never had to deal with this. . . ."

"And it would have spared us both a lot of joy. If we had gone our separate ways twenty years ago, we would have never gotten to deal with . . . this." Removing her hand from his head, she swept it broadly across the galaxy, trying to encompass the twenty years of good, warm memories that came before the last horrific weeks and months of pain.

"Question is, Brody, was it worth it?"

"Yes." She didn't so much as pause or stutter. "Staying away from you this past month has been the most difficult thing I have ever done in my life. Look at my nails, Elliot. I haven't chewed them for so long, people are stopping me on the street to comment on how nice they look!"

She stretched them out for his inspection. He took both of her palms in his.

"Wow," Elliot said. "I hadn't realized it was that serious."

And let both fall back into her lap.

She took no offense. She merely told Elliot, "This has been the most painful, torturous, agonizing four weeks of my life. And still, I would not even consider trading the twenty years that came before it, for anything. Joy, Elliot, has a price. It has a price that I, at least, am willing to pay."

He stood up. He took a step back, half-turning away from Deb so that he did not have to see her face when he asked softly, "Are you willing to pay the price of disappointment?"

"Meaning?"

He turned back. No matter how much he may have wanted to keep avoiding her gaze, Elliot knew that such a dodge was unfair to Deb. She deserved to inspect him head-on, as he revealed, "I don't know about you, but I've been fantasizing about what loving you might be like, for, oh, I'd say the aforementioned twenty years."

"I know. I think I've always known."

Elliot asked, "You called me a coward?"

She smiled weakly. "Right before I hurled that ashtray at your head, yes."

He stretched his arm forward, and, very lightly, brushed Deb's face with his fingers. "Well, you're right. Give the precocious little girl a teddy bear." Elliot pulled back his hand. "I am a coward. And I am scared of the disappointment that will inevitably crush us both, if reality fails to live up to fantasy."

"What's the matter?" Deb purred. "Seven months ago not pleasing enough of a dry run for you? Considering everything we had going against us, I thought our initial, inadvertent stab at converting fantasy into reality went rather well."

He sighed. "I wasn't talking about just sex, Brody. I agree, that part did go rather well. But sex is easy. It's the easiest part of any romantic relationship. All it takes is patience, practice, and, if you're not in the mood for any of those, a video. But it doesn't guarantee things working out in the long run. The arduous part is all the paraphernalia that goes on outside of bed."

"You mean like communication? Affection? Common interests? Shared values? Friendship?"

He all but stuck his tongue out at her. "Don't be cute."

"Correct me if I'm wrong."

Elliot sighed. "You are not wrong. And I am not stupid. You think I didn't fathom that this is what you were trying to explain to me with your charming mathematics metaphor, earlier?"

"I love a man who listens."

She'd said so dozens of times by now.

"I love you, Elliot."

"Elliot, I love you."

"Why won't you believe it when I tell I love you?"

"What do I have to do to convince you I love you?"

And, every time Elliot heard the word, it made his heart jump, and his brain spark and terminate like a computer hard drive in the midst of a reboot. It was hardly the optimal state from which to launch a coherent, victorious debate. So, to counteract the effect she had on him, Elliot tried to predict when that threatening word might come up. So he could brace himself for impact. Kind of like taking allergy shots composed from small doses of the allergen.

He'd gotten quite good at anticipating the common occurrences. He was actually starting to feel rather proud of himself.

And then, she so blithely tossed in her unexpected "I love a man who listens." How was Elliot supposed to guard against that?

As soon as his brain processed the word, it proceeded to do that rebooting thing, again. It would be a while before he was able to summon up something clever, again, so Elliot went with the one truth he knew to be valid under any circumstances.

Elliot asked, "What if I'm still scared?"

And ducked.

His brain may have been aqueous, but he always had a backup generator for his sense of humor.

"Very funny," Deb said.

Elliot straightened up, giving the ashtray on the coffee table a playful tap with his finger.

He said, "I am still scared."

"So am I."

"But you're willing to take this risk?"

"Yes."

"Why?"

"Because, right now, a future without you in it is infinitely scarier than any hurt I can imagine someday coming from you."

"Maybe your imagination needs an oil check," Elliot said.

"Maybe."

"Or, maybe, you can't imagine it, because you have never felt it. Until you understand what that species of pain feels like, how can you decide whether or not you're afraid of it?"

She didn't argue with him. She simply defined, "You mean the species of pain that you felt? Because of me?"

"The species of pain that I felt," Elliot concurred, though he couldn't bring himself to echo the last part.

Deb sat up straight in her chair. She squared her shoulders, and both hands dug into the piece's padded arms with such bearing, Elliot foresaw reupholstering in its future.

"Okay," Deb said.

It was as definitive—and obscure—a statement as Elliot ever heard. He felt as if they'd just jumped forward an hour into the future, and he'd missed some crucial development.

"Okay, what?" he asked.

"Hurt me."

Elliot's laugh sounded like a bark. He felt as if it had been burped out of him by an extrahearty slap on the back.

"What, you want *me* to throw the ashtray at *you*, this time?"

Deb argued, "You're right. How can I declare I'm willing to risk the anguish, if I don't really know what that entails? I want you to hurt me, Elliot. The way I hurt you. So, I'll understand. And so you'll take my subsequent decision seriously."

"You're being silly."

"I'm trying to prove my sincerity. I'd do anything for you, Elliot. Didn't I leave you alone when you asked me to?"

"You did." Which, actually, had rather surprised him.

"Now, I want to do something to make you trust me, again. I want to do something to convince you it's safe to love me, again."

She was trying to kill him. He'd suspected as much on many previous occasions, but now Elliot was certain. Deb was trying to kill him.

"Hurt me," she repeated.

Elliot sat back down on the couch. He crossed his fingers in front of him. He looked down at them, and then he looked up. He said, "Alright."

Deb blanched. A tricky feat, considering her complexion had already opened the day wavering between baking powder and chalk. She shrunk from his words as if they were a physical slap. But Deborah Brody was nothing if not a fighter. In front of Elliot's admiring eyes, she purged the initial shock from her system through visible force of will. Ordering reluctant muscles to lengthen to capacity, Deb bullied herself to sit up straight. She ripped open her clenched fists, pressing her palms into her lap, and, with one withering glance, made it clear that no trembling would be allowed. She lifted her chin, defiantly, and locked her eyes to zero in on Elliot's. This was not a woman willing to back down. This was a woman determined to fight to the death.

"Good." Her voice rang as clear and steady as a healthy pulse. "Go ahead," she said. "I'm ready. Hurt me."

The sight of her valor touched Elliot on levels of tenderness he never guessed existed. *Damn, and here he'd hoped there were no areas left in which Brody could hurt him. Showed what he knew.*

Softly, Elliot said, "I already did."

Confusion washed over her like a wave on a beach. Deb's hard-won confidence wavered. Her shoulders dropped just a notch as the energy she'd previously reserved for appearing strong found itself channeled to unscrambling his riddle.

"What?" She stammered, "I don't—I don't understand—"

"You didn't think I would, did you?"

"What are you talking about? I—"

"You didn't think I would hurt you. The whole time you were making me your very generous offer, you never actually thought I'd be capable of or willing to hurt you, did you?"

The fight drained out of Deb in stages. He could see it, like a teakettle emptying. "No," she admitted.

"It shocked you, when I said alright."

"I suppose, a little."

"That's because, your whole life—except for that one slip we'll write off to temporary insanity—you believed that I would protect you, and I would take care of you, and that, under penalty of death, I would never, ever hurt you."

A pause. Then, "Alright. Yes. Maybe, I did."

"That moment when you thought I actually would, though. What did that feel like?"

Understanding dawned quickly and visibly. "Betrayal," Deb said.

Elliot offered a soft, pedagogical, congratulatory nod of the head. "Now you know how I felt when the friend I thought I knew and could trust with my soul did something so unexpected."

She gave the matter some thought, summarizing, "You're afraid of it happening, again. You're afraid that, if you let me into your heart, again, I'll break it. Again."

"By George, I think she's got it." His tone was triumphant. A shame Elliot felt anything but.

Deb chose not to interpret his accolade as a compliment. She said, "So, there's nothing I can do to change your mind."

"That's what I've been trying to tell you from the start." He stood up, again, feeling like that children's doll, Bobo the Clown. No matter how many times you punch it in the face, it keeps coming back for more. Well, Elliot had no intention of coming back for more. He turned toward the door, meaning to leave this time.

Really.

But then, Deb's eyes widened, and she exclaimed, "That's it!"

Her enthusiasm caught him off-guard. He'd taken a determined step, one foot pointed toward the door. Her words stopped him in his proverbial tracks. Elliot pointed out, a touch insulted, "You don't have to sound so thrilled about it, Brody."

"The start," Deb echoed, speaking so fast she didn't bother to respond to his comment. She leapt breathlessly out of her chair, barreling straight to her point. "We can go back to the start."

"What do you mean?"

"I mean like—Hi, nice to meet you." She stood half a foot away from him, stretching her hand forward, looking for a friendly shake. "I'm Deborah Brody. What did you say your name was?"

Elliot stared at the formerly precocious, board-certified MD like she'd lost her mind. "Are you serious?"

"We start again. No history. No secrets. No pain."

"This is ludicrous," he said, taking a cautious step back from her at the same time as he—never precocious but also board-certified—couldn't stop himself from asking, "I mean, how would we even do something like that?"

She shrugged, blithe and so happy, Elliot almost expected her to start levitating off the ground at any moment. "How do normal people start relationships?"

"Are you saying we're not normal, Doctor?"

"I'm saying that our relationship, Elliot, is certainly not normal. We kind of jumped the gun on a couple of things, wouldn't you say? This time, I want to do everything by the book, the way it's supposed to be."

"The way it's supposed to be?" he repeated slowly, echoing the sounds without fully comprehending their meaning.

"I was out of circulation for twenty years, Elliot. You've got the experience, here, you tell me. How do normal relationships start? What do you do? That's what I want."

He was listening to her. Elliot knew he was listening to her, because he could feel the physiological processes clicking away in his ears, brain, and nervous system. Elliot couldn't believe he was listening, but he was. What was more fantastic was when he found himself responding.

"Now, let me get this straight," Elliot posed. "After twenty years, and one very eventful night . . . you want to go on a *date*?"

Deb said, "Yes."

Chapter Nineteen

Cary Grant was standing on her front stoop, again.

He still looked an awful lot like Elliot in a tux.

Not that Deb was complaining.

Elliot in a tux was a good thing.

He was also holding a bottle of champagne with both hands. He presented it to Deb, with a smile and a formal bow. "Happy New Year."

She felt underdressed by comparison. Deb was wearing only a long, black skirt, and a white cashmere sweater. Elliot hadn't told her where they were going, or what they were doing, so she'd had to dress monochromatically, and prepare for anything.

She hadn't prepared for this.

"It's March twenty-first," she pointed out.

"Indeed it is." Elliot gestured for Deb to take the champagne bottle, so Elliot could place both hands behind his back, and just stand there, waiting expectantly.

Deb did as he bade. The glass felt cool, and just a drop wet, along her hands. He must have chilled it for at least twenty-four hours before coming over. Elliot never did anything halfway.

"Okay," Deb said. "Now, I have a champagne bottle, and still no clue."

He held his hands out to the side, palms up, as if presenting her with a gift of the obvious. "It's Baha'i New Year."

"And you know this because . . ."

"Mrs. Pharsi told me when I did my follow-up with Adrian. Did you know the family practiced Bahaism?"

Deb admitted, "I did not know that."

"Bahaism originated in Persia, which is where they're from, by the way—well, it's Iran, now."

"That I did know."

"I thought that, in honor of Adrian Pharsi, and all the things that happened as a result of him, we'd celebrate New Year."

"You know how to? Celebrate Baha'i New Year, I mean?"

"Well, no, let's not get crazy. We're honoring the date, but I was hoping the celebration could be more, how can I put it—"

"*Love, American Style?*"

Elliot's face instantly darkened; his spirit, if not his feet yet, took a step back. "That's against the rules, Brody."

Ah, yes. The rules. They'd spent quite an epoch negotiating them. Per Elliot's conditions, if he and Deb were to start again, well, then, they really had to start, *again*. No history, no past, no issues, no bleeding wounds. Which, in tangible terms, meant no talking about history, the past, issues, or bleeding wounds. They were starting fresh. They were going on their first date. So, not only were they not allowed to discuss old, familiar things, but getting too newly familiar, too quickly, was also out of bounds.

Chastised, Deb grimaced. "Too much too soon?"

"We did just meet, after all."

"Right. Sorry." Deb stepped aside, making a grand sweeping gesture with her arm, down the length of her hallway. "Please, do come in, Dr. Elliot."

"Thank you, Dr. Brody."

She closed the door behind him. "How'm I doing?"

"*A* for effort."

Deb took Elliot's coat, and hung it up in the closet as neatly as she would any first-time visitor's. "When do you think we might progress to a first-name basis, Dr. Elliot?"

"When you invite me to, I suppose."

"Ah. I didn't realize that part was my responsibility." Coat draped securely on a hanger, Deb turned around. She bumped straight into Elliot, who'd come up behind her, quiet as the dark of space and, without warning or rule-change announcement, rested both hands on Deb's shoulders. He lowered his head, kissing her, lightly, informally, but all the same, unmistakably.

When Elliot moved away, he took Deb's breath with her. Her knees trembled. Then, since everyone knew the mouth could, and unfortunately too often, did, operate independent of viable brain function, Deb asked, "It's too soon for first names, but *this* is acceptable?"

Elliot smiled. He raised his thumb to his lips, and casually dabbed at the warm dampness of his mouth.

He illuminated, "I find the greatest obstacle to complete relaxation on any first date is worrying about that first kiss. Who makes the first move? When do I make the first move? How will it be, et cetera, et cetera, et cetera. . . . ? How are people supposed to chill and enjoy themselves, if they've got this guillotine swinging in the backs of their minds? My solution is to get that first kiss over with as soon as possible."

"I see," Deb said.

"Trust me on this one, Brody." Elliot winked. "I've been at this a long, long"—he sighed—"*long* time."

Something about that concluding *long* struck Deb as a touch too sincere to pass off as a gag. She let it pass, though, keeping her own tone light, airy, and by-the-book.

Walking down the hall to the living room, Elliot respectfully behind her, Deb, over her shoulder, tossed out, "You are welcome to call me by my first name, Dr. Elliot."

The pause that followed her invitation proved long enough for Deb to actually stop and turn around.

Elliot had frozen, mid-action in his tracks, left foot behind right, arm on his hip, lips crinkled to the side in concentration, head cocked, eyes focused on the ceiling. Slowly, he reflected, "I don't think I've ever done that before."

"Of course not." Someone had to follow the rules around here. "We've just met."

"Oh, yes." After a moment of standing frozen, Elliot, all of a sudden, came to life in double-time. He hurried after Deb to the kitchen. "Of course. I forgot. Sorry."

She opened a drawer by the sink, fishing for a bottle opener. When she found it, Deb passed it over to Elliot, along with the champagne. He stretched out his arms to take it from her.

Their fingers brushed each other as he gripped and she let go. Softly, Deb said, "Actually, you have called me that before."

Who am I, Deb? Who am I?

His question from the evening of Max's funeral reverberated so mightily in both their heads, the combined echoes proved deafening. And paralyzing. For a beat, they stood as they were, both of them clutching the champagne bottle as if it were the last tangible buoy on earth. Deb imagined she could feel the heat from their fingers melting straight through the intended chill of the bottle, burning holes in the glass and boiling the liquid inside it until the plug would explode from the unbearable pressure.

Naturally, it did no such thing.

This was the real world, after all, not *Ally McBeal*.

And in the real world, what happened was the beat passed, sans cartoon imagery.

Deb released her grip on the bottle, and Elliot, mundanely, took it from her. But, just in case, to prevent her hallucination from coming true, Deb asked, "Do you need a corkscrew?"

He tilted the bottle in her direction. "It's champagne, Dr. Brody. You don't use a corkscrew. You use your hands."

To illustrate, Elliot proceeded to twist and turn the cork with surgical precision, putting a little pressure here, a little pressure there, working with a combination of control and urgency. Deb could only watch with respect the sensual dance of his hands. Respect, and, well, alright, maybe something else as well.

She suppressed the delightful shudder the sight—with no help from her, she hastened to add—triggered inside her body. They'd only just met, after all. Deb had no business remembering a night, and a caress, and an indulged moan, that, according to their rules, never happened. Yet.

The cork snapped.

It shot in the air, bouncing off the ceiling.

Both leapt out of their skins, the anxiety barometer in the kitchen utterly disproportionate to the *boom*-triggered shock.

Why, it was almost like there was something else going on just below the surface.

But how could that be?

They'd only just met.

Luckily, whatever tension might have started slowly strangling them the minute both, ill-advisedly, stepped into that quagmire of this damned, first-name basis came to a blessed end as soon as the cork bounced off the ceiling.

And into Elliot's eye.

It was very difficult to remain sexually tense, when you were also laughing hysterically.

Wiping his eye with his fingers, trying to exorcise both the stray foam and the tears of laughter, Elliot observed, "This never happened to Cary Grant."

Deb, dabbing at him with a paper towel to wipe up the champagne he spilled on his tuxedo cuffs from the surprise, agreed. "It's not your fault. Cary must have had a stuntman do it for him."

Ominously, Elliot warned, "Don't patronize the bumbling, Dr. Brody. We're organized, we have a Washington lobby, and we prefer to be referred to as Inept Americans."

"Is this also part of your first-date ritual?"

He shook his head. "Not for a while, now."

"You mean, it actually used to be?"

Elliot accepted one of the paper towels from her, so he could finish the drying job along his chest. Deb wasn't going there.

Not on a first date.

He confessed, "Sort of. When I was very young—now, I mean very young—college, not even graduate school, I would always burn the first meal I cooked for a woman."

Deb, intrigued by the glimpse into the locked-off male psyche, asked, "Why? Oh, wait, is this a continuation of the why-you-never-learned-to-cook game plan that you told me about New Year's Eve? Uh . . . I mean, last New Year's Eve? The one three months ago?"

"Exactly. Women like seeing men helpless in the kitchen. It brings out their protective, nurturing instinct or something. It's a good way to get laid. And, as a bonus, you never get asked to cook again."

"That sounds stupid," Deb said. "How often did it work?"

"In theory, or in practice?"

"Practice."

Elliot grinned his *gotcha*. "All the time, baby."

Deb rolled her eyes. "And you're proud of this?"

"Listen to me, Brody. I am a doctor. I know what I'm talking about. Men cannot be held responsible for their behavior when it comes to schemes for getting women into bed. They suffer a medical condition that makes thinking rationally impossible."

"And what condition is that?"

Elliot's eyes twinkled. "Testosterone poisoning."

"Never heard of it."

"Hey, I warned you all those skipped days of school would come back and haunt you."

Deb shook her head. "You're an evil man, James Elliot."

"Oh, good," he said, and offered her a freshly poured glass of champagne. "We're finally really getting to know each other."

Deb accepted the alcohol, and, instinctively, tapped it forward in the toasting motion mandatory for such occasions.

"What are we drinking to?" Elliot asked.

Okay . . . That was a good one.

She considered the obvious: "To old friends." She considered the political: "To new friends." She considered the default, nonpresumptuous: "To friends."

But each seemed to come hand-in-hand with a potential, future quagmire of trouble. So, to be on the safe side, Deb went with the more nonpolitical: "To peace in the Middle East."

Elliot smiled. "And may God bless us, every one."

He swallowed his champagne in one gulp. He put his now empty glass down on the Formica counter. Then, he did nothing but watch Deb slowly sipping hers.

It was a very strange sensation—being observed while in the midst of doing something so mundane. Deb wasn't sure how to react. The close scrutiny made her feel like she should be doing something more. The whole thing unnerved her. She rubbed her thumb nervously along the stem of the crystal glass, and her teeth clicked against the rim.

Elliot did not resemble a person who was disturbed even in the slightest. He watched Deb sip, as if it were the most entertaining diversion in the world.

She felt compelled to ask the obvious. "What?"

"Nothing." His cool didn't flicker. "Just looking at you."

"Why?"

"My. It *has* been a while since your first date, hasn't it?"

"Looking is customary?"

"Looking is mandatory."

"You're really getting into this, aren't you, Elliot?"

"Wasn't that the point? Isn't that why you invited me?"

"Well, yes, of course." Time to tap dance. "I—I guess I'm just surprised. You were so, I don't know, obstinate?—is that the right word?—obstinate, about the possibility of our . . . our . . ."

"Go on. I can't think of a tactful way to put it, either."

"I suppose I didn't expect you to be so cooperative. To, you know, play along as, uhm, enthusiastically as you have been."

"I'm not being cooperative, Brody." He told her the absolute truth. "I'm being desperate."

"I don't understand."

Elliot sighed. "You know how much you want to convince me I'm wrong about you? It's nothing compared to how desperate I am to be convinced. You think I have an allergy to being wrong? No, Brody. Not this time, not tonight, and not about this. Please, prove me wrong. Prove that I'm wrong about you breaking my heart, again, and I will be the happiest mistaken bastard ever."

He told her this gospel with as much passion as Deb had ever seen Elliot reveal about anything.

But before she had a chance to respond or even fully process what he'd just confessed, Elliot turned his back on her, left the kitchen, and went off into the living room, to show her what else he'd brought for their celebration.

She followed, numbly.

As with all of his efforts, when Elliot pronounced March twenty-first ad-hoc New Year's Eve, he came prepared. Along with the champagne, he brought two plastic noisemakers—he blew first one, then the other, claiming it was imperative to test these things; a sandwich bag of confetti—he reached inside, and tossed a handful in the air, watching with a smile as the red, green, yellow, and blue dots wafted, like something out of a glamorous movie, into Deb's hair, on her cheeks, on her shoulders, and in her lashes; and a videotape of *Dick Clark's Rockin' Eve*.

Laughing as she spat out the confetti stuck—not nearly as glamorously—to her tongue, Deb popped the tape in the VCR. She watched a few seconds, then told Elliot, "It's from 1981!"

"It was all the video store had."

"What time is it?"

He checked his watch. "Ten-thirty."

"Perfect." She synchronized the tape with the clock. "We'll get to see the ball drop right at midnight."

"What do we do in the meantime?"

"It's your party," she reminded.

"You mean, I could cry if I want to?"

Deb made a face, and blew on the New Year's horn to mimic the buzz of a negative *X* on *Family Feud*. "That was baaaaaad."

"It's New Year's Eve. If old acquaintances should be forgot, doesn't that hold double for really old jokes?"

"So, you're what? Trying to get them out of your system?"

"Brody, I am trying to get a lot of things out of my system."

My, but that could be interpreted a lot of different ways. On the debit side, Elliot could mean he was trying to get a lot of old things, like several positive feelings he still nursed for her, out of his system. On the credit side, he could mean he was trying to get a lot of old things, like the sense of betrayal he still nursed for her, out of his system. The scales could slope either way, and Elliot, with his noncommittal tone and unremitting, cool demeanor, was not making figuring out his true meaning any easier.

Yet, nevertheless, he had thrown down the gauntlet. He'd told Deb he *wanted* her to change his opinion. He wanted her to convince him that she would not atomize his heart again, the way she had for twenty years. Where Deb came from, that didn't sound like a simple request. That sounded like a *challenge*.

And she was up for it. Deb felt like the past two decades of her life had been nothing more or less than a practice run to this ultimate moment, this ultimate test.

She would convince him. She would force Elliot to believe she wasn't lying or panicking or deluding herself. She loved him. Deb loved Elliot. And, now that she had finally admitted this truth to herself as well as him, the crippling, devastating conclusion she'd so foolishly leapt to months earlier was simply no longer possible.

The situation had changed. Only Elliot refused to believe it. He still expected Deb to change her mind about him. And he refused to, justifiably, put himself through that, again. Deb got it.

Consequently, she got that her task was simple. She needed to make Elliot see that he was wrong. And she needed to do it in the next ninety minutes. For, although Elliot hadn't specifically indicated a pumpkin time, Deb suspected that, going by the holiday he chose to relive, her unspoken deadline was midnight.

How considerate it was of Dick Clark to put a little clock at the corner of his screen, so she could keep track of just how much time she'd already wasted, and how little time there was left. The digital numbers scrolled backward mercilessly, showing Deb she now had an hour and twenty-three minutes to think of . . . something.

"Would you like to dance?" Deb asked.

"It is New Year's Eve," Elliot said.

He held out his arms, and Deb stepped into them, naturally and as if she'd been doing it for years. Actually, she had been. Just not in the real world, that's all. By default, their music was the rockin' of Dick Clark's Eve and, although it would seem to call for some serious getting down and boogying, both Elliot and Deb elected to interpret the hardest drumbeat with mellow swaying. They stood in the middle of Deb's living room, her hand on his chest, her chin against his shoulder, Elliot's fingers gently kneading the curve of her hip. Their thighs brushed against each other. Deb rested her cheek along the lapel of his tuxedo, relishing the cool smoothness rubbing her feverish skin. She could hear his heartbeat echoing in her ear, and feel his breath billowing the hair atop her head. It felt nice. Hell, who was she kidding? It felt amazing. Deb would have been happy to enjoy this version of the Eternal Dance forever.

But, she suspected, silence was not going to be the tactic to swaying Elliot. This was an intellectual battle she was fighting, here, not a physical one. After all, Elliot had never denied being attracted to her, and she—if truth be told—never doubted her ability to seduce him, should the demand arise. Tonight was not about breaking down simple physical barriers, but complex, psychic ones.

To that end, Deb shifted her weight slightly, so that she now looked up at Elliot. His face was so serene, so calm, so content, it made Deb wonder if maybe she hadn't already won him, after all. But she also knew she couldn't risk it.

Deb asked, "Elliot?"

"What?" His eyes perked open, going from sleepy contentment to caffeinated-alert faster than his beloved Lexus.

"Do you, uhm." She tried to remember what it was

people talked about on traditional first dates. "Do you remember New Year's 1981?"

"1981? Why?" His eyes snuck a peek at the tape, counting off its inevitable march to midnight. "Oh, right. I get it. Sure, I remember 1981. It was my first New Year's in medical school. You were there. That party we threw in the morgue?"

"Oh, yes. Oh, God." Deb buried her face in Elliot's chest. Eroticism had nothing to do with it, this time. This time, it was sheer embarrassment. "I cannot believe we did that."

"It's a UCSF tradition. All First-Year medical students are obligated to spend their New Year's at the morgue. Other schools offer binge-drinking for their hazing, we hang with the dead."

"It's a fine tradition. Everybody should kick off their New Year's smelling of formaldehyde, once in their life."

"And surrounded by defrosting cadavers propped up in chairs with party hats on their heads."

"And paper streamers wrapped around their waists, and noisemakers stuck in their mouths."

"The lucky ones got them stuck in their mouths," he reminded.

"True, true . . ." Deb propped her chin squarely on his chest. "That idiot who sat behind me in organic chemistry—Nichols, he did get very creative with what he judged an open orifice."

"Wasn't that also the night Saknovsky tried to demonstrate how tough he was, by drinking embalming fluid?"

"Yup. He kept talking about how, back in college, he and the rest of his wrestling-team buds used to do gasoline shots. Well, if he learned nothing else from med school, it was that embalming fluid is not gasoline shots."

"Is that moron even still alive?" Elliot asked.

"He's alive. He's the team doctor for the Olympic Wrestling Federation."

Elliot straightened his elbows, holding Deb at arm's length. "Please, tell me you're kidding."

It just so happened that she wasn't kidding. Deb'd read about Saknovsky's appointment in their alumni newsletter just last month. Nevertheless, if she had been kidding, Deb would have happily lied, to get Elliot to enfold her back into his arms.

She said, "It's true. He's on their national advisory board, and everything."

"God help America." Elliot ruefully shook his head.

But, doubt quelled, he did pull Deb closer to him, once again resting both his hands on her back, and absently rubbing the tender skin around her spine.

She shivered and burrowed against him. They continued swaying to music that was utterly inappropriate for the occasion. As far as Deb was concerned, the tunes could disintegrate to just the buzz of ear-bleeding static, and she would continue to stay right as she was, slow dancing with Elliot.

To that end, since reminiscing seemed to be soothing the savage beast—for now, and, God knew, Deb was not a whiz at quitting while she was ahead—she murmured, "Wasn't New Year's of eighty-one also the night Silverstein—who, by the way, I got a card from the other day, they had their fourth baby, another boy, one more and it's a basketball team—wasn't that when she finally got up the nerve to jump Levin, right there on the autopsy table?"

Elliot nodded emphatically, then mused, "I don't know who was more relieved she finally did it—her, him, or the rest of us. It was getting downright painful to stomach watching her dragging from place to place like a zombie, pining over him, wrapped in all that masochistic, stoic silence."

"Oh, you should talk," Deb teased.

"What do you mean?" She thought she heard a strange tightness in his voice, as if the breath had suddenly all been crushed out of Elliot's lungs. Yet, he continued swaying without missing a beat.

Deb told herself she was imagining things.

But, just to be safe, she kept her tone deliberately light and merry when she asked, "What was the name of that quiet girl—she went into oncology, later, I heard—the one who would turn bright red every time you walked by, or, God forbid, said a word to her?"

"You mean . . . Nielsen?"

"Right, that's the one. God, talk about pining in masochistic silence. She latched on to you like a parasitic virus. That little girl had it *bad* for you."

Elliot didn't say anything.

"You know," Deb continued. "Nielsen told everybody the two of you got together that New Year's. Behind the filing cabinets, or some other such nonsense."

"How can you be so sure it was nonsense?" He sounded almost offended by her assumption.

"Oh, I know, I know, you backed up her story to the letter."

"But that still wasn't enough to make you believe it? What did you want, Brody, pictures?"

"Oh, come on, Doc. Who do you think you're talking to, here? You, my friend, are a gentleman. If you had done it with Nielsen, you would have never blabbed about it. Kiss and tell is not your thing—you think I don't know that? The only reason you'd ever back up Nielsen's tall tale is because you didn't want her losing face in front of her classmates. It meant so much to her that we all think she'd had her love-struck way with you, that you played along. It's the kind of guy you are."

He parried, "You're so sure you know the kind of guy I am."

"Elliot," Deb said, "I know everything about you."

"For instance?" She could tell from his tone of voice that he didn't believe her. Well, Deb would show him.

She said, "For instance, I know the real reason you went into Pediatric Trauma Care."

"Big deal." Elliot shrugged. "Everyone knows that. Half our med-school class was there that day, and the other half heard about it through the grapevine."

Deb shook her head. A spot of her makeup rubbed off against the front of Elliot's tuxedo, and she dabbed at it with her finger. "Oh, no. I'm not talking about the reason everyone *assumes* you did it. I'm talking about the real reason."

"There was a real reason?"

Deb smiled. "Everyone thinks you decided to go into Pediatric Trauma after that day we were on ER rotation, and the EMTs brought in that little boy who'd been hit by a car and thrown half a block. He was clinically dead, but you spent an hour trying to restart his heart. You were like a man possessed. I mean, Roca finally had to order you to give it up, and, for weeks afterward, all you kept talking about was how that kid would have had a chance, if the ER had been stocked with kid-size equipment. A couple months later, you select Pediatric Trauma as your specialty. People who don't know you, they put two and two together and assumed some ipso facto algorithm. But I know better. I know you. You didn't decide to go into Pediatric Trauma because of a patient you lost. You went in because of a patient you saved."

Somewhere in the middle of Deb's flaunting her precocity, he'd stopped caressing her back. He even stopped swaying, and now stood rooted to the spot. Although his arms were still physically around her, Elliot's soul had fled. The look on his face was thoughtful, reflective . . . and obviously lost someplace so far away, he probably needed some kind of psychic passport just to get there.

For the first time in her life, Deb understood the meaning of her father's constant admonition: "Don't be too smart, young lady." Just look at where being smart had brought her.

She'd said something wrong, that part was obvious. She wished she knew what, but that was immaterial. She could put her time to better use trying to figure out how to extricate herself from this mess, and save the situation before it was too late.

By Dick Clark's clock, there were only fifteen minutes to go.

Elliot's arms were like dead weights on her shoulders. Deb slipped out of his embrace, disappointed when he didn't appear to notice—or care.

"Damn, I'm sorry," she said. Her natural tendency, when at a loss for words, was to speak faster, hoping that her audience would assume she'd just swallowed the correct ones in her haste to utter them. But speed wouldn't do in this case. She had only a finite quantity of coherency swimming in her head, and she didn't want to risk wasting it too quickly. So, rather than babbling, Deb forced herself to slow down, to enunciate each word, and to stall for time until the reinforcement—otherwise known as sense—arrived. "I broke your rules, didn't I? No talking about the past."

It took Elliot a long beat to come back to her. And, when he did, he looked down at Deb as if seeing her for the first time.

As if they hadn't just been standing so closely together that she could feel his every intake of breath.

As if the smell of her skin weren't still ironed into the silk of his tuxedo.

As if the kiss he'd just surprised her with in the closet, and the twenty years—and the seven months, that came before that—were all figments of a dream only she'd had.

"Is there any more champagne?" he asked.

"In the kitchen."

Elliot turned his back on her, and went to get it.

She wondered, was there a square that came before Square One? Because she really ought to know the name of the locale where she was standing.

When Elliot returned from the kitchen, sipping and checking his watch, Deb asked, "One more chance?"

"Brody . . ."

"Please. I know I'm making a fool of myself. But this is so important to me. Let's start, again. For the last time. I'll be good, I promise."

"Brody, I—"

"Elliot?" If she couldn't convince him, the least she could do was try and distract him. "Elliot, if you really just met me, right now, this evening, what would you think of me?" It was a distraction technique, plus, Deb honestly wanted to know. "Being married for so many years, I think I've lost touch with how other men see me. With how I come off, as a woman."

"You are a beautiful woman," he offered softly. But he also looked away as he offered it.

Her goal was to keep his attention. She was doing a bad job.

"Would you be attracted to me? I mean, if we'd just met."

"I'm going to let you in on a little secret, Brody. Men are attracted to all women. We're wired that way."

"So, I'm nothing special?"

"All women are special."

Deb crossed her arms, not even a little flattered. "You're a doctor, Elliot, not a lawyer."

"Right. I knew I was some kind of professional."

"You know what I would think, if I met you right now?"

Her query caught his attention. Elliot had been raising the champagne glass to his lips. It faltered on the way up. His gaze, once lost on the horizon, zeroed in on her with the speed of radar. He frowned. The lines in his forehead deepened, and Elliot cocked his head in her direction. For the first time all evening, she had his attention. And they both knew it.

Deb would have been delighted, if she wasn't also stymied.

There was a problem. She'd blurted her provocative query as part of a buckshot attempt to try everything and anything, hoping that, eventually, something would stick.

She hadn't expected something to stick so quickly. She would have planned for it. Still, Deb was a surgeon. She was trained to think on her feet. And improvise from the heart.

Moving slowly, lest a too-sudden action shatter the tentative spell her question had weaved between them, Deb lowered herself to a sitting position on the couch. Elliot remained where he was, the glass stuck in a no-man's-land between nonchalance and interest.

She'd operated on premature babies hardly taller than her hand. She'd brought clinically dead children back to life, and she'd held people's still-beating hearts in her palm. Yet, never had Deb felt more anxious about the life-and-death consequences of her actions.

The future depended on her subsequent words.

She thought that now would be a great time for

Deb to learn how to choose her subsequent words carefully.

Slowly, Deb said, "If I met you for the first time, tonight, I would think you were a very, very special man."

Well, so much for choosing her words carefully. She realized only after they were out of her mouth, how inappropriate they were. What if Elliot thought Deb was criticizing his earlier description of all women as "special"?

She hurried to cover up the faux pas. And no, she didn't need a reminder that that was the best way to ensure making another one.

"I would see a man who was decent, and kind, and intelligent. I would see a man with a princely heart and a noble soul, and with a vaguely twisted sense of humor."

Elliot smiled at that.

"I would see a man with the patience of Job."

Smile gone.

Tersely, Elliot said, "He sounds like a saint."

"No." This one, Deb knew the right answer to. "He just acts like a decent human being. Which most folks, out of unfamiliarity, mistake for sainthood."

On her second try, Deb struck double dimples. Elliot's smile was unhesitant, and unforced.

"Max . . ." He fondly identified the quote's originator.

"Max," Deb confirmed. "What can I say? When it comes to men, I guess I have a type."

"And what might that be?"

"I like nice guys. Like my husband. And my best friend."

He still hadn't budged from where he was standing.

She was running out of time. They both knew it. And not only because, on the tape beside them, Dick Clark was starting his half-a-minute-to-midnight countdown. At the buzz of the thirty-second mark, she began, "Elliot..."

He knew exactly what she was asking. And how badly she needed to hear the answer. To his credit, Elliot did not back down, take a step back, or in any other way attempt to duck the issue. All he said was, "Come on, Brody. You've had twenty years to make up your mind about me. I can't get twenty minutes?"

Deb pointed to the digital, on-screen numbers that suddenly seemed to have picked up speed like no-body's business. It wasn't her fault. The timetable was out of Deb's hands.

She sighed. "You have twenty seconds."

Chapter Twenty

Make that nineteen.

Eighteen.

Elliot looked at the ticking clock, and then he looked up at Deb. Without turning his head, he set his champagne glass down on a nearby table. *Oh, good, they were really making progress, now.*

"Brody?"

"Yes?" She struggled to keep from pouncing on the word and chewing it to bits like a playful puppy. Some dignity at the end of all this might make for a nice consolation prize.

Unfortunately, Deborah Brody wasn't exactly the type to seek comfort from consolation prizes.

"Can I ask you something a little . . . odd?"

Fifteen.

Fourteen.

Sure, why not? They had all the time in the world.

She cleared her throat. "You know you can."

Thirteen.

Twelve.

"Why did I go into Pediatric Trauma Care?"

It was the last thing she expected him to ask. And so she stammered, "I—I told you. I mean, I told you what I thought. What I assumed. I guess it *was* presumptuous of me, but—"

"You said it was because of a patient I saved."

"Yes."

Nine.

"What patient?"

Eight.

"Uhm—the old lady," Deb said. "The one who had all those pictures of herself around her room, from when she was young and a ballerina back in Russia, I think. The one who had the stroke, so she couldn't move."

"Mrs. Petkevitch?"

"Right. That was her name." Deb said, "I saw your face. You didn't want to resuscitate her. You certainly didn't want to leave her a vegetable. You thought that was no life for a lady like her. But you did what you had to do. You kept her from dying, and you left her trapped in that twisted knot of a body for God knows how long—she was still alive when we graduated, right?" Softly, Deb offered, "It killed you. I saw how it killed you. That's when you decided to work with kids. So you could save lives that still had a future, something to live for."

Elliot said nothing.

He just stared at Deb.

There was almost no time left.

And, once again, she'd clearly said something wrong.

Five.

Deb gave up.

"I am so sorry I let you down," she told Elliot. She wondered if she had said it so many times that he no longer even heard it. "I will regret it for the rest of my life. I know we've gone over this, and over this, until the words barely mean anything anymore. But, Elliot, do you think you could ever, ever forgive me?"

Three.

Two.

He kissed her.

Which was quite a neat trick, really, considering that a click earlier he'd been standing four feet away from her, and, now, here he was, arms around her shoulders, hands splayed against her back, mouth on hers.

She responded before her conscious reason even processed the development. Her arms automatically slipped beneath Elliot's, her fingers grazing his sides, then curving to curl up and around until she'd cupped the triangles of his shoulder blades. She balanced on the tips of her toes, straining to reach him, her breasts pressing against Elliot's chest, her hips kneading along his thighs, her leg slipping in between both of his.

His mouth consumed hers. Unlike before, he didn't leave even a sliver of opportunity for her to change her mind. There were no questions or doubts in this particular kiss. Only answers, only certainties. Elliot's tongue plunged inside her, seeking out Deb's equally willing one, and running his up and down the ridged, moist, eager sides of hers in a manner that made Deb yearn to both giggle and sigh simultaneously.

He sucked on her lower lip, breathing in so deeply as he did it, he might have been wanting to inhale her, whole. She couldn't breathe. That had always been a problem for Deb, actually. When she craned her neck up awkwardly to let a man kiss her, when she allowed him to cover her mouth completely, and, out of necessity, more often than not, ended up pressing her nose shut with his, Deb found it very difficult to breathe. That was why, early on, she'd developed a habit of breaking the kiss, and turning her head to the side, kissing the man's cheek, his ear, his neck, his shoulder.

She did it to take a literal breather.

But not this time, though.

This time, Deb decided she'd rather pass out first.

No how, no way would she be the first to break this kiss.

Elliot tasted of their earlier champagne, and he felt so warm, all Deb wanted to do was curl up against him and revel in the heat. This, she finally knew, was the way it was supposed to be.

This, she finally understood, was *meant* to be.

No. She would never be the first to stop this.

Yet, when Elliot, at long last, did, Deb wondered if she had made the right decision. At least, if she'd been the one to pull away first, she wouldn't have had to suffer the panic that gripped her when he did so. Had Elliot changed his mind? Again?

Deb told herself to look on the bright side.

Maybe he, too, was afraid of asphyxiating.

Her own breath returned in a rush, bursting out of her chest from where it had hammered, trapped, side by side with her burning question. "May I interpret that as a yes, Dr. Elliot?"

"You may interpret that." He held Deb at arm's length. His lips a touch swollen, his cheeks a touch flushed, his hair a touch mussed. In other words, a touch of perfection. "You may interpret that, Brody, as a 'Thank God.'"

His hands fell to his sides, and he surveyed Deb so intently, she fought the urge to squint, as if from a bright light. "You do know me, don't you, Brody? You know me better than anyone."

"I'd like to think so."

"I was so afraid," he said. "After you accused me, my whole world turned so sharply on its axis, I thought I was going to slip off and burn up in the atmosphere. I wondered how you could think me capable of such treason? I decided it must be because I was wrong. I'd always thought you knew me, but I guessed you really didn't. I blamed myself. How could you be expected to really know me, when I'd hidden such a huge, huge part of my true self from you, all of these years? My love for you, it *was* me. The bulk of me, anyway. And, since you didn't know about it, how could you know about me?"

"I did know about it, Elliot. I refused to admit that I knew, but I think, in my heart, I knew."

"That's what was holding me back. That's why I so adamantly refused to believe it, when you insisted you loved me. How could you love me, when you didn't know me?"

"Oh." Shocked air escaped out of Deb's throat like the plug being pulled on an air hose. Her legs shook. She had to sit down.

"That's what I needed from you, tonight. That's the proof I was searching for. Even if I couldn't exactly put it into words. I needed reassurance that you wouldn't change your mind and break my heart, again. I needed reassurance that, when you said, 'I love you,' you were saying it about the real me. Not the me I thought I'd allowed you to see."

"Oh, God." Deb covered her face with her hands, laughing and crying and kicking herself and kicking him. "You mean, if I'd told you I knew you were in love with me all these years . . . if I hadn't buried my head in the sand, and run away from my feelings, we could have avoided . . . oh, God, I'm an idiot."

"Technically," Elliot said, "I think we're both idiots."

Deb hugged herself tightly, palms rubbing her elbows until the friction all but ignited white sparks. She rocked back and forth, thinking and remembering and weighing.

Finally, she looked up at Elliot, and, as surprised to hear herself say it as she felt certain he would be to hear it, softly noted, "But we did the right thing all those years, didn't we?"

He didn't appear at all surprised. In fact, Elliot began nodding even before the thought was fully out of Deb's mouth. "We did the right thing."

"For Max."

"For Max."

"He was too decent of a man to hurt."

"I know I couldn't have lived with myself, if I had."

"I made him happy, didn't I?"

"You made him very happy."

"But, I—this, us. It's okay, too."

"Yes." Elliot sat down on the couch next to her, taking Deb's hand in his, rubbing the back of her palm. "This is okay. Finally, after all these years, it's finally okay."

"I love you," Deb said.

He looked into her eyes. He smiled.

"I know," Elliot said.

"Do you think Max would be happy for us?"

He sighed. "Brody, considering the hell we had to

go through the past few months to end up here, sitting like this, do you think we could have done it without a guardian angel?"

"So, you think he'll be okay with it?"

"I think being okay with it is a prerequisite for the wings."

Deb said, "I hope he's happy."

"Me, too."

"I'm happy."

Elliot squeezed her hand. "Me, too."

"It's not going to be easy."

"Except for Introduction to Calculus, I can't really think of anything in life that ever was."

"People *will* talk."

"Haven't you heard? I've got a foolproof way of dealing with people who say things I don't like."

"Punching them in the mouth?"

"Oh, so you have heard of it."

"And Morelli will probably find some way to spin this, so it makes us look bad in front of the Board."

"I am happy to provide that scurrilous little man with hours of entertainment. If he didn't have me to obsess over, who knows what innocents he might choose to wreak his havoc on?"

"You are certainly taking this well, Elliot."

"When I make up my mind, Deb, it takes an awful lot of effort to make me change it."

"I've noticed that. . . ."

They sat for a beat in silence. Then, shyly, she pointed out, "You called me Deb."

He nodded, to indicate it had been a conscious choice, and not a slip of the tongue. "Do you mind?"

"I—I don't know."

"You could try calling me by my first name. Go ahead. I'm a big boy, I can take it."

She laughed. Then, she told him, "You may be able

to take it. I can't. When you first came in tonight, and we were, uhm—"

"Acting like idiots?"

"I tried calling you James, when we were talking about being on a first-name basis, earlier tonight. Really, I did. I tried. But I couldn't. It didn't feel natural. That's not who you are. You're Elliot," she said softly. The words hung in the air, like an echo. "Calling you anything else feels weird."

"Yeah," he confessed. "For me, too. Calling you Deb, I mean. It feels weird, and it . . . tastes . . . different."

"How does it taste?" she asked.

"Like this," he said.

His second kiss didn't take Deb by nearly as great a surprise. For one thing, he was right next to her this time, not half a room away, and, for another, she'd been waiting for it for twenty years.

This was a kiss with no secrets. No lies. No hesitations, no denials, no subterfuge, no guilt, no uncertainty. This was just an uncomplicated, simple, sweet kiss.

Except that it was also so much more than that.

It was a kiss that tasted of the future. It was the first kiss of the rest of her life.

"You're right," Deb admitted when they finally pulled apart. She ran her tongue along her upper lip, savoring the taste for as long as the aroma still steamed from her mouth. "That does taste different."

"How about this, then?" Elliot dipped his head and, with his tongue, flicked the tender spot between her jawbone and her ear.

Deb inhaled sharply. His breath was so hot, she wondered why she didn't instantly burst into flame. And then, she realized she had. Only from the inside out.

"Scientifically speaking," Deb offered. "That's rather nice, as well."

"And this?" His mouth traveled downward, tracing a scalding trail of kisses down her neck, and beneath her chin. His tongue located her Adam's apple, and slowly, sensuously swirled a series of circles, each one growing tighter and tighter, until Deb felt like he was sucking all the air directly out of her.

Not that there was anything wrong with that.

"Not bad," Deb conceded. "But if we're to make this a truly scientific study, shouldn't we be taking notes?"

"Quite right." Without raising his head, and only turning an inch to one side, Elliot addressed a piece of imaginary technology. "Computer!" He gave the order into thin air. "Please take careful notes on the proceedings. Once we are done with this experiment"—he turned back to Deb, a question burning in his eyes—"we may want to repeat it?"

She smiled so broadly, Deb wouldn't have been surprised if the gossamer delight promptly ingrained a new set of dimples where once there had been none. "Oh, yes. Most definitely."

He cupped Deb's face between his hands, kissing her mouth, her cheeks, her nose, her eyelids, her forehead, as if attempting to commit each individual feature to memory. His tongue danced over her skin, licking and tasting and darting inside her ear, swirling in gradually tightening circles, his breath a whisper, his touch an embrace. He sucked on her earlobe, tongue tirelessly easing it back and forth inside his mouth in a rhythm that perfectly matched her heartbeat.

Every throbbing pulse point along Deb's body synchronized and centered, until she felt it pounding at the bottom of her stomach, the echoes resonating pleasure and promise and prospect in a myriad of directions. She wrapped her arms around him, pressing her body closer and closer, until she could feel even the faintest rise and fall of his chest, as Elliot breathed. She, who had always been so good with words, so dependent on them, found that there weren't any to accurately describe the sensations he erupted within her. And so Deb hoped that the moans escaping her throat in intervals would prove enough to let him know how happy his undertaking made her.

Elliot's head dipped, locating the sensitive spot at the base of her throat and sucking on it, softly, at the same time as his hands reached up to cup both of Deb's breasts, his thumbs matching the affection he was paying her neck with caresses of her nipples.

Every impulse in Deb's body was screaming for Elliot to hurry, please hurry. She wanted him to touch her everywhere, she wanted to feel his skin against hers. She wanted to feel Elliot on top of her and inside her and throughout her.

And so he had to hurry.

They had to hurry.

She tore at the buttons and zippers of his clothes, slipping his shirt off his shoulders as, with her own mouth, she drank in the sweet saltiness of Elliot's skin. She would have liked to take her time, she would have liked to savor every pore and every ridge and every texture. But they had to hurry.

"No, Deb." Elliot's hands let go of her breasts to wrap themselves around her wrists, halting her frantic attempts to undress him. He looked her in the eye, loving, compassionate, understanding, and, with infinite gentleness, reminded, "We don't have to rush."

She needed him.

She wanted him.

And there was no one and nothing to stop them.

Not now.

Not ever.

She reached for him again, smiling, eager, and—God, did it feel good—no longer afraid or ashamed.

"No," she repeated. "We don't have to rush. . . ."

"We don't. . . ."

"We don't. . . ."

"We don't. . . ."

Their individually whispered words wrapped around each other, coming together slowly and rhythmically and sensually, until both were repeating them, in unison, like a magical mantra.

Elliot took his time undressing her, savoring each gesture as if unwrapping a gift he already expected to enjoy, and so wanted to treasure every moment of.

Finally, they were lying nude and face-to-face, their arms and legs intertwined. Elliot's fingers danced along the side of Deb's body, stroking her outer thigh, her hip, her waist, her breast, her shoulder, her neck. He couldn't seem to take his eyes off of her, couldn't seem to stop touching her as if to reassure himself that she was actually there, that this was actually real. Because, no matter what Deb did, no matter how she nuzzled his chest with her lips, or gently grazed his back with her nails, or groaned as his mouth took possession of her swollen left nipple, he still didn't appear utterly convinced that this was it. That this was really for good and forever.

Which was why when Elliot briefly and regretfully turned away from her, sweeping the floor next to the couch with his free hand, looking for his discarded jacket and dipping into its inside pocket for a flash of square black plastic, Deb, raising herself onto one elbow, reached over and, gently but firmly, gripped his wrist with her hand. She shook her head from side to side.

Elliot looked at her, questioningly.

Deb asked, "When did you last give blood?"

"What? Oh . . . I—Three weeks ago."

"And you were healthy, then?"

"Presumably. They took the blood, and gave me cookies and juice for being brave."

"Any reason to suspect your status might have changed since then?"

"Not that I can think of."

"Then"—she pried the condom packet out of his hand, dropping it casually back onto his jacket—"we don't need this, do we?"

Elliot thoughtfully scratched his head. "Uhm . . . Brody . . . I think you may have missed another day of medical school, again."

She shook her head. She mouthed, "Nope."

"Brody . . ." The remainder of his question remained unspoken, but Deb could read it clear as day all over his face.

She said, "I want it all this time, Elliot. I want the whole deal. I want my job, *and* I want a life. And I want a family."

He swallowed hard. He looked Deb in the eye. He asked, voice barely audible, lest it betray him, "With me?"

She didn't say a word. She only nodded. And waited.

She waited.

And Elliot smiled. And, if a smile could release a breath it'd been holding for the past twenty years plus an eternity, he did that, too. They both did.

Deb thought the feeling that seized her when understanding finally dawned in Elliot's eyes about what exactly Deb was trying to tell him, was the greatest joy she would ever know in her life.

She was wrong.

That came later.

It came when, at long last, she allowed herself to hold Elliot in her arms, to feel his weight pressing on top of her, not crushing her, but buoying her. It came when she wrapped her legs around his hips, and sensed him move so deeply inside her that she could feel his presence in her every breath, in her every nerve, in her every thought. It came when she heard his breath catch, then quicken. It came when she looked up, stroking the sides of his face with her hands, feeling his lips nuzzle her fingers, his tongue caress her palms, his teeth click softly along her nails.

It came when she pulled him even closer to her, and when she whispered in his ear, just moments before she felt them both ready to tumble over the edge. "Oh, Elliot, my love, I do think this is the beginning of a beautiful friendship. . . ."

Epilogue

Their son was born with a dimple in each cheek, just like his daddy's—and a third one underneath his right eye, which seemed to come from nowhere genetically in particular. It was Francie, Deb's assistant, who, after cooing over the baby and bursting into tears at least twice, solved that mystery. She informed Elliot and Deb, "You know, people say when a baby is born with dimples, that means an angel kissed him on his way down from heaven."

Deb and Elliot exchanged looks, both thinking the same thing.

"An angel?" Elliot clarified. "You're sure it couldn't be a saint?"

Francie didn't understand why both doctors seemed so amused by the question, or why her answer of a hesitant "Well, I guess, yes, I suppose that's possible, too" seemed to make them so happy.

Later, though, there was nothing to misunderstand and quite a lot to reach for a tissue over, when Francie asked Dr. Brody what the baby's name was to be. It was Dr. Elliot who answered, though.

He told Francie his son's name was to be "Brody Elliot."

About the Author

ALINA ADAMS emigrated from the Soviet Union to the United States with her parents in 1977. Today she writes and produces television shows ranging from figure skating to movie premieres to soap operas. *When a Man Loves a Woman* is her second contemporary romance. Alina Adams lives with her husband and son in New York City.

Visit Alina Adams on the Internet:
www.AlinaAdams.com.